The Mayor of Jackson Square

Books by Greg Hunt

The Borderland Trilogy
Borderland
The Exiles
The Renegades

Ridge Parkman Series
Ride to Vengeance
Dewitt's Strike
The Haven's Raid
When Legends Die
Backtrail

Novels
Mission to Darkness
The Carroll Farm Fight
The Mayor of Jackson Square

The Mayor of Jackson Square

Greg Hunt

SPEAKING VOLUMES, LLC
NAPLES, FLORIDA
2023

The Mayor of Jackson Square

ISBN 978-1-64540-981-6

Thanks to my incredible buddy, David Tankersley, who, for fifty years, has always been there when the road started getting rough and I needed someone to help me keep going.

Chapter One

An hour ago Lloyd Ballou was asleep in a dark cocoon of long-distance travel, his jacket rolled up to pad his head from the hard glass window, the muffled growl of the bus engine as constant and reassuring as a mother's heartbeat.

Now here he was, curled up behind a dumpster like a discarded embryo, hurting in a dozen places and bleeding from some, barely able to harvest a few gasps of oxygen from the harsh stench of rot and filth rising up from the stagnant puddle where he lay.

He shoved his fear into its cage where he always tried to keep it, knowing it never disappeared for good. It was like a spirit that clattered a pot in the kitchen in the middle of the night, then sat down at your place at the table, patient, smiling, content to know you lay wide awake close by, wondering if the noise was real or only part of a dream.

He thought the punks that drove him into this predicament were gone, but some strange inertia kept him from crawling out to have a look. All he knew for certain was that right now he didn't have any fight left in him.

Then, as if this melodrama of tonight's bad luck was still incomplete, rain began to fall, sudden and hard like walking into a waterfall.

In his misery, it wasn't difficult to make a case for the fact that even this misfortune could be laid at the feet of his worthless bastard of a father, Billy Ballou. But what was the use? The staggering pile of Billy's transgressions already rose to forbidding heights. And besides, he was dead.

When Lloyd Ballou thought of his father Billy, an old photo his mother kept in a dresser drawer came to mind.

In the picture, Billy stood beside an enormous Cadillac convertible painted vivid blue and polished to a blinding shine. It was built back in the days when Caddies were as long as lumber wagons and had fins like killer sharks. Billy was in his twenties, lean and wiry, wearing jeans with rolled-up cuffs and a tight white tee-shirt. One hand clutched the neck of a quart beer bottle at his side, and a cigarette hung from the corner of his mouth. His thick dark hair was combed straight back, with some kind of grease to give it a sheen. Billy's grin was a little crooked, almost a sneer. Mischief and restlessness danced in his eyes.

The photo was thirty years old. Yet it was the way Lloyd still pictured Billy because that was how he looked the last time Lloyd saw him.

Either nobody told Lloyd Ballou that these bargain bus rides didn't end at traditional terminals like the familiar bus lines, or he just wasn't paying attention. In any case, he wasn't prepared to wake up from a dead sleep, claim his backpack and canvas tote, and be left to his own devices late at night in the parking lot of a plumbing supply company in a questionable New Orleans neighborhood.

"So what am I supposed to do now?" Lloyd had asked the driver as he manhandled the bags out of the luggage compartment and prepared to leave. "Is there any place close by where I can get a room?" Most of the other passengers who got off there either had a ride waiting, or had wandered away into the night.

"Beats me," the driver told him. He was an aging, overweight man in a rumpled blue uniform, surly of temperament and clearly uninterested in anyone's problems but his own. "I'm from New Jersey."

Lloyd just stood there, giving the man's back a hard stare. Finally the driver straightened up, digging a fist into a painful place on his back and making a face. "The river is over that way someplace," he said, waving an arm vaguely. "I think downtown is on the river, and the French Quarter, too."

Lloyd didn't bother asking how he would get there. During the minutes that the bus had been stopped, only a few cars had driven by, none of them taxis. No taxi driver was likely to cruise this neighborhood unless he was tired of living. He watched the bus pull out of the parking lot and turn onto the street, then hefted his backpack onto a shoulder and picked up his canvas bag. He stared forlornly in the direction the driver had suggested. The surrounding neighborhood was old, and probably on a downhill slide for decades. The streets were narrow and rutted, and the houses lay in tight, crowded rows. But at least some of the streetlights worked, and the area seemed deserted at this late hour.

Finding the river seemed his only option. He started walking.

The area he passed through began to change from run-down residential to run-down commercial. He tried to stop and stay in the shadows when he spotted the headlights of occasional vehicles approaching. Glancing into dark, narrow alleys, he wondered if there might be someplace down one of them where he could stretch out on the concrete, or maybe even a patch of grass, and pass the few hours until dawn, when people would be around to give him directions.

Even when he was a policeman back in Kansas City, with the steel of a patrol car wrapped around him, a loaded gun on his hip, a badge of authority on his shirt, and help only a radio call away, his nerves worked overtime when he cruised through areas of KC much like this. Patrolling with a partner helped, when you had one. Then you could talk the jitters away, and feel the confidence of knowing that you had backup just an arm's length away.

But when you were out there alone you studied each shadow for a lurking threat, watched each pedestrian and passing car to look for an arm rising and a hand with a gun in it. That's when you had to dig deep down inside to find the courage you needed to do your job.

As he rounded a corner, he was heartened to see the brightly lit outline of the downtown skyscape in the distance. It wasn't so far away, he thought. It looked like maybe twenty blocks, but it was probably farther. The size of the tall buildings distorted distances.

But even as he began to consider how good a crappy mattress in the first cheap hotel he came to would feel, his nerves were jolted by a wailing, desperate cry for help somewhere ahead. That was followed by a coarse, angry stream of threats, and finally a ripple of excited laughter. Lloyd slipped back around the corner, then stuck his head out, trying to see where the noise was coming from. He heard another blubber of pain, then more cold laughter, and the crisp smack of a fist connecting.

A blue sedan was parked halfway up the block, and Lloyd decided the ruckus must be happening out of sight on the other side of the car. Somebody was catching hell over there.

All of Lloyd's instincts told him to get out of there, to go beyond earshot of whatever was going on and try to erase it from his memory. In places like this, at times like this, there were only victims and predators, and there was nothing he could do to alter the natural order of things.

He wasn't a cop anymore. No car, no badge, no radio to summons help with a few cryptic words. He did have a gun, two in fact, wrapped in cloth in zippered bags, tucked down in the bottom of the backpack. But he wasn't about to haul one of them out to save some stranger from a beating. He knew enough about violent, chaotic situations like this to realize that with a gun in his hand, he might be the one who ended up behind bars, or shot up, or dead.

Better to find some way around this mess.

Then he heard another cry for help, cut short, probably by another punch or kick.

This is a mistake, Lloyd thought as he backtracked down the sidewalk to a battered dumpster tucked a few feet into an alley and stashed his backpack and canvas bag behind it. *You're going to regret this, dumbass.* He rummaged around blindly in the dumpster, and his hand came out with a four-foot piece of plastic PVC pipe. Better than nothing. *But what the hell.* Then he turned and went back around the corner, moving cautiously toward the blue car. His stomach roiled, and a metallic taste invaded his mouth. His heart pounded, and a strange tingling surged through his nervous system. These were old acquaintances that he hadn't shared company with in quite some time.

"Gimme his wallet. I don't trust you."

Their voices became clear as Lloyd approached. There were four of them, all young thugs, gathered around the moaning, bloody form of their victim like feeding beasts. None of the four had noticed him yet.

"Okay here, but I said dibs on the watch."

"Take it. It looks like a piece of crap anyway. Slam, you check his front pockets, and check his hands for rings."

"We got it all, Tats. So, what now?"

Lloyd stopped a few paces away, holding the PVC by his side. Their victim was the first to notice his presence, his eyes filled with hope and desperation.

"So nothing now," Lloyd said, trying to fill his voice with cop-style authority. "Take what you have and get going."

Four heads turned, and four sets of startled eyes full of distrust and surprise landed on Lloyd.

"Look guys. This is going to be a good night. We've got us another mark already."

The man nearest to Lloyd reached around to the back waistband of his jeans, and his hand reappeared with a gun in it, a cheap little automatic, but dangerous enough at this short distance. Lloyd swung the pipe at the man's wrist, and the popgun went flying. It went off when it hit the sidewalk, and the stray bullet punched a webbed hole the front glass of a store. Lloyd gave him another hard whack in the neck, toppling him over and leaving him growling in pain.

Two of the men rushed him, coming fast. Lloyd swung the pipe wildly, holding them at bay for a moment, understanding that if either of them was armed, or if the one who dived behind the car popped up with a piece in his hand, this fight was just about over.

"Run, mister. Go now!" Lloyd called out hurriedly to the battered victim. "Get out of here while you have a chance." He kept swinging, backing away blindly, trying to keep the pair in front of him from getting close enough to grab him or land a blow. The victimized man on the ground sat up, looking around as if the whole world appeared unfamiliar to him, then struggled to his feet and started away in a limping, clumsy lope.

Lloyd jabbed the pipe forward like a sword, doubling up one of his attackers. He drew it back for another swing, but a hand grabbed it from behind and wrenched it from his grip.

It was chaos after that. The fight unfolded so fast and painful that later it was hard for Lloyd to recall who did what to who. He was down on the sidewalk at one point, and he remembered the pipe landing across his midsection with the force of an axe handle. He caught one of them with a solid groin kick, and another, he thought, with a hard punch to the ear.

Somehow he managed to make it to his feet, and bolted away with the speed and determination of sheer desperation. His escape seemed to confuse them, and for a few critical seconds there was no pursuit. As he rounded the corner the only thought was to make it into the alley before they came along and saw where he went. The dumpster sat about a foot out from the block wall of a building. He wriggled in behind it and hunkered down. In a moment, footsteps approached the alley and stopped.

"Where's Tats? I though he was right behind us."

Lloyd's heart was pounding so hard and fast that he almost wondered why they couldn't hear it. His lungs were starved for oxygen, but he struggled to breathe evenly and silently.

"He's getting Troy into the car. But we can handle this guy, if we find him. Can't we?"

They were no more than ten feet away. But the alley was forbiddingly dark, and despite their tough talk, neither of them seemed ready to blindly explore it.

He's gone, dude. Run off someplace. Or holed up."

"I owe him for what he did to me with that pipe. I'll kill his sorry ass and enjoy the hell out of it."

"Yeah, I'll take a piece of that action."

Tough talk, Lloyd thought, but no walk. Hyenas only attacked in clans.

"Look, Slam. There's Tats with the car. We should get out of here, dude, before the cops come."

Lloyd couldn't see anything, but he heard the squeak of worn brakes as the car pulled up and stopped. Car doors opened and closed, and the driver gunned it.

Chapter Two

Dear Lloyd,

I got your address from a telephone book in the library, and I am writing you with news of your father, William Ballou.

I am your Great Aunt Charmaine in Houma, Louisiana. I don't expect that you know who I am, or that I even existed. I am your daddy's aunt on his mother's side, but seeing as how he left your mama so long ago, I don't expect that you ever knew much about your relations down here in Louisiana.

I write you today to let you know that your daddy died in the big hurricane that blew through here sometime past. This one was named Katrina, and was very hard on people in these parts. Maybe you heard about it. William lived in New Orleans at the time of the storm, but I don't know much about his life there. Afterward I kept praying that he would show up alive someday, because he never was the kind to keep in touch very much. But when I finally saw that his name was put on the government list, I knew I should start praying for his eternal soul up there in purgatory instead.

Maybe you don't care about him no more, or maybe you aren't even the right Lloyd Ballou. But if you are, I just wanted to tell you that he's gone because I thought you should know. And I wanted to let you know that whatever bad things he done to you and yours, he had a good side too, especially in his latter days.

In case you wonder what he looked like, I have enclosed a picture from the newspaper that he was in. He's the one on the left ladling soup out of the big pot.

You can write me if you want to, and I'll write you back.
Sincerely,
Your Aunt Charmaine Xavier

The bearded man behind the bar looked Lloyd over like he was some questionable species of vermin as he walked in and took a table near the tinted plate glass windows. And judging by the way Lloyd felt, if that's what the guy was thinking he wasn't far off at the moment. He waited at the table, glad to be off his feet at last, and surveyed the room as the bartender took his time washing a few more glasses. The only other people in the place were a man and a woman at the bar across the room. The two long-necked beer bottles in front of them told the couple's story. Last night wasn't over yet. Both were hunched, exhausted, and nearly comatose.

Eventually the bartender came over to the table and examined Lloyd up close.

"You win or lose?" the man asked. He had a dense, frizzy lumberjack beard, and his long, thick hair, streaked with gray, was tied back in a ponytail. His sleeves were rolled up, and he had a Harley tattoo on one beefy forearm.

"Call it a draw, I guess," Lloyd said.

"I s'pose it ain't no news to you that you look like hell, and you smell like a sewer. I wish you'd picked some other place besides mine to drag your stink into."

Lloyd raised his head and looked the man straight in the eye, each of them measuring the other. "But here I am," he said.

"You got any money?"

Lloyd took out his wallet, still reeking of dumpster sewage, and laid a twenty on the table. "That should cover breakfast."

The man laid a laminated menu in front of Lloyd, and waited while he looked it over. Lloyd ordered a breakfast special called the Oil-Rigger. "And give me a double-shot of something on the side. No, better make that two doubles."

"Jack okay?" the bartender asked.

"That should do the trick."

"The can's in back, in case you want to powder your nose."

A sorry sight greeted Lloyd Ballou as he set his bags on the bathroom floor and turned to the mirror. A red lump the size of an egg yolk had risen high on one side of his forehead, and both eyes were bloodshot, the skin around them just starting to darken. Blood had flowed and then dried on one cheek from a cut on his temple. The knuckles on his right hand were scratched and raw, as if they had been dragged across concrete, and his whole hand ached. There were other places that needed tending, but it wasn't something he could take care of in a barroom john.

He washed the blood and dirt off his face and neck as best he could with handfuls of soapy paper towels, then scrubbed the dumpster slime off his hands and forearms so he could at least eat. Everything else would have to wait.

When he returned to his table, a cup of coffee and highball glass of whiskey sat waiting. He downed a healthy swallow of the Jack Daniels, then followed it up with a big, tongue-scorching pull of coffee. Both of them went to work inside of him in their own specific ways.

"Come on, baby. Why not? I spent all my money showin' you a good time, ain't I?" The head of the man at the bar was shaved bald, his features puffy and red with exhaustion and alcohol overload.

"You full of shit," the woman said. "I seed you still had some twenties when you bought the las' round." She packed her mouth with fries from the basket in front of her, then washed them down with beer. Her pillowy form showed that she had sustained herself on that sort of diet far too long.

"Come on baby."

"You full of she-it."

The bartender brought Lloyd's breakfast on two plates, then went back and brought another cup of coffee. Lloyd tossed back the rest of the whiskey, then got him to refill that too. He tried to remember when he had last eaten anything, but the previous couple of days were only a blur in his head. The food and the whiskey conspired against his mind, and he started feeling like he was on the tail end of a marathon drunk.

"I ain't no crib girl. I never promised you nothin' did I? An' you prob'ly couldn't nohow, the way you so drunk."

"I'd sure like to try."

Lloyd ate for a while, trying to steer his mind away from the mess he'd gotten himself into the night before, and what lay ahead. Sometimes life just happened to you, and there wasn't much you could do about it. He had put away about half the food when the bartender brought his check to the table. "That twenty won't cover it, not with the Jack added on." Lloyd took out another twenty and gave it to him.

"Anyplace around here where I could rent a cheap bed?" Lloyd asked.

"Just follow the street outside a few more blocks and you'll be in the edge of the French Quarter. You'll see some places."

* * *

Lloyd took his flip-phone out of a side pocket of his backpack and was pleased to discover it still had a little charge left. He checked the time, a little past seven, and then put it away. Around him on the narrow, busy streets and sidewalks of the French Quarter, everyone else was just starting their day, but all he could think of as he plodded along was sleep.

Glancing down a side street Lloyd spotted a weathered sign announcing, “Rooms for Rent.” Smaller type underneath promised, “Reasonable Rates. Day, Week, Month.”

A bell jangled as Lloyd opened the door of the narrow, aging, three-story building. His black biker boots clumped on the worn wooden floor like dropped books. The ten by ten lobby was stark, empty, and not particularly clean. There was a counter at the far side, and an open door behind it that seemed to access a small apartment. Cooking odors, cigarette smoke, and television noise drifted out the doorway.

The ground rules of the place were posted in a jumble of hand-lettered notices on a wall behind the counter. “Rent due on time—No Credit!” “Not responsible for stolen property.” “Replacement keys $10.” “No prostitution on premises.” All valuable information, Lloyd thought.

A woman with blond hair and blue highlights came out of the back room and stood behind the counter. Canned laughter swelled and subsided behind her. She held a lethargic baby perched on one hip. She was young, but her eyes spoke of a hard life so far.

“We’ve got two vacancies,” she said, looking at Lloyd like he was something that needed flushing. “A sleeping room for eighteen a night, one ten a week, or a studio for thirty a night, one eighty a week.”

The baby began to whimper. The woman shifted it around to the front, tugged up her knit shirt on one side, and offered the kid a breast.

“I’ll take the studio for a week,” Lloyd told her. “I’m feeling like a high-roller today.”

“Yeah, we get a lot of those in here,” the woman mumbled.

The third-floor walk-up was about what Lloyd expected—cramped and grubby, furnished with curbside cast-offs. It smelled like a high school locker room. The bathroom was at the end of the wooden walkway outside, and you got clean bed linen, a towel, a bath cloth and a small bar of soap once a week, whether you needed them or not.

But the price was right, and he wouldn't be here long. It would do. He dropped the sheets on the decaying mattress, stripped down to only his jeans, and headed down the walkway to the shower.

He turned the water on scalding hot, and stood for a while just letting it pour over his varied aches and pains and wounds. The experience was pleasure and punishment at the same time, like stepping up to do the right thing, and then taking a beating for his good deed. Life had its tradeoffs.

Chapter Three

It was impossible not to hear his parents arguing through the thin walls of their tiny rented house. Lloyd was only eight then, but his recollections of that tumultuous time stuck with him.

Billy was working in a storm window shop, and Lloyd's mother Carol stayed home to tend their two young children and newborn baby. They were short on money, and that's usually what the fights were about. Carol thought Billy spent too much on his cigarettes, his beer, and his car when bills were always overdue and there was never enough food in the house.

Before Carol got pregnant with Benjamin, Lloyd used to hear other, gentler sounds through that wall, sounds that he scarcely understood but found reassuring and vaguely exciting. All that stopped when the baby started to swell Carol's belly, and never seemed to resume after little Bennie was born.

When they argued, Billy always withdrew behind the same verbal defenses. He was under a lot of pressure with a wife and three kids to support. A man needed to relax once in a while with a smoke and a brew, didn't he? How was he expected to get to work if he didn't have wheels? If she didn't like the way he did things, maybe he should just get the hell outa Dodge.

Sometimes when it seemed like it would never stop, Lloyd would slip out of the bedroom where his little sister and baby brother were sleeping and go to the living room. There on the sofa with an afghan pulled up over his head, the voices were not so loud.

Billy had been there for all of Lloyd's short life, and Lloyd refused to consider the idea that he would ever actually leave.

Until he did.

The sound of a rattling doorknob set off a flood of alarm signals in Lloyd's brain and nervous system. Instinctively his right arm reached out, his hand closed over the grip of the Ruger on the bedside table, and he drew it to him. He sat up abruptly on the side of the bed and jacked the action once.

He had no idea where he was. The doorknob rattled again, and somebody mumbled something incoherent outside. It was nighttime now. He could tell that much. His body was damp with sweat, and his nakedness made him feel somehow vulnerable. The leavings of an interrupted dream still roiled in his brain—the blood, the pain inflicted and received, the confusion and fear and the pointlessness of it all.

A wobbly form shuffled by the window on the walkway outside his third-floor room, a dark silhouette beyond the curtains, and Lloyd's finger withdrew from the trigger guard.

New Orleans. A cheap flop-house room. A throbbing head. An aching belly. Knuckles that felt like they had been dipped in acid.

He ejected the bullet from the cylinder and put it back in the clip, then laid the Ruger aside. It probably wasn't a good idea to keep it so easily accessible, he thought. These days, when dreams and realities sometimes merged into a puzzling mish-mash, the risks were there. A 9mm bullet didn't know and didn't care whether it was dispatched by the hand of a man awake or asleep.

At his feet lay a jumbled pile of his belongings. He fished around until he found a shirt and a pair of jeans that seemed to stink a little less than the others, and pulled them on. A trip to a laundromat registered on his mental short-list, but for now he just felt like going out and having a look around. According to his phone, it was ten o'clock. He had slept for fourteen hours.

The street the flop-house was on was empty and docile, but Lloyd was drawn by the lure of the lights and music and people a few blocks down. As he merged with the throngs on the crowded sidewalks and blocked-off streets, he felt a calm anonymity settle over him. At a sidewalk stand he bought a beer in a huge plastic cup, and spilled half of it when a girl with a glassy, drunken smile and dozens of strings of cheap plastic beads around her neck plowed head-long into him. She and her girlfriends laughed hilariously, then plunged on.

This was the New Orleans you saw on television, Lloyd thought. A carefree montage of music and crowds and celebration, a rowdy, drunken party that never stopped. And here in the middle of it, it was almost possible to believe that was true, at least for the moment.

It was easy enough to imagine his father Billy, the twenty-something Billy from the picture, plugged into this environment. The liquor and music and women and wildness made it his sort of place. It was about living in the moment, with no pesky memories or guilt to spoil the experience.

There was too much noise for Lloyd to hear his phone ring, but he felt it vibrate in his jeans pocket. He rounded a corner and took a few steps up a side street, shielding one ear as he raised the phone to the other.

"Where are you? It sounds like fun!"

"Believe it or not, I'm on Bourbon Street."

"Bourbon Street? In New Orleans? What you doing there?"

"Road trip," Lloyd said. He didn't feel like explaining his real mission to his ex-wife Kelly. She wouldn't have cared anyway. "So what's up?"

"Not much at all. Robert is in D.C. this week taking some kind of evidence class, and I was feeling bored. I just thought. . . But I guess if you're a thousand miles away, it's kind of out of the question, isn't it?"

"It should be out of the question anyway, Kelly. We both know that." Lloyd wasn't sure who he despised more at that moment, her or himself. He knew that if he was back home something would probably happen. It usually did when she called him up like this, when she got that soft suggestive tone in her voice and he realized that she was his for the taking, at least for a night or maybe only for an hour.

"Are you getting any action down there?" Kelly asked.

"I just got here," Lloyd said. "I'm walking around checking things out."

"Where are you staying?"

"I've got a room. Nothing fancy, but I don't plan on spending a lot of time there anyway."

"Big bed?"

"No, it's more like an army cot."

"That would be alright, I guess," Kelly teased. "We always tangled up tight anyway, didn't we?" Lloyd felt the old feelings yet again. It wasn't love anymore, or at least not the kind of romantic love that people believed they needed to make their lives complete. But there was still something, and she knew she had the power to use it against him any time she chose. "How long will you be there?" she prompted.

"I haven't decided," Lloyd told her. All he had to do was tell her to come. She would tell the necessary lies to Robert, if he cared enough to listen to them, and within a few hours . . . "I want to see the sights, eat some good food, get drunk at least once. I needed a little getaway, from everything and everybody."

"By yourself. I get it," she said. The softness left her voice and in an instant she was again the woman he divorced. She didn't like being refused.

"Yep."

Lloyd used to tell himself that one day he would make it to New Orleans, especially in his younger years before the responsibilities of work and marriage and bills, and his mother's growing illness, rearranged his life's priorities for him. In his mind it seemed to represent a place to escape every burden, every care. It was a place where booze flowed from a tap perpetually open, where music revealed life's secrets, where women were like ripe apples on a tree, and where every drunken moment was filled with pointless jubilation.

But here he was, and none of that was happening. Maybe it was because there was one burden that he could never possibly leave behind. It was the simple realization that his life was only a tangled mess so far, and there was still no sign of redemption on the horizon.

Or maybe it was simply because he had gotten the crap beat out of him less than 24 hours ago, and his body still ached and stung and throbbed in a dozen places. Maybe he just needed to come back another night.

At the far end of Bourbon Street, he bought another walking-around beer and turned around, hoping he could remember the way back to the humble, cruddy flop-house that he would be calling home for the next few days.

* * *

The next morning started early, and Lloyd left his room with a renewed sense of purpose. He had slept well. The aches and pains were diminishing, and the bruises were starting to fade. If he would focus on what he came here to do right up front, then he could enjoy what New Orleans had to offer with a better attitude.

The concierge in one of the big downtown hotels gave Lloyd directions to the Times Picayune, but advised him not to go it alone on foot, even in the daytime. Lloyd turned down the offer of a taxi, and managed the ten-block walk without incident.

His father's aunt Charmaine hadn't provided any details about the newspaper clipping she sent. There was no date, and he didn't even know for sure that it had appeared in the New Orleans paper. But at least the photo had a credit, Marc Tabor, and that was a starting place. Fortunately Tabor still worked at the Times Picayune.

Tabor was a scruffy, impatient, artsy type in his mid-forties. He received Lloyd in his work room, a dreary, windowless cell in the newspaper's inner sanctum. The room was an orderless dumping ground for all the miscellanea and refuse from the photographer's careless, random, hectic existence. Finding a place to sit was out of the question, but Tabor made it clear that he only had a minute to spare anyway.

"I remember taking that shot," Tabor said. "Normally I would have sent my intern out for that kind of drivel, but a copy editor broke her sweet little coed heart, and she went running home to Corpus Christi." As he talked, he rummaged through a six-inch stack of photos and proofs on his desk, as if something of great importance was buried there somewhere.

"The caption says it was taken at a place called the Union of Hearts Mission," Lloyd said. "I looked in a phone book and I can't find it. I thought you might be able to tell me where it is."

"Somewhere north of Claiborne, I think," Tabor told him. "But that area got hit pretty hard during Katrina. It might not be there anymore."

"You wouldn't happen to have an address, would you?"

Tabor turned to Lloyd and rolled his eyes in consternation. "That was some time ago," he explained impatiently. "Do you have any idea how many places I've been in this city and how many pictures I've shot since I took that one?"

"No idea at all," Lloyd said. He had to put some effort into controlling his own irritation now. "But here's the deal, Mr. Tabor. One of the men in that picture is my father. He's been missing since the hurricane, and this is the only real lead I've got. I'd appreciate any help you could give me."

There was no use talking about the rest of it, Lloyd thought. Tabor didn't need to know that Billy Ballou was a sorry bastard who abandoned his family to a forlorn, difficult future, and that Lloyd was only here to find out if his father might have left something behind, money, property, anything, that he could claim to help his mother fight the cancer that was dining on her organs. It wasn't the kind of family business that you just spilled out, especially to a creep like this.

With a martyr's sigh, Tabor shoved crap aside until he unearthed a keyboard and exposed most of a computer screen. He typed standing up, pulling up files and scrolling through them in machinegun succession until he found what he wanted. Looking over his shoulder, Lloyd saw that the photographer was consulting some sort of assignment log that he apparently kept.

"There! That's it," Tabor said. "Union of Hearts Mission, March 29. 1442 St. Antoine Street. The building was about to fall apart then, and it's probably nothing but a heap of firewood now. If that."

"It's more than I had before," Lloyd said. "Thanks a lot, Mr. Tabor."

"No problem," Tabor said. Without looking up, he dropped directly into his email, and a message there immediately caught his attention. He ignored Lloyd as he took notes on a scrap of paper. "Okay, I've gotta go. An alligator that someone lassoed beside a canal in Metairie is calling to me. Maybe it will break loose and eat somebody's dog while I'm out there. A shot like that would get me on the front page." He snatched up a few thousand dollars' worth of gear and was out the door before Lloyd had the chance to say more.

A guard in the lobby provided Lloyd with a street map and circled his destination on it. During the long walk to St. Antoine Street, Lloyd realized that moving freely around New Orleans would be a problem. He didn't mind the walking, but without knowing the city it was impossible to know what areas he could or could not walk into with impunity.

He had considered riding the Yamaha down from Kansas City. A road trip would have been good for him, and it certainly would have spared him from the throw-down that he'd taken part in that first night. But now that he was here, he was glad that he hadn't brought the bike. If he had to worry about a backpack of jeans and underwear being stolen, where could he have safely kept a seven-thousand-dollar motorcycle? And what small fortune would it have cost?

The walking did give him a chance to experience the flavor and personality of a different part of the city, apart from the charm, glitz, and come-on of the tourist areas.

Katrina had not been kind to the neighborhoods he passed through. Maybe half of the low-end bungalow homes were either repaired or in the process. Countless others still stood vacant, in the same condition they were in when the storm passed and the flood waters were finally pumped out. Some were ravished shells, others hopeless piles of rubble. High water marks on the walls of some buildings graphed the terror and destruction from block to block—three feet here, five there, some places even higher.

The few businesses that remained were all small, barred, run-down liquor stores, seedy markets, car repair shops, thrift stores, beauty shops and the like.

The building at 1442 St. Antoine Street had indeed suffered the fate Marc Tabor predicted. Plywood covered the gaps where doors and windows had been. The building was collapsed at one end. The outside walls in front still bore the spray-painted codes showing that rescuers had searched the building and no corpses remained inside.

Wading through waist-high weeds, Lloyd walked the perimeter of the building, peeking past the loose plywood sheets. There was nothing but rubble and chaos inside. Nothing on the building indicated what it had been. But a notice stapled to the wall beside the front door revealed what it was now. Condemned.

Kim Chi Market was located a few lots down St. Antoine from the abandoned mission. It had survived Katrina and was open for business, although the walls and roof were a patchwork of old and new building materials. Inside the light was dim and the air was rich with the amalgam of myriad food odors, both routine and exotic. The shelves along the two narrow aisles were packed with goods, most labeled in a variety of foreign languages and unrecognizable Asian script.

A slim Asian woman behind a counter on one side was ringing up tortillas, bologna and beer for a young Mexican who looked like he had spent the morning in a muddy trench. They didn't speak to each other, and probably shared no common language except that of the currency they were exchanging. Lloyd waited for the man to leave before approaching the counter.

"Sorry to bother you," he said. "I wanted to ask you about a building down the street, the one that used to be Union of Hearts Mission."

"You're not bothering me," the woman said, smiling. Somehow it surprised Lloyd that her voice revealed no trace of accent. "Yes, I know about the mission." She appeared to be a little older than him, petit and shapely, serene in some unique, timeless Asian way. "They never tried to reopen it after the hurricane. Like a lot of other places in this city."

"Do you know how I could contact the people who ran it?" Lloyd asked.

"I'm sorry, but I don't," the woman told him. "This was my parents' store, but they went to my brother's home in Shreveport just before

Katrina, and afterward they never came back. They're old, and putting it all back together again would have been too much for them."

"And you weren't here then?"

"No, I live in Montreal. I came down here after the hurricane to get the store repaired and back in operation so I could sell it for them. They came here from Viet Nam thirty years ago, and this store is all they have. I thought it would be temporary, but it's been months now, and no offers yet."

"I'm trying to get some information about my father," he explained. "We haven't been in touch for a long time, but I believe he might have worked at the mission at one time." He didn't bother taking out the newspaper clipping. "Could I leave my cell phone number with you? Maybe someone who stops in the store might know something about the mission and who ran it. His name was Billy Ballou."

"I'll be glad to keep your number, and I wish you luck," the woman said. Then her eyes softened, and she added, "But I advise you not to hold onto too many false hopes. There were so many people who left and never came back, like my mother and father. And so many others who died and were never identified, or simply disappeared."

As he started back toward the French Quarter, Lloyd realized that the afternoon was waning. When he reached Rampart Street, he caught a bus that took him to Canal, the main downtown thoroughfare, and felt relief at being back on somewhat familiar turf as night fell.

Chapter Four

Lloyd's mother Carol went through a lot of men after Billy left. She was honky-tonk sexy, she put out, and her standards weren't all that high. Finding men was easy, and ditching them was not a problem either because she never let any of them close to that tender, vulnerable core she reserved only for her husband and children.

For a while after Billy left they all played "Daddy's Coming Back" although it grew harder to maintain the façade as the first few anxious months passed. Lloyd knew the game was finally over when a handsome, hard-partying, out-of-work carpenter named Jerry carried his sparse belongings into the house in two black garbage bags and hung his prized possession on the wall behind the couch, a black felt painting of Waylon, Willie and Johnny.

There were other transients, some nice, some rotten. Even after the family moved and he got his own room, Lloyd sometimes slept in the room with his little brother and sister and kept a paring knife under his pillow. He grew up knowing a lot more about the good and bad in people than most boys his age had to deal with.

Out of necessity, Carol got a job as a department store clerk, and worked her way up to shift supervisor. They began to live better than they had when Billy was still around, although for a long time his very absence continued to be like a separate entity in their home.

Other men might keep their beer in the refrigerator, sit in the extra chair at meals, and sleep in Carol's bed, but they were still Billy's chair, Billy's bed, and Billy's woman.

Lloyd took a seat at the dark end of a stale little bar that lured him in with a Randy Travis song. It was near where he was staying, so no matter how drunk he decided to get, he could still find his way back to bed. Only a handful of other people were in the place, and none seemed inclined to force their conversation on him. He ordered a Bud in a bottle and set to work staring at the accumulated crap behind the bar.

He had known what Kelly was like when he married her, but like every other idiot who tied up with a woman who was more than he could handle, he thought that all she needed was the love and security of marriage to somehow get fixed. There was a shallow sort of satisfaction now in doing to Bob Bollinger what Bollinger had done to Lloyd when Lloyd was married to Kelly. The only difference was that Lloyd had cared, usually too much and sometimes violently, but Bollinger didn't seem concerned. From working around him on the force, Lloyd knew that Detective Bollinger always had his own action going on the side, married or not. Cops like that usually didn't allow their spouses the same privileges, but maybe Bob was different.

So Kelly was still Lloyd's problem, even though they were divorced. Lloyd felt like a guy sitting in a truck bogged to its axles in mud. You could gun it and spin the wheels all you wanted, but you still weren't going anywhere.

When his first beer was nearly gone, the bartender brought him another one without being asked. She knew his type.

"Life just keeps coming at you, doesn't it?" she said with a dry half-smile. It was in her job description to find out if these quiet, moody types needed to get something off their chest. She took some ones from the cash Lloyd left on the bar and rang up his drink.

"I guess so," Lloyd said. It felt good to have a little human contact, but he didn't know what else to say. She finally moved down the bar to wash a couple of empty glasses in a deep, steaming sink.

Outside the open front door a steady flow of people passed. A few glanced curiously into the dim recesses of the bar, no doubt imagining its inhabitants as hopeless drunkards wasting their health and the remainder of their lives. Lloyd was on the inside, and he felt like he fit that description.

He and Kelly had wanted children, but now Lloyd was glad they hadn't produced any. He despised the thought of going to Bollinger's split-level on Saturday morning to pick the kids up for some manufactured outing so he could dilute his guilt at being an absentee dad. He was still young enough to bear fruit with someone else. Thirty-eight wasn't all that close to the grave. But with who? There was no one in his life, no one in the wings, no one even on a distant horizon. And he wasn't trying either. That might have something to do with it.

When the time came for another beer, the bartender brought him one and took another shot at conversation. Maybe she was bored. "First time in New Orleans?" she asked.

"I've been meaning to get down here for years," Lloyd said, offering his own version of a smile so she'd know her company was welcome.

"Business or fun?" She wore her light brown hair straight and long, a style that she should have moved beyond in her twenties. She just missed being pretty, something about her mouth, Lloyd decided. But he liked the little lines that crinkled at the corners of her eyes when she smiled.

"Family business," he told her. He didn't offer more, and she didn't probe.

"Where you from?

"Kansas City."

"Really? I've been there. I drove through there several years ago with a friend. We loved the Plaza District, and it seems like we ate some kind of barbecued beef at every meal, even breakfast. That's about all I can remember of Kansas City."

"Well we've got a little more than barbecue to offer. We've also got beef steak, and roast beef, and ground beef," Lloyd teased. "How about you? Where are you from?"

"Cincinnati. We made our four-way chili out of your beef, so it really is a small world, isn't it? But I've lived down here for seven years. New Orleans suits me." She offered him that smile again, quick and engaging. "I'm Betsy, by the way," she said, extending her hand to him.

"Lloyd." Her hand was damp from the dishwater, and her grip was firm.

"So now that we're buds, Lloyd, I want to ask you something. What are you doing sitting in a dump like this when all of New Orleans is right outside that door?"

Lloyd had to smile at that. "I had something to think over," he offered.

"And how's that going for you?"

"Not worth a damn," he admitted.

"Okay then, it's settled." As she talked, Betsy tipped his bottle up and poured the beer into a plastic cup. "Get out of here. Go take a stroll down Bourbon Street and check out the action. Maybe if you're lucky you'll get to see some pretty woman show off 'the girls' for a string of beads."

"I took that walk the first night."

"That's not enough to take it all in. So get back out there."

"Well I just . . ." Lloyd began tentatively.

"I mean it, Lloyd. Beat it."

Not sure why, Lloyd found his way to Bourbon Street, beer cup in hand, and again made the trek to the opposite end of the quarter. But nobody showed off anything he was interested in seeing. The long day of walking and the beers were starting to take their toll. Supper was a questionable foot-long hot dog from a street vendor, and after than he had nothing but sleep on his mind.

En route back to his room, he came across a large open plaza and gardens that the locals called Jackson Square. The area was defined by a majestic old cathedral and a museum at one end, and two stately, block-long, symmetric buildings on the flanking sides. In the center of the garden area, lush with banana trees, palms, and well-tended beds of flowers and foliage, was an enormous statue of a military hero, sitting astride a rearing steed and waving his hat in victorious celebration of some bygone battle. General Jackson, he presumed, and thus the name.

A cluster of black men had gathered at a bench near the ornamental iron fence that surrounded the central garden grounds. They laughed and talked together, sipping from beer cans and pint bottles concealed in damp paper bags, pretty much ignored by the tourists who flowed past a few yards away.

Then one of them picked up a dented trumpet, turned toward the tourists strolling past, and sputtered out a few shrill, startling notes.

It was like a signal. The others gathered up a variety of battered instruments -- trombones, saxes, and the like -- and within seconds they had plunged into some blues standard that Lloyd recognized vaguely. A small crowd began to gather and gawk, listening with broad interested grins and snapping photos.

Lloyd sat on the stone steps of the cathedral, back from the crowd, to take in the scene.

The makeshift band played with more enthusiasm and volume than talent, but they were good enough to please their impromptu audience. After a few numbers, the man playing the trumpet stood up and closed the set by squeezing out one pure, piercing, prolonged note on his sad old instrument. Then he stumbled back and half sat, half fell onto the bench.

The crowd cheered and applauded. A few went up and dutifully dropped dollar bills in a battered plastic bucket on the flagstones in front of the bench. A cute young blond in yellow stepped forward boldly and sat amidst the grinning musicians while her girlfriend popped a flash in their eyes.

Lloyd noticed movement to one side of him and figured he was about to be hit up for a handout. The young man who approached put him on his guard. His sleeveless shirt revealed arms decorated from wrist to shoulder with elaborate, but not particularly artistic, tattoos. Coming up out of his shirt and onto his neck, like some stealthy beast going for the jugular, was a fire-breathing, multi-colored dragon. His head was shaved bald, and a snake lay coiled on one side of his scalp.

When Lloyd was on the force, they used to call this type "CITs," or "convicts in training." Their fates were already written in the book of life, but they just hadn't found their way to the prison gates yet.

The stranger sat down on the steps at Lloyd's side as if they had just partnered up. "Gimme a smoke, man," he said. Even that simple statement seemed somehow challenging.

"Gave 'em up," Lloyd answered.

Silence hung in the air between them as the young man took Lloyd's measure. "You a cop?"

Lloyd turned his head and gave him a hard look. He had a good one when he needed it.

"If you're a cop, you've gotta say so if I ask."

"You watch too much TV, kid."

"What do you need, man? Whatever it is, I bet I got it, or I can get it for you."

Lloyd turned again and glared deeply into the street weasel's blood-shot eyes. He had dealt with and arrested dozens of throwaways like this before, heard their ritualistic protests of innocence, ignored their exaggerated squalls as the cuffs bit into their wrists, tolerated their flatulent threats, and tracked their migration from street to court to jail, and all too often, back to the street.

But Lloyd wasn't a cop anymore. He was just a guy trying to listen to a little music.

"Just beat it, kid," Lloyd said, his voice controlled and neutral, "before I get really sick of the sight and the smell of you."

The tattooed young man pulled back, and Lloyd thought he would leave. But that would have been too smart.

"Nobody talks to me like that on my own home turf," he challenged. He flung a discordant string of epithets at Lloyd, but Lloyd let those just fly on by.

What worried him more was the hand that the kid had just snaked around behind. It wouldn't be empty when it came back in sight.

The knife was one of those long, thin, spring-loaded jobs that makes a small hole but goes in deep and does lots of damage.

Lloyd swung a hard, backhanded blow that caught the kid just under one eye and sprawled him back. His head bounced on the flagstones with a satisfying thump and he lay still.

Lloyd picked up the knife with his handkerchief, placed one foot on the blade, and snapped it off.

"You shore cole-cocked him, didn't you?" a voice said from the side. "You figger he's dead?"

Lloyd saw the kid's chest rising and falling smoothly. "No, he just got sleepy all of a sudden," he said. He looked up and saw a disheveled man in his fifties standing over him. He stood askance, one leg shorter than the other, and his filthy clothes were little more than rags. He had a brown-toothed grin, obviously relishing Tat's current condition. What surprised Lloyd even more though, was that nobody else in the vicinity seemed to have noticed the knockout. The tattooed young man looked just like another drunk sleeping it off.

"You'd best move on outa here, suh," the cripple advised. "That boy there, he's mean as snakes, him an' that bunch he hangs with. They'll be on you like hornets when they see him laid out like that."

"He seems pretty peaceful now," Lloyd noted with a half grin. "But I trust your advice. I'm sure the cops pass by here from time to time, too."

"Plenty of 'em. But I ain't seed nothin'. Nobody around here ain't seed nothin'. Like you say, ol' Tats he just got sleepy."

Lloyd had already stood up to leave, but that stopped him cold. "Did you say Tats? Is that his name?" He stared down at the unconscious man on the ground, deciding that he needed to remember him.

"All we know him by. You met him before?"

"In passing, but it was dark, and neither of us bothered with introductions." He wondered if Tats remembered him, but decided he didn't. This little encounter would have gone differently if he had.

Lloyd didn't pause to look back until he was at the far edge of the plaza. A nice-looking couple in casual evening clothes were diverting around the still, prone form on the cathedral steps, hardly glancing down and never pausing. New Yorkers, probably, and used to seeing bodies lying around.

There was no blood and no fingerprints. The only witness was a crippled drunk whose memory banks probably cleared themselves anew after each night's bender.

This episode was over.

Chapter Five

Over time some of Lloyd's earliest memories achieved an odd duality. They were both precious and painful. He could not have imagined at the time that the most ordinary moments would become such haunting treasures.

He could remember watching an A&W carhop clip the metal tray on the driver's side window of Billy's Caddy. Just father and son, out for a treat on Saturday afternoon. No exotic delicacy could have matched the odor and taste of those paper-wrapped cheeseburgers, washed down with gulps of root beer in a mug so cold that the drink froze slushy on the inside of the glass.

Like watching it on a screen, he could see his mother spreading a blanket on a grassy spot in Swope Park while his father carried a cardboard box of food and cold soda pop from the car. The picnic menu was always the same, always tantalizing—cold fried chicken, potato salad, dill pickles, chips, loaf bread, and pineapple upside down cake.

On popcorn night Billy went out and rented a movie, usually something with fast cars and gunplay, and Carol popped huge quantities of popcorn and heated cans of Campbell's Chicken Noodle Soup on the stove.

They never made the trip to Talladega like Billy promised, or drove down to Branson for a week as Carol dreamed of doing. But they did sit together on the living room floor on a snowy evening, dropping handfuls of popcorn into steaming bowls of soup while Burt Reynolds risked his foolish neck to get a truckload of Coors beer into Georgia.

Like disheveled castaway mannequins, the scattering of homeless men slumped in the comfortable padded chairs on the back side of the public library reference room. All had books open in their laps, although some couldn't have explained the meaning of a third of the words on the pages in front of them. Pretending to read was the cost of admission. Some dozed, and others stared lethargically at nothing in particular.

It was probably the same in libraries all over the country, maybe even the world, Lloyd realized. If you lived on the street, the library was a good place to keep warm on cold days, or to cool down on the hot ones. It was safe, quiet, out of the weather, and a place where you could be around creatures of your own species, even if you didn't know them, talk to them, or even give a rat's ass what happened to them the minute they walked outside.

Off to one side a uniformed black security guard kept casual watch over the crew of regulars, occasionally crossing the room to wake one of them up when nodding off turned to full-fledged snorting, snoring sleep.

Lloyd took a seat at one of the computer terminals on a long table. A placard on the monitor announced that it provided "Internet Access." He clicked an icon on the screen, and a web browser popped up.

At least those three months of computer training after he left KCPD hadn't been wasted, he thought. It might not have landed him *an exciting, rewarding career in the growing high-tech industry*, but at least it had equipped him to access the limitless storehouse of information available on the internet.

His first search was the most obvious one. "William Maurice Ballou". Remarkably, those three names were not linked together in that particular order anywhere in the countless mega-zillion terabytes of information around the world to which this little machine provided a window. "Billy Ballou" got plenty of hits, hundreds in fact, from around the country and the world.

"Billy Ballou New Orleans" was also a bust. There were pages of hits offering dozens of context references using some or all of the four words in practically every combination and order, except the one he needed.

Deciding on a different tactic, he located a "White Pages" site. He searched for Billy Ballou, then William Ballou, with the location as Louisiana. He got a few hits for each, and began listing the addresses and phone numbers before realizing that these listings were not likely to included home addresses for dead men.

After a frustrating, unproductive hour at the computer, he took a break and bought a cup of coffee at the snack bar near the library entrance.

There was just too much information available these days. During whatever time Billy had lived in New Orleans, he must have left some record of his presence. He had to live somewhere, own a phone, hold a job, drive a car. All that information was out there somewhere in the measureless, interlinked cosmos of information on the internet. But what was the key to finding it?

He felt his cell phone vibrate in his pocket and took it out. The caller was unfamiliar to him. C. Charron. Finally he answered.

"Mister Ballou? Lloyd Ballou?" It was a woman's voice, vaguely familiar.

"That's me," Lloyd said.

"This is Casey Charron."

"Sorry, but do we know each other?"

"You came by my family's market yesterday."

"Yes ma'am, I remember. I just didn't know your name."

Well it's actually Kim Chi, like the market. But people shortened it to K.C. when I was a child, and eventually it became Casey. Charron is my married name."

"I see."

"You asked me to call you if I learned anything about the mission that was down the street from our business. I think I might have something for you."

"I could sure use it, Mrs. Charron. So far all I've done is run into walls."

"I called my brother's home in Shreveport last night to check on my parents," she explained, "and I remembered to ask them about the mission. They were very familiar with it. They didn't remember your father, but they did tell me about a kind, pretty lady who worked there. The closest they could come to pronouncing her name was *Sha-Ray*. But their English is still not so good, even after all these years. Could be Sharon, or Sherry, or god knows what else."

"Did she run the mission?"

"No, that was someone else, and I do have his name. You can't be in this part of Louisiana long without hearing about J.T. Raintree."

"I guess I haven't been here long enough, then," Lloyd said.

"He's runs some kind of medical charity operation for Central American children, and I guess he also runs some places like the Union of Hearts Mission here in New Orleans. He's all over the television asking for donations, but I've never paid much attention to him. I didn't know Union of Hearts was one of his facilities. I hope this is some use to you."

"It's a lot more than I had five minutes ago," Lloyd told her. "Did they tell you anything else about the mission?"

"Nothing that would probably help you. My mother said that sometimes the homeless men who ate at the mission would come into the market afterward and try to steal beer or cigarettes. She would run them out with a broom, but she never called the police. She said their lives were already *một biển khổ*. A sea of suffering. Just like in Viet Nam."

"Your mother sounds like a sweet lady," Lloyd said. "And you're kind for going to this much trouble for a stranger too, Mrs. Charron."

"I love my parents very much, and I sympathize with your search, Mr. Ballou. I wish you good luck in trying to find out what happened to your father."

Back at the computer, Lloyd had no problem finding information about J.T. Raintree. He spent the next three hours exploring link after link, learning everything he could about the man's humanitarian endeavors, both here in New Orleans and in three Central American countries.

Raintree's charitable organization was called Hearts Across the Gulf. Its main endeavors were apparently the children's clinics that he built, staffed and supported in Honduras, Guatemala, and Belize. But he also supported some local charitable operations such as the ill-fated Union of Hearts Mission. He relied heavily on television for his fundraising, and in video clips that Lloyd played, it was obvious that Raintree's organization excelled at the gut-grabbing-guilt appeal. One clip he watched was filled with images of chillingly disfigured children, and shabby old men rummaging through garbage cans. Meanwhile a soothing female voiceover assured viewers that only their generous contributions could end this suffering.

Another featured Raintree himself, holding a legless child on his lap amidst a backdrop of board shacks, donkey carts, and muddy dirt streets. In earnest tones, he explained to his viewers how they could help provide the medical care little Carlotta needed for about the same amount that they spent on their morning coffee. He was a fiftyish, khaki-clad man with a thick crop of dark wavy hair, sincere eyes, and a persuasive pulpit voice.

How and why did a man like Billy Ballou end up working with a do-gooder like this? Lloyd wondered. Billy hadn't been exactly the type to devote his time and energy to helping anyone but himself, or to give a damn about the suffering and deprivation of children—not even his own. Lloyd had to wonder if there might have been some kind of angle for Billy in this business. Maybe he had found a way to skim a little out of the offering baskets, or maybe he was banging the pretty lady who was whipping up the mission soup.

Lloyd wasn't able to find any personal contact information for Raintree, which wasn't surprising. Instead he sent a message to the Hearts Across the Gulf web page, using an online form provided for donor contributions in the "Pray for me!" box. He briefly explained his search for Billy, and gave his cell phone number and a Yahoo email address that he seldom used or even checked.

During the walk back to the French Quarter, which Lloyd had already started to think of as home turf, he made a call that he hadn't been looking forward to.

"Mid-Continent Truck," a clipped voice answered.

"Vic? It's me, Lloyd."

"I sure hope you're calling to tell me you'll be back to work tomorrow, kemo-sahbee."

"I'm still in New Orleans, Vic. It's taking longer than I thought it would to find out anything about my old man."

There was a pause, and Lloyd knew Vic was building up steam. Most of the time Vic Moretti was good company and a good boss, but he had a temper like a blasting cap.

"Hellfire Lloyd! You know what a bind I'm in right now. With Terry locked up and Booker out 'till his hemorrhoids get better, I've got over a week's work backed up in the lot. You could be earning double-overtime right now. When I let you off you told me you'd be gone three days, or four tops. So now what are you telling me? You'll be back when you get damn good and ready?"

"I'm telling you I don't know. I've got a few vacation days piled up, don't I? I'll use that." Lloyd had learned that there was no use responding in kind when Vic went off like this. The best tactic was to stay calm, stand your ground, and wait until the yelling passed. Lloyd expected that someday his boss would probably fall over as dead as an axle right in the middle of one of his tantrums. But that was his business.

"You won't use shit, old son! You haven't got any damn vacation days because you haven't got any damn job. Not anymore!"

"Don't do something stupid like firing me, Vic, just because you're pissed off. We both know I'm the best mechanic in your shop, and your most reliable employee. I'll get this wrapped up as fast as I can and then I'll be back to work."

"Go screw yourself, Ballou. Come back whenever you damn well please. I'll have two checks waiting for you," Vic growled as he hung up.

Lloyd shook his head, sighed, and stuffed his cell phone down into his jeans pocket. He probably wouldn't go back this time when Vic called him and offered to give him another chance not to screw things up. Vic had fired him twice before, and both times had sweetened the deal just enough to convince Lloyd to return. He liked the big, vigorous, explosive Italian, but he was tired of staying cool and trying to be reasonable while Vic ranted and cussed and threw wrenches across the shop.

Nothing Lloyd put his hand to ever seemed to provide permanence and direction.

Joining the Army a year out of high school had seemed like a great choice for a smart young kid stuck at home with not much to fill his time but a crappy construction job and the same crowd of non-college-bound misfits that he'd hung around with in school. Military life appealed to him, and even the long stint in Iraq had been bearable, despite the heat and boredom and daily risk. He began to see a future for himself as a soldier. There was always at least one war going on out there somewhere, sometimes more, and you couldn't beat that for job security. But three months in the stockade for breaking the jaw of a training sergeant cured him of that ambition. He was lucky to get out of lockup after such a short time, and even luckier to leave the Army with only a general discharge instead of a dishonorable. What made the JAG reasonable was the little matter of what the perverse sergeant had done to get his jaw broken.

Lloyd fell back into construction when he got out, but then a friend of his mom's current boyfriend got him an in with the Kansas City Police Department, and they were hungry enough for new recruits that somehow his military record was overlooked long enough to get him into the academy. He liked the work, enjoyed the brotherhood, and his stint in the middle-east had prepped him for the kind of risks a cop had to face.

The night of the shooting, Lloyd had picked up an extra shift for a buddy and was patrolling alone. Kelly had called earlier to say she was waiting up for him, with all the throaty innuendo that came with such a late-night call. His thoughts ranged no farther ahead than cruising to the end of his shift, then heading home to a warm bed and a warm woman.

He wasn't the one who took the original shots-fired-officer-down call just after eleven, but he was second on the scene.

He found a fellow officer, a paunchy unpleasant patrolman named Clymers, down, bloody and unconscious. Clymers' rookie partner, Bookman, knelt at his side, holding a pressure bandage to a wound low on Clymers' considerable belly, looking wild-eyed, rattled, and through being a cop for the night.

Three more units joined Lloyd in less than a minute, and they began to work their way around both sides of a house where the shooter had fled.

Later, none of them actually knew whose bullet took down the old man who stood in the dim moonlight behind the house, firing a shotgun in blind panic and shouting incoherent threats into the darkness of his own back yard. They only knew that one cop was already down out front, and none of them wanted to be next. Despite the tragic end, no one doubted that they had followed procedure. The old man had refused their commands and fired again. Not knowing who he was, they put him down.

Twenty minutes later other units drug the hoodlum who actually shot Officer Clymers out of some bushes two blocks away.

Lloyd was embarrassed at the flood of selfish personal relief he felt days later when he learned that the bullet that killed the homeowner hadn't come from his gun. He wasn't the one. He'd be okay. He could stay a cop. But not being the killer didn't exonerate him in the eyes of the activist community group that took up the cause. Their first demand was for the arrest and trial of all four officers involved, but everyone knew that was just a blustery opening salvo to get press coverage. Weeks later the settlement they finally agreed to with city leaders left the old man's widow a wealthy woman, and cost the four cops their badges and reputations.

The next pillar to topple for Lloyd was his marriage to Kelly, who found no fulfillment in trying to help her disgraced ex-cop husband try to regain his footing and get on with things. She had her own needs, didn't she?

Seconds before his finger tightened on the trigger that night, Lloyd Ballou was one of those men for whom the elements in his own personal galaxy seemed to have miraculously assembled into something worthwhile and lasting. But four months later he was sleeping on a couch at his sister's, wondering what the world happened.

* * *

Betsy the bartender wasn't on duty that evening, and in her absence, the little bar where she worked reverted to a seedy, unpleasant den for drunks and creepy loners. Slumped in a dark corner in back, a decaying old man who looked like he had washed up on the river bank with the rest of the flotsam was putting away beer after beer, lost in incoherent debate with the spirits that haunted him, swilling down the pathetic, dwindling windfall of crumpled bills that lay on the table in front of him. A couple came in and found a table near the window, assessed the environment and menu briefly, then reconsidered and left without ordering. Occasionally young people in small groups dropped in momentarily to replenish their walking-around beers. The bartender was a lank, sullen guy, devoid of interest in his customers. During his off moments he slouched at the end of the bar leafing through a worn magazine called Chubbies, sipping from a coffee mug that he replenished occasionally from a Jägermeister bottle.

Lloyd ate a grilled cheese and a bowl of chili, mainly because he was here, and they had food, and he had to eat somewhere. It was dark by the time he left, late enough to go back to his room and try to sleep, he decided.

A hard-looking woman in her forties was behind the counter when Lloyd entered the boarding house. She eyed Lloyd suspiciously, but seemed to know he belonged here and didn't challenge him. Through the open doorway in back television applause crested and faded. Lloyd glimpsed the clerk who had checked him in that first day, wearing a black bra and baggy knit sweat pants. With one arm she held the baby perched on a hip, and with the other hand she tipped a beer can back and chugged. Feeling Lloyd's gaze on her, she met his eyes without expression, tugged up a fallen bra strap, and turned her attention back to the television.

In his room Lloyd checked the contents of his duffle, then checked the splinter he had wedged under the edge of the air vent to let him know if anyone had bothered with it and perhaps found the hiding place of his arsenal. Everything was as he had left it. No intruders, no thefts, and no evidence that the maid had dropped in recently.

After a shower in the communal bath down the hall, he settled on his bed and tried to will himself to sleep. The air in the room was stale and moist, and his mind roiled with random thoughts and worries. An unpleasant, uncertain future seemed to loom before him.

He thought about calling his sister Kat, but imagined her trying to get supper on the table for her husband and put the kids to bed, cradling the phone on her shoulder while she multi-tasked, only half listening.

Instead Lloyd stared up at the white planked ceiling in his room, its splits and water stains dimly illuminated by the glow of the city outside the dirty window. He thought about the quiet, plump neglected middle child, who had become a plump tramp and hellion in her teens and early twenties, and was now the plump complacent wife of a devoted dullard husband named Paul. Each of her five kids had different fathers, three by previous husbands who had been as wild and worthless as she was at the time.

Lloyd and Kat had not been close during the rampages of her teens and twenties when she made it her goal to mold her own life according to the only example she had ever known, their mother's. He had done what he could for his little sister in the absence of any real parenting, but in the end, he had only been father enough to provide a convenient target for her anger and rebellion.

Paul Scorby, the clumsy kid that everyone must have dumped on all his life, the gentle clod whose career choice was car detailing and janitorial work at a Pontiac dealership, couldn't have been a more unlikely choice for Kat at a point in her life when her own horrendous choices and the odious burden of providing for five children on a clerk's salary had nearly ground her to dust. But somehow they had come together, and somehow it worked.

Kat had few recollections of their brother Benjamin, who died at four. She remembered even less about their father, who left when she was a toddler. She was fortunate in that at least. For his part, Lloyd never felt that he could completely move clear of the haze of shame and guilt he felt about little Bennie, or the bitterness that was his father's only legacy.

Chapter Six

They used to play in the creek all the time. In most places it was just a six-inch rivulet of water winding across a bed of limestone and flint. In the occasional pools, Lloyd and his friends would catch minnows with their hands, or turn over slabs of rock and watch the crawdads scurry desperately backward to their next safe haven. The crumbling dirt banks were steep but navigable, if you were old enough and tall enough.

He didn't usually take Bennie or Kat down to the creek with him. His pals didn't want the little kids hanging around, and if either of them got wet or dirty, he had to clean them up.

After school that day, as always, he was supposed to watch his brother and sister until his mom got home, which could be in time to fix them supper, or maybe after the bars began to close. It was a tedious responsibility for an eleven-year-old.

They were watching TV, and Lloyd couldn't have honestly said whether Bennie was gone five minutes or half an hour before he finally noticed. Road Runner and Bugs Bunny came on back to back, and they always held his attention, even the episodes he had seen countless times before.

When he finally realized that his little brother was not in the house, the search took only a short time. Instinct drew him to the creek. Bennie lay face down at the edge of a pool, his head half submerged, his fine black hair riffling in the gentle current.

In that first instant, Lloyd convinced himself that his little brother was just getting a drink. He even called out, "Bennie don't! That water's dirty! It'll make you sick!"

But the water had already done far worse to the little four-year-old.

The hours that followed were a terrifying swirl of tears, grief, guilt, and official process. It confused Lloyd when the police focused their blame and scorn on his mother instead of him. Lloyd had been in charge. It was his fault. She hadn't even been there. They located her in some bar and raced her home. Already drunk, she burst from the squad car, wailing incoherent denials as she stumbled to her child's lifeless body.

Late, very late that night as Lloyd lay exhausted in his bed, fighting sleep, terrified of the ghouls and horrors that awaited him there, he almost convinced himself that none of it had really happened. It had been a dream, a petrifying, horribly realistic dream. If he got up now and went in the other room, he would find Bennie tangled in the sheets, one foot hanging off the bed, sleeping his innocent sleep. But he didn't go.

Sometime during that endless night, Lloyd finally came to the certain conviction that neither he nor his mother was actually to blame. It would not have happened if Billy hadn't left them. They wouldn't be living in this slummy rental. His mother would be a normal parent, at home every night, not drunk and whoring around with whatever man would tolerate her. And Bennie could have gone on living the life that Billy Ballou's cowardly abandonment had stolen from him.

When Lloyd snapped awake, he thought it must be almost morning, although it was still dark outside. He felt as if he had slept for hours. His watch read 11:12.

The musty odor and dampness in the tiny room seemed to pollute the air he breathed. He swung his legs off the side of the bed and sat up. In the distance, barely audible unless you listened for it, someone was playing a trumpet. Footsteps clumped by on the walkway outside, and the outline of a tall dark form moved past the closed curtains. Moments later, the walls transmitted the noise of a flushing toilet.

Lloyd was wide awake. He reached for his jeans.

There were still people hanging around in the big courtyard in front of the cathedral in Jackson Square, but the environment had changed. Drunks trooped forward determinedly, intent on finding the next bar or simply reaching their beds before unconsciousness claimed them. The more respectably sober moved with the purposeful air of people who don't want those they passed to know how threatened and vulnerable they felt. The regulars who malingered there clustered tribe-like in small groups on the benches, drinking and smoking, talking among themselves, surveying strangers who passed for their potential as threat or mark.

After his first reconnaissance pass across the square, Lloyd stopped in a small market for a pack of cigarettes and a cheap lighter, then returned to Jackson Square.

Loitering on the same bench was the same group of men who had played the impromptu blues set the night before. There with them was the crippled man he had spoken to, and a wasted old woman, dressed in tattered layers of men's clothing, so far gone that she leaned in dreary-eyed stupor against the man beside her.

With a lit cigarette in his hand, Lloyd sidled toward them. All eyes settled on him as he neared, and the relaxed conversation faded.

"How you fellas doin'?" Lloyd asked. "I heard you play last night. You sure know how to make music."

"We jus' play 'cause we can't kick the habit," one of the men offered.

"An' for the dollars them white folks drop in the bucket," another added. "A man need some drinkin' money, don't he?" He and the others shared a chuckle. "Say, you got another one of them?" he asked Lloyd, pointing to the cigarette he held.

"Sure." Lloyd offered up the pack and lighter. It went around the group, and the pack came back to him nearly empty. Some had taken two. Tobacco, the great bond builder.

The man who had trilled out the high notes on his trumpet the night before was sleeping on one end of a bench, slumped on one elbow. He cradled the horn against his chest, his fingers on the keys as if he might recover from his stupor at any time and start blowing out some notes.

"That there is Brass Man Jake," one of the other men offered.

"That horn of his looks like it's been through the wars," Lloyd said.

"Claims Louie Armstrong gave it to him back in the fifties when they was playin' together in a club over in Algiers," the man told Lloyd. "Got a whole story built around it. But I don't believe no such nonsense. I figger he paid a few bucks for it in a pawn shop. Or stole it someplace."

"Well I can witness it's still got some music left in it."

"Yeh, so does Jake, 'til that gin gets a good holt."

On the force, Lloyd had learned a simple secret for getting along with street people like this. Just acknowledge that they exist, and treat them like normal people. Once they trusted you, that's what they usually turned out to be.

He took a seat on the bench beside the old woman, far enough away, he hoped, that he wouldn't carry any of her stink away with him. She slurred something unintelligible at him, and he handed her the pack of cigarettes. Smiling, she tucked it away inside her rags.

"Name's Lloyd," he told no one in particular. "I just hit town a couple of days ago. My first time in New Orleans."

Some of the men offered their names in return, but Lloyd caught only a couple of them. Sly was the man who had been talking to him, and the cripple was Chester.

"That there's June Bug aside of you," Sly said. "She usu'ly a bit livelier, but she had herself a pint of gin a while ago."

"So where do you folks spend the night?" Lloyd asked.

"They's places around. Some good, some not so good. You lookin' or just curious?"

"I'm in a boarding house right now. But I might be looking if my money runs out."

"Wal, there's places. You got a need, you let us know," Sly told him.

"I stay at my brother's when his ol' lady let me," Chester said. "But if I come back drunk, she locks me right out on the street. She can tell jus' lookin' at me."

As they chatted, Chester gave no indication that he recognized Lloyd from the previous evening when Lloyd gave the skinny, tattooed kid a time out. Yet there was something about the way the man looked at him, as if they shared a secret bond.

Harsh laughter rolled toward the group from the direction of the nearby cathedral. Four youths in their late teens or early twenties, three guys and a girl, were clustered there smoking and roughhousing with each other. One of the guys seemed to be pestering the girl, grabbing at her skirt. She aimed a sudden kick at his groin, but he managed to dodge it and they all laughed again, even her.

"Do you know that bunch?" Lloyd asked. He scanned the group looking for Tats, but the light was poor and he couldn't tell if the tattooed man was among them.

"Them boys is trouble," Sly said guardedly. "We leave them alone, an' they leave us alone, most times."

At another bench several yards away, three women and two men who had been relaxing there began to gather up their assorted belongings and start away. Their age, clothes and hair tagged them as throwbacks to a bygone hippie era. Earlier one of the men, a lean wrinkled specimen with a wiry hillbilly beard and a frayed black stovepipe hat, had manned a fortune teller's table.

In the other direction, waiters from a corner restaurant started closing latticed shutters over the windows. Inside, someone turned a recorded blues track off. Lloyd realized that he hadn't even been aware of the music until it stopped abruptly.

Joining the migration, the group Lloyd was with also began to assemble their sad, motley collection of instruments and black trash bags. Somebody shook the trumpet player awake, and Sly and another man tugged the drunken woman, June Bug, to her feet. She stood with their help, and remarkably, began to walk.

"We goin' down by the river," Sly explained. "You take care now, tobacco man. Maybe we see you again one of these nights."

The four young people over by the cathedral had disappeared as well, and suddenly the open plaza was temporarily deserted. Blocks away the cacophony of noise from Bourbon Street could still be heard, sending out its siren call to all the music lovers, pleasure seekers, and drunkards within earshot.

But Lloyd thought he was tired enough to get back to sleep now.

* * *

Lloyd tracked the staggering progress of a drunken man about half a block ahead of him on Royal Street. He wore a wrinkled gray business suit, now defiled with an enormous stain down the back. He had reached that point of intoxication when walking straight was no longer an option. Staying vertical was challenge enough.

This stretch of Royal was empty and quiet. Lloyd had no idea how safe or dangerous the area might be. He decided to follow the drunken man for a while and make sure nothing happened to him. It amused him to think of the guy waking sometime tomorrow, sick, hung over, miserable and filthy, with no idea that a guardian angel had seen him safely back to his hotel the night before.

The blow to his back, low on the right side, was sudden and unexpected. It hurt like the blazes, but lacked the necessary force to knock him down or debilitate him. Someone grabbed his arm, swung him around and flung him into an alley. In the darkness he tumbled over a row of trash cans and went down amidst a noisy clatter and the stench of scattered garbage.

He only had an instant to register the presence of people standing over him, three or four at least, before the kicking and beating started. Lloyd rolled away, curling one arm up behind his head and taking most of the abuse on his back and legs. They grunted and cursed and snarled as they passed out the pain, and in the chaos, Lloyd thought he could hear a woman someplace close by, encouraging them on and laughing hysterically.

Lloyd's hand found one of the metal garbage can lids, and he swung it behind him wildly. Somebody yelped, and his attackers scrambled back a step or two. That instant of reprieve was all he needed. Rolling over, he swung the lid back and forth at their shins, and connected a couple of times, eliciting growls of pain.

The alley was almost completely dark, but he could see now that he was up against four of them, none of which seemed to be seasoned or particularly aggressive fighters. Strength in numbers was more their style. He made it to his feet again, and when a couple of them came at him, he managed to catch the closest one in the side of the head with the metal lid. After that, the fight was pretty much over.

"Come on, guys," one of them said. "I think we taught him his lesson."

What lesson? Lloyd wondered. He thought he recognized the voice of one of them from days ago when he sought refuge behind a dumpster.

They scrambled out of the alley like rats released from a box, and by the time Lloyd staggered to the street they were just disappearing around a corner, howling and laughing at their victory. By the time they told this story tomorrow, they would have left Lloyd broken and bleeding on the paving bricks, begging for his life.

But what was the lesson? Lloyd wondered. *Don't walk down an empty street at night in New Orleans without a baseball bat or a .45? Or maybe, when you see a staggering drunk on the street, leave him to suffer the punishment fate decrees.*

It pissed Lloyd off that for the second time in less than a week, he found himself brushing the dirt and garbage off his clothes and skin, surveying what kind of damage the crew had done this time. He pulled his shirttail up and wiped something greasy and fishy smelling off his face, nearly gagging as he realized some of it had gotten into his mouth.

By tomorrow morning he would hardly be able to walk. Again. But at least nothing seemed to be broken, and he didn't think he was bleeding anywhere. These guys were amateurs, not like the two Chicanos from the mean side of Houston who jumped him in the stockade and convinced him that when one of their *compadre*s decided that he wanted your pork chop at supper, the best decision was to hand it over. Those two fellows had known how to hand out a beating.

Back in the boarding house, Lloyd again found himself letting the hot water in the shower beat on his battered back and legs until the tank was empty and the stream turned lukewarm, then cold.

Maybe, he thought, the lesson was that you didn't snap off the blade of a fellow's favorite switchblade without expecting to get tossed into an alley and knocked around for it.

Chapter Seven

You didn't have to be tough to survive in the neighborhood where Lloyd grew up and the schools he attended. Not unless you had a mom like Carol Ballou.

Lloyd never was the toughest kid in school. In the early grades that distinction went to Dana Andrich, a stocky, overbearing bully with crew-cut hair and an ever-present band of stooges. His dominance on the school bus and playground generally went unchallenged.

In junior high it was another boy that everyone simply called Salino, a kid from the hillside Sugar Creek slum overlooking the smoldering city dump. Salino was two years older than his classmates because of early failures, and it was said he had actually been locked up at 14 for stealing a car.

But even their type learned the consequences of saying the kind of things about Lloyd's mom in front of him that everyone else usually said behind his back.

The feud between Lloyd and Dana Andrich dragged on for five hostile years, and each time they tangled, Lloyd came a little closer to winning the fight. He and Salino fought only once. Salino won, of course, but Lloyd's unflinching loyalty to his mom impressed his opponent, and afterward they became friends. With a father in prison and a mother who earned money to feed her five kids just about any way she could, Salino understood.

The ringing phone dragged Lloyd reluctantly out of his deep, dreamless sleep. When he reached for his cell on the bedside table, he felt like someone shot a jolt of electric current up his back.

"Mr. Ballou? I waited 'til late morning to call so I wouldn't wake you. But it seems like I did anyway," a man's voice said. There was an unspoken accusation in the tone that soured Lloyd from the start. He recognized the resonate voice of J.T. Raintree from the internet video clips he had watched the day before.

"It's okay," Lloyd said. *For the second time in a week, I got the holy crap kicked out of me last night so maybe I deserve a couple of extra hours in bed,* he thought.

"Then you are Lloyd Ballou, Billy Ballou's son?" Raintree asked.

"Yes sir, that's me."

"This is Reverend J.T. Raintree. Excuse me if I sound surprised, Lloyd. Billy never mentioned having a family. He was such a loner, and when we were around each other, we usually just talked about the work at hand."

"We live up north," Lloyd explained. "My mom and my sister and me. He and mom split up a long time ago, and we lost track of him."

"I see," Raintree said. He sounded distinctly uncomfortable, almost annoyed. He'd probably prefer to spend his time telling some big donor about how bow-legged, malnourished Central American orphans had to eat dead cats to survive. "My staff passed your email on to me, Lloyd. I thought it was only proper that I call you personally since your father used to work for me. What can I do for you?"

"I'm really not sure, Mr. Raintree," Lloyd admitted. "I got word recently that he died in the hurricane, and I came down here to find out what I could about him."

"Well, if you'll permit me a moment of selfishness, Lloyd, I'll admit that I'm glad you already know that Billy's gone on to be with our Savior. I dreaded having to deliver that sad news."

"I understand."

"Your father was a good man, Lloyd. A dedicated servant of the Lord, and a valuable worker at one of our local outreach missions. He's sorely missed by his coworkers and friends here, including me." After an uncomfortable pause, Raintree went on. "Would it be rude if I ask again what I can do for you?"

"No sir, it wouldn't," Lloyd said. "Since Billy worked for you, I'm wondering if you might have time to sit down and talk to me for a few minutes. I'd really like to know more about what he was like, what kind of work he did, who his friends were, where he lived . . . that sort of thing."

"Well, I . . ." Raintree stalled. He clearly didn't want to meet with Lloyd. That might simply be because he was so busy, but Lloyd got the sense that it was something else entirely.

"I'm sure your schedule is always full, Reverend Raintree, with all the good works you have going on. But a man's only got one daddy." He felt silly playing that card, as if he actually gave a hoot in hell about his old man. But sometimes you did what you had to.

"I supposed we could arrange something," Raintree conceded. "I'm spending the day in Baton Rouge today. I'm actually on my way there now. But I could get my secretary to move things around on my schedule tomorrow."

"That's kind of you, Reverend. I won't take up too much of your time."

"Then come for breakfast. Say eight tomorrow?" He gave Lloyd an address, and Lloyd wrote it down on his hand.

He was glad Raintree hadn't suggested that they meet today. It was going to take some effort before he could stand up straight again.

* * *

Raintree's house was in the Garden District, a twenty-minute trolley ride southwest of the French Quarter. This genteel, upscale slice of the city was worlds away from the rustic, crowded, commercialized French Quarter. The streets were flanked by ancient live oaks and magnolias, and the houses were set well back, their manicured lawns and landscaping protected from intrusion by tall brick walls and wrought-iron fences.

Reduced to miniature scale, J.T. Raintree's two-story Victorian house would have looked just right sitting on a young girl's dresser. It wasn't as large as some of the enormous period-piece mansions Lloyd had seen during the trolley ride down the St. Charles Street common ground. Still "Cedar Manse" as the place was named, was sufficiently genteel and ostentatious to testify to its owner's success, at least in the material world.

The wrought iron front gate was chained, and Lloyd couldn't discover any way to gain the attention of anyone inside short of shouting. Exploring down a side street that bordered the house, he discovered a drive-through gate that sat open.

Inside the gate a three-car garage and a dense ten-foot hedge blocked any view of the back yard of the house. Lloyd hesitated in the driveway, then started toward a stone archway that promised a way through the hedge. He was, after all, an invited guest, and this seemed to be the only way in.

The back yard of Cedar Manse was secluded and luxurious, a refuge clearly designed for privacy, relaxation and entertainment. There was a swimming pool on the far side, with flagstone patios, a covered bar at one end, and clusters of recliners scattered about. Closer to Lloyd, flower beds in full exotic bloom surrounded a patch of lawn that looked as healthy and well-tended as a putting green. A stone fish pond with a waterfall dominated a back corner.

A woman was in the pool, swimming smoothly and vigorously toward one end. Lloyd stopped, not so much to watch her as because of the sudden feeling that he might be an intruder after all. When she reached the end toward the house, the woman climbed up out of the water and wrapped a towel around her slim, healthy frame. She glimpsed Lloyd, registered surprise at his presence, and hurried toward the back of the house.

At that moment, Lloyd was too dunderheaded to even try to explain that he was invited here, and wasn't just some meatball off the street coming to gawk, rape or pillage.

Less than a minute later a man came out the same door that the woman had just entered. He came straight toward Lloyd, his stride determined. He stopped a few feet away, and something about his stance indicated that it might take considerable effort to get past him if he didn't want that to happen.

"What do you want?" he asked, not belligerently, but with no particular cordiality.

The man was slightly shorter than Lloyd, but broader at the shoulders and narrower at the waist. A bodybuilder, Lloyd decided, and darned proud of the sculpted body he has worked so hard to achieve. He wore light loose trousers, and a dark silk shirt that must have been custom made for his buff dimensions.

"I came to meet with J.T. Raintree," Lloyd explained. "I was out front, but I couldn't figure out how to let anybody know I was there. So I came around back."

"Name?" With his dark hair, ruddy skin, and dark brown eyes, Lloyd took the man to be from European stock, perhaps Italian or someplace farther east. He might have been handsome, except for some unsettling quality that lurked behind his steady, expressionless stare.

"Lloyd Ballou." He was growing weary of being treated this way, but saw nothing to gain by letting it show. Pec-Boy here appeared to be some sort of security or bodyguard, and they were paid to act like blocks of ice and to suspect everyone. "I'm here at Reverend Raintree's invitation," Lloyd added.

"Okay, follow me." He led Lloyd across the lawn, past the pool and into a glassed-in room built onto the back of the house. It seemed to serve as both a sun room and greenhouse. There were comfortable looking couches facing the pool and yard, and a luxurious abundance of plants hanging from the ceiling, on racks along the glass walls, and in a scattering of large pots on the floor. The air in the room bore the rich moist scent of a damp tropical forest.

J.T. Raintree entered from a doorway at the back of the room to greet Lloyd with a warm handshake and a broad smile. "Welcome to Cedar Manse, Lloyd," Raintree said. "You gave Leila quite a start coming in the back way like that. I live a fairly public life, and we get our share of unwelcomed visitors from time to time. We usually keep the back gate locked, but my bodyguard, Rudy Soyez, left it open this morning so the housekeeper could get in. She's running late." Lloyd glanced around and saw that the bodyguard had disappeared, possibly to rectify his oversight before any more riff-raff wandered in.

"I started out front, but that gate is chained, and I didn't see a bell or an intercom," Lloyd explained. "I couldn't find any way to let you know I was here."

"That's by design," Raintree said. "Generally, I don't receive visitors here at my home. Come over and sit down."

They sat at a glass-topped table near the back window, overlooking the pool and grounds. There were place settings for two, and a decanter of coffee sat in the middle of the table. Raintree poured for both of them, then offered cream and sugar.

"You'll need plenty of cream," the reverend said. "This is our native chicory coffee, and I like it strong enough to eat the chrome off a bumper."

"Bring it on," Lloyd said.

"You know, you don't bear a lot of resemblance to your daddy, Lloyd. He was thinner than you are, and his hair was darker."

"I guess I took after my mother's people from north Missouri," Lloyd said. "Brown hair, brown eyes, big boned. Pure mid-western stock."

The young woman that Lloyd had seen coming out of the pool came in through the door in back, carrying a tray with a variety of breakfast offerings. She had slipped into a pretty yellow sun dress with lace at the sleeves and hem, very feminine. Her short blond hair was still moist from the swim.

"Leila, this is Lloyd Ballou," Raintree said. "Billy Ballou's son. Leila is my personal assistant, secretary, business manager, sounding board, and the only person in this outfit who seems to be able to keep me on track and on task from one day to the next."

"Pleased to meet you, Lloyd," Leila said as she began transferring the food from her tray to the table. She delivered scrambled eggs, grits, fried ham, biscuits, gravy, and fruit, enough food for half a dozen people. "I didn't know your father very well, but everyone always spoke highly of him. I'm sorry for your loss."

"Thanks for that," Lloyd told her. "And I'm sorry I scared you before."

"Forget it. I like to take a quick swim first thing in the morning before I start my work. I'm used to being out there alone, and you surprised me."

As she left, Lloyd trailed her out with his eyes. She had a nice figure, but didn't flaunt it, and nice legs, although her hem line was at a modest knee length.

"She's a looker," Raintree said, noticing how Lloyd's attention had strayed. "But I hired her for her experience and organizational skills. I'm not one of those preachers who think God gave him some special dispensation to bang the hired help or the ladies in the flock." He began shoveling food onto his plate, and Lloyd followed his example without invitation.

"I wasn't thinking anything like that, reverend," Lloyd said. "I just enjoy the sight of a pretty girl, coming and going."

"Well, God didn't say we couldn't look at 'em, did He?" the preacher chuckled. "Just not with lustful intent."

As they began to eat, Raintree brought the conversation back to the topic at hand. "So, you want to hear about your daddy," he said. "Let's see. When I first met him over at Union of Hearts, he looked more like one of the poor lost souls we were there to minister than he did a volunteer. Dressed kind of shabby, needed a haircut, and generally run-down looking.

"But when he introduced himself and told me he was there to help out, I could tell right away that I was completely wrong about him. A woman named Sarah Bradley was running things day-to-day for us at Union of Hearts. We trucked the donated food over, and she made sure the volunteer staff cooked and served it, and that the place was cleaned up afterward. There were no overnight sleeping facilities there, so the people would just wander in, eat their fill, and then go back out on the streets again.

"Your daddy was with us for a year, maybe less, and I paid him a small salary. Not nearly as much as he was worth, mind you, but we are a charitable organization, and we stretch our contributions as far as we can."

Lloyd resisted the urge to glance around the place they were in, but he wondered how much stretching was involved in paying for this house and this lifestyle.

"He never talked about it, but I got the impression that at some point in his life, Billy himself had probably lived the kind of desperate life out on the streets that these people we serve were living. He had a connection with them that most of our volunteers, no matter how big their hearts might be, could never develop. Most of these poor lost children of God are more used to being treated like the crap on somebody's shoes than they are to being looked at and talked to like what they really are—living, breathing, thinking human beings with the holy spark of life and a God-given eternal soul deep within their breasts."

Raintree paused to take a drink of coffee and a mouthful of food, as if giving Lloyd time to admire his eloquence. And the words did have an impact on Lloyd. They confused him. He wanted to ask the preacher if there was a mistake here somewhere, and if they were definitely talking about the same Billy Ballou. How could one man walk away from his own family, cursing them to a life of unhappiness and desperation, then come down here and treat bums off the street with such empathy and compassion?

There had to be a catch. What was in it for Billy?

"Of course, he wasn't one hundred percent saint," Raintree went on with a chuckle. "But then who is? I never saw it firsthand, but Sarah told me he used to come in drunk once in a while, even first thing in the morning, like he was on an all-nighter. And he got in a few scuffles, usually with some first-timer that came in loaded and got out of control with the staff. Sarah said she got scared when that happened, because when Billy started fighting, all his good sense left him and he didn't know how to stop swinging even after he had won."

Lloyd remembered his mother talking about that. When they were dating, Billy had fractured the femur of a rival with a tire iron.

"He was arrested for one fight, and it took us a week to get him out of jail. He might have served some real time for that one, but the homeless man he beat up stole some drugs and sneaked out of the hospital, so we got the charges dropped."

Picturing Billy behind bars put him back in character, Lloyd thought.

They ate in silence for a minute. This was the best meal he'd had since he hit New Orleans. The coffee was growing on him, too. He thought he might try to find a cheap coffee pot for his room, although appliances were forbidden.

Finally, Raintree asked in a quiet voice, "Would you like for me to tell you about the day he died? Or should we skip that part?"

"I can handle it."

"Okay then. When the evacuation order went out, I told all my staff and volunteers to get out of New Orleans, but some of them wouldn't go. Your daddy was one who chose to stay. We all knew that some of the homeless would show up at our missions if they didn't have any other place else to go, and my people, God bless 'em, still felt a need to serve even with the worst storm in decades barreling down on them.

"We had a plan to distribute emergency stockpiles of food, water, blankets and medical supplies to the missions, for several days if need be. But of course, once that old gal roared ashore and the levies started crumbling, no plan but the Lord's was in play. We tried to send trucks out from the warehouse, but it was useless. If they weren't stopped by the floods, they were mobbed and looted on the street and the drivers had to flee for their lives.

“I tried to get out there during the storm, but it was just no use. It would have been suicide. So instead I cowered here, feeling as guilty as Judas himself because I was dry and safe.” He ran a hand back through his thick brown mane to express his discomfort at the memory, and a look of suffering came into his eyes. “In the middle of the hurricane, I spent hours on my knees praying for the safety of my people, and for the countless other tragic witnesses to the fury of God’s nature.”

“So did Billy die at Union of Hearts?” Lloyd asked.

“No, not there, although others did,” Raintree said. “We actually don’t know where he died because his body was never found and identified. All we’re really sure of is that if he had survived, he would have returned to us and gone back to work.”

“I see.”

“About thirty people tried to ride out the storm at the Union of Hearts Mission,” the preacher continued. “It was a mixed group, some homeless, and some local residents, mostly women and children and the elderly, who felt like they would be safer at our mission than in their own homes. Sarah Bradley, Billy Ballou, and another volunteer, Chas Kirchner, were there to take care of them as best they could. Sarah told me that even during the storm, others kept showing up, and they took everybody in.

“Sometime during the hurricane part of the building collapsed. Chas and a couple of others were killed outright, and several more were injured. It must have been a terrible scene, simply horrifying. But there was worse yet to come. After Katrina had done her worst, the looters and criminals showed up and pretty much took over the place.”

During another dramatic pause, Raintree let the imagined horror of the incident contort his face into a mask of sadness. It made Lloyd uncomfortable to watch him.

"Your daddy managed to get Sarah out of the mission and back to a safe haven in the French Quarter. But Billy didn't stay there with her. He told Sarah that he had to try to find some help for the injured people still at the mission. When he left her, that was the last any of us saw of him."

"So nobody really knows what happened to him?" Lloyd asked.

"Not to him, or to hundreds of others like him, swallowed whole by the storm and the days of chaos that came after," Raintree said. "He might have gone back to the mission and been killed by the looters and street thugs. Or he might have simply been randomly murdered on the street, an anonymous victim. Or he might have drowned. Only God knows."

"It sounds like he died well at least. Trying to help," Lloyd said. It sounded weak and detached, and Raintree gave him a questioning look.

"Why do I get the feeling that you still need more, Lloyd?" the preached asked. "You still have questions."

Lloyd considered that for a moment, then decided to just lay it all out there. Why not?

"Like I told you on the phone, Reverend Raintree," he said, "Billy left us a long time ago, and never looked back. Our family lived through a lot of difficult times because of that, especially my mother. I'm glad that he found something worthwhile to do here in his last days, and I suppose I'm sorry that he's dead.

"But the truth is, that's not the reason I came down here. I have a much more selfish motive. My mother Carol has cancer, one of those that can drag on for years before it finally takes you out. It's already cost her everything she has except her life, and it will take that too, soon enough. When I heard that Billy was dead, my first thought was to wonder if he left anything behind that I might use for her care. A house, a car, life insurance, savings, anything that I could turn into hard cash. They never divorced so she's still his wife. She would be entitled to it."

As Lloyd spoke, Raintree nodded sagely, as if it was a situation he had seen many times before and understood well. Lloyd could see no hint of judgment on the man's face, and he appreciated that at least.

"Okay, it's all becoming clearer to me now," the preacher said at last. "If I was in your shoes, I'd probably do the same. But I'm not sure how much help I can provide. We don't carry any insurance on his level of employee, which we term 'paid volunteer. ' He didn't own a car as far as I know, and I'm guessing he didn't own a house either. We probably have an address on file. Leila can give you that. And she should have his social security number. Your mother might be able to make a claim on that if you can find some legal proof of death. That's probably all."

"It's a couple more steps forward," Lloyd said resolutely.

Raintree glanced at his watch, and stood up. The meal and the meeting were over. Two men came in from the main house and stopped a few feet away at a respectful distance. The reverend introduced the man who intercepted Lloyd in the back yard as Rudy Soyez, his bodyguard. He didn't look like the type to line up and start singing, "Onward Christian Soldiers" but a man like Raintree would need protection. The other, an aging black man named Oscar Breach, was Raintree's driver.

"Stay here and finish your coffee, Lloyd," Raintree suggested. "I'll have Leila pull that information for you and bring it out." He shook Lloyd's hand warmly. "It's been a pleasure to meet you," he went on. "And for your own sake, don't carry around too much bitterness in your heart, son. If you do, it might not leave room for anything else. Your daddy was just a man, with a bad side and a good side, like all of us. I was fortunate enough to see him at his best, but I don't guess you know much about him except the bad."

After the three men left, Lloyd sipped at his lukewarm coffee and admired the sun room, the backyard pool and the gardens. J.T. was certainly doing alright for himself. There must be some pretty good money to be made in the sick kid business.

He saw the three men come out the back of the house by another door and head for the garage. Soon, through the opening in the thick hedge, he caught a glimpse of shiny black fenders passing out the gate. A Mercedes, he noted. A big one. Pretty good money indeed.

Eventually Leila came back out with the information Lloyd had requested.

"This is the last address we had for your father," she said, handing Lloyd a folded piece of paper, "and his social is on there, too. I wouldn't hold out much hope that the house is still there."

"I forgot to ask Reverend Raintree about this woman he mentioned, Sarah Bradley. It sounds like she and Billy must have worked closely."

"She was wonderful sweet woman," Leila said.

"Was?"

"Oh, she's not dead or anything. But she's no longer with The Hearts organization. I think the tragedy of the hurricane and the stress of everything that happened at the mission was just too much for her. She gave up her volunteer work with us, and we haven't heard from her in quite a long time."

"Could you help me contact her?" Lloyd asked.

"I couldn't give you that information without her permission," Leila said. "It wouldn't be fair to her."

"Well maybe you could call her. Tell her who I am and why I'm here, and give her my cell phone number. Then she could decide whether or not she wants to talk to me."

"I'll consider it, Mr. Ballou."

They left the sun room, and the secretary walked with him as they headed for the back gate.

"It looks like this place did pretty well during the storm," Lloyd suggested.

"Better than some, but there was a lot of damage. Trees down, broken windows, and over two feet of water covering the yards. Fortunately, the house is high enough that the water didn't rise above the foundations. But that little sun room where you ate breakfast was a shamble. Broken glass, mud, ruined plants, you name it. It's all been repaired now."

"It must have been terrifying, even in a relatively safe place like this."

"I'm sure it would have been," Leila said, "if I had been here."

"Oh, I just assumed . . ."

"I was one of the fortunate ones who was able to get out in time," she explained. "We didn't leave until the very last day, but eventually we were able to make it to Meridian where my family lives. But getting back in was even harder. They weren't allowing anybody to return. Finally, four days after the storm, we were able to ride back to the city on a National Guard helicopter because we ran a relief agency."

"We?" Lloyd asked.

"J.T. and me. He was eager to get back into the city."

Chapter Eight

Kelly used to send occasional pictures of herself to Lloyd's phone, even after they were divorced. She took them in everyday settings and her messages were generally light and chatty, scenes captured and transmitted to him as if he might be wondering what she was doing at that precise moment. He thought she must believe that somehow they could maintain an easy-going friendship despite their difficult past and the pain they had caused one another.

Once she sent him a full-length shot of herself, standing nude before a mirror that hung on the back of her bedroom door. There was something almost artistic about her casual posture and demure smile. Her tight, sleek body was just as he remembered it. Her gaze seemed to communicate to him.

Lloyd was sitting on the couch in a cramped, cluttered apartment when the picture reached him. For an elusive instant he almost thought that he finally understood why she did these things. She had thrown him away, willfully and without hesitation. But she still thought of him, still had regrets, sometimes even wanted him back.

Then in the picture's shadowy background he noticed Bob's dim image lying on the bed several feet away, raised on one elbow, leering happily at her nakedness.

Lloyd almost deleted it, then changed his mind. He would keep it to occasionally remind him of the casual cruelty that can exist in those who once were closest to you.

After leaving Raintree's house and taking the trolley back downtown, Lloyd planned to locate the address Leila gave him and see what remained of the place where Billy once lived. He wasn't sure what he would be looking for, but it seemed to be the next logical step. If the neighborhood wasn't completely wrecked, maybe he would find someone who had known Billy—a neighbor, landlord, shopkeeper, somebody.

But as he entered the edge of the French Quarter a man outside a parking garage on Peters Street stopped him and asked him if he'd like to make ten dollars an hour for a few hours of work. He supposed his worn jeans and faded mechanics shirt made him look like a ten-dollar-an-hour sort of man.

The man ran the garage for one of the nearby hotels, and one of his employees hadn't shown up. For the next few hours Lloyd washed and waxed the cars of hotel guests in a dim, damp back corner of the building. He left the place at eight that evening with an unexpected windfall of ninety extra dollars in his jeans. Lloyd wasn't exactly broke, not yet, but the money was draining from his checking account in Kansas City at an unsettling rate. There was nothing coming in to replenish it, and nothing to fall back on.

He was worn out and ready to go to bed early after treating himself to a better than usual meal, which he now felt he deserved and could afford. He had a place in mind that offered twelve-dollar steak dinners and two-dollar long necks. He'd have no trouble sleeping tonight.

Glancing in a plate glass window as he strolled down Decatur, he saw a face he recognized. It was Betsy, back behind the bar where he first met her a few days before. On impulse he went in.

"Hey Missouri!" she said with a smile. "What happened to you? Did you fall in the river?"

Lloyd realized how disheveled he must look. His shirt and jeans were wrinkled and damp from the day's work, and his hair was finger-combed back to keep it out of his face.

"The last time I saw you in here you ran me off," Lloyd said. "I didn't know if you'd allow me to come back."

"Long as you've got money in your pocket, baby boy," Betsy said. She remembered his brand and set a cold one in front of him. "Where have you been?" The place was empty at the moment, and she leaned her elbows on the bar, giving Lloyd her full attention, as well as a casual peek down the front of her shirt. That was probably good for tips.

"I stopped in the other night, but you were off. That other guy who works here is a real charmer, isn't he?"

"Kane? He creeps me out. I hate working doubles with him because he's always *accidentally* rubbing against me. One night I told him if he didn't stop, I was going to tase his stiffie and drag him out into the alley with it. He'd be right at home back there with the rats and roaches."

Lloyd took a long drink of the beer, feeling the relaxation flow over him.

How's the 'family business' going?" Betsy asked.

"I'm making a little progress," Lloyd reported. "My father went missing after Katrina, and I've been trying to find out something about him." It surprised him that he just spilled it out like that to her. But that's what people did with bartenders, wasn't it?

"That's tough, Lloyd. I'm sorry to hear it. But it's not such an unusual story in this city."

"It's not so bad. He left us a long time ago, when I was a kid, and I haven't seen him since."

"Do you think he's dead?"

"I don't think there's any doubt. But there's no body to prove it," Lloyd said. "I'm trying to find out if he might have left anything behind that I could use to help my mom. She's not doing so well right now." Without thinking about it, he dumped the whole load on Betsy—Billy's abandonment, Carol's cancer, the letter from Charmaine Xavier, and his own decision to come down here and do some nosing around. He even told her about losing his job. It could have just been an act of professionalism, but Betsy listened as if this stuff really mattered to her.

By the time he finished talking, Lloyd's second beer was empty, and Betsy was popping the cap on a third. A young couple came in and stood at the end of the bar while Betsy refilled their tall plastic cups with draft beer, then she returned to her station in front of Lloyd.

"What kind of food do you have in this place?" Lloyd asked.

"Nothing the health department would approve of," Betsy said.

"I was on my way to dinner when I saw you through the window. I stumbled across a day's work this morning, and I haven't put anything in my stomach since breakfast. Except water and this stuff," Lloyd said, raising his beer bottle.

"Well Hemingway insisted that beer is food," Betsy told him. "And who are we to argue with Hemingway?"

"Steak is food, too."

"I'll tell you what, Lloyd. Hang around here and knock back a couple more until I get off. Then we'll go someplace and do something."

"Does 'something' include food?"

"Sure. I don't feel like going home, but I don't feel like hanging out by myself either."

"I'm pretty grubby," Lloyd warned.

"It's okay," Betsy laughed. "You'll be right at home in the kind of rat holes I'll be dragging you into."

* * *

The room Lloyd woke up in looked like an artist's studio in imminent danger of being reclaimed by a nearby jungle. Canvases, easels, paintings, sketches and artist supplies of every description were scattered all about, and the floor was a riot of paint spills and splashes in every conceivable color. Flowers and lush, sprawling foliage plants cluttered the tabletops, the floor, and the narrow balcony outside an open set of French doors. Only a path of sorts led from the bed where he and Betsy had slept, to the kitchenette and front door at the other side of the room.

He stretched lazily on the bed, judging by the sunlight spilling into the room that it must be mid-morning. Betsy was nowhere in sight.

Sex with her, and the exhausted sleep that followed, had been unfamiliar and somehow out of sync, as it usually was with strangers. After their first hour out together last night they had both known they would end up here like this. There had been no negotiation, no seduction. When the time came, they just strolled here to her small apartment on the end of the quarter where the locals lived, climbed the narrow creaking stairs to the second floor, and did what people do. Even strangers.

Lloyd vaguely remembered Betsy getting up during the night and standing by the French doors, staring at the deserted streets outside. She had cried quietly for a little while before finally coming back to bed and molding herself tightly against him. It was as if he could actually feel the yearning and remorse subside within her as she drew comfort from his physical presence beside her. They both slept deeply and restfully after that.

His clothes were in a jumble on the floor. Lloyd heaved himself up and pulled on his boxers, then went to the window and stood looking out. New Orleans was awake and active outside on this bright, clear Saturday morning. It had rained overnight, and the breeze blowing in the open doors was warm and humid, rich with the odors of the city.

He didn't even want to consider yet what last night meant, or if it meant anything at all.

Betsy returned, bringing coffee and beignets. She pushed back plants and tubes of paint until she made room for them to eat on a small table by the kitchenette.

"I hope this is okay," she said. "I'm not a breakfast person, or even a morning person. Lunch is usually my first meal of the day."

"It's fine," Lloyd said, breaking off a piece of beignet and shaking the excess powdered sugar off of it. The coffee was thick and strong, much like the coffee J.T. Raintree had served him. "I didn't even know you had gone out."

"You were in a coma when I got up. Even the sound of the shower didn't bother you, and those old pipes growl like a foghorn."

"Being tired and drunk and freshly laid will do that to a man," Lloyd grinned.

"Well, I'm glad you're up now," Betsy said, "because I've got to get going in a few minutes. A gallery down on Royal has some of my pieces on display, and the tourists are more inclined to buy a painting when they get to chat with the artist."

"We were together all evening, and you never mentioned that you were an artist," Lloyd said. "I don't even remember seeing all this stuff when we came in last night."

"It was dark, and you had other things on your mind," Betsy said, winking at him.

While Lloyd nibbled at a beignet, drank his coffee, and watched, Betsy went to the corner of the room that served as her boudoir and changed into something sufficiently artsy, a long full peasant skirt and a loose, brightly colored blouse. She was well into her late thirties, or maybe even early forties if she was taking care of herself. She was not a girl anymore by any measure, and her body had begun the inevitable thickening of middle age. But that hadn't mattered last night, and it still didn't this morning. There was something about that quick, pretty smile, those lively knowing eyes, the way she seemed to just adapt to things as they came. She moved with a smoothness that said she was comfortable being who she was, and she had a mid-life loveliness that Lloyd found elusively appealing.

He finished his coffee and most of a beignet, then went over and pulled his clothes on. They left the building together, pausing on the sidewalk outside for an awkward parting.

"You never did get your steak last night," Betsy said.

"I forgot all about it, but there's always a steak to be had someplace. This was better. Thanks for letting me tag along with you, Betsy. And thanks for . . . well . . ."

Betsy laughed lightly and stood on tiptoe to kiss his cheek. "You know where to find me," she said, and turned away.

* * *

The tiny frame house on Jacquelyn Street a few blocks northwest of the French Quarter sat in a row of low-end hovels gutted by the storm and apparently not worth anyone's time or money to reclaim. Few had any remaining doors or windows, and weeds had grown tall and lush in the tiny abandoned yards.

Billy's house, like all the others, had suffered the indignities of looters, then vandals and squatters, after Katrina had done her worst. Nothing of any value or possible human use remained inside. But Lloyd felt the need to give the place a thorough inspection nonetheless.

The floors were littered with the expected refuse—beer cans and liquor bottles, empty food cans, sodden newspapers, condoms, syringes, and so on. In one corner of the room that might have been the bedroom, a rotting, waterlogged mattress lay rolled up against a wall. The toilet, sinks, stove, refrigerator, and even the kitchen cabinets had been ripped out and hauled away. The inside walls and ceilings were chopped up and the wiring behind them stripped out. It was amazing, Lloyd thought, what desperate people managed to steal.

He tried to imagine Billy making his home here, furnishing it with shabby second-hand furniture and dollar-store accessories, fixing simple meals, watching television, going to bed at night and getting up in the morning. What had it been like for him? What had he thought about when he was home alone, when he stretched out on his bed and the world grew dark and quiet around him? Had demons from his past haunted him, or did his thoughts roam no farther than what he had done that day, and what he would do the next?

It was useless to come here, Lloyd realized. He didn't know what he had expected or hoped for, but there was nothing left here, no sign that Billy Ballou had ever inhabited this tiny space, no lingering shadow of his restless, ambiguous spirit.

The closet door fell toward Lloyd as he pulled it open. It was the same story inside. The floor was heaped with soggy rags that had once been clothes, perhaps Billy's. A startled rat scurried toward a back corner and disappeared.

He saw a mashed, decaying shoebox to one side and gave it a lethargic nudge with his shoe. If it had once contained anything of value, its contents would be long gone by now. But there was something inside. Lloyd knelt and brought the box out into the light.

He retrieved a handful of damp, decaying photos, and immediately realized that this effort had not been completely wasted. He had never seen the top picture before, but he instantly recognized the people in it. His mother Carol, young, pretty, and happy once more, stood on the top porch step of a simple white house, holding baby Bennie. In front of her was little Kat, smiling for the camera, and Lloyd himself, wearing a childish imitation of the smirk he had learned from his father.

The next few pictures were of people he didn't know, an old man standing with a shotgun in the crook of his arm, three old women posing side by side in front of a flower garden, a young woman, pretty except for her crooked teeth, a child of four or five sitting at the top of a playground slide.

The final picture returned Lloyd to familiar territory. He and Kat were sitting on the front porch steps of yet another rundown rented house eating ice cream. He recognized the house. It was the one with the creek running along the back boundary of the property, the house where they lived when Bennie drown.

Then it struck him. Billy had left them long before they moved into that house, years before. So how had he gotten this picture of Lloyd and his sister? Could Carol have sent it to some old address, or to some member of Billy's family? It didn't seem likely. If she ever had any such information, she would have gone looking for him.

On one edge of the photo was a shiny, blurry object that Lloyd finally realized was a car's side mirror. Then he got it. Billy himself had taken the picture. He had come to their house and parked across the street. He had taken the picture of his daughter and son, but then lacked the courage to get out and declare his presence to the family who missed him so much and needed him so badly.

"What a weasel," Lloyd murmured. Billy Ballou could feed all the bums he wanted, mold himself into a shabby saint in the eyes of these people here, even save a woman from rape and murder in the midst of a hurricane. But he could never undo what he had done, or truly change what he was.

Lloyd put the photos in his pocket and headed for the door, wanting nothing more at that moment than to get out of this filthy, hateful place.

Chapter Nine

By all rights Lloyd should have been a drunk. The children of many drunks were, especially if they grew up neglected and ignored in a love starved home as he had. It just seemed to be the natural path to start down early, and not many were able to turn things around once they began the journey.

Sure, he drank, mostly beer, occasionally too much, and rarely way too much. But he never remembered reaching that point when he couldn't stop, when he woke in the morning anticipating that first drink of the day, and went to bed at night stupid and stupefied, unable to raise another glass or can. He had never signed away ownership of his soul to the stuff.

He had seen enough drunks in his life to understand that if the fates had done him one single favor in thirty-eight years, that was it.

He wondered sometimes what it might have been like for his mother Carol, and for all of them, if she hadn't gotten her head stuck in a bottle trying to forget the pain of Billy's abandonment. "Better" was as far as he ever got with it.

June Bug was eating something out of a crumpled, greasy wrapper, but Lloyd couldn't quite figure out what it was. A sandwich maybe, or shrimp, or possibly just some random, edible garbage culled from a trash can during her rambling migration here to Jackson Square.

She was almost clean today, and smelled far better than she had the only time he saw her here several nights before. She had on a long-sleeved plaid shirt and a pair of faded jeans that almost fit. Her wiry salt-and-pepper hair was pulled back and held with a rubber band. She wore a piece of green ribbon tied around her head, and a matching green bow was perched flirtatiously above one ear. Lloyd knew the improvements were probably the result of a brief sojourn in rehab, or maybe just a stay in a shelter someplace.

"I wisht my Mayor would come back. He alls brought me somethin' good to eat. Better'n this trash can crap. He was the best husband I *ever* had," June Bug insisted. A rivulet of something that looked like mustard ran down her chin as she spoke. Her accent had a southern twang, Alabama, possibly, or Mississippi. "An' I had lots of husbands. Maybe about a hunnert of 'em."

It was late in the evening, and finally beginning to cool down after a steamy afternoon. Foot traffic had been fairly heavy, but now it was beginning to wane. The musicians on the benches nearby were getting too drunk to play for the tourists, and some of the fortune tellers and artists were starting to pack their wares and leave.

"What made him such a good husband, June Bug?" Lloyd asked.

"He watched out for me. Made people leeb me alone," she explained. "If I was drunk, he'd take me someplace where I could sleep safe. Sometimes he'd keep my stuff for me so nobody would steal it. An' he give me stuff. Cigarettes and bologna, stuff like that. But not no gin, though. Didn't like me drinkin' gin when I was around him. My Mayor."

"Was that his name? Mayor?" Lloyd knew better than to ask her to try to spell it.

"Yup. My husband. His name was Mayor."

Lloyd had been hanging around the Jackson Square area for a couple of hours, sipping on beers, talking to whoever was willing to talk, absorbing the flavor of the place. He felt comfortable here with these people. For the time being, they were the closest thing he had to friends.

"Mayor, he called my daughter Sissy in Tecumseh, to get her to take me in an' gib me a home. But she wouldn't have none of it. Said it was too hard for her, and it wasn't no use anyways. Said her kids was scared of me, an' her husband said he'd leeb if I came back again. I guess she's right. I ain't been a good person, I s'pose. I never did right by that gal her whole life. Not really.

"But my Mayor, he was different. He always took care of me. Like a husband, an' I sure do miss him."

The other night when Lloyd first saw June Bug, filthy, slumped over and drooling, babbling drunk, she appeared to be an ancient old relic. But now, cleaned up and a little more sober, he realized that she was younger than he thought, mid fifties, perhaps.

"So where is he now?" Lloyd asked.

"Who?"

"Mayor. Your husband."

"Gone. Long gone now. When the hurricane came, they took a bunch of us in a bus over to Houston. We stayed in this big place with a thousand people, and they gave us blankets and water and food to eat. But I didn't like it there. I stayed sick all the time, and couldn't get no gin to help my guts. I blew that place soon's I could and come back here."

"But Mayor was gone when you got back," Lloyd surmised.

"Yep. Gone as hell. I never could . . ." She stopped unexpectedly as something behind Lloyd caught her attention. A guarded look came into her eyes.

Lloyd turned and saw two uniformed New Orleans policemen walking casually toward them. The younger of the pair was about Lloyd's height, haughty in his crisp blues, twirling his baton carelessly by its leather strap, clearly impressed by his own authority. His partner was several years older, a paunchy jaded veteran.

The two cops stopped in front of Lloyd and June Bug. The younger one grinned at them and said, "So, you found yourself another husband, huh June Bug?" He spoke with that unique local accent that, to the untrained ear, sounded almost like Brooklynese. He shifted his gaze to Lloyd. "Hadn't seen you around before. Where you from?"

"Kansas City." Lloyd told him. "Have we done something wrong, officer? We're just sitting here talking."

"No, nothing I can see," the cop said. He reached out with his baton and rapped the paper bag that held Lloyd's beer. It fell off the bench and emptied on the flagstones. "But if you're thinking about tapping this one, I hope you brought a pocket full of latex." His baton whacked June Bug's leg, and she winced in pain.

"We're just talking, nothing more," Lloyd said, keeping his tone neutral, his temper in check.

"That's good, cause June Bug here, she's got every kind of clap and crawly crotchety thing they ever gave a name to. Don't you, June Bug?"

June Bug's eyes were diverted down to her lap. "Caught most of 'em from you, Pepper," she muttered under her breath.

Pepper's partner chucked, but Pepper didn't seem accustomed to having his jokes turned around on him.

"Is that so?" the cop said. He tapped the woman's knee with his baton, then hit her knuckles when she reached out to protect her legs. "When you backtalk me, old skank, you know what's going to happen." As he spoke, he kept hitting her with his baton, not hard enough to break bones, or even hard enough to bruise, but certainly hard enough to hurt.

"Look, she didn't mean anything," Lloyd said. With this type he knew he wasn't going to get anywhere, but he couldn't bear to sit there and just let it happen.

"Stay out of it, unless you want some of the same," Pepper said, glaring at Lloyd.

"Well, better me than her," Lloyd said, "if you feel like you've got something to prove."

"Come on, Pepper," the cop's partner said. He touched Pepper's shoulder, but Pepper shrugged away. It was a dangerous mix, Lloyd thought. A smug cop with a temper, and a stick.

"Let me handle this, Gautier," Pepper growled. "You know we can't let this kind backtalk us. They gotta respect the badge." He drew his arm back and this time Lloyd could tell that anger would fuel the blow. As he swung forward, Lloyd reached out and caught his arm in mid-swing.

He couldn't have made Pepper any angrier if he had pissed on his shoe.

For a moment Pepper simply seethed. Then, through clenched teeth, he ordered, "On your feet, Romeo." Lloyd stood carefully, realizing that at this moment he was one wrong word or deed away from plenty of pain, and maybe a trip to jail on charges that would be concocted on the way. "See that little alley over there?" the cop said. "That's where we're going. That's my church and we're going to have a little come-to-Jesus talk."

In the alley Lloyd got about what he expected. A hard shove against the wall, some tough trash talk about respect, several painful whacks with the baton. He knew Pepper's type, even worked with his kind from time to time, and he knew the young cop's biggest problems concerning respect probably started in the squad room. He might not be worthless enough to kick off the force, but nobody believed he had the sand to do the job right when the flame touched the fuse.

Lloyd also recognized the partner's type. Gautier just put in the hours, tried not to stir things up too much unless Pepper seriously crossed the line, and waited it out until the next rotation when he was almost certain to draw a better partner.

Lloyd did what was called for under the circumstances, and left the alley with nothing more than an aching gut and a slight limp from a painful whack to the side if his knee.

He was going to have to keep an eye out for that pair now, especially Pepper. He'd do the same again if he got the chance. That's who he was.

June Bug was gone when he got back to the bench. Smart move on her part. Lloyd sat down and pulled his pants leg up to look at the egg-sized lump that had raised on his knee, then retrieved his beer from the ground and drank what remained in it. Just another balmy summer evening with the locals.

"I seed that rat bastard Pepper slammin' on you." It was Chester hobbling over to commiserate with him. "We all hate him when he comes around. An' we scared of him, too. There ain't never no tellin' who he'll choose to pick on from one time to the next. Po-lice, he says. Respec', he says. Humph!" He summarized his contempt by spitting on the flagstone. "His daddy in gov'ment."

"Just for one crazy second it crossed my mind to feed him that night stick," Lloyd grinned. "But then I listened to my wiser angels."

"Well, even just thinking about it can give a man some satisfaction," Chester laughed. He sat down beside Lloyd, and Lloyd offered him the last cigarette in the pack he had brought along. June Bug had taken all the rest, confiscating three or four each time Lloyd offered her one.

"June Bug was talking about somebody named Mayor that used to watch out for her," Lloyd said.

"Yep, a good man," Chester said. "Used to come around some evenings, maybe bring us some food. She got it in her crazy old brain that they married 'cause he was kind to her, an' didn't nobody mess with her when he was here. Not even Pepper, mos' times. But he never showed back up after Katrina. God only knows . . .

"Sometimes it gets rough livin' this street life," Chester said. "A person get hurt, maybe even die, an' don't nobody even care except maybe some other throwaways like him."

Across the way on another bench, a young man began strumming a guitar. It was a soft ballad of some kind, a tune that Lloyd didn't recognize. It could be something the guy was making up then and there.

"But there's some good things too," Chester said. "Sky above, earth below. No boss man tell you 'do this, do that.' No bills to pay, no windows to wash, no car always needs fixin'. Somebody's always gonna give you a little money for a drink or a bite to eat.

"And sometimes you can just let your soul connect with the world. That's when I let the poetry come out."

"So, you're a poet, Chester?" Lloyd asked.

"Not like them poets in books an' schools," Chester said. "I'm just a poet in my soul. I don't write nothin' down, an' I don't hardly remember none of it from day to day. I just let it out, and by and by it flies away on the breeze."

"That's downright spiritual. I'd like to hear something."

Okay, let's see now." He closed his eyes for at least a minute, and when he opened them again the words started coming.

Quiet man with a hurt knee. Looking for something.
Thinks he knows what, but he don't know.
Soul locked in deep down,
Sometimes hard to remember it's even in there.
Sometimes wishes he could cry.
But that ain't what he needs.

As he got into it, Chester raised one hand like a spiritualist beseeching the powers above. His gaze was so unwavering that it made Lloyd uncomfortable.

Hope run off to the woods like a sick old dog.
Won't come when you call him.
"Dream woman won't sleep with a man
that won't dream before he sleeps.
"Feet numb from all that walkin'.
"Seeds drying out in his hand."

Across the way a couple of Chester's cronies were elbowing each other and chuckling. They were too far away to hear his words, but no doubt they had seen him run through this routine with targets of opportunity many times.

Sons and mamas, girls and their daddies.
Always thought there would be something to hold onto.
But it all changes.
Change is all that don't change.
Better listen up if you hear the voice.
First time could be the last time.
Might be somethin' you need to know.
Might just be the wind.

A wide grin broke out on Chester's face as soon as he finished. Clearly he was proud of this talent.

"Did you come up with that just now?" Lloyd asked.

"Sure. It just comes out of me. Sometimes it makes sense and it's sort of spiritual, like you said. Other times it's just a load of crap. That's when people look at me kinda nervous and walk away. The crazy cripple."

"Well I liked it, Chester."

"A'right, then buy me a beer," Chester suggested with an unabashed grin. He seemed used to asking for fair value in trade. "The little grocery's still open up the block. I'll wait here so I don't slow you down."

Lloyd got an overpriced six-pack of cheap beer and brought it back to share with the group. They sat around for a while enjoying the cooling evening air and talking a little, but not about anything in particular.

Sly had two days' work starting Monday, helping a bricklayer patch a foundation over on Desire. Chester had made up with his sister-in-law so he'd be sleeping on a bed tonight with the luxury of a box fan keeping him cool. He described the big breakfast she always fixed on Sunday morning, but to pay for it he'd have to take a shower, put on some of his nephew's clean clothes, and go to church with the family.

By midnight just three of them remained. The various vendors had all cleared out, and few people passed by that weren't staggering drunk. Sly seemed in no particular hurry to leave, nor was another fellow who, an hour before, had slumped over sideways on a bench and fallen asleep. As near as Lloyd could tell, his name was Jo-she, or something along those lines.

Lloyd wasn't drunk, but he felt remarkably mellow. The beers had calmed the dull ache in his battered stomach and leg. He actually looked forward to the cramped little rooming house bed, and figured that he'd probably sleep deep enough to ignore the thumping passage of his neighbors on the walkway outside his room.

Across the way he saw shadowy figures in the alley where Pepper had taken him for his lesson in respect. At first, he wondered if the two cops had returned, and if he should go ahead and leave before they came over. But it was three people, not two, and as they came out into a little better light, he saw that it was two young men and a young woman.

Eventually the three sat on the concrete steps in front of the cathedral, smoking and drinking from plastic cups, and talking quietly among themselves. The two young men flanked the girl on either side, as if vying for her attention.

She was pretty, about twenty Lloyd guessed, but wasted and kind of frazzled looking. She wore a halter top with a short denim skirt, and her legs were long and slender. One of those guys was bound to get lucky tonight, Lloyd figured.

That made him think of Betsy, but only for a moment. Then something else caught his attention.

One of the young men over there with the girl was Tats, the guy who had earned a pop in the face by pulling a knife on Lloyd. He didn't seem to recognize Lloyd, which was a good thing for all of them.

After surreptitious looks around, Tats passed something off to the other guy, and soon after the other guy got up and walked away. Not long after that, Tats fished something out of his jeans pocket and handed it to the young woman. She looked at it briefly in her palm, then tossed it into her mouth and washed it down with a drink of beer.

If she hadn't been prime pickings before, Lloyd thought, she would be when that stuff kicked in, whatever it was. He couldn't hear what they were talking about, but he could tell by Tats' body language that he had started his selling job. At first she would just laugh and shake her head, but he was persistent.

After a few more minutes of conversation, Tats stood up and reached out his hand. The young woman allowed herself to be pulled to her feet, still grinning and giddy. She was none too steady on her feet, but Tats slipped an arm around her waist and they started away.

It was none of his business, Lloyd told himself. He didn't know the girl, and she looked old enough to be responsible for her actions, or irresponsible, if that was her choice. But it still bothered him, maybe because of his brief experiences with the worthless slug she was with.

"I think I'll make a sweep up to Bourbon Street, and then probably call it a night," Lloyd told Sly. "You got this guy covered?" he indicated Jo-she with his thumb.

"If he wakes up, I take him with me," Sly said. "Elsewise, Pepper can wake him up later with that stick of his."

Tracking somebody strolling down Bourbon Street late Saturday night was about as easy as falling down stairs. Tats' companion was enthralled by the crowd and the night life here at the decadent epicenter of the French Quarter. She paused to dance in the street to the raucous music blasting out an open club door, and managed to spill most of her drink on herself and a couple of drunk revelers. She snagged a necklace of plastic beads tossed her way by a partier on a balcony above, and donned them like they were pearls. Tats got her another drink from a street-side vendor, and she spilled that one too. She stood beside a mime and tried to match his pose, then made Tats drop a dollar in his box.

Tats was patient, but made sure they didn't linger too long in any place. He seemed to have a destination in mind, but the girl didn't appear to know or care where they were going.

Most of the strip joints were on the downtown end of the quarter, strung out along the last three blocks before fantasyland ended and the real city began. Pretty young girls that didn't seem old enough to even enter such places stood like bait just inside doorways, wearing wisps of fabric, high heels, and way too much makeup. Barkers who could have been hired straight out of the drunk tank worked the sidewalks, annoying every man that passed with their overbearing invitations to go in and take a look.

Lloyd knew what lay inside. The undersized drinks would cost three times what they should, and the women would make it clear from the start that you had to be willing to part with some cash if you wanted to truly enjoy the merchandise. But if you had the cash, anything was possible.

Wearing the uniform back in Kansas City, he had hauled all types out of places like this—drunks and drug dealers, under-aged girls, prostitutes, perverts, and every other flavor of garden variety punk. Out of uniform, he and his buddies were sometimes patrons, too.

Just before the French Quarter party district ended, Tats steered the girl down a side street. The crowd immediately thinned and the noise level diminished. Lloyd fell back a few more paces, then sat down on the sidewalk like a drunken loiterer to watch.

One side of the street was lined with old two- and three-story brick buildings. Most looked vacant, but a couple appeared to be under renovation. The ground floor of the buildings on the opposite side of the street contained low-end eateries, bars, and small businesses of one sort or another, most closed at this late hour.

Toward the far end of the block, Tats pulled open a heavy metal door and ushered his young companion in. The burst of rock music that splattered out when the door opened was clipped short when it swung shut. Lloyd got to his feet and headed that way.

The place was called Club Les Girls. On the marquis above the door, a neon woman twisted and wiggled spastically. The windows across the front were darkly opaque, with bars to protect them, and the heavy metal door looked sturdy enough to withstand an RPG attack. The windows facing the street on the second and third floors above were either blackened or covered with heavy blinds.

Standing in the shadow of a big metal dumpster across the street from Club Les Girls, Lloyd weighed the risk of going in. Despite their close encounters recently, Lloyd thought Tats wasn't likely to recognize him, and there was no chance that anybody else in there knew him.

With very little cash in his pocket, he couldn't afford to sit around and drink for long, but they wouldn't let him stay if he didn't drink. And what would it accomplish? He should just go on back and go to bed. Tats had latched onto a wasted chick, had brought her to a strip club to get her primed for the main event, and that was that. So what?

But those old cop instincts still tugged at him. There was something else.

He sunk back into the shadow of a dumpster and sat down. He could wait. That was something Lloyd was good at.

There wasn't much traffic in and out of Les Girls. Once when a party of swaying, stumbling men in crumpled business suits stood with the door open, arguing about whether to go inside, he got a glimpse of the interior. Long hardwood bar to the left, tables and chairs filling the center of the room. The stage with its poles and other accoutrements was probably to the right, out of his line of sight. A few men were seated here and there, a few women strolled about looking for opportunities.

A couple of flirtatious women in lingerie came out and dragged the men inside, and the door swung closed again.

Tats reappeared a short time later, now alone. He paused on the sidewalk long enough to light a cigarette, not noticing Lloyd in the shadows across the street. Then he turned left and started away.

But what had happened to the girl? Lloyd wondered. Had she finally figured out that she was a fox keeping company with a sewer rat? Had someone inside made her a better offer? Or had she finally reached full alcohol and drug saturation and passed out? Lloyd decided he wanted to know.

He crossed the street and entered Les Girls. Business was slow, and two women were in his face almost immediately. One introduced herself as Satin, the hostess. She introduced him to the other woman, Crimson, and explained that Crimson would get him settled in with a table and a drink. There was no warmth or connection in Crimson's fixed stripper smile.

Lloyd smiled at them like a pilgrim freshly arrived in the holy land. "That sounds just fine, ladies," he said, slouching and slurring. "But would you mind if I stopped by the can first? I need to pay the rent."

He started toward the back of the bar, taking his time. On the stage a skinny girl with long blond hair and an odd, disconnected look in her eyes, was going about the routine process of shedding her clothes for a table of men near the stage. Occasionally one of them hooted and tossed some money at her feet.

Tats' companion was at a table in a dim back corner, a drink in her hand, sitting with three other women. Two of her companions were about her age, barely dressed, laughing and talking with her like she was one of their own.

The third woman at the table interested Lloyd more. She was older than the other three, and the tight black silk dress she wore didn't look designed for easy removal. As the others chatted, her eyes constantly swept the room, keeping track of everyone there and everything that happened. She'd be the floor boss, Lloyd thought. Her gaze tracked him briefly on his way to the john, then moved on. He felt relieved not to have rated any particular notice.

Crimson was waiting nearby when he came out of the men's room. "Come on baby, I saved our best table for you," she cooed, caressing his chest softly with her fingers. "What are you drinking?"

"Actually, I don't feel so hot," Lloyd mumbled. "What's that saying? Wine on beer? Or is it beer on wine?"

"Oh crap. Are you going to puke?"

"Maybe . . . maybe I need to just go on back to my room."

"Good idea, Jack," Crimson told him, suddenly all business. "We sure don't want to be cleaning up after you in here."

Lloyd lurched for the door, and no one tried to delay him. Once outside, he turned in the same direction Tats had gone and set a course for the boarding house.

The girl hadn't jilted Tats, and she hadn't passed out. She was in the middle of a job interview, although she might not yet be fully aware of it.

Among his other street enterprises, apparently Tats was also a talent scout for Club Les Girls. As Lloyd strolled down the dim, deserted street, he had to wonder what price a cute young woman in her early twenties went for these days.

Chapter Ten

Lloyd remembered slivers and bits of the things his father said about his own childhood, although at eight none of it had much relevance to him. Houma, Roulade, Bayou Justine, and Terrebonne Parish could have been places on another continent, or the names of craters on the moon.

He vaguely remembered that Billy was bitter toward his father. There had been some sort of falling out over a houseboat and a shotgun and a dead bird dog. Billy seldom mentioned his mother unless it had something to do with food, or their house, or whippings, or making him go to school until he was old enough to drop out on his own. There was an older brother, killed in an oil rig accident, but Lloyd couldn't remember his name. And there was a grandfather who hardly spoke a word of English, played the fiddle at community gatherings, and got drunk every night of the week.

Lloyd much preferred the stories Billy told about playing pirates on the bayou with his friends, or going out in a pirogue and catching redfish and baby alligators and washtubs full of crabs and shrimp. It all sounded like high adventure, and Billy had promised to take him when he got a little older.

By the time Billy was old enough to buy an old clunker and keep it running, he was ready to leave home. Thinking back on that now, it was no surprise to Lloyd. Billy was the kind who always left.

The two-lane paved road leading south out of Houma passed through flat, wet, useless looking country. On both sides were broad expanses of brush-filled swamps, interspersed with patches of impenetrable, soggy looking forest clinging to islands of slightly higher ground. It wasn't like any terrain Lloyd had ever experienced, and he wondered what it must be like when one of those big storms like Katrina blasted in from the Gulf across flat country like this. Much worse than anything the Midwest had to offer, he imagined, even if you threw in the tornadoes that Kansas seemed so fond of spinning across the state line into Missouri.

He'd gotten a cheap deal on a one-day car rental from one of the smaller outfits, but he couldn't help thinking how much more enjoyable this trip might have been if he had his legs wrapped around his bike instead being folded into this tiny yellow sub-compact.

The little settlement of Roulade stretched thinly along a half-mile strip of highway a dozen miles south of Houma. Most of the houses were small, some built with heavy timbers anchoring them to the ground, shutters for every window, and white clapboard siding to reflect away the stifling Louisiana heat. A boat of some type was visible at almost every home, and some of the houses had docks reaching out over the deep green canal that seemed to parallel almost every road and highway in this part of the state. There were a few businesses of the expected variety, gas stations, groceries, restaurants, bars and bait shops.

Lloyd wanted to call ahead to let his father's Aunt Charmaine Xavier know he was coming, but she had not included her phone number in her letter, and directory assistance couldn't help him. So he took his chances.

He pulled into the first service station at the northern edge of Roulade and got directions. Charmaine Xavier lived in a wood frame house on a quiet side street that dead-ended at a still, green bayou. The house and grounds looked well maintained. The spreading branches of a live oak shaded the house and part of the yard, and two thick, fresh stumps showed that there had been more trees until recently. Evidence of Katrina's work was everywhere.

Lloyd parked on the edge of the road and followed a gravel path to the front door. He knocked once on the screen door, then waited a minute and knocked again. The inside door was open, and through the screen he could see a small, neat parlor.

"Hold your garters out there, Raymond," a woman called out from somewhere inside the house. "You know how slow I get around."

Eventually a woman came through a doorway in the back of the room, moving slowly toward the screen door, pushing an aluminum walker ahead of her. On the drive over from New Orleans, Lloyd had tried to calculate how old Aunt Charmaine might be, but knowing so little about their family relationships, it was hard to tell. His best guess put her in her eighties at least.

"I swear, Raymond, for a man who hardly ever shows up anyplace on time," she scolded as she shuffled across the room, "you sure are in an all-fired hurry this morning." It wasn't until she came right up to the screen that she looked up and saw that her guest was not who she expected.

"Goodness me, you're not Raymond," she said, tilting her head curiously to the side as if to get a better look.

"No ma'am, I'm not. I'm Lloyd."

A moment passed, and Lloyd saw the curiosity on her face slowly change to recognition, then shock and surprise. Time might have diminished her body and etched its roadmap on her features, but with one look into her eyes, Lloyd could tell that his aunt's mind was still clear and sharp. "Oh my!" she muttered. "Oh my, it really is you, isn't it?"

"Yes ma'am," Lloyd said quietly.

"I can see your daddy in you, boy. I might have recognized you even if you didn't tell me your name." Lloyd doubted that, but let it go.

"Come here, Lloyd, and give your Aunt Charmaine a great big hug." She pushed the screen door open and raised her arms to him. It proved awkward with the walker between them, but she pulled him down to her level, wrapped her bony arms around his neck, and kissed his cheek.

"Come in, come in," Aunt Charmaine said. "I'll get us some tea. I'm so happy that you've come to see me."

Lloyd followed her into the house. The parlor they crossed was crowded with well-used furniture, and the rugs were worn thin from decades of traffic. The floorboards creaked and gave slightly beneath his feet. But the place was clean and neat, smelling of apples and vanilla.

She led him into a small kitchen with vintage appliances and a chrome table and chair set reminiscent of half a century before. She took two quart canning jars from a dish drainer and filled them with ice, then retrieved a pitcher of tea from the refrigerator. It was thick and dark, and smelled like tea and raspberries. Her hands quivered as she poured, and the weight of the pitcher seemed to be about all she could handle.

"I was hoping you would answer my letter," Aunt Charmaine admitted. "But I didn't dare hope that you might actually come all the way down here to see me." She wore a faded cotton house dress buttoned up to her neck. The hemline fell several inches below her knees. Old age had most likely diminished her height by a few inches already. Her hair was the color of old aluminum, short and combed straight back out of her way.

"I'm sorry I didn't write you back," Lloyd told her, "but your letter did start me thinking, and that's why I came down here to check things out. I've been in New Orleans almost a month now, but I don't have a car, and this is the first chance I had to get over this way."

"Just like him," Charmaine said. "One day I went to the door, and there he was. Just standing there, grinning that crookedy grin of his. You know the one." Lloyd knew. The picture grin.

"That was three years ago," Charmaine said. "And once he got here, he stayed for six months. Do you plan to stay that long, Lloyd?" she teased.

"I guess not," Lloyd smiled. "I just rented that little car out there for the day. If I don't get it back by eight tonight, I have to pay an extra day."

"Well, no matter," Aunt Charmaine said. "The important thing is that you're here now and we finally got to meet. I know why you came."

If you know that, then you're ahead of me, Lloyd thought. He sipped his tea, savoring the mingling of bitterness, sweetness, and a fruity under taste.

Outside the screened kitchen door another large oak shaded much of the back yard. There was a small, neat garden situated where it would catch the afternoon sun, its rows lush with thick green foliage and abundant summer produce. A wooden bench swing was mounted on poles beneath a sun-bleached canvas canopy. At the farthest limit of the yard lay the still, olive drab waters of a bayou, perhaps the same Bayou Justine that Billy had talked about. Lloyd wondered if the alligators and other swamp creatures ever strayed up into the yard to sample the garden produce, or perhaps an occasional house pet.

"Your daddy left Roulade when he was just sixteen, you know," Charmaine went on. "His daddy said he probably wouldn't make it out of the parish before that rusted old Pontiac broke down, but I guess he made it that far, and a whole lot farther. It was two years before any of us heard a word from him again. Then finally he wrote his mama to tell her he was working on the oil rigs over in Oklahoma. That worried her some, because his brother Jean was killed on one of the rigs out in the Gulf."

"I remember hearing him mention that," Lloyd said. He could see that he wasn't going to have to coax information from his great aunt.

"Jean was a few years older than Gui, but Gui was crazy about him, followed him around like a puppy when they were kids. Things were never quite the same for any of them after Jean was killed."

"You called him Gui?"

"Oh yes, that was what we always called your daddy. It's his Cajun name, short for Guilliam. I don't know why he finally decided to go by Billy instead. Rebellion, I guess, but I never could get used to it.

"But anyway, he was gone all that time, just sending a letter once and again, maybe with a ten-dollar bill for his mama, or showing up for a week or so every few years. We couldn't get in touch with him when his mama died, or later on when his daddy passed. But I don't know if he would have showed up for Philippe's funeral anyway. Those two never could get on. It's the main reason why Gui left in the first place."

A knock sounded on the front door. "That must be Raymond," Aunt Charmaine said. "He was supposed to be here at ten, but he's always late." She shuffled out of the kitchen with her walker, and Lloyd heard them talking at the front door. She didn't sound happy, and when she returned, she was shaking her head with disgust. "He was supposed to weed my garden today, but he claims he twisted his shoulder helping somebody lift a boat. That Raymond Beauchamp is about as much use as dull scissors. But he's all I've got to help out with things around here."

"Why don't I weed the garden?" Lloyd suggested. "I'd like to do something for you while I'm here."

"No, I couldn't let you do that."

"Sure you could, and I need the exercise." He stood up as if the thing was settled, and she rose too, surprised and pleased at his insistence.

The ten by twenty foot garden patch was filled with a broad assortment of ripening vegetables. Lloyd found an old hoe by a shed and set clumsily to work. Carol hadn't exactly been the gardening type when he was growing up, and he knew very little about what he was supposed to do. Aunt Charmaine dragged an old lawn chair close to where he was working and settled in. She seemed to notice his inexperience and offered occasional advice. "Just chop the grass and weed in the middles, and loosen the soil up. That's all it needs."

Lloyd soon got the hang of it. Once in a while he cast a cautious glance toward the bayou. The garden hoe would be a sad weapon against a full-grown alligator. But Aunt Charmaine seemed unconcerned.

"Just like when your daddy was here," the old woman noted with a sad smile. "That summer when he stayed with me, I had the best garden in years. We filled up on fresh tomatoes, cucumbers, peas, beans, onions and watermelons at every meal, and there was still plenty to put up."

"Did he ever explain why he finally came back home and stayed for six months after being gone so long?" Lloyd asked.

"Not really, and I never asked," Aunt Charmaine said. "But I have my ideas about it."

"What are your ideas?" It felt surprisingly good to Lloyd to be baking and sweating in the hot Louisiana sun, calling on muscles that had been too long inactive. He glanced toward the swamp and saw the water ripple near the bank. He waited, wondering if a long black snout full of teeth would surface. But it was just a fish rolling near the top of the water.

"I think he was just tired. Mind, body and soul. Tired of going from place to place all his life. Tired of so many beds, and so many jobs. Tired of always leaving people behind and never looking back. People like you, Lloyd. Tired of being who he was, maybe."

"So he came home," Lloyd said.

"Yes, he finally came home," the old woman confirmed, "even if everything was changed, and almost everybody he knew was dead or old, or didn't even remember who he was. Even if he wasn't the same cock-sure, hell raising Gui Ballou who left here forty something years ago."

For the next hour Lloyd worked steadily in the garden, as his back slowly turned the color of a glowing stove burner and his arms and shoulders began to ache like they were lined with hot lead. All the while the old woman told a steady stream of stories about their family, and young Billy Ballou's adventures and troubles here in the swamp country of southern Louisiana.

Lloyd learned that his grandfather Philippe had worked for years as a commercial fisherman, and later opened a small shop where he repaired boat engines and cars. Billy had practically grown up in that shop, which accounted for his love of cars and his talent for fixing them. But he had learned other things from his father too. Philippe was a hard drinker and an unrepentant womanizer.

"My sister Roxy put up with a lot more from Philippe than I ever would have from my husband Miles," Aunt Charmaine said. "Miles knew what would happen to him if he ever came home stinking of whisky and chippies. I always had more sand than Roxy, and it seemed like she couldn't imagine any kind of life except the one she had. But she never enjoyed her life. Those boys didn't grow up in a happy home."

When he finished his work in the garden, Lloyd rinsed off with the backyard hose and put his shirt back on. He was already feeling prickly across his shoulders and arms, and he knew he'd be dealing with a full-blown sunburn by tonight. But it felt good to work so hard, and he resolved once again, to get back into some kind of daily exercise routine as soon as he got back to New Orleans.

Aunt Charmaine put together a lunch from leftovers in the refrigerator. She served bowls of reheated gumbo thick with shrimp, lumps of crab and sausage, chunks of tomato, okra, and other vegetables. On the side were sandwiches made of white bread, mayonnaise, and slices of fresh tomatoes an inch thick. There was a bowl of watermelon chunks, and another of cucumbers, onions and jalapenos in vinegar. The tea pitcher was apparently bottomless.

"Your daddy worked a lot on my house while he was here. He put on a new roof, and he painted everything that didn't move, talk or grow. It was a lifesaver to me. I'd gotten way too old to do those kinds of things for myself, and there wasn't anybody else to do it for me. Not anymore.

"Sometimes I'd go out while he was working and just sit in the shade to keep him company. We talked a lot. Or at least I talked a lot, and he talked a little.

"He never just told me much outright about his life, but sometimes there would be a name here or there, or a little story that put him in a particular place at a particular time. I figured out that he'd been in prison in Kentucky, but I'm not sure what for. Car theft, maybe."

"Did he talk about us at all?" Lloyd asked. "About my mother Carol and my little sister Kat? I wonder if he even knew my little brother Bennie died?"

"I think he knew, but I don't know how. Sure, he talked about you, and how you would be a grown man now, and wouldn't know him from Adam if you met him on the street. And he talked about the others, too."

"My mother and sister?"

"Yes, them and some of the others, too."

"What others?" Lloyd asked.

"Why, his other wives, and his other families," she said.

Lloyd froze with a spoonful of gumbo halfway to his mouth and looked up at her. "Other families?"

Guilt washed over the old woman's face. "I'm so sorry, Lloyd. My old brain must be working way too slow," she confessed. "Somehow I thought you knew. But how could you? And now I've spilled it out just like that."

The possibility had never occurred to Lloyd, but it made immediate sense to him. He himself was evidence of the fact Billy Ballou was the kind of man who married, brought children into the world, and then drove away. Why wouldn't he do the same thing more than once? Serial husband. Serial dad.

"What do you know about the others?" Lloyd asked. "Have any of them come to see you like I did?"

"No, none of them have come. I sent three letters when I decided he was dead and that someone might want to know. But the other two came back."

Lloyd had trouble wrapping his mind around the possibility that he might have half brothers and sisters that he never knew, and never would. But then he remembered the strangers in the pictures he had salvaged from Billy's house, and realized that he might have been gazing at blood relatives.

"Gui didn't feel good about all that," Aunt Charmaine said. "Not any of it. I got the feeling sometimes that his heart was just full up with regret. But what could he do about it? Come to your house and say, 'Hi I'm your daddy and I'm sorry that I left you.' "

"I'd have knocked his teeth out," Lloyd said coldly.

"Any of you would have. He knew that, and I think it ate at his heart that he had hurt so many people, and done so many terrible things, and there was nothing he could do about any of it. He'd have to carry it right into the grave with him, and probably on beyond."

Screw him and his guilt, Lloyd thought. But he didn't say it. None of Billy Ballou sins were the fault of this kind, simple old woman.

"He was a heartsick man, Lloyd," Aunt Charmaine said quietly. "It's probably why he got wrapped up in all the things he did over there in New Orleans."

"I met with J.T. Raintree," Lloyd said, "and he spoke highly of Billy."

"Gui didn't seem to share the same opinion of Reverend Raintree," Charmaine said. She spoke the man's name like it put a bitter taste in her mouth. "He said Raintree lived too well on the money people donated, and he didn't like the men that the reverend kept around him. But he thought that what he was doing was worthwhile, and that's why he stuck with it. That's why he eventually moved to New Orleans, so he could spend all his time helping the poor and the homeless."

"Did he ever mention a woman named Sarah Bradley?"

"Sarah? Oh yes. He even brought her over here with him once. She was a kind, lovely woman. They were only friends, but they were very close."

"They were together at the mission during the hurricane, and Raintree said Billy saved her life."

"I know. She told me. She came over to see me after things had settled down," Charmaine revealed. "She told me the whole story about how he saved her from the hoodlums at the mission, and how he got her to safety before he disappeared."

"Do you know how I could get in touch with her?" Lloyd asked. If Raintree's secretary had ever passed Lloyd's number to her, which he doubted, then she must have decided not to call.

"I've got a phone number she gave me before she left, but I'm not sure she hasn't gone away someplace. She said the whole thing had been too much for her, and she was leaving New Orleans."

It was late afternoon, and Lloyd realized that he would have to go soon if he wanted to get the little yellow tin can back to the rental agency on time. But he promised to return when he could. He wanted his sister Kat to know what he had discovered here, and he was already plotting how he might convince her and Paul to bring the whole brood down for a visit.

Aunt Charmaine insisted on packing food for his trip back to New Orleans, although it was only an hour and a half drive. She fought back tears as she maneuvered the walker down the gravel path to the road.

"I think your daddy was a sick man by the time he moved back to New Orleans, Lloyd," she said. "Not just heart sick, but really sick. Maybe that's why he was trying so hard to make some kind of change in his life, to make a difference to somebody while there was still time."

"Maybe so," Lloyd said. But it was hard for him to even consider that the man he had spent most of his life despising could have undergone such a miraculous transformation. He didn't want to believe it.

"That last time he left," Aunt Charmaine said, "I stood right here seeing him off, just where we're standing now. And there was a look in his eyes, like he knew . . ." She paused, searching for the right words, and then gave up. "No, that's just silly I guess, and I'm just a silly old woman with too much imagination."

During the drive back to New Orleans, Lloyd called the number for Sarah Bradley that his aunt provided. After several rings a woman answered. Her voice sounded tentative, and when he identified himself, there was a long pause, then the connection was broken. He called back, but of course there was no answer this time. He left his number anyway.

Chapter Eleven

Getting women had usually been easy for Lloyd. That at least was one talent he had inherited from his father. But finding the strength to truly cherish them and keep them was quite another matter for both father and son.

The problems for Lloyd usually began when he started caring for a woman, or she for him. It was perplexing that these two things rarely seemed to happen in any logical pattern. At first even with Kelly, her early giddy professions of love had sent shivers of panic through him that triggered all his flight instincts. He never understood that knee-jerk reaction within himself, although he had seen it manifest itself far too often.

But with Kelly he made the perilous decision at last to stay put, take the risk, and see what came next. He had never regretted that choice, especially during their first few years together, when their love grew deep and strong. When it all started to go bad, he began to feel the burden of many regrets, but he never did regret that for a time he had freely granted a woman the power to break his heart if she chose to do so. Eventually Kelly exercised that option.

Even now Lloyd found a miserable sort of consolation in the fact that, unlike Billy, at least he had stuck it out to the end.

In a small apartment crammed with so many manifestations of Betsy's passions, pastimes, and eccentricities, Lloyd understood the challenge she must face when she decided to straighten up her home. But he could see that she had made an effort. No dishes were piled in the sink, adequate space for two diners was available on her small cluttered table, and the bed was made. In the tiny bathroom a clean hand towel hung on the rack by the sink, and the clothes, underwear, and towels that carpeted the floor during his previous visit were nowhere in sight.

"Keep your expectations low about the food," Betsy warned, stirring a pot of pasta on the stove. "I'm the kind of cook who can simultaneously catch a potholder on fire in the oven while spilling the spaghetti sauce on the linoleum. My cookbook has about three things on it. Scrambled eggs, peanut butter and banana sandwiches, and spaghetti from a jar." She looked good tonight in her simple yellow dress and apron. She wore little yellow flowers and sprigs of baby's breath in her thick brown hair. It was a flower child sort of look that harked back to the seventies, and it was a good fit for an unconventional spirit like Betsy.

"Since its dinnertime, I guess it's safe to assume we're having spaghetti," Lloyd said.

"If we're lucky."

The heat of the day was waning, and the fresh breeze filtering in through the open balcony doors stirred the blooms and foliage of the multitude of plants in the room. From outside he heard the sounds of traffic, and the conversations of people walking by on the banquette below. Lloyd had intentionally eaten a light lunch so he would have a good appetite for whatever Betsy decided to serve.

"A gallery on Royal sold one of my paintings yesterday," Betsy announced casually. "It was a still life of an orchid in a beautiful crystal vase. Very detailed. One of my best, I think." She poured more wine into her glass, then added a splash from the bottle into the pot of sauce simmering on a back burner. The Ragu jar sat on the counter nearby. At least she was up front about it.

"So are we celebrating that tonight?"

"Partly. But mostly I just wanted to see you again. I enjoy hanging around you."

"Yeah I'm such a charismatic guy. Divorced, unemployed, and nearly broke. All the things on any woman's A-list."

"You left out the fact that you really need a haircut, and you dress like a mechanic."

"Which I was, when I had a job."

"To be honest, Lloyd, I haven't thought much about why I like you. But I guess it's because you're . . ." She searched briefly for the word she wanted, and finally came up with one. ". . . because you're genuine."

"That sounds like a compliment, but I'm not sure what it means," Lloyd said.

"Me neither," Betsy admitted. "From that first night in the bar, after we talked for a while, I could see that there was something different going on inside of you. Most of the men who come into that place alone are as easy to read as the want-ads, but it took a lot more effort to begin to get a fix on you. And I'm not sure I'm really there yet."

She drained the spaghetti in a colander in the sink, then started putting their meal together on two mismatched plates.

"When I'm working in that bar and I have the time," Betsy went on, "I can squeeze a life story out of just about any loser that staggers in the door. It helps sell booze, and it's good for tips. But when it's a story about love, and one way or another most of them are, it usually feels like I'm hearing the same damn thing over and over again. Even my own tale of woe is pretty much like all the rest. But you actually interested me."

"I'm not seeing it, I guess," Lloyd said. "There's nothing new about how Kelly and I botched things up."

"No, it wasn't that. It was this thing about your father, about how he had left your family a long time ago, and now after thirty-something years you're still hot on his trail."

"Even though he's dead," Lloyd said, "and probably washed on down the river a long time ago. Talk about a cold case."

"That's it. I just figured it out," Betsy said. "He's dead and gone, and you know that. But you're still looking for him." She replenished the wine in both their glasses as she went on to explore her new discovery. "I called you genuine a little while ago because I just couldn't seem to hit on the right word, but I think I'm going to take that back now. My new word for you now is haunted."

Lloyd rolled his eyes, took a drink of wine, and twisted a bite of spaghetti onto his fork. It was not nearly as bad a dinner as Betsy had warned, but he knew his standards were low. This kind of stuff, and far worse, was what he survived on back home.

They were halfway through the second bottle of wine by the time they carried their glasses out on the balcony and settled on the wicker loveseat. A large hanging basket of English ivy hung directly above him, its dangling tendrils annoying the top of his head when the breeze stirred them. Above the balcony rail a dozen other baskets partly blocked the view of the apartment balconies across the street.

Night had nearly come, and the passers-by on the sidewalk below were beginning to get drunker and louder. *When the Saints* was playing someplace in the distance, up toward Bourbon. In the French Quarter it always seemed to be playing somewhere, like background theme music to the lives of the people who lived here. Business in the bar on the ground floor across the street was picking up. It was a lot like the place where Betsy worked, dim and anonymous. Lloyd had downed a few beers there, and found it satisfactory.

"You're going to think I'm crazy when I tell you this," Betsy said. She was slurring just a little, and a shy, almost sleepy smile embraced her eyes and mouth. Since Lloyd had arrived over an hour earlier, she had outpaced him two glasses to one with the wine.

"This sounds good," Lloyd smiled. Any topic besides him and his screwed-up life sounded good. "When it comes to female company, the crazier the better as far as I'm concerned. And just a little bit slutty doesn't hurt, either."

"Okay, but you were warned," she told him. "This is not some Ouija board nonsense, or a dream I had. I really believe it, so don't make fun of me."

"I promise."

"When I first came here seven years ago, a gallery owner named Andre Harp over on Royal agreed to display some of my paintings for a month and see if anything sold. He and his family lived out in the suburbs, but he kept a tiny little attic apartment here in the Quarter. For when he worked late or partied late, he said. I ended up bunking in there for a few weeks, and sometimes he stayed there, too. There's the slutty part, in case you were looking for it. But I didn't really mind. He was a decent looking guy, just a few years older than me. He finished quick, he didn't snore, and he wasn't jealous if I spent time in other company besides his.

"After he'd sold a few of the pieces I brought with me, and I picked up some steady work in a florist shop, I started looking for a place of my own. I scoured the ads and walked the streets for two weeks. I really wanted to live in the Quarter, but every place I looked at was either too small, or too nasty, or too expensive. Then finally I found this place."

"When do we get to the crazy, spooky part?" Lloyd asked.

Betsy took a sip of wine and a couple of drops dribbled onto the front of her dress. She looked down at the stain, but apparently decided to ignore it.

"A ghost brought me to this building and told me that she wanted me to live here," she said at last.

"A ghost."

"Cherie. I wasn't really aware of her until after I'd moved in, and I didn't know her name for a long time after that. But I knew something strange was leading me here from the first day that I took a wrong turn and started down this street."

Well, she had warned him, Lloyd thought. He tried to act serious, but it sounded goofy to him.

"I turned down this street by mistake, and just happened to see the sign by the door downstairs. It was late on a Saturday night, but the manager answered my ring, and he brought me up and showed me the apartment. Another couple had left a deposit, but they never showed back up again, so he said I could have it right away. I wrote a check that night, and moved my stuff over from Andre's place the next day."

A dozen whimsical responses came to Lloyd's mind, but he had made a promise to her.

"Crazy, right?" Betsy prodded.

"Who's to say? Just tell me the rest of it."

"Since that first day, from time to time I've had this tingly feeling when I was here. At first it was scary, but finally I got used to it. It wasn't until months later that the whole story began to come together. Back in the early 1800s this building was the home of a crazy old Creole widow. After she died, they discovered that for years she had kept one slave after another imprisoned in a back room. She got off on torturing and starving them until finally they died, and then eventually she would go out and buy another one. Apparently, her household servants knew about it, but I guess they were just glad it wasn't them chained up back there, and they kept their mouths shut."

"And Cherie told you that she was one of those slaves?"

"Not directly. I had to find out on my own. I got curious and started doing some research on the house. I found her name in the public archives, and I knew it was her. That explained so many things that I had been feeling, and knowing without really knowing."

"Okay, I'll give it to you. Crazy as hell, Betsy."

She smiled a little at that. "I know," she said. "But it doesn't change anything."

"Does she live here with you?" Lloyd asked. "Like a roommate or something? Is she here right now?"

"No, it's not like that. Sometimes I just feel like she's here. I feel a little chill, and the hair stands up on my arms, and I know I'm not alone. I think I've seen her shadow a few times, and once I thought I saw her silhouette against the curtains in the middle of the night."

"So, you don't sit down and have little chats over a glass of wine, then?"

"No, but she does communicate in her own way. Think about how terrible the last weeks or months of her life must have been, and the horrible way that she died. Sometimes, usually in early morning hours when things are quiet and the rest of the world is asleep, I know that she led me here so that she wouldn't be alone and afraid anymore. And she shares that same feeling with me."

Betsy turned her head away and stared out into the distance, as if her gaze was fixed on some faraway place that only she could see.

Lloyd was surprised to feel chill bumps raise on his arms, then fade slowly away. Why not? he thought. If he was crazy enough to come all this way to search for a dead man who was so thoroughly gone that even the memory of his time on earth was slowly fading, why couldn't

Betsy have her ghost spirit to keep her company in this little sanctuary of paints, canvases, potted flowers and hanging baskets?

She had gotten it right. They were both haunted in their own way.

In bed that night Betsy added more detail to the bare-bones description of her relationship with the gallery owner, Andre Harp. Their involvement, however it might be described, had not ended when she found her own place, with the aid of the dead slave spirit Cherie, and had moved out of the his oh-so-convenient little French Quarter garret. It had, in fact, only become deeper and more complex over the ensuing months and years. It struck Lloyd as such a cliché fable that he was a little surprised that a smart, sensible woman like Betsy didn't recognize the futility of it early on. But eventually she had, and that was why Lloyd was sharing the cramped and lumpy little twin mattress with her instead of that other man.

Over time Betsy and Andre had fallen in love, and she had brought Andre the sort of happiness that he thought he would never be lucky enough to find again. That was his line, and she bought it. He planned to divorce his wife so that they could be together without all the secrecy and clandestine antics.

When his kids got old enough to grasp the concept of a failed marriage, Andre had moved out for a time, living a Spartan sort of life in his tiny bohemian French Quarter apartment. But eventually he was compelled to move back when legal and financial issues arose regarding ownership of the Royal Street gallery. That was two years before, and he never left again.

Three months ago, Betsy had finally broken up with Andre, and she was over him now. Her insistence on that was so strong that Lloyd had to wonder who she was trying to convince, him or herself.

Her story told, her secrets revealed, Betsy fell asleep in Lloyd's arms. But Lloyd lay awake for a long time afterward, eventually extricating his numb arm from beneath her, and rolling away a little to reduce the exchange of body heat and sweat between them. He watched the stir of the curtains in the breeze and the dim play of lights through the myriad jungle of plants as cars passed on the street below. It wasn't that hard to imagine shadowy spirits drifting pointlessly to and fro about the room.

Getting women was usually pretty easy for Lloyd, but he still wondered why he had ended up with this one. Pretty, free-spirited, and even somewhat slutty women were abundant enough here in the Quarter. Betsy was broken, but perhaps fixable. Something about that appealed to him, although he wasn't quite sure what it was.

Toward dawn Lloyd was drawn up from deep sleep by his bedmate's quiet sobs and whimpers. She reminded him of a frightened child. She muttered in the meaningless speech of sleep, and at one point she called him *Ma Cher*. There was a ghost in here alright, but it had nothing to do with a murdered slave girl.

Maybe it was time to go home to Missouri, he thought, as her crying subsided and he drifted back asleep.

* * *

Lloyd got up early, and Betsy woke as he eased out of the bed and padded barefoot across the squeaky floorboards to the bathroom. When he came back out a few minutes later, she had coffee brewing in an ancient percolator on the stove. Soon they were sitting at the table sipping a sweet, strong brown brew of half milk, half chicory coffee, and munching on slices of toasted French bread slathered with a thick layer of peanut butter.

Betsy didn't have much to say, and Lloyd could tell she was hung over. Her eyes seemed sunken, rimmed with blue-gray shadows, and occasionally she raised a hand to press against her temples. It was no wonder, he thought. Her share of the night's consumption was nearly two bottles of the cheap red that she seemed to keep in stock, and right now her body was probably crying out for water, aspirin, and the oblivion of a few more hours of rest.

"I'm going back to that place where I washed cars before and see if I can pick up some more work," Lloyd said. "If he'll let me, I'll work a double shift and won't get off until late." Betsy raised her eyes from her coffee mug and nodded, not seeming capable of speech just yet.

"That was fun last night," Lloyd said. "Kind of weird, but interesting."

"Don't take me too seriously, baby," Betsy said. She cleared her throat to get rid of the crackle in her voice. "I think some of my circuits got crossed up somewhere along the way, and you never know what's going to come out of my mouth sometimes when I've had a few."

"Well I'm still getting to know you, Betsy, but I like you."

She gave him a dreary smile and reached out to pat his hand.

* * *

The second shift at the hotel parking garage didn't end until past nine at night. Lloyd had been smart enough to bring along a towel and fresh clothes this time, and dropped in a bathroom to clean up and change before stopping at the small parking garage office on his way out. The shift manager paid him in cash out of a locked desk drawer, counting out $130 that no government agency would ever require a share of. Then he invited Lloyd to take a seat at a worn metal desk across from him. The desk was cluttered with stacks of paperwork, a land-line phone, and two cell phones that seemed to ring constantly. Several hand radios were charging in a rack behind him, and the remnants of the manager's carry-out supper were stuffed into the trash can at his side. His name was Beau Lagarde, a man of about fifty, with a Cajun accent so thick that he might have wandered up out of the bayous just the day before.

"I keep an eye on my people, even the casuals, and I can see that you stay at it and give me my money's worth when I give you a shift," Lagarde said. "I don't know anything about what's going on with you or what brought you here, but I do know that you work circles around the drunks and street trash that I usually send back there to the car wash bay. This job could probably turn into something better for you if you're interested and plan to stick around for a while."

Lloyd hadn't expected this, and didn't know quite how to respond. "What do you have in mind?" he asked.

"Well, nothing to write home to mama about," the man said. "Maybe start out as a valet if you've got a driver's license and don't mind putting your real name on a little paperwork. Park and fetch. That kind of thing. And then see where it goes from there."

"I've told you my real name. That's not a problem. I'd have to become an employee then?"

"A temp," the manager said. "The pay's not that much better, but the tips can be decent on a good day."

"To tell you the truth, Mr. Lagarde," Lloyd said, "when I came to New Orleans, I didn't expect to stay more than a few days, and I still haven't figured out how long I'll be here. But I do appreciate the offer. Can I let you know later?"

"Maybe. But I need somebody now, and if it's not you, I'll need to know that in a day or two."

"Okay, fair enough."

Lloyd couldn't help feeling a little flush when he left the hotel garage, even though he knew the $130 in his pocket wouldn't go far in this city, and he should probably squirrel it away with the rest of his dwindling bankroll for rent and necessities. He thought about calling Betsy despite the late hour, but she had told him she was going out with friends to celebrate the sale of her painting, and she hadn't dropped any hints that he would be welcome to the party.

So, what *was* he going to do, stay or go? He wondered. The business about his father seemed to have run into a dead end, and he felt certain that there was no bank account, car, house or unexpected 401K that he could claim and cash in on his mother's behalf. When he died, Billy had only seemed to be one rung up the ladder from the homeless derelicts he was dishing gruel out to at the mission. Even if there had been any sort of estate or insurance to claim, how could he possibly find it or prove his mother's right to it? Billy wasn't exactly the last-will-and-testament type.

But what prospects were there to go home to? A shabby little apartment when he could scrape together a deposit, and another greasy wrench job just as bad as the last one. There wasn't that much difference in status, pay, or future prospects, whether he was parking rich people's cars, or popping the hoods and changing plugs for them. It occurred to him that his own situation wasn't really that much different than Billy's during his last days here in the Crescent City. But at least he hadn't left a wife and kids destitute back in Kansas City, as Billy had, not unless you counted Kelly, who was not his wife anymore, and certainly was not destitute.

The only thing that showed any hope of tipping the scales for New Orleans was Betsy. But he wasn't even sure he would stay interested in her after he understood the full scope of her craziness, or she would want him to stick around after she made her own similar discoveries about him.

He strolled west, toward the downtown area, searching for someplace dim, dull and smoky where he could drink cheap and postpone having to make decisions about anything at least for the rest of the night. That was one of the great things about the French Quarter, he thought. There was a bar for any sort of mood or pocketbook.

As he rounded a corner, he realized that he was just down the street from Club Les Girls, the strip joint he had followed Tats to a few days earlier. Pausing for a moment, he watched the neon dancing girl above the door thrust one glowing red leg out, then pull it back. She had probably been doing her little dance up there for decades, Lloyd thought, and a couple of the florescent tubes that formed vital parts of her anatomy no longer lit up. The heavy steel door of the bar was propped open tonight, perhaps because of the heat, or possibly to give passers-by a tantalizing, sinful glimpse inside. A dreary, used-up looking woman in a skimpy, tasseled outfit stood just beside the open door, smoking a cigarette and looking at her phone.

There wasn't much foot traffic down this narrow side street on a weeknight, and Lloyd figured it must be her turn to park it outside and try to lure in suckers. She looked up as he walked closer, lowered the phone, and put on a cold smile.

"How about it, fella?" she asked, physically stopping him with a hand in the middle of his chest. "You like girls, don't you? We got some inside you need to check out." Her bright red lipstick was smeared on her right cheek, probably from talking on the phone. The confusing smell of perfume, cigarette smoke, sweat, and something ephemerally sexual permeated the air around her.

Lloyd started to brush on past her, but didn't, not really understanding why. He glanced into the dim interior of the bar, catching a glimpse of a woman on stage swinging around the proverbial brass pole.

“Two for one drafts,” the woman offered, “and hot chicks doing things you probably never seen before in your life. No cover.” Her phone made two deep vibrating sounds back to back. She raised it and looked down just long enough to see who the call was from, then turned her attention back to Lloyd. The girl inside on stage hooked one leg around the pole and leaned so far back that her head touched the floor behind her.

“Two for one drafts, fella. This is anything can happen night, and you look to me like a player.”

“Okay, you convinced me,” Lloyd said, feeling like a mark already as he turned toward the door. The woman led him inside and guided him to a table on the far side of the room against a wall. It was darker there, away from the scattering of other men in the room, and not very close to the stage. Lloyd realized she was staking her claim on him, and it made him a little uncomfortable.

“What’s your name, handsome?” she asked. “Mine’s Electra.”

“It’s Lloyd,” he told her.

“What’s your pleasure, Lloyd?” she asked.

“The drafts will be fine,” Lloyd said.

“Okay. Back in a flash. Don’t go anywhere, baby.”

While she was away at the bar, he had a better chance to look around. Over at the bar one of the girls was gyrating between the spread legs of a young man about college age while his two companions leered and goaded. Two other men in rumpled suits and loosened ties sat right down by the stage, drunk beyond reason, tossing dollar bills toward the performing stripper every time she did something noteworthy.

The two plastic cups of beer that his personal handler returned with were small, not more than eight or ten ounces, Lloyd guessed, and each had a two-inch head of foam.

“That’s eleven, not including tip,” Electra announced with a smile.

Lloyd gave her a dismayed look, but didn't say anything. A man should pay for his own stupidity without complaint. He pulled out a twenty and handed it to her.

"Can I keep the change, handsome?" Electra asked. She eased up close so her body made intimate contact with his shoulder, and her fingers, still wet with beer, traced their way through his hair.

"Give me a five back," Lloyd told her. His brain did some simple math. One hour of work today paid for one cup of tepid beer tonight. What the hell was he thinking, and why was he even here? During his adult life he had been in dozens of places like this, on duty and off, and this one held no allure for him. So why had he come in?

"I'm the best dancer in this place," Electra said. "It's only twenty for a dance at your table, or forty if you want to go in back where there's more privacy."

"I bet anything-can-happen-day happens back there," Lloyd said with a grin.

"Let's just say that you get your money's worth," Electra said. "And then some."

"I guess not, honey," Lloyd said. "But thanks anyway."

"What the hell, it's a slow night. Just thirty to go in back."

Lloyd gave her another smile and shook his head. "I'm just not flush enough for that kind of fun tonight. Take my advice. You shouldn't waste even one more minute of your time on me."

"Sure, I get it, Lloyd," she said. There was no anger or resentment in her voice. "Just doing my job, you know?" She turned and left, joining two other girls at the bar who sat sipping cokes, watching the front door, and waiting their turn at bat.

The song that was playing ended, and the girl on the stage, now completely naked, wrapped up her routine. She gathered up her tips and clothes from around the stage, and had a brief tug of war with one of the suit guys over possession of a pale blue wisp of a garment. Finally, she moved gingerly down the narrow stage steps in her four-inch heels.

The voice of the strip joint god briefly filled the room. "How about a big round of applause for the lovely Tanya, ladies and gentlemen!" A couple of the men and all the girls at the bar clapped obediently, but without enthusiasm.

"And now Club Les Girls is proud to bring to the stage our very own sexy, sultry, seductive Sultana! Let's give her a warm welcome! Sultana!" There was another patter of applause that died out abruptly when the next dancer mounted the stage.

A woman like that should give some thought to finding a new line of work, Lloyd thought as he raised one of the cups of beer and drank. It was warm and flat, and some tiny insect was struggling desperately to survive in the foam head. He lifted it out with a finger and flicked it away, wiped the finger on his pants, and drank again. Damned if he could afford to waste this expensive stuff.

As the music started again, Sultana began to parade around the stage with some fluidity and grace, despite her large round belly and fat-wrapped arms and legs. Lloyd was surprised to see that she was a competent dancer, chubby or not. But her routine struck him as about as erotic as a plastic bag of Jell-O. It was advisable for some people to just keep their clothes on in public. In fact, most people, probably.

"Hello sailor. How's your drink?"

Lloyd looked up and discovered a woman standing just to his right. Her eyes seemed to lock onto his and hold them captive for an instant.

"Could be colder," he said, "but beer is beer."

The woman nodded knowingly, and a hint of a smile swept briefly across her face. "One of the coolers under the bar where we keep the kegs has gone out . . . again. Everything in this place is a thousand years old. Everything but the people, and some nights I feel that old myself."

The woman was, in fact, noticeably older than the other women there, in her mid-forties perhaps, although it was hard to tell in the dim light where he sat. She wore a long, light blue gown of some filmy, see-though material, cut low in front and back, and slit nearly to her waist on one side. Lloyd guessed that she must have been a heart-stopping, man-crushing beauty in her younger days, and even now she had the kind of fading loveliness that was hard to tear his eyes from. There was something about her eyes, the way she kept them fixed on his, that was unnerving.

"Mind if I join you?" she asked. "Don't worry, I won't hit you up for a drink. I brought my own."

"I'd enjoy the company," Lloyd said. He couldn't help but feel somehow flattered, although he understood that she probably hadn't come over just because she decided that here was a man she needed to know better. He pulled a chair back from the table and she slid smoothly into it, putting her drink on the table in front of her.

"Thanks, it's a slow night," the woman said, "so I thought I'd come over and check you out. I'm tired of sitting over at the bar listening to the girls bitch about who has the most worthless, lazy, asshole boyfriend." Lloyd glanced again at the women at the bar, and thought one of them looked somewhat like the girl that Tats had led here from Jackson Square. It had only been a short time past, but if that was her, already the changes in her life had no doubt been profound.

"I'm Lloyd," he said, holding out his hand to his companion.

"I'm Marta," the woman said, taking his hand with soft, delicate fingers. Her arm was slim, and for the first time he realized how thin her entire frame was under the blue dress. "At least in here that's what everybody calls me. Outside that door I'm Mary Lucchesi, simple little Italian girl from the Ninth Ward."

"I bet it's been a long time since all you were was simple little Mary," Lloyd said. "There's plenty of mystery in those pretty eyes of yours. And plenty of danger too, I'll bet."

That little smile flittered across her face again, and again her eyes held his. "I don't know what you're talking about," she said lightly. "What mystery?"

"For starters," Lloyd said, "here you are sitting with me, concerned with my two thimbles of beer, when I'd be willing to bet those two guys down by the stage are breaking another hundred every fifteen minutes or so. Shouldn't you be over there where the cash is flowing?"

"I leave that to the girls. I give my time and attention to anyone I choose," Marta said, "and right now that's you." She turned her gaze to the suits down front, letting Lloyd get a quick glance down the front of that sheer blue dress. Nice chests and a flat belly, but her ribs stuck out. All the dieting she ever needed probably came from pills and needles, but he didn't think she was on anything now. Those eyes were too clear and piercing. After a reasonable time, she brought her attention back to him.

"I'm not complaining, mind you," Lloyd said, "but why me, Marta?"

"I run this place," she said calmly, "and Electra said you smell like a cop. Are you a police officer, Lloyd?" She asked the question so calmly that she might have been asking him for the time or wondering if it might rain.

"I worked fourteen hours today and I'm sure I must smell like something. But not a cop."

"Not law enforcement of any kind? DEA, FBI, ATF, Code Enforcement, anything like that?"

"Nope, not even animal control, or toilet inspector."

"Sorry, but I've got to make sure sometimes, Lloyd. We've got our rules here, but these girls didn't grow up genteel and proper in the big houses down St. Charles Street, and they're here to make money. Some of them do it any way they can, rules or no rules."

"I used to be a cop," Lloyd said, not sure why he let that particular piece of information slip out. "But that doesn't count, does it?"

"No, it doesn't count," Marta smiled. "But it might explain why you've got the look. Who were you with?

"Kansas City PD."

"And . . .?"

"The sky fell on top of me."

"Well that's too bad for you, I guess," Marta said. "But I have to say they're not some of my favorite people. When they come in here, any of them, on duty or off, nothing good ever happens. But at least now that we've got that out of the way, we can relax." She waved one of the girls over and ordered another beer for Lloyd. "An Abita. Tell Buck one of the really cold ones in back, the ones he stashes back there for himself."

"What's your last name, Lloyd?" she asked.

"It's Ballou."

"Like Cat Ballou. The movie?"

"Yeah. That was my sister's nickname in high school, but she hated it."

"It sounds Cajun. Is your family from around here?"

"My father was, but I was born and raised in Kansas City. We lost touch with him a long time ago, and I came down here because I found out he was dead. I wanted to see if I could find out something about him, but I haven't learned much."

"When I was fifteen, my daddy washed overboard off a shrimp boat during a storm," Marta said. "It's not an easy thing, but at least I had some good years with him growing up."

"We didn't have very many good years, before he left or after," Lloyd admitted. "But that's all history, now, isn't it?" He picked up the beer and chugged, trying to pull his mood back up. "What do they say down here? *Layzay lay bonton* something?"

Marta's mood was definitely lightened, and she laughed at his clumsy abuse of the local French patois. Now that she had established that he was no threat to her business, she did in fact seem to be enjoying his company. A glance toward the bar and a quick nod started another beer on its way.

"Then what comes next for you, Lloyd?" Marta asked. "Are you going to stick around here and see what else you can dig up about your daddy, or just let it go?"

"I don't know. There are a few more things I could follow up on, but I'm not sure there's any use in it. And my family's back in Missouri. But a guy did offer me a job here today. Not a great one, but . . . hell, I don't know."

Marta reached out and laid her hand on his, her fingers soft and cool. "You'll find your answers," she said. "And in the meantime, why not just relax and have some fun? You're in New Orleans, for Pete's sake. It's like Disneyland for hard partying, decadent adults."

Lloyd was surprised to hear himself laughing out loud for the first time in a long time. He looked into those eyes again, and it seemed somehow as if she had touched the right place to make all his worries go away, at least for a little while.

Over the next half hour as they continued to talk, a scattering of customers came and went. The suits left after getting directions from one of the girls about how to get back to their hotel. A creepy guy at a table near the back slinked out, and another creepy guy slinked in and took a seat at the bar. Two middle-aged couples in shorts and tee-shirts claimed the table that the suits had been sitting at down front by the stage. They ordered multi-colored drinks with straws and fruit, and Electra danced directly in front of them, not stopping until she was right down to bare skin. The women seemed at once embarrassed and fascinated by the performance, and the men tossed some cash up on the stage.

Marta kept the beer coming, and Lloyd started wondering if he was unknowingly running a tab. He had worked through lunch, thinking he would eat after he got off, and the beer in his empty stomach was starting work its magic on his mind and body.

One of the girls came over to tell Marta she had a call, and she excused herself, promising to come back. Lloyd decided it was a good time to pay the rent.

Facing the back of the bar, Lloyd saw a dim, narrow hallway on the right where he realized the private dances took place. One of the girls was just now leading one of the college boys out of that pleasure din, holding his hand with one of hers, and clutching a wad of rumpled cash in the other. The drunken young man looked dazed and disoriented, like he had just returned to earth from an alien abduction.

In the center of the back wall was a door that led to the dancers' changing room. It was open, and inside Electra was getting back into her little outfit after her stint on stage.

Lloyd headed to the left, past the end of the bar, where the bathrooms were. He was surprised at the unsteadiness of his steps, and now that he was up and moving around, he felt like his bladder might explode. He opened a door in back and entered a nearly-dark hallway about fifteen feet long. There was a door at the other end, with light showing under it. Ah, his destination, he thought. Moving forward carefully, he came to the door and tried the knob. It was unlocked, therefore unoccupied, and he pushed it open.

But instead of all the standard men's room paraphernalia, he realized he had stumbled into what looked like the small back office of the club. Two desks were crammed into the cramped space, along with a couple of chairs, and various pieces of computer equipment. A man was sitting in a chair, leaned back with his feet on a desk, and Marta was sitting on the other desk a few feet away, apparently having a conversation with him. Both looked over, startled by the interruption. Lloyd's two-second take on the man was that he was fortyish, husky, rumpled gray trousers and golf shirt, and definitely not pleased to have an unwelcome stranger barge in so unexpectedly.

Marta came over and pushed Lloyd gently back out into the hallway, pulling the door closed behind her. "What are you doing back here?" she asked as she steered him out of the doorway and closed the door behind her. Clearly his intrusion made her jittery, although Lloyd couldn't see why.

"Sorry, I thought it was the head," Lloyd explained.

"One more door down," Marta said, pointing him back to the hallway. "I just have to talk to this man about some business, but it should only take a minute."

Standing at the urinal, savoring the sweet relief of the moment, the image of the man's angry face came back to him. It was his scowl that made him seem somehow familiar, but Lloyd couldn't imagine where he might have seen this man before. If Tat's visit here was any indication, all manner of unsavory characters probably passed through that little back room. Maybe the guy was the owner of this place, or bagman for the owner, or some kind of security. The cop side of Lloyd's mind stirred up any number of shady possibilities.

When he went back out, Marta was waiting for him at the end of the bar. "Feel better?" she asked. Her smile and her good mood seemed to have returned now that they were back out front.

"Yep, that did the trick," Lloyd said. "But it's been a long, hard day, and I'm beginning to feel those Abitas. I think I should start back to my place while I can still find it."

"I understand."

"What's my tab?"

"It's my treat tonight," Marta smiled.

"Well thank you, ma'am, and thank you for the entertaining company."

Marta walked him to the front door, then stepped outside with him. "Listen here, Lloyd Ballou, if you make up your mind to stay in New Orleans, why don't you let Mary Lucchesi take you around one of these days to see some of the sights? We could go anywhere you want. Are you interested in ghosts, or cemeteries, or alligators, or old plantation houses? Anything you'd like to do is fine with me. I think I'd enjoy hanging around with you, Lloyd. We could ride down the river on a boat, or do some damage to a big bucket of crawfish. Anything you want to do."

"Well that is awfully nice of you, Mary," Lloyd said, curious but somehow touched by her offer. "If I decide to stay, I'll take you up on that."

Marta put one hand on his shoulder and gave him a soft kiss on the cheek. Then she slipped a business card into his shirt pocket. "My personal cell number is on the back. Call me any time."

Lloyd nodded and smiled at her.

"And if you want my advice about your daddy, I'd say just let it go. Katrina took a lot of lives, and left a lot of grief and misery behind. But after a while, people have to get on with their lives."

"I know, and thanks for the advice."

"I'd like to see you again away from here, so give me a call."

"I'll do that."

Lloyd thought about Marta for most of the walk back to his squalid little sleeping room. He was flattered by her unexpected attention, but also puzzled by it. He assumed that some women like her probably led normal, straight lives outside the flesh shops where they worked, but the offer to be his tour guide in her daytime persona had caught him off guard. Was she playing him, he wondered, and if so, to what end? Or was the whole thing as simple as she made it appear? She had made a new friend, liked him, and wanted to see him again, well away from the greed and sleaze of her workplace. It could happen, he supposed.

Eventually the man in the small back office returned to his thoughts. He only got a brief glimpse of him, but something in the back recesses of his mind kept telling Lloyd that he had met this man, or had at least seen him before. Maybe it would come to him when he least expected it, he thought. He had never been one of those cops with instant recall of the name and face of every thug, suspect, and lawbreaker he'd ever crossed paths with. But he did believe that, at least for him, the answers were usually back there someplace if he just had patience and let them work their way to the front.

So now there was a woman name Marta, who could be another reason to stay, or another to go.

Chapter Twelve

Lloyd was eleven the first time he found his mother sodden and unconscious on the front porch of their rented house. Earlier that night she had put the younger kids in bed, then told Lloyd she was just going out with some friends for a little while. He could stay up late and watch TV if he wanted, and she'd be back soon. She popped some corn for him, and left a cold Coke in the fridge.

Later he couldn't have said what exactly woke him up or what time it was. All he really knew as he stirred awake was that there was a test pattern on the TV, and a warm, indistinct fear coursing through his body like his own blood. But she had left him in charge, and he knew he couldn't just pull the afghan up over his head and hope sleep would return.

Whoever had dumped Carol Ballou at the curb hadn't stuck around long enough to see her safely inside. She must have fallen coming up the steps, and once down, simply curled up on her side and let oblivion claim her. The back of her skirt was darkly stained with pee, and the side of her head lay in a small puddle of vomit. The smell about her was indescribable, and for a terrifying instant, Lloyd wondered if she was even alive. Then he saw her back and shoulder move slightly with her slow, irregular breaths.

The front of her blouse, and the underwear beneath, had been ripped open, as if by some violent hand, and one breast sagged out, oddly misshapen upon the peeling planks of the porch. The nipple was dark brown and rigid in the chilly night air, and for a terrible, guilt-ridden moment Lloyd could not tear his eyes away from it.

Sometimes in a dream, or even in an unguarded moment, that scene still returned to him unbidden and unwelcome. The sights, the smells, the horror and disgust . . .

He somehow got her inside, and far enough into her bedroom to close the door, although getting her limp form up onto the bed was impossible. She emerged the next morning just before noon, crimson-eyed, shuffling and oblivious, the rich, rancid scent of alcohol still oozing from her pores.

She never mentioned that night, probably because she didn't remember any of it . . . not how she got home, how she got in, or why she woke on the floor soaked in her own urine and stomach bile. But Lloyd remembered it, and many more nights like it that were yet to come.

It was dark outside when Lloyd woke on the narrow, lumpy cot in his small rented room. It had rained earlier, one of those short, sudden, inundating downpours, and now the humidity was so thick it felt like a person could drown in it. His skin, clothes, and bedding were sticky with sweat. He tried to remember when he last showered, then pondered whether to take one now before going out. Even if he did, he knew his skin would be slick again before he got back to his room, and he didn't think he had a clean shirt anyway.

In the minutes before he woke, he had dreamed of his little niece, Charity. Dressed in a winged fairy costume, she had been wandering his room tapping his sparse belongings one by one with her glittered plastic wand, announcing with each tap, "This is not real. This is not real. *This is not real!*"

"If nothing here is real, sweetheart," Lloyd had asked her with some amusement, "then what is real?"

The long look she gave him seemed to contain all the wisdom and sorrow of the ages, and Lloyd was suddenly struck with a sobering chill. The child slowly raised her toy wand upward, toward the vent in the ceiling where he had hidden his guns.

They were shorthanded at the hotel garage. He had taken a late shift the night before, working as a parking valet driver, then got up early this morning and went back to his car washing duties. Afterward he came back here and piled into his bed with no thought of food or drink or rudimentary hygiene.

Although he didn't feel particularly rested, he was fully awake now, his mind filled with thoughts of food. He swung his legs off the bed and turned on the dim bedside lamp, realizing that he didn't even need to put his shoes on because he had fallen asleep still wearing them.

Before going out, he looked up at the ceiling, noticing the chip under the edge of the vent, remembering Charity's silent, sober declaration. He had not checked on the two handguns since he put them up there a couple of days after his arrival. But now he pulled a chair over and stepped up on it. The weapons were there, right where he put them, and he left them there undisturbed.

He stripped the sheets and pillow case off his bed, then on his way out he dropped them off at the front desk. The night clerk on duty tore herself away from the television in the back room and came out, resenting the interruption.

"He don't lub me! That's why he lebe me alone ever night and take his junk over to that white trash ho!" The wronged woman on the TV, easily a three-hundred pounder, was shrill with righteous offense.

The desk clerk turned her head to see if that accusation would trigger the mandatory brawl for this episode. As she turned her head, Lloyd got a good look at the tattooed creature crawling up out of her tee-shirt, up her neck, and into her hair. He thought it was either a mythical dragon or a deformed rendering of a clawed paw.

"Thursday's your sheet day," the woman said, still looking around at the TV, just in case. "Cost you two dollars extra if you get 'em early."

You should prorate that fee," Lloyd said. "Since I'm just two days early, it should only cost me sixty cents or so."

The clerk deigned to look at him then, her face deadpan, and repeated, "Two dollars."

"Alright, I'll pick them up on my way in."

Outside he took a right and walked toward the river for a few blocks, then made another right onto Decatur. By the volume of foot traffic and the condition of the random drunks passing by, Lloyd realized that it was earlier in the evening than he thought. He stopped in a little shop to buy a muffaletta, one of his new favorites, a tall-boy, and a pack of generic cigarettes. The crowd at Jackson Square wasn't picky about their smokes. He munched on the sandwich and slugged the beer as he threaded through the evening crowd.

At the benches in front of the cathedral in Jackson Square, three of the old jazz men were blowing out a standard on their tarnished horns. A small crowd had gathered, and their bucket on the flagstones contained several crumpled bills. Nearby, a younger man in jeans and a brown polo shirt was just putting his clarinet away in a case. He had apparently been sitting in with them. They knew him and seemed to accept him, but they didn't offer him a share of the tips. He was here for the experience, and years from now at parties he would brag about how he used to go down to Jackson Square and play the real stuff with the legends.

Lloyd sat down on a bench a few yards from the performers, just outside the perimeter of the small crowd that had gathered. He took a big bite of the muffaletta and washed it down with a slug of beer, wishing he'd bought two cans, or even three.

Before coming to New Orleans, about the only music he listened to was country and classic rock. But now, just into his second month here in New Orleans, he was beginning to develop more of an appreciation for the jazz and blues which were bedrocks here. That was especially true when he wandered over here to Jackson Square, where the music was live, and the performers had spent the majority of their long lives with this stuff flowing through their veins and out their instruments.

The crowd was a mixed bag of tourist types. A young couple sent their little daughter shyly forward with a contribution. Brass Man Jake gave her a wink and somehow managed a warm sideways smile behind the mouthpiece of his tarnished trumpet.

Two cops, one the tough nut who had roughed him up a few weeks ago, strolled by on the flagstones. The one named Pepper was twirling his baton by its lanyard, performing an elaborate routine that occasionally caused passers-by to give him a wide berth. Lloyd still remembered the sharp bolts of pain that stick had delivered to his leg and chest, and diverted his eyes away, just as the other regulars did, so he wouldn't call attention to himself.

Lloyd recognized the tune the men were playing, but didn't remember the name. It didn't matter. He leaned back against the bench and took another drink of beer. An occasional gust of air cooled the fresh sweat on his face and arms.

"They on a roll tonight," a man said nearby, "drawin' a crowd and everything."

Lloyd looked up at Chester, the street poet, and said, "Hey, my friend. I haven't seen you for a while."

"Been over to Chalmette," Chester explained, taking a seat beside Lloyd on the bench. "A nephew of mine had a crawfish boil for his baby birthday, and I took a bus over. But I never stay for long, no more'n a day or two, 'cause his wife, she think I ain't no damn good."

He gave Lloyd a little grin and added, "But I don't hold it 'gainst her, cause she right."

Lloyd took another bite from the muffaletta, then noticed Chester eyeing it. "I like these things, but they're too big for me and I always waste half. Here, you want to help me finish it?" Chester accepted the remainder of the sandwich and the rest of the tall-boy beer as well.

"Much obliged," Chester said. "I brought some food back from my nephew's house, but it's all gone now, and my gov'ment check don't come 'til Thursday. My ribs been rubbing my backbone."

Lloyd turned his attention back to the musicians. When the tune was finished, Brass Man Jake announced that they were taking a little break, and went forward to collect the cash contributions. It was then that Lloyd first noticed the still figure sitting in the shadows of a sagging banana tree about ten feet behind the bench where the musicians were, leaning against the stone and cast-iron fence that surrounded the inner garden area of Jackson Square.

"Who's that back there?" Lloyd asked. "Just somebody settled in for the night? They must be loaded if they can sleep through this commotion."

"That's June Bug," Chester said quietly. Sitting with her knees pulled up and her head lying forward on her folded arms, she looked almost like a pile of rags and refuse. "She don't be feelin' so good," he went on, "but she say she don't want no help. Just want to be left alone. Beat up, I think, an' maybe raped." He paused, then added, "But I don't know 'bout raped. How bad off a man have to be to take him some of that?"

They sat looking over at her for a few moments, and in all that time she made no movement, showed no sign of life. Lloyd considered the possibility that she might already be dead. But if Chester had spoken to her earlier . . .

"Sad ol' bag of rags, just lookin' in the window with a candle in it."

As Chester began, Lloyd recognized his companion's poet voice and stayed quiet.

"But maybe the man inside don't know she come from there a long time ago.

"Don't recognize nothin' he ever made. Maybe he just think . . ."

Chester paused, then looked at Lloyd, shaking his head. When he spoke again it was in his regular street voice. "Nope, it ain't there to-night. No use tryin'."

"So, we just sit here and do nothing?" Lloyd asked. He could feel his frustration rising at the detachment in Chester's voice. He seemed more disturbed that his poetry wouldn't come together for him than he did about the fact that an injured person sat suffering just a few yards from where they were.

"What you want to do, mister?" Chester asked. Lloyd could tell that he too was annoyed. "Maybe you could take her to her house, which she ain't got. Or you could take her to the hospital in your car, which I bet you ain't got, and pay the doctor for her with money I also bet you ain't got. What you want to do? Just tell me that?"

"I don't know. Something. At least tell the police."

"Okay, you go catch up with Officer Pepper up the street and tell him June Bug in trouble. Maybe he'll take her to jail, where she get beat up some more, or maybe he'll just save some time and whale on her here, like he done before."

Lloyd just stared at him, disturbed by his words, but unable to dispute anything he said.

"I been over there twicet already, but she run me off. Say she cut me if I bother her again. Maybe if Mayor was still around . . ." Chester said. "He'd know what to do, how to help her. But he gone."

Lloyd watched the still form of the derelict woman a moment longer, knowing he couldn't just leave her like that. With no plan, he got up and started over to her. As he drew near, he thought that if she wasn't dead, she already smelled that way.

"Hey June Bug," Lloyd said, sitting on the sidewalk a foot or so away from her. "It's me, Lloyd. How are you?"

Without moving she mumbled something which he thought might be, "Go way."

"I heard you're not doing so well," he tried. No answer. "Chester said somebody hurt you."

"He beat me up an' banged me hard," June Bug mumbled. "I cut him on the arm, but he done me anyway."

"Not Chester," Lloyd said gently. "He wouldn't do that to you."

"Not him. That other fella. I don't know who. Down at the river someplace. I can't think. My brains all scrambled. Leave me be."

Lloyd felt the impulse to comfort her, to at least reach out and touch her filthy hand, but the idea of it was at the same time repulsive to him. A stew of foul odors hung like fog around her, nearly gagging him.

"Guess what I've got, June Bug?"

She mumbled something that Lloyd thought vaguely was a curse or threat.

"I've got some cigarettes," he said. "I've got a whole pack, just for you."

That got her attention. She stirred for the first time, turning her head on her folded arms until she could look at him. Then he got a better idea of the extent of the violence she had suffered.

Lloyd took out the pack of cigarettes, making a show of opening it in front of her. She watched the movements of his hands with anticipation as he took one out and reached for the plastic lighter in his shirt pocket.

"Sit up a little more so you can smoke, June Bug," he prompted her.

The simple act of raising her head clearly caused her pain. Even in the shadows under the banana tree her injuries were starkly apparent. Her features were bruised and swollen. Her right eye had swelled nearly shut, and dried black blood crusted on a split upper lip. The worst of her injuries were on the right side of her face, and the cop in Lloyd automatically deduced that her attacker must have been a lefty. But that was a clue without any value to anyone.

Lloyd put a cigarette between his lips and lit it, then took a single draw. He hadn't smoked for a long time, but the taste, and how he felt when it entered his lungs, reminded him why it had been so hard to give the damn things up.

Lifting the old woman's nearly limp right hand, he put the cigarette between her first two fingers and guided it to her lips. She took a deep drag, and the glow cast an odd red accent on her face. It seemed like the undamaged side of her mouth almost tried to smile as she drew again.

As soon as Lloyd released her hand it fell away, and the cigarette landed in her lap. He retrieved it before it could do any damage.

"Maybe I'd better help you with this," he said. The smoke drifted lazily out of her mouth and nose. She hardly seemed to be breathing.

So what now? Lloyd wondered. He looked around but didn't spot any uniform cops. And if it was Officer Pepper that he had to go to for help, he had to agree with Chester. He and his partner weren't likely to do much. All that seemed to be left was to call nine-one–one, but he wondered how long it would take them to get here, and where they might take her when they loaded her up.

He pictured June Bug lying ignored on a gurney in the halls of an overcrowded public hospital emergency room packed with injured screaming kids and shot-up gang bangers.

Lloyd reached out and gave June Bug a draw on the cigarette. Her eyes were closed, but she still acknowledged the pleasure of it with a soft sound in the back of her throat.

"She got some people someplace." Chester had come over finally, and was standing nearby. "She told me oncet, but I don't recollect where. Atlanta maybe, or Alabama. Or Dakota. Somethin' with an 'a'."

"She told me she was from Mississippi, or was it Alabama? I don't remember either," Lloyd admitted. "Some little town I've never heard of." He saw the street poet eyeing the cigarette pack and handed it up to him. Chester tapped out four or five, then gave the pack back.

"That's right. Mis'sippi," Chester said. "She said if I know it when she die, she want me to tell them she gone. She gave me a piece of paper."

"With a phone number on it?" Lloyd asked.

"Don't know," Chester answered, somewhat sheepishly. "I put it in my billfold and forgot about it 'til now. Probably still there."

Chester's ancient leather wallet nearly disintegrated as he pulled it out. It was over an inch thick and half its contents spilled out into his hand as he opened it up. Lloyd tried to stay patient as the old man began fumbling through the fistful of cards and folded scraps of paper. The only thing that seemed to be missing from the mix was any sign of paper money.

Maybe this was the solution, Lloyd thought. If he could reach some member of June Bug's family, maybe they could take over, or at least tell him what to do.

"Nope. Nope," Chester mumbled as he examined each item and crammed it back into the tattered wallet. Then finally he announced, "Ah hah! I think this is it."

He handed a folded, disintegrating cocktail napkin to Lloyd. The writing wouldn't win any penmanship award, but it was legible enough. The name was Sissy Marks, followed by a phone number. Lloyd didn't recognize the area code, but it wasn't the New Orleans 501.

Lloyd turned back to June Bug. He gave her another drag of the cigarette, then stubbed the butt out on the cobblestones.

"Who's Sissy, June Bug?" He asked.

The old woman raised her head and blew the smoke out through pursed lips. Her arm rose haltingly and her fingers moved to her lips as if to take another puff, but of course they held no cigarette.

"Who's Sissy?" Lloyd asked again. "Is she your daughter, or your sister? Do you know Sissy?"

"You take my fag?" June Bug asked.

A short distance away, the high tawdry wail of a trumpet rang out. After a few solo notes, the other instruments began to join in. The old men had started their next performance. Chester had already meandered off in their direction, still holding the tall-boy Lloyd surrendered to him.

June Bug again folded her arms across her knees, then rested her head on them, retreating back into her own little cocoon of suffering and solitude.

"I'm going to call Sissy and tell her that you need her," Lloyd said, nearly shouting. "Don't worry, we're going to get you some help."

The tip bucket was back out, and a small audience was gathering to hear the old men play. Brass Man Jake had hit the gin bottle during their break and was blowing a few sour notes, but the spectators didn't seem to mind. This was the real stuff.

Lloyd skirted the crowd and walked toward the Cathedral where it was quieter. He punched the number from the cocktail napkin in his cell phone, and a woman answered on the fourth ring. Her voice had a raw edge to it.

"Hello, is this Sissy Marks?" Lloyd asked.

"No it is not," the woman said curtly. "Who is this?"

"This is Lloyd Ballou, and I'm calling from New Orleans." He started to use "patrolman" in front of his name just to get her attention, but decided against it. "Is Sissy Marks there? Can I speak to her?"

"This is Sissy Gilley," the woman said. In the background Lloyd could hear a kid squalling. "Melissa, can you please do SOMETHING with that baby? Jeb, get down from there right this minute!" When she finally returned her attention to the phone, her tone was harried and inpatient. "Who are you? Are you selling something?"

"No."

"My name used to be Sissy Marks. So how did you get this number? What do you want?" The baby had stopped crying, but Lloyd could hear a girl's voice asking her something. "Take him into the living room for a minute. Can't you see I'm on the phone? What do you want Lloyd?"

"There's a homeless woman here," Lloyd said. "I don't know what her real name is, but everybody calls her June Bug. She's . . ."

Without warning Sissy Gilley simply exploded on the phone. Her voice rose several decibels and the words spilled out in a staccato. "You mean that damn drunk bitch is still alive?"

"Just barely."

Well go tell her for me that I never want to hear from her again. Tell her that I just can't go through all of that again for the umpteenth time."

"All of what?" Lloyd asked.

“Getting in the car, again, and driving to whatever jail or charity hospital she’s in, again, and bringing her back here to try to get her straightened out. Again.”

“Are you her daughter?”

“I was,” Sissy said. “But I gave up on her completely after the last time. I tell people she’s dead, and I thought by now she would be.” The shrillness had left her voice, and she was speaking quietly now, probably because of the children. But her tone still held a cold detachment. “She had a big part in wrecking my last marriage. Over and over I’d bring her back here to Tecumbah, bring her into our home, and try to get her into rehab or whatever. Finally, that last time when she caught our house on fire, my other husband just had enough. He left the night of the fire, and she disappeared the next day. Took the cash out of my purse, and Melissa’s piggy bank, with her.”

“I’m so sorry to hear that, Mrs. Gilley,” Lloyd said. His voice caught unexpectedly in his throat and tears welled in his eyes. “My mother’s been a drunk since I was nine, so I understand. I raised my little sister practically by myself.”

Sissy sighed heavily, as if she might be marshaling the resources to go on. “You know, then,” she said. “You sound like a nice man, Lloyd, and I know you’re trying to do what’s right to help her. But some people are just lost, you know? And you can’t do anything about it.” A bond had formed during this brief conversation, and now she needed his forgiveness.

“I understand,” Lloyd said, “and I think you’ve made the only choice you can.” He heard sniffling and knew she was crying, but probably trying to hide it from the children.

“My new husband thinks she’s dead,” Sissy said softly, her voice breaking. “He’s a good man, works hard, and he loves me and the kids. I don’t want him to know I lied to him.”

"I'll do what I can, then," Lloyd said, "and I'll try to get in touch with you when I can. If you don't want to know anything more, just don't take my call. I'll understand."

As he turned back to the open cobblestone plaza, he realized that the band had stopped. They were absent from their customary bench, their instruments left scattered behind. Another crowd was gathering now, a few yards farther away, back where June Bug now lay slumped on the flagstone pavement.

Lloyd understood what had happened. He started that way, shoving past a collection of gawkers.

Chester was kneeling beside June Bug's crumpled body. It appeared to Lloyd that she must have struggled to her feet, but made it only a few steps before stumbling and hitting her head on the sharp edge of a low brick wall as she fell.

"She dead. She sure 'nough dead," Chester said quietly as Lloyd knelt beside him. Chester had covered the old woman's shoulders and head with his own filthy jacket.

"Are you sure?" Lloyd asked. "Did you check for a pulse, or heartbeat?"

"No need. I know dead when it's this plain." Chester raised the corner of the jacket and let Lloyd have a look.

June Bug lay on her stomach, with her head turned awkwardly on the side toward them. A rivulet of thick dark blood had seeped out from under her head onto the flagstones beneath her. It sparkled even in the dim light. Her right eye, the only one the crowd could see, was opened and unblinking, staring at nothing of this world. Spittle seeped from the corner of her open mouth.

"Pore ol' gal," Chester said quietly. He reached out and closed her mouth and her open eye. "There. She don't look quite so spooky now," he explained to Lloyd.

Most of the onlookers held back from the body, out of respect or perhaps fear. When Lloyd realized that one crass gawker was taking video with a small camera, he kept his head averted. He felt like going over and feeding it to the guy, but the time wasn't right for that.

A young woman separated herself from the crowd and took a few tentative steps forward. She was 18 or 20, wearing a white cotton blouse and denim shorts.

"I called nine-one–one," she told Lloyd and Chester. Her eyes stayed fixed on June Bug in grim fascination.

"Thanks. That's kind of you," Lloyd said.

I said a prayer for her, too," the girl said. Tears glistened in her eyes. "She's with Jesus Christ up in heaven now."

"I ain't so sure she lived the kind of life that take her up to see Him," Chester said skeptically. "But wherever she goin', she dere now."

Lloyd wondered if Chester might be about to cut loose with one of his poems, but his muse was nowhere around now. He thought that later he might ask Chester to come up with something. It might be the only eulogy this sad wasted soul received.

"They told me there were officers in the vicinity," the girl offered, "and somebody would be here soon."

The surprised look that Chester gave her seemed to startle her, and she backed away, her civic duty completed.

"Officers comin', be here soon," Chester told Lloyd, an edge in his voice.

"Well, somebody's got to take charge here," Lloyd reasoned. "I don't know what to do, and I don't guess you do either."

"Officers with questions," Chester said. "Officers need to know what happened here, an then don't believe what they hears. Maybe somebody knock her down. Maybe somebody steal her stuff. Maybe somebody need to go 'long with them an' talk some more."

"Oh shit!" Lloyd muttered. His thoughts had been going in an entirely different direction, looking at things from a cop perspective, but of course Chester was right. And Pepper was walking the beat tonight.

They both rose together, Chester taking a heavy grip on Lloyd's arm to steady his aged knees. He turned left and blended in with the gaggle of old music men nearby. Lloyd went right, skirting the crowd, and a hundred or so feet away he sat down on the end of a bench. At the other end was a young couple sitting close together, talking quietly, seemingly unaware of the excitement nearby. Nobody in the crowd seemed to have noticed his departure, or at least nobody was looking at him now. A few people were beginning to leave the scene of June Bug's death to continue their night out in the Quarter.

Over near the corner of Chartres and St. Peter, two policemen came in sight, seemingly in no hurry. It was Pepper and his partner. Lloyd slouched down a little more on the bench and lowered his head, just another faceless nobody getting a little sleep.

Pepper's partner, a different one tonight, knelt beside June Bug and drew Chester's jacket aside. With any luck, Lloyd thought, they'd leave it there so Chester could retrieve it later. While Pepper got on the radio, his partner checked the body for vitals, then looked up at Pepper and said something. Pepper nodded, then passed the word on through the microphone clipped to the epaulet of his uniform. When he was finished, he turned his head and stared down at the dead old woman at his feet. He said something to his partner and grinned broadly, pleased with his own joke, but his partner didn't share in the amusement. Instead he looked up and said something that wiped the grin right off of Pepper's face.

Lloyd decided that he liked this guy, and might have liked to partner with him back in the day.

They searched June Bug's clothes and pockets, but seemed to find little of use to them. Then the partner again covered June Bug's head and shoulders with Chester's jacket. That thing was going to stink when this was all over, Lloyd thought. But then, Chester was a walking montage of unpleasant smells himself.

The ambulance arrived fairly soon and the crew loaded June Bug in back with practiced efficiency. Again, one of them checked for vitals, but it was an unnecessary protocol at this point.

The old music men had been passing around a bottle in a paper bag, watching the goings on from a distance. But as the ambulance crew went about their tasks, the old men picked up their instruments and begin to play. The tune started slow and bluesy, the sort of mournful dirge that sounded appropriate when death came calling. Then, as if in unspoken agreement, they all stopped playing at once, letting their last notes dissipate like smoke.

A six count later, the high note that Brass Man Jake blew from his trumpet was as startling as a fire alarm, rude and shrill, glass shattering and mesmerizing. It set the pace and tone for the rollicking jazz number that was to follow.

The ambulance driver, a middle-aged, white-uniformed black man, slammed the rear doors of his vehicle closed. Up until this point he had performed his duties with detached professionalism, but now he looked up at Jake and the rest, smiled approvingly, and waved his understanding. He half walked, half danced around the side of the ambulance to the driver's door and gave the musicians another wave before climbing in.

There were many ways to honor the dead, and this was how they did it in New Orleans.

When the excitement was over and this end of Jackson Square returned to its normal late-night lethargy, Lloyd did actually doze off for a while, dreaming in sad, tragic snippets that dissolved from his memory the instant that he woke.

The whole bench was his now, the young couple gone. So were Chester and the jazz men. A few drunks and late-nighters still strolled or staggered by, and here and there sleeping homeless men were sacked out on benches and on the bare flagstones. Faint music from at least two different directions drifted to him on the humid night air.

Lloyd took out his phone and stared at it for a moment. He felt an obligation to do something, as if this particular tragedy required one final act. But he dreaded the idea of calling that sad confused woman, especially this late at night.

Finally, he sent a simple text message to her number. "It's not a lie anymore."

Then, hardly thinking, he chose another number and hit call.

"Hi mom. Sorry to call you at this hour, but I know you stay up late. How are you?"

"Not so good tonight, son." Carol Ballou's voice had that dreamy lethargic quality that spoke of strong meds and prolonged suffering. "It hurts something awful tonight, honey, but I still got two hours before they'll give me anything more."

Instead of going back to toss and turn atop the damp sheets in his musty cell, Lloyd walked the two blocks to a corner grocery and bought a couple more tall boys. He knew it probably wasn't such a good idea, but he hoped the alcohol might calm the dreary demons inside his head.

He returned to the spot where June Bug's sorry life had ended, sat down on the flagstones a few feet away, and popped the tab on one of the beer cans. It was ice cold going down, and almost immediately began to spread a welcome calm.

A stain of vile body fluids marked the spot where the old woman sat when Lloyd helped her smoke the last cigarette of her life. A few feet farther away another dark puddle, this one blood, showed where she had fallen and died.

Lloyd turned his face away from these grim reminders and took another drink.

A few times in his police career Lloyd had worked scenes like this. When derelicts were found dead, little or no interest was shown in the actual cause. It was as if whatever happened to them had been their own fault, and they deserved whatever fate served up to them. He had felt no particular sadness about any of them that he could recall. These were the world's throwaways, the ones that made you feel a little better about your own life, even if it seemed pretty crappy most of the time. The paths that led most of them to this sort of end were littered with terrible luck and terrible choices, and sometimes it seemed like death was the only mercy and the only relief they had been shown for a long, long time.

What was different this time? Lloyd wondered. What made him feel now that there should have been something more he could have done? He had no reason to feel guilty. Calamity and death stalked people like June Bug, hovering in the shadows, waiting to pounce. And yet, the feeling he had was real.

He drained the first can of beer and popped the tab on the second one. The beer was helping. The vague hunger he felt before was gone, and the clarity of his thinking was starting to fuzz around the edges. He welcomed that.

Hell, everybody and everything had to die, one way or another. Billionaires choked on rare delicacies in lavish dining rooms. Sweet old grandmothers tripped and hit their heads on table corners. Innocent kids caught random bullets in the head from guns fired blocks away. People who had everything to live for ended it all with ropes and knives and bullets and pills. Little boys drowned in shallow puddles at the bottom of creeks.

The stench of the spot where June Bug sat began to made Lloyd a little queasy, so he got up and moved away. The bench where he sat earlier was occupied by a sleeping man who cradled his shoes in his arms and rested his head on a bundle of clothing. His snoring was irregular and rumbled damply with phlegm.

Lloyd began to think that maybe he could finally sleep. It was reasonably safe out in the open here in the Square, and the police didn't start rousting anybody until dawn. The air was cool and comfortable, but he knew he'd never be able to rest on the hard, bare flagstones with nothing to put under his head. So, it was back to the room. He wondered if he would be able to get his two-dollar linens this late at night.

He skirted around the fenced middle commons of the Square and walked south toward Decatur and the Mississippi River. Cafe du Monde was straight ahead, still pulling in a decent crowd even at this late hour. Dodging through the steady traffic on Decatur, he found an empty table on the far side of the cafe's large covered patio.

The young man who came to take his order had a limited grasp of English and a heavy Eastern European accent. But good communication skills probably didn't rank high in the employment interview at a place where ninety-nine percent of the customers ordered exactly the same thing.

When his order of beignets and cafe au lait arrived, Lloyd picked up one of the hot, freshly fried pastries and took a big mouth-scorching bite. The thick dusting of white powdered sugar peppered down onto his shirt and jeans. Next came a drink of the sweet, creamy, lukewarm chicory coffee.

An unexpected trill of female laughter somewhere to his right caught his attention and he looked around, curious about why it sounded familiar.

Betsy didn't notice him from where she was sitting. She was dressed for a night on the town, wispy red dress, heels to match, hair up, and more make-up than he had ever seen her wear. The man beside her had his chair pulled up close, one hand placed possessively on her inner thigh.

Lloyd figured this had to be the storied Andre Harp, semi-wealthy art dealer, giver of joy and yearning, thief of self-esteem, teller of punishing lies, the unfortunately irresistible lover. He was taller and leaner than Lloyd had somehow imagined him, a few years older, and hardly as handsome. He was square-jawed to a fault, his eyes seemed a bit too small, and his thinning brown hair was annoyingly immaculate. But then, Betsy had never really described him to Lloyd, and there were no pictures of him on display in her tiny apartment, at least when Lloyd was there.

There were three other couples at the table, and they seemed to be reviewing tonight's escapades. The conversation was raucous and lively, punctuated liberally with bursts of laughter. Clearly their evening had been more enjoyable than his own.

Betsy hardly seemed to be the same person he had come to know. The smile never left her face, and she had a giddy, fulfilled air about her that he had never witnessed. Her eyes turned moony and intimate the instant that they fell on the man beside her. She slid her hand under the table to rest on top of his, as if acknowledging his right to anything she had.

In that instant Lloyd felt like he understood all the puzzling aspects of the time he had spent with this woman, the ghostly glides to the open balcony doors in the middle of the night, and the tears that sometimes flowed as she slept beside him. She was one half of a soul mate pairing, but the other half of that mysterious spiritual bond remained tantalizingly out of reach. The magic clearly wasn't there for Andre Harp. He was just a married man getting a little on the side.

Lloyd scooted his chair around so his back was to the group and began to watch the varied pedestrian traffic flow by on the sidewalk a few feet away. He ordered a second cup of coffee and sipped it slowly as he finished his beignets. At this time of night nobody seemed to be in a hurry to get where they were going, nor was he.

He heard chairs slide on the tile floor behind him, and the chatter of the group moved his way. Hanging onto Andre's arm, Betsy passed so close that the soft fabric of her dress brushed his shoulder, but she never knew he was there.

Chapter Thirteen

Lloyd sank into numbing isolation after being fired from the Kansas City Police Department. Until his termination, his life centered on being a cop, and all of his friends were cops. Then suddenly he was permanently expelled from that fraternity. He knew that if he ever tried to go back to the watering holes and eateries where he and his brothers in blue once congregated, he would be treated as an outsider, or worse, a pitiable hanger-on.

The three other cops who left the force for the same transgression as Lloyd had all landed on their feet, more or less, but the humiliation of what they had gone through kept them from wanting to buddy up. Mark Finch started up a lawn service, and was now running four crews. Lonnie West went to work for his father-in-law installing aluminum siding. Tony Achelle had started up his own detective service, and Lloyd had actually worked for him for a while. It wasn't such a bad gig when you got used to it, tailing cheating spouses until you snapped the money shot, and setting traps for small-time thieves ripping off their employers. But a time came when Tony couldn't make payroll, and he let Lloyd go.

Lloyd drifted through a couple of security guard jobs after that, but the pay was lousy and something about wearing a uniform but no gun seemed phony and embarrassing for a man whose blood was still a slowly fading shade of blue.

Eventually he hired on with the auto repair shop where he used to take his and Kelly's cars in better times, and soon he realized that he had stumbled into a trade that actually suited him and paid a decent wage if you worked hard enough. He couldn't see himself making a career of it or, God forbid, ever thinking about opening a shop of his own, but by then he was beginning to condition himself not to think too far ahead or aim too high.

For all those years that he was a cop, married to Kelly, with two cars and a nice little mortgaged bungalow, Lloyd Ballou was always confident that this was the life he was meant to live. Now he wondered if he would ever savor that feeling again. It was unnerving to realize how close he was at this moment to being out there on the street, just like Chester and Brass Man Jake and all the rest.

Was that why he was drawn to their company, he wondered. Was some instinct telling him he'd better get street savvy, just in case? Or was it something even more elementary than that? Was it simply that he had found a new band of comrades who had fallen so far themselves that they no longer judged anyone?

It was late Saturday afternoon, as hot as it was going to get, and the French Quarter shops, bars, restaurants, markets, streets and sidewalks were bustling with sweaty tourists and locals. Lloyd was in search of a good meal at a reasonable price, and then, without giving it much consideration, he figured he would go where he usually ended up when he was out and about. For now, and maybe forever, the little dive bar on Decatur where Betsy worked was off limits, but Jackson Square was always there.

They had been shorthanded recently at the hotel garage and Lloyd had put in a grinding 42 hours in the past three days, but now he didn't have to go back in until noon Sunday. Without making any promises, his boss was beginning to break him in on some of the supervisor's tasks, and even let Lloyd cover for him during breaks. His days of car washing seemed to be over for good. Within the limited perspective of that little employment microcosm, things were looking up, and his rise from ten dollars an hour to fourteen, plus a steady flow of tips, seemed meteoric. He had his biggest paycheck to date in his wallet, and had enough folding money left, mostly ones, that he wouldn't even need to cash the check for the next few days, not until the room rent was due. He wasn't ready to buy stock or look for real estate yet, but at least he was breaking even now and didn't have to hit on his dwindling checking account in Kansas City.

Lloyd had slept late, so tired that even the heat in his room didn't bake him awake until nearly five in the afternoon. He started the day out with a cold shower and clean knit shirt and jeans, enjoying the fresh feeling that he knew would only last a short while once he hit the streets.

He wandered for a while, buying a to-go cup of coffee and a couple of scones at a trendy, tiny joint along Esplanade. The girl that served him was colorfully tattooed, and wore her cornflower colored hair in a spiky Mohawk. She was flirty and vivacious, knowing it improved tips from guys like Lloyd, who went in there not so much for the coffee as just to get a boost from her broad smile, cheerful chatter and tight shorts. Her name was Brindle, and she lived in back with her boyfriend, who ran the place. Both were musicians chasing the big break.

He sprang for a real meal in a little meat-and-three joint frequented by locals, and tipped the waiter a few bucks up front to ensure that the helpings were generous. He had the leftovers bundled up, knowing there would be somebody down on Jackson Square who wouldn't mind at all if the chicken fried steak, corn, green beans and scalloped potatoes were all jumbled up together.

Life was sometimes a matter of measured expectations, Lloyd thought. Somewhere in New Orleans, at that same moment in time, there was someone eating a two-hundred-dollar steak dinner with a twenty-dollars-a-glass wine who wouldn't enjoy their dinner half as much as he had enjoyed his.

Without really thinking about it, Lloyd re-routed his path so he didn't go down Decatur, past Betsy's bar, on his way to Jackson Square. Night was setting in, and a pleasant breeze was blowing in from the river. It would be comfortable later, good sleeping weather, and he thought he might head back to his room a little earlier than usual. The hurried grind would not start back up at the hotel garage until tomorrow.

In mid-block down a quiet side street Lloyd noticed half a dozen people clustered together, staring down a narrow alley between two dilapidated buildings. Drawing nearer, he realized they were staring at a shabby, slumped figure sitting a few feet down into the alley, his back against one wall and his pulled-up knees nearly touching the other. His head lay forward on his folded arms.

Lloyd's thoughts flashed back to the death scene of June Bug just a few days ago, and the curious crowd that had encircled her. The man was sitting much like June Bug sat when Lloyd found her. But unlike her, this man was crying. Desperate, pathetic, mournful sobs shook his shoulders and chest, and in his overwhelming grief he didn't seem to know or care that people were standing just a few feet away looking on.

"We just found the old friggin' dude here like that," one of the onlookers told Lloyd, as if to establish his non-involvement. He looked to be about nineteen or twenty. His head was shaved clean and shiny, but he was working with limited success on a patchy beard. A remarkable array of colorful, unidentifiable tattoos flowed up both arms and into the sleeves of his tee shirt. He held a battered guitar case in one hand, and a stained white apron in the other. "I was just like walking down the friggin' sidewalk goin' to my friggin' job, you know dude, when I like found him sitting out here. Then these other dudes came up, but we don't know like what to friggin' do for him."

Lloyd glanced at the young man, realizing that there was no useful information in what he'd said, and he *like* didn't require a *friggin'* answer.

Lloyd knelt beside the crying man and put a hand on his shoulder. "Hey brother, are things all that bad?" he asked. "Is there something you need, something that we can do for you?"

The odor that drifted up from the man labeled him as a street person, as did his worn, dirty clothes and worn-out shoes. His graying black hair was a nappy tangle. His bawling diminished as Lloyd patted his shoulder. He raised his head and looked up, his lined, chocolate features gleaming with tears.

"Do you need help?" Lloyd asked. "Are you hurt or sick?"

The old man looked Lloyd's face over and a spark of recognition lit in his eyes. "I know you," he said. "You Chester's friend." His breath was rank.

"Sure, I'm Lloyd, Chester's friend. And you're Jake. Brass Man Jake."

"Yup. The Brass Man hisself," the old man confirmed.

"Dude, you friggin' got this?" the bald kid asked. Lloyd raised his head and saw that most of the onlookers had already moved on. "I gotta like book, you know?"

"Sure, I'll take care of him."

Lloyd turned his attention back to Jake and asked, "So why are you here, Jake? Just sitting in an alley crying like this?"

"They took my horn," Jake explained, his voice heavy with grief. "They snatched it right out of my hands, and run off with it. Them street punks." Lloyd pictured the dented, well-worn trumpet that Jake used when he played with the others. It looked like something you could pick up at Salvation Army for a few bucks, but clearly it had far more value to Jake.

"I blowed The Saints outa that thing a million times. I been blowin' Louie outa that horn half my life." His eyes filled with sad despair, and fresh tears welled. "I get my gin money with it."

"Did you tell the police?"

"What use is that?" Jake said. "They ain't gonna help no ol' back-street nigger ginny like me. 'Sides, he says he kill me if I tell the police. And I know he mean it."

"Then you know who did it?" Lloyd asked.

"Sure, I know. It was that white trash hoodlum, that sonofabitchin' devil Tats. Him and his bunch. Just broke my heart. That horn mite near all I got in this ol' life."

Eventually Lloyd coaxed Jake to his feet and they started away, moving at the old man's shuffling pace. Something about this whole thing got under Lloyd's skin, and he could feel the cold anger rising inside. Weren't these people's lives hard enough without street punks like Tats and his bunch making them even more miserable? Where did these vultures come from, and what made them the way they were?

Along the way, he decided that at least this time the offense would not go unchallenged. You couldn't fix all the evil in the world, but sometimes you could fix little pieces of it.

They stopped once for Lloyd to go into a little shop for beer and cigarettes, as well as a few other small items he thought he might need later. When he got back to the sidewalk where Jake waited, the old man accepted the cigarettes but wouldn't have anything to do with the beer. He was a gin man.

When they got to Jackson Square, Jake wouldn't sit with the other players, shamed by his tragedy, so he and Lloyd went to a bench nearby. Lloyd gave him the leftovers from his dinner. The old man accepted it and ate a bit with the plastic fork, but mostly he only pretended to eat. Then he pretended to be finished, and Lloyd set the foam container aside.

"Brass Man. Brass Man. Brass Man Jake.
Wash dishes all night and never break a plate."

Lloyd and Jake looked to see Chester approaching. As he drew near, Chester took in the scene in one scanning glance. The two men, the pack of cigarettes in Jake's hand, the sack of beer beside Lloyd's shoe, and the foam to-go box on the bench.

"Things not so good tonight, Chess," Jake said. "I'm feelin' low, low down, brother man."

"Wassa matter, Jake boy?"

Jake looked up and his eyes twinkled with fresh tears. He tried to speak, but his voice broke.

"Those boys stole his trumpet," Lloyd explained. "The one I had a run-in with, and his bunch."

"That Tats, he's a mess, a'right," Chester confirmed. "A mess of trouble, that boy."

Chester sat down on the bench and finished off the leftovers while, at the other end, Jake leaned forward, elbows on knees, head down, having a private conversation with himself. Lloyd popped a beer and watched the other old men prepare for their evening activities. When Chester finished eating, licking the foam container clean, Lloyd gave him ten ones and sent him off to get some gin for Jake. It was clear the old man would be needing it more and more as the evening went on.

When Chester returned, he and Brass Man Jake huddled together at one end of the bench, talking in low tones, both sipping from half-pint bottles Chester brought back with him. Lloyd, feeling suddenly like an outsider, sat at the other end of the bench and watched a crowd gather as the music started up with one of the standards.

Moments later, he heard Chester's voice rise, and recognized his poetry seer voice taking over. Chester had one hand on Jake's forehead, and Jake himself, eyes closed and head tilted back, seemed to have drifted into some sort of trance. Lloyd watched the two old men in fascination.

Bokor comin' for the white boy, Jake.
Take him off to see Baron Samedi.
He hear the drums and he see the dance.
No-headed chicken run all over, blood a'spurtin'.
Smoke an' blood an' dead man's eyes burnin' straight through.
That boy just thought he seed black before that night come.
Soon he wish the gators eat 'im.

Chester's second verse was in some kind of patois that Lloyd didn't understand, but from the slight nods of Jake's head, it was clear that he understood his friend's prophesy. Then finally Chester switched back to his flavor of street English.

The dark ones come across the big water jus' like us come.
Come over deep in our bellies,
Hide inside our souls,
Where massa never know they dere.
Dark as a grave, no heart in 'em.
Love to see the blood run down.
Love to see the eyes sew shut.
Eats the screams with a spoon, like grits an' butter.
Love to fill a man up with scare

'Til he got no room left in 'em.
Love to make a man so dead he never die.
Only costs a little, but you always gotta pay.

Chester lowered his hand and looked over at Lloyd to favor him with a quick wink. It took Jake a few seconds to come around, but when his eyes finally opened, he seemed at peace.

Sometime after ten, as the foot traffic began to thin, Tats and a couple of his toadies arrived down a side street and began mingling with some of the younger people on the plaza. Lloyd figured they had goods to sell, and was not surprised when he saw Tats lead somebody into the shadows of the alley beside the cathedral.

Lloyd reached in his jeans pocket and took out the two rolls of nickels he bought in the convenience store, one for each hand. He wandered over toward the alley, stepping into the shadows just as Tats and his latest customer were finishing their transaction. Tats stuffed some cash into a pocket and gave Lloyd a dark look, but didn't try to leave. His two companions were nearby and he felt confident in their numbers.

"Brass Man Jake wants his trumpet back," Lloyd said simply.

A little sneer came over Tats' face. Lloyd figured he had already started sampling some of his own wares, making him cocky. "Don't know what you're talking about," he said. He turned his head toward one of his cohorts, and the guy sniggered obligingly.

"Just give me the old man's horn and I'll leave you alone," Lloyd said. "That's the easy way."

"That there's a kind and generous old nigger man. He gave it to me. It's mine now."

"Spare me the bullshit and just give it back." Lloyd kept his voice quiet and even, knowing the shadowed threat a soft tone could convey. His eye's never left Tats'. "Why make a big deal out of this? You've had your laughs by now. It's just a beat-up old trumpet, but it's important to him. You couldn't get ten dollars for it if you tried to pawn it, but I'll give you twenty right now."

"Fifty," Tats said. He glanced at his buddies and winked.

"Alright, fifty," Lloyd said. "Just because it'll be simpler than doing it the other way."

"How about a hundred, then?"

"Is it in that bag over there?" Lloyd asked, pointing to a backpack leaning against the church wall.

"It's there," Tat's said. "So how about two hundred and we got us a deal?"

"How about I just take the bag and everything in it?"

The young man on Tat's right was taller and huskier than his two companions. Lloyd vaguely recognized him from that first night, and saw by his stance that he thought well of himself. His fists balled, and he took one step forward with what was meant as a threat. "How about if I just . . ."

Lloyd had learned way back in middle school that fistfights like this started suddenly, and usually ended fast. His opponent seemed unaware of that reality, probably using his build and height advantage to end most fights before they started.

The clip on the jaw that Lloyd gave him was clearly unexpected. It was a solid, no-nonsense punch, precisely aimed, and aided substantially by the roll of nickels cradled in his palm. Lloyd followed that up with another punch just below the breast bone that was intended to make breathing an all-consuming preoccupation for the next few moments. Gasping for air, the man staggered back until he bumped the wall behind him. His eyes stopped fixing on anything in particular, and he slid slowly down the wall until he was sitting limp on the flagstones. He wasn't quite knocked out but was clearly stunned. He wouldn't be a problem again until he got his breath and senses back, and probably not even then.

Lloyd recognized Tats' other companion as well. He was fumbling with his back pants pocket, probably trying to fish out that same little automatic he'd tried to pull on Lloyd before. But Lloyd didn't wait long enough to find out. He was a little farther away, so Lloyd's arm was fully extended and his right fist was moving fast by the time it connected. The kid fell straight and hard, not even conscious enough to try and break his fall. His head hit the flagstones with a dull thump.

Lloyd turned to point at Tats and said, "Okay numb-nuts, fight or flight?" The last two or three seconds had wiped the sneer from Tats face, and his eyes were wide as he surveyed his defeated entourage. Lloyd was between him and any possible escape route. He made the next best choice and took a hesitant half step backward.

"I'm getting kind of tired of dealing with you, kid," Lloyd said. "You're so ignorant and cocky, you could have had fifty bucks in your pocket and be back selling your shit already. But you chose this instead. Give me the Brass Man's trumpet, or get ready to sit down hard like your buddy over there." Then he added, "And if your hand comes out of that pack with anything but a beat-up old horn, you can plan on waking up in the hospital while they're trying to figure out where all the pieces go."

When Lloyd turned to leave the alley, trumpet in hand, he saw Chester standing a short distance away, chuckling to himself, wearing a grin that lit up his face.

"I seen a thing or two," Chester said as they started back toward the bench where Brass Man Jake sat, "but I never seen nothin' like dat." He chuckled and added, "Nor maybe seen nothin' I enjoyed more."

"I guess we didn't need your hoo-doo spirits this time," Lloyd said.

"Aw, I don't believe none of that voodoo crap, but the tourists eat it right up, an' it seems what ol' Jake needed tonight. He growed up way, way back in the swamps, where the people still believers. Tole me oncet when his mama die, he an' his daddy burned her to ashes down in her grave so nobody couldn't zombify her. But if I did believe, then maybe I be thinking you the hoo-doo man tonight. Just like Mayor hisself mighta done oncet."

"June Bug's Mayor. Again."

"That's the one. He gone now, but you here in his place."

"I'm not here to fill his shoes, Chester, nor probably man enough to do it." It puzzled Lloyd why the old man kept bringing up this man, to whom they all seemed to owe such loyalty. "I'm carrying around too many problems of my own to want to take on anybody else's load."

It didn't take more than half an hour for a couple of policemen to show up, and they headed straight for the bench where Lloyd was sitting. Lloyd had just a moment to wonder how Tats might have gotten word to them, then realized it didn't matter. He had a problem now.

Pepper was with another partner tonight, a young woman who tried to look tough and serious, but barely pulled it off given her height and build. This prick went through partners faster than any cop Lloyd had ever seen, for obvious reasons.

Pepper had his nightstick in his hand, twirling it in cone-shaped circles at his side. He stopped in front of Lloyd and said, "We heard there was a little trouble tonight. Some young men were assaulted and robbed."

"Can't help you officer," Lloyd answered. "The only robbery I know of is the theft of an old man's trumpet. But he has it back now." He didn't rise and kept his voice even, not wanting to give Pepper any good reason to reacquaint him with that stick.

"One of them is in the hospital getting checked for a concussion," Pepper said. He raised the stick and pointed it at Lloyd. The guy had a weird fixation with his stick, Lloyd thought, which led to all kinds of amusing speculation. "And they said you did it."

"Look, they mugged one of these old men and stole his trumpet." He might as well get it all out there, he decided. Maybe Pepper's partner might have a little more sense, even if Pepper had his mind already made up. "You know these men, officer. Nobody could help him get it back unless I did it. I offered to buy it back, but they wanted to fight instead. It's not my fault if they were not very good at it."

"Did he report the theft to the police?" the female officer asked. The name tag on her uniform read "Thibodeaux."

One of the band members, the one known as Sly, stepped unexpectedly forward and said, "They said they gonna kill Jake if he tells the police. He's just an old man, and he was scared."

Pepper turned to Sly, not expecting this kind of back-talk from one of these men, and clearly annoyed by it. "Are you sure you want to get into this, old man?" he asked, emphasizing his words and authority with taps on Sly's shoulder as he spoke. "Chances are we're going to haul this man in for assault, and you're welcome to go along if you want."

"He didn't do nothing but what was right," Chester said from somewhere behind Lloyd. He hadn't quite worked up the courage to step forward, but still had his say.

Pepper looked up at Chester, then scanned the others with his glare. He was more used to seeing these people slink away into the shadows when he was around, and didn't quite know how to react to this newfound courage.

"Come to think of it," Lloyd said, "maybe you should take me in so I can explain all of this to your sergeant. They can come along as witnesses. And we can also talk about how that crew is out here several times a week, peddling their drugs on your watch."

Pepper turned back to Lloyd, his grip tightening on the nightstick as his temper rose. This was a new reality to him, a rebellion of the peasantry, and he responded instinctively with anger. Only a light touch on the shoulder by his partner seemed to restrain him from swinging the weapon at Lloyd. "He's not resisting, Donald," she said quietly, "and I won't lie for you."

After another hard glare at Lloyd and his haltingly courageous cohorts, Pepper turned and stalked away.

Thinking back later about the two encounters during his walk back to his room, Lloyd realized that he had caught a glimpse of the old Lloyd Ballou tonight. That must mean he was still in there somewhere.

Chapter Fourteen

Home. In his early years the word had never stirred the same sort of feelings in Lloyd Ballou that it did in people who lived normal lives. Home was where you ate and slept and kept your clothes. Home was a third-floor walk-up plagued by roaches and noisy neighbors. Home was a run-down two-bedroom house where the pipes rattled in the walls and cold air seeped in around every window and door. Home was cleaning vomit off a toilet bowl.

There was a time that seemed oh-so-brief when he and Kelly had been together and happy in their own little nest. But now even that seemed like an episode in someone else's life, someone else's home.

It didn't surprise Lloyd that he kept delaying going back "home" to Kansas City. From eight hundred miles distance, he felt like nothing but problems and unresolved disappointments awaited him there. Guilt dictated that he should go back for his mother's sake, to be around during the last fleeting months or years of her life. But even that image was flawed. Half the time he had to remind her who he was when he walked into her room, and he didn't have any resources to improve her circumstances. The hard side of him, buried deep in his heart and never given voice, wondered if what she was suffering through now might be fair payment for the life she led.

He had to go back, because Kansas City was home. But not just yet. He had a job here, such as it was, and companions, such as they were. Kansas City could wait until he was ready.

Lloyd climbed in behind the wheel of the yellow Nissan Sentra, started the engine, and sat there long enough to watch the car's owner leave the valet parking area. She glanced back briefly before going through the automatic doors and entering the hotel's lower level. She tossed back a smile aimed straight at him. On the small piece of paper she had given him with her ten-dollar tip, she had written a brief note. "Rm 518, 10 pm tonight. Call first."

Lloyd chuckled to himself as he crumpled the paper and tossed it in the back seat. At least this woman was better looking than the other one who hit on him a couple of weeks ago, barely over forty, nice face, decent figure, and mischief in that twinkling smile.

He drove the car down to the reserved valet area, parked it, climbed out, and locked it up. As he started back up the ramp he heard squealing tires approach and sidestepped between two cars. Jorge roared by, again mistaking the lower level garage for a freeway. The young Costa Rican hadn't banged up a car yet, but in the dim, crowded catacombs behind the hotel, it was only a matter of time.

Phone reception was iffy back there, but when he got up higher Lloyd saw he had a missed call. His first thought was of his mother, then of Betsy, then of his sister Kat. It was a New Orleans area code.

For the moment there were no customers at the curb waiting for their cars, and none pulling in, so Lloyd stepped outside the parking entrance. A light drizzle had just started, but standing tight against the building no water reached him. That also kept him out of sight so his boss wouldn't know he was malingering.

He called the number back and a woman answered. "Hello. Someone called me from this number just a few minutes ago, but they didn't leave a message."

"That was me," the woman said. She spoke with a soft, slow creole accent, very pleasant, but hesitant. "Is this Mr. Ballou? Lloyd Ballou?"

"That's me. And you are . . ."

"This is Sarah Bradley, Mr. Ballou. You called me over a month ago seeking information about your father, and I'm afraid I wasn't very cooperative at the time."

"Sure, I remember you, Mrs. Bradley," Lloyd said. Then, chuckling, he added, "And I agree you weren't exactly a fountain of information at the time. You seemed afraid of something."

"I was afraid, and I still am," Sara Bradley admitted. "My hands started shaking when I dialed your number, and my heart's pounding just talking to you."

"I guess I don't understand, Mrs. Bradley. Who are you afraid of?"

"No, not on the phone," she said in a hushed, almost conspiratorial voice. "I changed my phone number, but they could still be listening. I know they followed me, not for a long time now, but I don't want to take any chances."

Lloyd didn't know how to respond to that level of paranoia.

"Your call has weighed on my mind all this time," she went on. "And I finally decided that you deserved more. You came all this way to find out about your father, and I might be the only one who could tell you what you need to know. So afraid or not, it's the Christian thing to do, and my obligation."

"I do appreciate that, Mrs. Bradley, and I'm anxious to hear more. The thing is, I'm at work right now, and my boss will be looking for me in a minute."

"That's fine. I'd rather have this conversation in person anyway," she told him. "Are you working tomorrow?"

"I'll get off if I need to. Maybe we could meet someplace."

"Since all this happened, I hardly ever come into New Orleans at all, and I never go near the French Quarter." *Since all what happened?* "Do you have a car?" she asked.

"No."

"Alright, I'll pick you up. I'll choose someplace safe where we can talk. I'll call you tomorrow morning from another phone and tell you when and where."

* * *

Lloyd stepped down from the antique green trolley, and then waited for it to clatter on past before crossing the tracks and the neutral zone between the two opposing lanes of traffic. He waited again for the traffic to clear before jogging across St. Charles in mid-block.

The cloak and dagger precautions Sarah Bradley was running him through seemed amateurish and unnecessary, but one thing was sure. Her fear was real, even if it was wrapped in such extremes of paranoia. He wondered what sort of kook he might encounter when she picked him up.

He crossed to the corner of St. Charles and Calhoun, turned right, and walked two blocks, as instructed, looking over at each passing car to see if it was the charcoal Audi she said she would be driving. After waiting no more than a couple of minutes, a burgundy sedan came down Calhoun and stopped at the curb near him. The passenger window slid down, and the woman driving leaned over in the seat. "Lloyd Ballou?" she asked.

"Yes."

"I'm Sarah Bradley. Please get in."

Lloyd got in, closed the door and buckled up. She seemed to prefer the anonymity of the back streets, narrow though they were, and drove south nearly to river before turning left, back in the general direction of downtown.

"I was looking for an Audi," Lloyd said. "But this is . . . what, a Buick?"

"I decided to bring my husband's car at the last minute. He was a Buick man, born and bred just like his dad. I realized that they know my car because I always drove it into the city, but they weren't likely . . ." She stopped and looked over at Lloyd, an unexpected half-smile playing across her face. "By now I guess you've decided I'm as batty as a barn loft. And you could be right. But your call triggered something. It all began to come back, even after so long, and I just started . . ." She left the sentence hanging.

"It's not my job to judge you, ma'am," Lloyd said. "I don't know anything about you except that you were Billy's friend at the mission where he worked. And now I guess I also know that something about his death is scaring you."

Despite her quirks, Lloyd somehow found himself becoming comfortable with this woman, even interested in her. She appeared to be in her late fifties or early sixties, aging well, and nicely dressed in khaki slacks and a silk blouse. With only a touch of makeup and uncomplicated shoulder-length hair, mixed gray and brown, there was something about her that spoke of simplicity and gentility.

"So where is this safe place where we're going to talk?" Lloyd asked.

"I thought this might be a good opportunity to visit your Aunt Charmaine's. You do know who she is, don't you?"

"Yes, I do now. A letter from her is what brought me down here, and I've been out to meet her once. I didn't even know she existed until about three months ago. And I didn't know Billy had settled in down here, either."

"I'm sorry for that," Sarah said, as if she shared the fault for his father's failings. "After we became friends, Billy told me a lot about his life, both the good and the bad. He needed somebody to talk to, perhaps to confess to, and I was there."

"All I knew was the bad stuff," Lloyd said. He tried not to let the bitterness creep into his tone, but nonetheless realized it was there. And why not? "So were the two of you . . ." He searched for the right word. "Involved?"

"Oh heavens no," Sarah said, almost laughing at the suggestion. "After my husband Harold was killed by a homeless man several years ago, that was it for me as far as romance was concerned. And as for Billy, I think he had wounded and wrecked his way through so much of his life that at this point, he didn't want to risk hurting anybody else. It was comfortable for us, with no expectations on either side."

"All I know at this point about Billy," Lloyd said, "is that he was working at a mission, had a little house, and disappeared sometime during or after Katrina. It seemed like a pretty simple story . . . at least until I got ahold of you."

"But he didn't just work at the mission, Lloyd," Sarah said quietly. "He also went out on the streets at night, sometimes in the worst neighborhoods, doing what good he could find to do. I can't tell you much about that because he seldom talked about it. It was like some force, perhaps the Lord Himself, drove him out there. No, your father's life was far from simple."

"I'm starting to understand that, Sarah. But what's all this business about you being so afraid?" Lloyd asked. "Who are you afraid of, and why?"

"Oh dear, where do I start?" she said, as if to herself. Her eyes went to her mirrors, first the one on the driver side, then the rear-view, as she had been doing frequently ever since Lloyd got in the car. When Lloyd had rented a car and gone out to see Aunt Charmaine, he had started the trip driving west on I-90, but Sarah seemed to be taking another route and avoiding the interstate. He didn't recognize the streets and highways she was using.

"I was a volunteer supervisor at the Union of Hearts, although none of us had any real titles. Billy and I were the most reliable people there as far as showing up regularly and getting things done. I believe they paid him a small salary, but I'm sure it wasn't very much. But Reverend Raintree's organization ran the business side, and someone from his office was out there two or three times a week to check up on things. Occasionally when he was in town the Reverend himself would come, and at least once a week his security chief, Rudy Soyez, stopped over. He gave me the shivers, and I only talked to him if I had to."

"I know what you mean," Lloyd said. "Our paths crossed once at Raintree's house. He's not the kind of guy you buddy-up with."

"They had a little room in the back of the mission that they always kept padlocked. They called it the office," Sarah went on. "I had a key to the outside door of the mission and to the room where the groceries were stored, but not one to the office door. We didn't think much of it because none of us had to do any paperwork and had no need to get in there. They had the food delivered, and we prepared it, served it, and cleaned up after. The whole operation was very casual, but it got the homeless fed, and that was what we were there for.

"Sometimes Rudy or one of the others would give Billy extra jobs to do, like driving a truck to pick up the food if the regular delivery driver had more than the usual number of stops. He also did some odd-job maintenance work from time to time. And that's how he got a look into that office. He was up in the attic trying to pinpoint a leak in the roof, and he crawled right over the office. The light was on in there, and he was able to peek down through a crack between the ceiling boards."

"And what did he see?" Lloyd asked.

"Oddly enough, cartons of children's toys and various kinds of souvenirs. The room was half full of them, and little else. Some of the cartons had Spanish writing on them, which seemed to indicate that they were being imported by the Reverend's organization. Importing that kind of cheap goods is one of his income streams, and in a place like New Orleans there's a steady tourist market for them."

"But why store them in the back room of a food kitchen? You'd expect a big organization like Raintree's to have actual warehouse space to use."

"They do have a warehouse, so we wondered about that, too. But what puzzled us even more was that we never saw anybody take anything in or out the room while we were there, so they must have been doing it at night."

They were passing into a more rural area now, with scattered houses up on stilts and set back from the road. Small runoff canals paralleling the road, and the slightly higher ground was a wasteland of scrub brush and dead tree trunks.

"I was content to let well enough alone," Sara said. "I was working there for an entirely different reason, which was to help the homeless. I did it as a tribute to my husband, and as a living act of forgiveness to the anonymous, miserable human being who took him away from me. I felt like it was God's command to me. Whatever J.T. Raintree wanted to store in his little locked room was no business of mine. But Billy couldn't leave it alone. He just kept going over it in his mind, and once he confided in me that the only solution he could come up with was that it was something illegal. I told him I thought he was crazy. This was *J.T. Raintree* we were talking about. The man who tended to the homeless and hungry across south Louisiana, and the man who delivered vital medical care to urchins and orphans all over Central America."

Sara paused, and when she spoke again her voice took on a quiet, introspective tone. "Now I wish I had listened to him more closely. If I had, I might have been able to do something, or at least stop what happened to Billy when he found out the truth."

This was the reason for Sarah Bradley's fear and caution, Lloyd realized at last. And if this narrative was heading where he suspected, she might have just cause to feel the way she did. Instead of asking the myriad questions that were swirling in his head, he let her continue at her own pace.

"Lloyd, have you ever thought about how sometimes people's lives can pivot on the smallest of things? You turn left instead of right, or pause to tie your shoe, and the whole world changes?"

"Not really," Lloyd admitted. It wasn't the kind of thing he was likely to spend much time pondering. "But I suppose it's true."

"Your father made one of those choices. We were cleaning up the mission one evening, just he and I, and he brought up the subject of that locked office again. I told him we'd probably never know what's going on, and that it wasn't really our concern. But he wouldn't let it alone. He decided on the spot to spend the night in the mission and see if anyone came. He made a little pallet for himself in a broom closet off the kitchen. And it might have worked if he had heard them before they heard him.

"It was his own human frailty that made the difference, I suppose. He bought some beer in that Asian store down the street, and he got drunk sitting there in that dark little closet. It's almost ludicrous to picture it in your mind. When he finally went to sleep, it was one of those deep boozy stupors, and I guess it was his snoring that got him caught. They heard him through the walls and went to check it out.

"It was Rudy Soyez, and he had brought a couple of helpers along with him to carry the boxes out to a van. Billy said he actually knew one of them, and said I probably would too if I saw him because he came in here occasionally to get a free meal. He had so many tattoos that he looked like he'd been dipped in an ink well. Neither of us knew his real name, but people called him Tats."

Lloyd felt as if a curtain had been suddenly pulled aside, and a whole new landscape came into view. Tats worked for Soyez . . . Tats the Jackson Square street dealer. Tats the strip joint recruiter. Then another realization came closely on the heels of the first one. That night in Club Les Girls, this was why the man he glimpsed in the back room with Marta had seemed so familiar. Despite the brevity of the moment, he was sure it was Soyez! So many possibilities began to race through his brain that it was hard to turn his thoughts back to what Sarah was saying.

"Billy said he pulled a full-on drunk act and tried to babble and lie his way out of it, but didn't think they believed him. They shoved him around a little bit, but he got out of there as soon as he could. He called me that night and told me how he had messed up, and he was afraid to come back to work. After that I didn't see or hear from him for a few days. I was worried sick, and I began to wonder if they'd done something terrible to him. Maybe even killed him. Then finally he got word to me that he was in jail.

"I sent my lawyer over there, and he found out Billy was charged with child molestation. Billy said he had never even met the thirteen-year-old girl he supposedly molested, but I guess she was willing to tell a believable story for the right price. They had him good.

"The next day I had a locksmith come out and open the office. If there was anything in there, I was determined to hand everything over to the police. But it was empty. Both Reverend Raintree and Soyez stopped coming to the mission after that, but once in a while I would notice a man in a car parked down the street. Then after my lawyer got Billy out of jail, I sometimes saw the same car, the same man, watching my house. I was scared to death, but I decided that the best thing for me to do was just go about my normal routine as if I didn't know anything about what happened." She paused, then added quietly, "It never occurred to me until later that the lawyer I sent to help Billy linked me to him and the whole ugly mess.

"All that happened while Katrina was sweeping across the Gulf, gaining strength with every mile, and then she hit New Orleans head-on."

* * *

When Aunt Charmaine didn't answer their knocks, they went around back and found her there. She was sitting on her walker seat out in the middle of the garden, leaning awkwardly forward as she pulled weeds, humming what sounded like an old hymn.

"Oh my goodness!" Sara said with some alarm. "If she falls out of that chair, she'll break her neck."

"I'd guess she's been doing things her way all her life," Lloyd said, "and isn't about to stop now."

The old woman struggled back upright when she heard them approaching. She pulled the brim of her straw hat down to shelter her eyes from the blazing midday sun and squinted, trying to make out who her visitors were.

"It's me, Aunt Charmaine," Lloyd said, a little overly loud. "Your nephew Lloyd. And I've brought along someone who wanted to see you. It's my dad's friend, Sarah Bradley."

"My goodness gracious me!" the old woman beamed. She held her arms open to them, and each leaned forward and hugged her in turn. She was slick with sweat, and the skin of her arms felt like damp paper as they wrapped around Lloyd's neck. "Come on, let's go in the house. I made a big pitcher of tea for lunch, and there's still plenty left."

Aunt Charmaine stood up and led the way, pushing the walker with surprising agility up the ramp that Billy had built onto the back of the house. It would be a mistake to describe the inside of her house as cool, but the windows were open, the fans were blowing, and it was out of the sun. As women will, Sarah pitched right in, taking down quart canning jars from a shelf as Charmaine retrieved ice trays from the freezer. As they moved into the living room with their drinks, the old woman was expressing her delight at their unexpected visit.

"I'm sorry that it's been so long," Lloyd said, "But I've got a job now, and I'm working some long hours. And I still don't have a car."

"Don't worry about it for a second, honey. You young folks are busy with your own lives, and I'm just happy to see you here now."

Lloyd glanced over at Sarah and saw her amusement at being included in with the "young folks."

"But you really shouldn't be out gardening in that sun during the heat of the day," Sarah said. "You'll get heat stroke."

"Can't just sit around," Charmaine explained. "Too much to be done around this place, and now with Raymond not around anymore, it's all on me. Not that he ever got that much done anyway."

"What happened to Raymond?" Lloyd asked.

"Went out frog gigging one night, and just never came back. The sheriff's deputy found his boat a couple of days later, but he wasn't in it, or nowhere around. The gators don't let much go to waste deep in the swamps where he was."

"That's too bad. For him and for you."

"Well, Raymond made his own fate, just like the rest of us. The deputy found his cooler chest, with several beers still in it. They figure he got so drunk he just flipped over the side."

They chatted for a while about mundane things, and Lloyd told his aunt about his job at the hotel garage. Sarah talked little about her own life since she had been here last, but of course mentioned nothing about Reverend Raintree and the odd goings on at the mission. When his glass was empty, Lloyd volunteered to take over in the garden, and his aunt didn't hesitate to accept his offer.

While the women sat in the shade of the back porch, Lloyd found a hoe and went to work. They seemed to find plenty to talk about, and occasionally he would hear snippets of their conversation that let him know that they were talking about Billy. It was easy to tell that they were fond of one another, nearly as comfortable with each other as family. By the time he had finished with the weeding, his back, neck, and arms were crimson, and his muscles ached. He figured he had sweated out every last drop of the quart of tea. As he walked back up to the porch, he saw that his aunt had dozed off in her rocker, her head tilted to the side and her mouth sagged open, snoring softly. Sarah was just sitting there, watching her with a gentle, peaceful smile.

"She wanted us to pray together, just like we used to do when I came to visit," Sarah said softly. "But somewhere along the way, she just dozed on off."

"A prayer?" Lloyd asked. "What were you praying for?"

"A lot of things," Sarah said. We even prayed for you."

"There's a lost cause if I ever saw one." He tried to make his words sound light, but the whole subject made him uncomfortable. Whoever tried to pray his sins away had some hard work ahead. Even the patient, gentle smile Sarah gave him jangled his nerves, and he was glad when she changed the subject.

"I guess it's time to go," Sarah said. The sun was down into the treetops. "It'll be well past dark by the time we get back to New Orleans, and then I've got another long drive on to my house. But I do need to get over here and see Aunt Charmaine more often. I'm the last of my line and don't have any relatives left alive. I like to think of her as my aunt, too. I wonder if she would consider coming over to live with me when she's too old to take care of herself?"

"My guess is that she plans to go on living here in this little house right to the end," Lloyd said. "But you could ask. I'm impressed that you would even consider such a kind thing."

"My husband Harold and I tried to live our faith, although we weren't always successful."

They roused the old woman gently, and gave her a few moments to gather her wits. She wouldn't even consider letting them go without carrying away some of the bounty from her garden. She went with them out to the car, again setting a snail's pace over the gravel with her walker.

"There is just one other thing I want to ask, honey," Aunt Charmaine said as they stood by the open car doors. "Do you know how Billy died, Sarah?"

"I honestly don't know, auntie," Sarah said. She began to tear up right away. "All I can tell you for certain is that he saved my life. He showed up at the mission in the middle of the storm. There were a few of us there, me and a handful of homeless men. The building was blowing down around us, but we didn't know what to do, or where else to go. I've never been so scared. We already had casualties, including a man who worked with us named Chas Kirchner, and there was nothing I could do to help anyone. I was sure I was going to die soon. Billy took me out of there, and somehow got me to a friend's house on Esplanade. He carried me most of the way, especially when the water got deep. Once I was safe, he left again, and never came back."

By the time she was finished, both women were brimming with tears, and even Lloyd had an unfamiliar and unwelcome lump in his throat.

"I'm so proud of that boy," Aunt Charmaine told them, smiling through it all. "My little Gui."

Sarah was quiet for the first few minutes after they left Aunt Charmaine's house, and Lloyd let her have her solitude until she was ready to talk again. It was dusk now, and he could tell that she was nervous driving along the narrow roads.

Eventually he broke the silence by asking, "Would you like for me to take over the wheel at least until we get onto some better roads?"

No, it's fine," Sarah said. "It's my eyes. I don't have good night vision anymore, but I'm fine for now. Maybe later."

The silence returned for a moment, then Sarah turned her head and gave Lloyd a quick look. "I didn't tell her everything," she said. "I just wanted to share the best parts with her, but not the rest."

"Good call," Lloyd said. "But I'd like to hear all of it, if you feel like telling me."

"Sure, it's your right to know everything. I was just waiting to . . . well, honestly, I don't know what I was waiting for."

"Maybe to get a better fix on me," Lloyd said.

"Yes, that's part of it." She looked over at him again, her eyes probing, and then had to swerve the car off the shoulder and back onto the pavement.

"After Billy got me to my friend's apartment, I begged him to stay there at least until the worst of the hurricane had blown past. But he kept talking about those people we'd left behind at the mission. He said he knew some of them, that they were his friends and he had to try to help them. And he had a crazy idea.

"He told me that he knew where the Union of Hearts Mission warehouse was over near the Superdome, and said that if he could get there, he could take a truck, one of the big ones, and drive it back to the mission."

"With a hurricane right on top of the city, and people dying on all sides," Lloyd said, "he was going to drive a truck through the floods and rescue a bunch of homeless guys. Yeah, I'd say that idea qualifies as crazy."

"He said he had to try," Sarah said quietly. "He was going to break into the warehouse and load the truck up with food and water. If he made it to our mission and got the survivors out, then he was going to try to make it to one of the others, maybe the one out by the airport, or the one in Chalmette. But he never made it back out to even the first mission building. A few days later I talked to two of the men who had stayed there. Enough of the building remained standing to keep them alive, but there was no food or water. After the storm blew past, the gangs came in, but there was nothing to steal. If Billy hadn't come to take me out, I can hardly imagine what might have happened to me at that point."

Lloyd could imagine, and it was ugly.

"But Billy's body was never found?" Lloyd asked.

"No. I finally got my courage up and called the Reverend Raintree, but he said he didn't know anything about Billy's whereabouts. I told him about Billy's plan, but he said the water was too deep at the warehouse for anybody to get in there, or for anybody to drive a truck out. After the first minute or two, I knew he wasn't interested in talking to me. Even if he did know something about Billy, he wasn't likely to tell me about it."

"Do you know where the warehouse is?" Lloyd asked.

"Yes, but if you're thinking about going there, I'll save you the time. I drove by there when the water went down and the streets were usable again. It was just an empty shell."

Chapter Fifteen

There was a girl in high school named Rosalee Gold. She transferred in during Lloyd's junior year and was in two of his classes, although she seemed to be at least a couple of years older than Lloyd and his classmates.

No one knew much about her. He could tell that she wanted to fit in, wanted to make friends, but that was not in the cards for her. She lived in a neighborhood called Pumpkin Creek, where a sea of ramshackle houses spread haphazardly up a steep hillside, overlooking a refinery that clotted the air with a nearly toxic amalgam of petroleum odors and waste product burn off.

Rosalee was reasonably pretty, and her buxom figure guaranteed her plenty of first dates, but few seconds. She was a pariah with the girls, who both envied and despised her for the mature curves that always drew attention to her. She came to school bruised up far too often, but always had a good excuse if anybody bothered to ask why, which seldom happened.

Late in the school year, Lloyd had his own first date with Rosalee. The plan was simple enough. Go to the drive-in, win her favor with fries and Cokes and Junior Mints, get as far as he could get, and show up at school with bragging rights the next day.

With the car windows down, he could hear the shouting inside as he pulled up in front of her house, and in a moment she came scooting out like a kicked dog. A beer bottle flew out the open screen door after her, but missed. Once inside the car she tried to be fun and chatty, good company for her date, but the tears just wouldn't stop running down even as she faked her smiles and made up lies about what just happened back there.

Instead of going to a drive-in movie, they had their fries and drinks in the side lot of Texas Tony's drive-thru. They sat there talking for over three hours, until the manager finally came out and told them they had to buy something else or leave. Their car-hop was complaining.

Rosalee ended up telling Lloyd dark things that she might never have shared with anyone before, tales from a desperately miserable childhood wreathed in poverty, abuse, and neglect. Even Lloyd had trouble matching Rosalee's horror stories with his own descriptions of his alcoholic mother, runaway father, dead brother, trashy sister, and the steady stream of worthless men who had passed in an out of their lives like bums in a soup kitchen line.

The next day at school they passed one another in the hall and their eyes met, but neither of them said a word. Both of them seemed to sense that there was too much pain between them, and neither might ever be able to save the other.

Lloyd was slumped on a bar stool at a lively little back-street joint called Machismo's, sort of watching "the game." Atlanta was playing New Orleans, and it seemed to be a big deal to the crowd around him. There was a decent sprinkling of women in the half-drunk mob, but most of the rowdy fans around him were men, roaring wildly and sloshing their drinks on one another when the Saints did anything to cheer about. Lloyd thought it probably wouldn't take much to get the crap beat out of him if his fellow revelers knew his preference was the Falcons. Or they might even do it if they knew how little he cared which side won. He hadn't bothered to follow sports with any real interest since he stopped hanging around with his cop buddies.

This joint was too young for him, Lloyd decided, but it was as good a place as any to put away a few before going back to his room. Most of the women were attractive enough, looking good even in their slouchy week-day-out team tee-shirts, jeans and backward caps. But he felt old in here, imagining the amused looks he'd get if he tried to talk any of them up.

It was way too noisy for him to hear his cell phone ring, but he felt the vibration in his pocket and took it out. The area code was 816, a call from Kansas City, but he didn't recognize the rest of the phone number. He always took calls from Kansas City because of his mom.

There was no use trying to answer while he was inside, so he shoved his way through the crowd, savoring the decrease in decibels when the door closed behind him. He touched the number on the screen to call back.

"Hello lover." In spite of his own internal resolve, he felt an undeniable happiness when he heard Kelly's familiar greeting. Then Lloyd felt a quick ping of jealousy when he wondered if she called her new husband the same thing.

"I didn't recognize the number," Lloyd said. "You must have a new phone."

"No, just a second one," Kelly said. "I call it my *private line*."

"That's not a good sign."

"No. That, and a lot of other things," Kelly said. She sounded sober tonight, which somewhat surprised him, and he gave in to the pleasant feeling of simply hearing her voice. "But that's not why I called," she went on. "If I want to bitch about my husband, I've got plenty of girlfriends for that. I called to see what you're up to."

"Pretty much the same stuff that I've been doing ever since I got here. Eat, sleep, go to work, drink a few. Then start over. I found a decent job that pays enough to get by on, but I won't be staying around here much longer. I don't think I'm going to dig up much more about Billy."

"Kelly laughed and said, "Actually I meant *what are you doing right now*?"

"Hanging out in a bar. I'm pulling a twelve-hour shift tomorrow morning, six-to-six, so I'll be heading back to my room soon."

"Well, the thing is . . ." Kelly hesitated. "A couple of my buddies and I have been planning a trip to New Orleans. But one of them got sick, and the other one had a family deal come up."

"So just change the date," Lloyd said. "There's some kind of jazz event coming up in two weeks, and a seafood festival the weekend after that. There's always some kind of mischief for you and your girlfriends to get into down here."

"Well, the thing is . . ." Kelly said again, with an even longer pause. "The thing is, Lloyd, that I came on anyway. I put Robert on a plane last night and then started right out from the airport. He knew about the trip, but he didn't know my friends had backed out. And I'm pretty sure he doesn't know you're in New Orleans now. If he did, he would have raised holy hell about it. I drove straight through."

"And you're here now?" Lloyd asked. "That's over eight hundred miles! You must be a zombie."

"Well, I put the car on cruise control and caught a couple of hours of sleep on the last leg down from Memphis." It was an old joke between them.

"And you're here now?" Lloyd asked again.

"At the Chateau Plaisir, right on Bourbon Street. From my balcony I can watch drunks throw up on the street, and tomorrow night I plan to be one of them."

Lloyd didn't know what to think, let alone what to say. His own feelings caught him completely off guard. He was happy that she was here, happy that he would soon see her, and truth-be-told, happy that hers and Bob's marriage was possibly crashing.

"You are coming over, aren't you, lover?" Kelly asked.

"Sure, I guess so. But I should go by my room and clean up first. I'm still in my work clothes."

"Just come," Kelly said. "I'm wearing the same clothes I've been in for the past thirty-six hours, so you couldn't be any grubbier than me. I really, *really* want a drink, more than a shower or anything else, but I'm afraid to go out on the street by myself. I'm afraid I'll just pass out in some alley and get dragged away by a pervert."

"Alright, I'm just a few blocks away. What's your room number?"

* * *

Even in her rumpled driving clothes, unbathed and unkempt, Lloyd's ex-wife still managed somehow to look good. She always seemed to have a certain style about her, a presence of some sort that defied description. As she wrapped her arms around him in the hotel room doorway, her face revealing her pleasure at seeing him again, Lloyd felt happier than he had in a while. He fought the notion that he felt that way because he was still a little bit in love with her.

No, not anymore. Not after what they'd put each other through.

"So where do we go for that drink?" Kelly said, dragging him into the room and closing the door. "I'm just dying to try out something sweet and fruity and tropical, something that will kick my butt, but who cares? And I need to eat, too. I've been surviving on gas station crap all the way down."

It was a nice room, costly he was sure, but more stylish and spacious than most of the rooms in the hotel where he worked. The furniture was fake period stuff, mostly white, and as billed, a pair of curtained French doors opened onto a wide balcony with a third-floor view of Bourbon Street below. Lloyd wondered how loud it got in here at night, and then whether he was about to find that out tonight.

Kelly went on talking as she walked into the bathroom to run a brush through her hair, but it was pretty much a lost cause. "You're right, you smell like a lumberjack, lover. I guess I'm not much better, but hey! I bet everybody smells like that down here in this heat."

"Not always," Lloyd said. "We coon-asses wash up at least a couple of times a week, whether we need to or not." Two little one-dose liquor bottles from the mini-bar sat open and empty on a table. She had been priming the pump, he thought. "I'm thinking they've got the perfect drink for you just a few blocks from here at Pat O'Brien's. It's called a Hurricane."

"Oooo, yes! I've heard about those. I want one!" She fogged the air in the bathroom spraying herself with some sort of cologne, then came out ready to go. On the way out the door she slipped her room key and a couple of hundred-dollar bills in Lloyd's shirt pocket. "I might turn out to be an expensive date," she said lightly.

Lloyd didn't protest, knowing that he only had a few bucks on him, probably not enough to get them through the first hour. And besides, it gave him some sort of twisted satisfaction to think that he would be spending Bob's money escorting Bob's wife around The Big Easy.

It was mid-evening now, and many of the revelers along Bourbon Street, and throughout the French Quarter, were deep into their various over-indulgences. Pat O'Brien's was crowded, and there was a long waiting line to jam into the main room where two singing pianists were pounding their keys and belting out an endless collection of barroom standards. Lloyd took Kelly into a side bar which was also full, but not quite as chaotic. He ordered two Hurricanes and they appeared almost immediately, served in tall branded glasses.

Kelly's face lit up when she saw the drink, and her smile widened even more after her first long taste. "I've come to an important decision, lover," she said, leaning toward Lloyd and nearly shouting above the crowd noise.

"And what's that?" Lloyd asked.

"You'll be my designated driver tonight. In a little while, I'll have no business getting behind a wheel."

"Not much chance of that since we're on foot."

"Alright, you'll be my guardian angel then."

Despite Lloyd's warning that the drinks were half rum, Kelly belted down her first Hurricane way too fast, then commandeered his, which he had hardly started on. He ordered another one, then had the bartender pour both their drinks into tall carry-out cups.

"Come on, let's go walk around so you can get a taste of the Quarter," he suggested. He knew he had to get her out of here or she'd be down on the floor in record time. This place tended to have that effect on the uninitiated.

Kelly had never been to New Orleans, and she was captivated by the atmosphere. She stopped at one point to flirt with a cluster of grizzled, leather-clad bikers. Their expensive rides were lined up at the curb in front of a dim little dive bar that spilled out a cacophony of music and loud voices like a broken dam. Lloyd just stood back and let her go at it. Despite her declaration, he wasn't her guardian anymore. But the husky, bearded men took her in stride, used to being trifled with by drunk female tourists who wanted to dip a toe into the wild side. Lloyd knew that most of them were accountants, mechanics, system analysts, grocery managers and the like, and probably even some cops in the mix, donning these personas occasionally just because they liked bikes and enjoyed looking tough. Lloyd smiled, thinking of his own grubbies back in Kansas City, leather pants and all.

Kelly was done with them in a few minutes and came back over to Lloyd. She tossed her empty cup at a trash can and missed, then reached for his, stumbling clumsily against him in the process.

"A little food might be a good idea," Lloyd suggested. "How about slacking off until you get something solid in your stomach?"

"Sure, something greasy and delicious," Kelly laughed. "But in the meantime . . ." She reached again for Lloyd's cup and this time he let her take it. The rum in the Hurricane wasn't being greeted well by the beers he'd put away earlier, and he could see that one of them was going to have to stay somewhat lucid as the night progressed.

Kelly's greasy dreams came true in a side-street seafood joint that Lloyd had heard good things about. It was blessedly quiet in the back booth the waiter led them to, and Lloyd had to stop Kelly from ordering half the menu. She ended up with a Fisherman's Feast, a long oval platter piled high with deep-fried seafood delights. Lloyd ordered chowder and oysters, thinking he could nibble from Kelly's platter once she took the edge off her ravenous appetite. Kelly ordered a scotch while they were waiting for their food, and a bottle of wine to accompany the feast.

"If I was with Robert, he'd never let me order anything like this," Kelly said as the waiter delivered their food to the table. She seemed to be having trouble focusing her gaze on anything in particular, and her smile was bleary. "He says I'm getting fat."

"Fat? I'm not seeing it."

"He's such a bastard sometimes," she went on, biting a hushpuppy in half. "He calls me names and cusses me like a dog. I see now why he had three wives before me."

"I told you that," Lloyd reminded her. "Bob Bollinger has a temper like a cherry bomb. But you were so sure you could handle him."

"At the time, I wasn't in the mood to believe anything that came out of your mouth, mister."

"I also told you he liked to slap women round when he got hot. Has he started that stuff with you yet?"

Kelly laughed out loud at that question. The diners in the booth across from them looked up, then exchanged quiet comments to one another. "He did once, but then he experienced an awakening," she said. "He split my lip open good, and gave me two black eyes. But the next morning he woke up with a bullet hole in his pillow. I took it down in the basement and shot it with his own gun, then took it back up and slid it under his head."

Lloyd had to laugh at that. "But even after that, you two still stayed together?"

Kelly took a bite of food and a long drink of wine, then looked across the restaurant at nothing in particular. When her eyes returned to Lloyd, she had teared up. She didn't realize how loud her voice was getting, but when she answered Lloyd's question, the nearby couple looked up again.

"I still thought I was in love with him." Then her eyes followed Lloyd's across the aisle, and she noticed the pair in the other booth glaring their disapproval. "Don't make me come over there," she said. Wisely, the man and woman developed a sudden, urgent interest in their bowls of chowder.

"I didn't know what to do anymore," Kelly admitted. "I've spent a lot of time trying to prove to myself that I made the right choice, and that I was better off than I was with you. But I don't love him, not even a little bit. Sometimes I think we should have had an affair behind your back, and then when I got to the point where I despised him, I could just walk away. But no, that would have been too easy. Now I have to wake up every morning and turn my head away from the man I'm married to. I have to try to slide out of bed before he can get his disgusting hands on me. And what am I supposed to do about that, lover boy?"

Lloyd had no answer so he just sat there, watching the tears run down as she blew her nose into the heavy green linen of the restaurant napkin.

"You're hitting it pretty hard tonight after that long drive down from Kansas City," Lloyd said.

"Seems like I always hit it pretty hard these days," Kelly said, looking up at him and almost managing to smile. "And still it's not hard enough."

She attempted to refill her wine glass, trying to show that she was in charge of at least that, but her grip on the bottle failed. The half-empty bottle rolled across the table, spilling its contents onto Kelly's shirt and lap, then clattered onto the floor and into the aisle. When the waiter came over and saw what kind of mess Kelly had made, and had become, he tried to give Lloyd a stern, accusing look. But Lloyd countered with a challenging stare of his own, and the waiter retrieved the bottle and went away without saying a word. He came back a moment later with their check, although they were far from being finished eating. Lloyd spotted a man in a dark jacket standing a few feet away, clearly a manager of some kind. He got the message. Dinner was over.

* * *

Lloyd sat on the edge of the bed in Kelly's hotel room, enjoying the relative quiet following the nightly reverie outside along Bourbon Street. After a restless three or four hours of almost sleep, repeatedly interrupted by the pointless celebrations outside, he wished that he could get back to sleep now. Most of the lewd neon lights were extinguished, the music ceased, and it was still too early for the big, growling garbage trucks and street sweepers to begin their daily invasion. The glowing clock on the bedside table gave the time at 4:12 am. He thought about taking a shower, but wondered why he should bother when he had to put on the same smelly clothes until he got back to his room and found something clean.

Kelly lay as still as a corpse at the foot of the enormous bed, wearing what she had on last night, ketchup smears, wine stains and all. She had crossed into the void about halfway back to the hotel. When he finally got her back to the room, he simply piled her onto the bed, legs hanging off, one shoe on, one lost along the way, and there she laid still. She reeked with the stale stench of alcohol seeping from her skin. The smell carried him back to a similar incident in his mother's life long, long ago.

Lloyd had already called in to work to let them know he wouldn't make it today. He wasn't sure what that would mean when he did show up, but at the moment it didn't seem important. Finding another job parking cars couldn't be that hard to come by in this city.

He had a feeling that he never thought he'd feel again. Kelly needed him, at least for today, and somehow, completely illogically, he thought he owed that to her. He wouldn't abandon her, not in the condition she was in.

He made coffee, retrieved the newspaper outside the door, and spent a long time on the commode. When he finished, he looked distastefully at his pile of clothes on the floor by the bed, then reluctantly put them on. He thought he could probably go back to his place, clean up, and easily be back before she woke.

But when he went back into the bedrooms Kelly was sitting up at the foot of the bed, leaning forward, elbows on her knees, hands covering her face.

"By any chance did I get run over by a bus last night," she asked, her voice muted behind her palms.

"No, but when you passed out on the way back I was ready to throw you in front of one." Lloyd filled a hotel glass with water from the bathroom sink, and she gulped it down eagerly. While he went back to get her a refill, Kelly fumbled around in her suitcase for her hangover kit—aspirin, vitamin C, and saltines. She was no stranger to mornings like this.

"I lost a shoe someplace," Kelly noted. "But at least I didn't throw up. What's this stuff on my shirt?"

"Wine, and some other souvenirs from dinner."

"Wow, it's getting worse. I hardly remember anything after we came out of Pat O'Brien's. Some guys with motorcycles, and maybe some shrimp or something. I used to remember every stupid, humiliating thing I said and did when I got shit-faced, but not anymore. Maybe it's a blessing, huh?"

"Maybe." He fixed her a cup of coffee and took it into the bathroom while she stripped off her clothes and scattered them on the floor. She tried the coffee as the water heated in the shower. It was so strange, Lloyd thought. This was like a thousand mornings when they had been together, so ordinary and natural for both of them. But now she was another man's wife, and this kind of thing should feel illicit.

"I'm going to my place to clean up and change," Lloyd told Kelly. "It wouldn't be a bad idea to get more sleep if you can. That's what I'm going to do. I'll call you about ten."

* * *

Lloyd sat across the table from Kelly, watching her spread marmalade on a half slice of buttered toast. She had easily polished off a breakfast of waffles and fried chicken, along with two cups of rich dark chicory coffee and half a pitcher of ice water.

She was clean and made up now, hair neatly brushed, wearing crisp white shorts, sandals, and a loose blue tee-shirt. No one would have guessed that just a few hours before she was limp, pathetic drunk, not unless they got close enough to see her blood-shot eyes and to smell the day-after drunkard's stench that still oozed from her smooth, pale skin. Even the cologne she wore couldn't conceal it.

"So how much of an ass did I make of myself last night?" Kelly asked.

"Not so much," Lloyd said. "As tired as you were, I should have known better than to start you off on Hurricanes."

"That's right, I blame it all on you, lover boy."

"But it looks like you're none the worse for wear now."

"We functioning alcoholics know all the tricks," Kelly said lightly, looking up and smiling at him. "I like that term, don't you? It's so much better than falling down drunk, and there's something about it that makes it seem like it's not my fault."

"Is that what you are now?"

"Seems like it. I don't go to meetings or anything like that, but I'm too deep in to lie to myself." Kelly's smile didn't quite fade away, but her voice became more contemplative. "Lloyd, my life has been so royally screwed up for so long that it's a wonder I don't keep a fifth by the bed to get a jumpstart in the morning."

"I'm sorry, Kelly," Lloyd said, not quite knowing why.

"And you should be," she said unexpectedly. "Because you were, and probably still are, a big chunk of the problem."

That comment hit Lloyd like a sucker punch.

"No, that's not really fair," Kelly said softly. "I shouldn't have said it like that."

"You shouldn't have said it at all. It's been a long time since I played any part in your bad decisions. It was you that got mixed up with that grease ball while we were still married, and you that walked out on me and ended up married to him!" The restaurant was empty of other customers this late in the morning, but the blue-haired waitress behind the counter gave him a sour look.

“I know,” Kelly said. “And I’m paying the price now for all the stupid mistakes I made. But did you ever ask yourself why? Did you ever wonder whether any of the bad times we’ve been thought, together and then apart, might have been partly your fault too?”

“You left me at one of the worst times in my life, Kelly. When I needed you most? You abandoned me.”

Kelly’s eyes locked on his, but it was impossible to read what was behind them. She went over and paid the check, then headed straight for the door. Lloyd got up and followed. They walked without talking down an empty cobblestone side street, wandering in the direction of the river.

Finally, after nearly a block, Kelly broke the silence. “I hope you’ll be glad to hear that I don’t plan to be a worthless mess like I was last night much longer.”

“I am glad,” Lloyd said. His anger was past, and he was beginning to regret what he’d said. The time for lashing out with words like that was long past.

“I’m facing some hard truths about myself, Lloyd, and I’ve got a plan working. I talked to my dad and he said I can move back to Wichita for a while, maybe start some classes at the little community college.”

“How long will you be able to stay with that old bastard before you decide to smother him in his sleep?”

“A while. He’s better now that he’s gotten old. Some of the rough edges are worn down. But I’ve got to go someplace. I’ve got to get away from Bob. We’re just hacking each other to pieces, and if we keep going on like we are now, there won’t be much left of either of us worth saving. He’ll probably welcome my leaving. I think he’s already got wife number five swimming around in the shallow water someplace close by."

Across the Mississippi a dark, towering line of storm clouds obliterated the blue sky, pounding Algiers and the marshlands beyond with their watery onslaught. Occasional bursts of lightning backlit the storm clouds like camera flashes, revealing, if only for an instant, how translucent and ephemeral this impressive act of nature truly was.

"Did you have any doubts when we got married, Lloyd?" Kelly asked.

"None that I can remember. But it's only natural to have some doubts about a thing like that. I probably did."

"Was I a good wife?"

"My best answer to that is, you were until you weren't. Same for me as a husband, I guess."

The storm would blow by to the south of them. For now, they were safe from its fury. He could get her back to her hotel without either of them getting wet. And he realized, suddenly and unexpectedly, that after today he might never see her again.

"Did you think it would last forever? At least at the beginning?"

"I had my hopes. But the examples that I had in my life taught me that it doesn't always go that way."

"Aren't we still supposed to believe it, though?" Kelly asked. There was poignant despair in his ex-wife's voice that Lloyd felt like he had never heard before, something that made him believe that at this moment he was getting a glimpse of something deep within her core.

But he had no answer to give her.

Chapter Sixteen

Joe Burks' tumble into hell was a cautionary tale for Lloyd Ballou. They rode as partners off and on at the KCPD, and for Lloyd, Joe set the bar for what a cop should be. Twenty years Lloyd's senior, Joe had decades of wisdom and experience, and didn't mind sharing it. He could be as tough as old leather when he had to be, but wasn't one of those stick-swinging bullies that waded in roughshod at the slightest provocation. He could have gone up in the ranks, but like Lloyd, preferred the streets.

The one-car accident that killed his daughter Stancia hardly looked worse than a routine fender-bender, but she died at the scene from a freak chest injury. Joe's wife Shirley had been fighting lung cancer for years, but after Stancia's death she gave up the fight. Within months, she lay beside her daughter in Mt. Washington Cemetery.

Joe didn't give up, didn't retire or put a bullet in his temple. He soldiered on, tried to fulfill his duty to live his life, but it was damned hard even for a big tough cop like him. He came to work smelling like booze, and once Lloyd caught a glimpse of the quart bottle of Maker's Mark in Joe's locker bag. Over time, he needed even more relief than that.

Stopping by one night at the squalid tomb that had once housed the Burks family, Lloyd was the one that found Joe dead. Joe had a gut-deep hatred for drugs, and heroin was at the top of his list. But when the time came, he also knew where to get his hands on some.

Everyone had their inner demons to battle, and everyone had their own breaking point. And sometimes it was hardest to see it in the people you were closest to.

Lloyd knew it was a stupid thing to be following Tats and his sidekicks around the dim, nearly deserted, back streets of the French Quarter, and even more foolish to follow him on into Les Girls. But he thought he could pull it off. His cap was pulled down, shadowing his eyes, and he hadn't shaved for a few days, which he thought would be disguise enough in the dim interior of the sleazy strip joint. He recalled from a two-week intro to undercover class that sometimes less disguise was better than too much.

Once inside, the punks had gone straight back to the office, and Lloyd settled in at a table along the wall opposite the bar, in the darkest corner he could find.

He didn't have a plan, or even a purpose. After spotting Tats and his crew a few blocks away down Chartres, he just fell in behind them on curious impulse. His conversations with Sarah Bradley had jump-started his interest in finding out what happened to Billy, and had helped him finally make up his mind not to go back to Kansas City yet. He knew Tats wasn't about to cough up any information about what had been going on in that locked room at the Union of Hearts, what connection he had to Rudy Soyez, or if he knew anything about what happened to Billy Ballou the day Katrina came to town. But if there was any information to be had, this seemed like the place to start. If he saw Tats leave this place with one of those backpacks, as he had before, Lloyd thought he might find out what was in it.

It was late, and the girls weren't as aggressive as they had been before. He drank a small, warm seven-dollar beer, and then a nine-dollar one, amused at the price fluctuations depending on which girl delivered his drink. The music stopped and the apathetic girl who had been gyrating on stage gathered up her scattered garments and went toward the back. The room was quiet for a minute, then the music started up again, and another dancer who looked all of fifteen made her way down front. Appraising her briefly, two men seated near the stage got up and wobbled out. She wasn't much to look at, and danced like she was sailing on a cloud of cocaine, or something even worse.

Lloyd couldn't work up any interest in what was happening on that side of the room. In fact, he was starting to wonder over the past few days whether he should give up women entirely for a year or so, or more reasonably, maybe six months. Or three. He could be celibate for a while until the bitterness diminished and the confusion started clearing in his head. How long did it take to detox from women?

The time spent with Kelly was a befuddling experience for him. Until then he had it all neatly compartmentalized so he could simply put it out of his mind and move on. But then . . .

Quiz Show Moderator—Lloyd, tell us what happened to your marriage? In twenty words or less.

Lloyd—She left me when I needed her most. She had an affair with my friend. She's a slut.

Moderator—Congratulations, nineteen words. Now the lightning round. Are you glad this happened?

Lloyd—No.

Moderator—Do you want her back?

Lloyd—No.

Moderator—And what have you learned from this experience?

Lloyd—I'll take a pass on that one.

As she was getting ready to go home, a day earlier than she planned, Kelly had told him that she was still in love with him, but could never picture them being happy together again. She may have meant it to be some kind of consolation, or maybe a rebuke, but it only added to his confusion. Weren't people who were in love supposed to be together?

Isn't that how life worked? But on the other hand, there was the case study of Billy and Carol Ballou. If people were intended to learn from the example of their parents, then he was where he should expect to be right about now.

Lloyd glanced toward the back end of the bar and saw two people step out of the doorway in the corner. One of them was Marta, the slim, silk-clad manager, the one who called herself Mary Lucchesi and offered to morph into a sweet, simple Italian girl and take him on the guided tour of the real New Orleans. The man with her was one of Tats' cohorts, the one Lloyd had doubled up and put down during the recent trumpet affair.

They were both looking at him. In a moment, the man leaned his head down and said something to Marta, then turned and went back through the doorway. Marta went over to the bar and spoke to one of the waitresses sitting there.

Lloyd turned his attention back to the stage, where the young dancer was just wrapping up her routine. Okay, you did something incredibly stupid, Ballou, but now you've got to be cool and smooth. Pull your hat down and think you won't be recognized? Slick move.

A waitress came over and brought him another beer, one he hadn't ordered, and laid a cocktail napkin in front of Lloyd. "From Marta." She said. Looking up at her gave him a chance to glance over toward the doorway again, and what he saw was not encouraging. Soyez was standing there now, with both Tats and Lloyd's punching bag at his elbow. From their expressions, it didn't appear likely that any of them would come over and welcome him to Les Girls.

Lloyd gave the girl a ten and she left without offering change. He glanced at the note. "Leave while you can. When we go in back." He palmed the note as he was taking another drink, and crushed it in a ball.

Once outside, Lloyd made for the nearest alley and wormed his way under a pile of cardboard boxes. When he confronted Tats and his guys in the alley beside the cathedral he had handled them easily enough, but he'd caught them off guard, and they weren't the real deal anyway. He had an idea that with Soyez, there was no such thing as off guard . . . or unarmed.

He froze when he heard the men come out the front door of Les Girls just a few yards away, imagining them looking both directions down the street, speculating on which way he went.

"Musta run," somebody said.

"Okay, get the car."

* * *

Lloyd spent the night under a clump of bushes in the tiny front yard of a home across the street from the flophouse where he stayed. He had no reason to believe they knew where he lived, but thought that if they did, they might come by here at some point to see if he came back. Getting any rest was impossible, curled up like a worm under the bushes. Every late-night passer-by and every car that drove down the narrow, one-way street startled him awake. Around three in the morning it rained for a while, and at six the homeowner's dog started barking at him through the front windows.

Exhausted, Lloyd gave up the watch and crossed the street. He was nearly asleep before his head hit the pillow.

For the first few nights after the incident at Les Girls, Lloyd climbed up on his chair and retrieved one of his hand guns, a cool and reassuring bedtime mistress, then returned it to the hiding place in the ceiling each morning. But eventually he gave up that routine. It was a nuisance, morning and night, and what would he do some night if he was startled awake and felt the pistol ready in his hand? Start blowing holes in the walls, or blast some luckless transient walking by on the balcony outside his door? It was silly, he decided, as silly as that miserable night he had spent in the bushes across the street waiting for the boogey man to show up.

He pledged never to set foot in Les Girls again, but eventually started going back to Jackson Square once in a while. He spotted Tats and his buddies in the distance a couple of times, but left them alone. Occasionally one of them might throw a hard look in his direction, but that was about it.

Lloyd thought he was ready now to pack it up and go home. More and more, the way forward seemed pointless and obscure. In the chaos of a cat five hurricane, his father had simply been swallowed up, along with uncountable others. At the point of her greatest fury, it was easy enough for mother earth to do away with a single frail, recyclable, human body, as if it had never existed at all.

For now, he would just keep his head down and go about his routine, Lloyd decided. He would give his notice at the hotel parking garage, and make one more trip out to see Aunt Charmaine. He would give Sarah Bradford a call, and maybe even stop by the bar on Decatur and say good-bye to Betsy. It would be good to see his mom, and he'd crash on Kat's couch again until he got a place of his own. There was always some sort of job available. With a dry laugh, he realized that he even had a new career path to explore. Parking valet.

* * *

They were waiting for him in the darkness of his grubby little sleeping room, sticks and bats at the ready. Lloyd had his door only halfway open when he smelled the cigarette smoke inside the room. He took a short step back, but not fast enough to avoid the first stunning blow. The bat raked down the side of his head, then landed full-force on his right shoulder. Lloyd staggered back against the railing and began a clumsy backward retreat down the balcony. He tried to raise his arms to ward off another blow, but only his left arm responded to the command. His fingers locked instinctively around the descending bat, and he snatched it out of the surprised attacker's grasp.

It worked to Lloyd's advantage that they had brought along too much manpower to do the job effectively on the narrow balcony. One or two, hiding in the shadows inside the room, armed with bats or knives or even guns, and smart enough not to smoke while they waited, could have taken him down easily. But there were five or six of them, shoving and stumbling as they tried to get into the fight. Lloyd slammed the butt end of the bat into one man's face, flattening his nose and eliciting a primal scream of shock and pain. Blood was blurring the vision of Lloyd's right eye, and his right arm no longer seemed to be a participating part of his body.

Something hit his left thigh, sending shocks of pain the full length of his leg, but he didn't quite go down. He swung bat down and heard the satisfying snap of bone.

"Get ahold of him! Grab that bat!" That was Tats, from behind the others. Every battle needed a general.

Lloyd swung again, taking out a light fixture mounted on the wall. Another blow struck his right arm, but he hardly felt that one. His right eye was useless now, and he could feel the strength leaving his body. He was scarcely aware of what was happening when a tall form, arms splayed, plunged at him. As the man's arms encircled Lloyd, the balcony rail gave way behind him. In mid-air they swirled and writhed like divers, and an instant later they landed in a tangle of limbs and body parts on the flagstone patio two floors down.

Lloyd could feel no movement or sign of life from the body beneath him. His mind was hazy and he seemed to hurt everywhere. He felt no inclination to move a single muscle.

From somewhere he heard voices, and struggled to open his left eye a little. Dimly, in the distance above, he saw heads leaning over a balcony, looking down.

"Holy shit! That's gotta be a back breaker! Are they dead?"

"How would I know? They look dead to me." That was Tats. "But we were s'posed to kill him anyway. Soyez said."

"But not Slam."

"That's just his bad luck. I never did like that sum bitch anyway. He always thought he was tough, but he don't look so tough now, does he?"

"Not all twisted up like that."

A light came on someplace nearby, but Lloyd decided not to move while they were still up there.

"Man, we gotta get outa here before the cops come, Tats. Are we gonna try to take Slam with us?"

"Hell no. Do you want to try to carry him around like that? They're both dead. We did what we came here for, so let's haul ass."

"Well, we've got to do something about Richard's face. His nose is smashed, and he's bleeding like a chicken."

From some other direction Lloyd heard a woman's voice, half afraid and half mad. "Hey what's going on out there? I already called the cops. You're going to have to pay for that busted railing."

"Let's go, Tats! The cops will be here."

"Alright. Get Richard up off the floor."

There were some frantic mumbling noises, probably the injured man above trying to talk.

"No, we can't take you to a hospital, but we'll figure something out. Get up and come on."

Lloyd let his head loll to the side. The boarding house desk clerk was standing on the top step of her first-floor apartment, wearing a pink bra and sweat pants stretched up over her clearly pregnant belly. She had a baby perched on one hip, and somewhere in the dim room behind her another child started bawling. "Hold on! You're gotta pay for that busted rail . . ." she called out to the fleeing men. She didn't see Lloyd and the dead man beneath him, prostrate in the shadows of the unlit, weed-ridden courtyard.

Lloyd managed to make it to his knees, then braced himself on the arm of a decaying wooden recliner and groaned to his feet. He tried a tentative step and nearly went down again. His right arm swung at his side like a clock pendulum, but the feeling was starting to come back. He looked down with his one available eye at the man at his feet. His limbs were twisted at impossible angles, and his eyes were open, taking in the swaying branches and the stars above with a fixed, unblinking stare. Puddles of blood were pooling on the flagstones beneath his skull and midsection. Lloyd's thoughts went for an instant to June Bug.

The woman with the baby had gone back into her apartment and closed the door. It was dark again in the courtyard. Lloyd stumbled toward the back wall, amazed that his legs managed to carry him, eating the pain. He had been hurt before, but never like this, and he wondered foggily whether he was going to die.

Lloyd had lived here for weeks before he discovered the rusting wrought iron gate, concealed behind a labyrinth of lush vines that had overtaken the back wall of the courtyard. Rust had paralyzed the hinges, but the gate was open just enough for a man his size to squeeze through.

Later Lloyd could only attribute his rescue to nothing less than an act of God, or at least a *cause majeure*. He had been making his way slowly and doggedly in the general direction of Jackson Square, but had started getting a panicky, desperate feeling that he had lost his way. The only people he had encountered at this late hour were two staggering drunks who greeted him with slurs and laughter, not even seeming to notice that the whole right side of his body was soaked in blood.

Eventually he stopped and leaned against the brick wall of a closed restaurant, convinced that he didn't have it in him to go another step. He would have to stop here, and maybe die here, and neither prospect seemed that upsetting at the moment. Anything was preferable to the pain.

There was something almost mystic about the figure that appeared down the block, stocky and dark, limping and staggering slowly along, backlit and almost seeming to glow because of the streetlight behind.

His pace picked up slightly as he spotted Lloyd leaning against the wall, seeming to sense his desperation and despair. Lloyd realized that this man was drunk too, mumbling to himself, but there was something familiar about his crooked, halting gait and the deep texture of his voice.

"Boy, is that you? Lloyd Ballou?"

"'Fraid so, Chester."

"What cement truck you fall in, boy?"

"A fight. Fell off a balcony." Lloyd was struggling to stay conscious, to stay upright. "A dead man there, and the police were coming. Baseball bats. I smashed a guy's face. Damn, that felt good. Then we broke the rail, me and the dead guy. It was Tats' bunch."

"Lloyd, we gotta get you to a hospital. You all busted up."

"Can't do that, Chester." His thoughts were all fuzzy and he wasn't sure why now, but he knew his mind was already made up. No cops.

"Then maybe you die."

Okay, then maybe I die."

Chester studied Lloyd's battered, bloody face and body for a moment, and then with a solemn nod he showed that he understood.

"Come over here and I see what I can do." Chester helped Lloyd back into the recesses of an alley, lit by a single bulb above the restaurant's back door. He helped Lloyd slide to the cement, then went away for a moment. When he came back, he carried a bucket and a couple of filthy white aprons.

As Chester dipped one of the aprons into the bucket and began cleaning up the side of Lloyd's head, it took Lloyd a moment to recognize the odor he was smelling. Then it came to him from way back when he had just joined the Army. It was the smell of a mop bucket, rich with a mixture of Lysol cleaner and the potpourri of all the disgusting things someone was likely to mop up off a dining room floor. But the water felt good on his head and face, and for the moment that's all that seemed to matter.

As he worked, Chester dropped into his other voice. At the moment, it almost seemed to Lloyd that the old black man was reaching out and finding some greater truth to what had happened tonight.

The Debil he come for Lloyd Ballou,
But Lloyd Ballou say no he will not go.
Still got too much to do.
Blood to spill an' bones to mend.
Hearts to bleed and hate to end.
Still got to find hisself,
'Fore that ol Debil haul him away.

"Anyplace else you bleeding 'sides your head?" Chester asked, coming back to himself.

"I don't think so. But I'm hurt inside. Some broken ribs, maybe."

"Big long cut on the side of your head, and your ear is all tore up. A good doctor could probably fix that good as new. If you had one."

Chester tore a long strip from the second, dry apron and tied it around Lloyd's head. Somehow Lloyd felt a little better just having the open wound tended to, but all the other places were still broadcasting their presence. He tried his right arm and was able to lift it a little, but pain shot up into his shoulder when he did it.

Chester leaned back on his heels and surveyed his handiwork. "We'll figure it out tomorrow," he said. "Least you won't bleed to death. My brother's wife mad as hornets 'cause of something I done, so we can't go there. But I know a place, bes' we can do tonight."

Chapter Seventeen

When he was eleven year's old, not long before Bennie left them, Lloyd's mother picked him up from school early one day. She wouldn't tell him why, but when he saw the somber expression on her face, and then saw his younger sister and brother already in the car, he knew it was nothing good. She didn't drive home, and after a while he started getting the feeling that she was just driving around randomly, with no destination in mind.

"I've got homework, Mom, and a civics test in the morning," Lloyd offered at one point. Kat and Bennie had fallen asleep in back. Carol had stopped and bought them all snacks, and now Bennie's cheese curls were scattered all over the back seat. Carol didn't even bother to complain about it.

"I'm sorry, but I can't think about that right now, sweetie," his mother said, her voice distracted and tentative. Lloyd looked over at her, and was startled to see her eyes welling with tears. "Maybe you won't be going back to school for a few days. We'll just have to see." She was gripping the steering wheel with both hands, holding it tightly as if someone might try to snatch it from her. She looked scared, and Lloyd felt the fear transfer to him, like a shared electric shock.

"Why, mama?" he asked. "Ever since you picked me up, all you've been doing is just driving around. Is something bad happening? Why can't we just go home?"

"It's hard to explain," Carol said. "Some men are there and they're carrying out all of our stuff . . ." A sob gripped her throat, and for a minute she couldn't go on. "Lloyd, sweetie, do you know what 'evicted' means?"

"When they kick you out with all your stuff?"

"That's right, son, and that's what's happened to us. Because I couldn't stay caught up with the rent. So, for a little while, we'll be sleeping in the car while I get enough money to rent someplace else for us to stay. But we can make it fun. It can be just like camping out. It'll be okay."

Lloyd had never been camping, so it was hard to imagine what that would be like, nor could he have ever predicted what the next three months would eventually be like for them. Later when he thought about that time, he always thought of his fielder's mitt, which he assumed had been dumped by the street with everything else they owned. For years afterward he despised the illogical mental image of some other kid out there in center with his mitt on, catching the high fly that he was meant to catch.

When Lloyd felt the tug on his foot, jarring him out of nearly comatose sleep, he pulled his leg back and kicked out reflexively. The old man who was on the other end of the kick let go of the shoe he was trying to steal and scooted away a foot or two. He cursed Lloyd profusely and unintelligibly. Lloyd raised up onto one elbow and looked down. His other shoe was already gone, and he assumed the old man already had that one.

Lloyd lay on a damp, stinking bundle of filthy rags, which in turn rested on a bed of rough limestone gravel. As near as he could figure out, he was under some sort of riverside pier. Rows of round concrete pilings rose around him, and no more than three feet above his head was an expansive concrete slab extending out toward the river. The stench of filth was almost unbearable. No more than three feet from where his head had rested was a clump of fresh human waste. Trash and debris of every kind was strewn about, and weeds grew up scraggly but determined through the gravel bed. Down a steep slope, maybe thirty feet away, the restless, greenish brown waters of the Mississippi lapped against the muddy, slime-covered shallows.

Other men were scattered about under the pier, some sleeping, others sitting in small clusters or alone. A few seeming to be eating God-only-knew-what, and one or two were smoking. Off to one side, a man in dirty rags that passed for clothes drained the last drops from a flat liquor bottle, then tossed it carelessly aside.

Lloyd didn't feel like moving, but in the interest of making at least a feeble show of self-defense in this seemingly hostile environment, he struggled to sit up. For the first minute, his head swirled and throbbed so badly he thought that he might pass out again. He reached up and felt the blood-crusted apron that Chester had tied around his torn scalp and mangled ear last night. The worst of the pain came from there. It was all coming back to him now—the attack in the doorway of his room, the baseball bat landing hard and merciless, the sickening sound of the decaying lumber of the railing fracturing, the horrifying fall, the feel of the broken and lifeless body beneath him on the cobblestones, the agonizing trek through the dark, empty streets . . .

The old man cackled and held up Lloyd's other shoe, mumbling some unintelligible taunt. Lloyd thought he made out the words "guts" and "chicken-shit." The man's face was a rock garden of gray-green tumors, some as big as the tip of a thumb, and his tongue seemed to protrude when he made his pathetic attempts to speak.

A rustling sound caught Lloyd's attention and he turned his head to the side to see Chester making his way awkwardly across the stones, moving painfully on his hands and knees toward him. He had a large white paper bag which he moved carefully ahead of him as he crawled. Even above the stench of the place, Lloyd could smell the tantalizing aroma of coffee.

"Figured you might could use something this morning after the hard night you had," Chester said with a wide grin. "Jus' had to wait 'til daylight 'fore I go out so maybe nobody mess wit you."

"Chester, I could kiss your whiskery old cheek," Lloyd said.

"Don't need no nonsense like that," Chester laughed. He carefully unloaded the sack, taking out two tall cups of coffee and several cheap, cellophane-wrapped pastries. "You bought it anyway. I hadn't had a dime in my pocket for three days, so I took your wallet. Safer with me anyway, 'cause somebody woulda stole it while you was asleep."

There was still no strength in Lloyd's right arm, so he accepted the cup with his left. He pried the lid off and scalded his tongue with the first sip, deciding it was the best stuff he had ever tasted. "That old man down there stole my shoe," he told Chester. "I've still got the other one, but I don't think I've got the juice to go down there and take back the one he got."

Chester looked over at the diseased old man, who lifted Lloyd's shoe up accommodatingly and cackled at the two of them.

"Leonard, you old wart-face piss bucket," Chester said. "This here my friend. One shoe ain't no good to you, so you just as well give it back."

Leonard waved the shoe playfully.

"I give you one of these here," Chester said, displaying a cellophane wrapped honey bun, "And you give him the shoe."

Leonard said something past that swollen, diseased tongue, which Chester miraculously seemed to understand. "A'right then, how 'bout I give you one of these," Chester said, offering the cheap pastry again, "*and* I don't come over there and bash that nasty old head of yourn with a rock?"

The thief seemed to approve the bargain, and crawled forward a few feet until he was near to Lloyd and Chester. He handed Lloyd his shoe, then reached out and snatched the pastry from Chester like a starving hyena. As an afterthought, Chester also held out his coffee to the old man. "I already had me some up top," he explained to Lloyd. Lloyd doubted it, but understood that it was in Chester's nature to do something like that.

They watched the old man rip the cellophane off the pastry and gobble it down, licking the wrapper once he was finished. "Don't s'pect old Leonard be around much longer," Chester said quietly after the old man had crawled away. "'Sides them things on his face, whatever the hell they are, he bleedin' inside. You can see it on his britches."

As Lloyd ate his breakfast, Chester began taking various things out of his pockets, a wallet, a knife, a key, and finally a phone, all Lloyd's. "I took your stuff with me, but I wasn't stealing, I promise," Chester explained. "These boys down here, they mos'ly not bad, but just hit rock bottom. They rob a sleeping man if they get a chance, maybe hurt him bad if they have to."

"What is this place?" Lloyd asked. "Where are we?"

"It's where a man come when he got no place else to go. No law, no rules down here. Everybody just do what they need to do to stay alive. Maybe not quite hell on earth, but just about the last trolley stop 'fore you get there. Down here prob'ly where June Bug got herself so bad hurt 'fore she die."

"And here I am now," Lloyd noted bleakly. He shifted around to a better sitting position, and a bolt of pain shot up his left leg, nearly as intense as the pain he felt when one of Tats' thugs slammed a baseball bat into it the night before.

"Well maybe not for so long," Chester grinned. He picked up Lloyd's phone and showed it to him. The case was cracked, and the screen was a spider web of shattered glass. "I figgered it was busted, but I try it anyway. Ain't much I can do for you, an' I don't know how bad you hurt. If the police are after you like you think, you need someplace, and somebody more than me.

"So, I push the button on that busted phone, and like a miracle somebody's phone ring somewhere. Don't know who or where, but it was a nice lady that answered. I told her who you was, and how you hurt and got no place to go, how you need a friend an' maybe she was one. She ast a lot of questions 'bout how you got hurt and how bad. Didn't tell her much more than I had to, nothin' about that dead man a'tall. I told her you thought you'd be in plenty of trouble if the police put their hands on you. Finally she said okay, she help you if she can."

Sarah Bradley! Lloyd never thought of her, and probably wouldn't have called her even if he did. The one Ballou man she got involved with had drawn her into more danger than she deserved, and he certainly wouldn't have asked her to get into the middle of another mess with yet another desperate Ballou. But if she had volunteered to help, as Chester seemed to be telling him . . .

"Don't know who that woman is, Lloyd Ballou, but you got yourself an angel, seems like."

"I know her, and she is," Lloyd said quietly.

With Chester's help, Lloyd made his way to the edge of the underside of the concrete pier. His joints and muscles were stiff and painful, and at times it felt like he hadn't tried to walk for months. Taking inventory as he hobbled along, one arm over Chester's own feeble shoulders, he decided that his left leg must not be seriously broken, but just horribly bruised, or possibly fractured. He wasn't sure quite what a concussion would feel like, but he thought he might have one, and thick, dark blood was once more oozing out from the improvised bandage. He didn't even want to think about how messed up his right shoulder and arm might be.

Chester left him just under the edge of the pier while he made his way up the steep path, through the weeds, to the top. A vague memory of this place, from last night in the moonlight, started coming back to Lloyd. The pier was perhaps a hundred yards long, extending out over the river's edge so barges could move up close and take on cargo. At the far end of the pier was an aging warehouse, dark and foreboding last night, seemingly abandoned. Close by on the end where Lloyd waited, a tall chain link fence sealed the area off, running right down into the water. But someone had cut a gaping gash in the wire and peeled it back so now a person could cross right through without hardly bowing their head.

The wait seemed long to Lloyd, and he began to wonder if something had happened to Chester. If that was true, what would he do? Lloyd wondered. His phone had miraculously worked that one time for Chester, but now it appeared to be dead and worthless. If he went up top on his own, where would he go, and who could he ask for help? If he fell into the hands of the police, there was a good chance that he would be held responsible for that bloody, twisted corpse in the courtyard outside his room. If Soyez had been able to engineer the rape charges against Billy, how much of a problem would it be for him to get Lloyd tagged for murder?

At one point two young men approached from under the other side of the pier. One was white, one black. They were equally ragged and filthy, but looked fit and healthy, and they assessed Lloyd with predatory gazes as they approached.

Lloyd looked around and picked up a fist-sized rock in either hand, knowing that if they attacked, any defense he tried to make would be pathetic. But they saw him pick up the rocks, and maybe it would make them think.

"Dude, somebody bashed you good," the white one said, pointing to the bloody rag on Lloyd's head.

"A couple of cops," Lloyd said, hoping that this might earn him some cred with the pair. "I'm hiding out down here 'cause I think I hurt one of them."

"Hope so," the black one said. "Got a cigarette?"

"Wish I did. Or money to buy some."

The two seemed to decide a bloody casualty like him wasn't worth the effort to mug, and followed the worn path through the weeds a few feet away. When they were just past, the black one stopped unexpectedly and turned his head back toward Lloyd, giving him yet another appraising glance. His hand went up to his shirt pocket and took something out, which he tossed in Lloyd's direction. Then they went on, out from under the pier and up the hill.

Lloyd picked up the cigarette from the ground beside him, looked at it, and then looked over where the men had gone. You just never could tell about people, he thought, sticking the cigarette down in his shirt pocket. It would be a nice treat for Chester, if he had any way to light it.

He heard a man and woman talking up above half a minute before he actually saw them, Chester's voice familiar and distinct, and the woman's quiet and tentative.

"Sorry ma'am to bring you down into a terrible place like this," Chester said. "No place for a nice lady, for sure. But he just down there a little piece more."

"It's alright," the woman said quietly.

"Bes' keep an eye out so you don't step in nothin'."

Lloyd watched their feet, then legs, then torso's as they worked their way down the path, Chester in the lead, holding her hand and pointing out places not to step. Lloyd took a deep sigh of relief as he realized that help had arrived. Maybe things would be better soon.

Then it struck Lloyd that the woman Chester was leading was not Sarah Bradley. She was smaller in stature, noticeably younger, and her hair was shiny black in the morning sunlight. When they stopped for a moment and Chester pointed Lloyd out to her under the edge of the pier, Lloyd realized that she was Asian. Her face was completely unfamiliar to him.

"Here's your angel, Lloyd Ballou," Chester said, beaming.

"Good morning," Lloyd said tentatively, still trying to sort this puzzle out in his foggy brain.

"I'm not sure why I agreed to come here, Mr. Ballou," the woman admitted straight out. She had no accent, which somehow surprised him because she looked like she should.

"Did Sarah send you?" Lloyd asked.

The woman took a tentative step forward, puzzled herself, studying Lloyd's battered head and his ragged, bloody clothes. "I don't know who Sarah is," she said.

"Then how . . .? I mean, why . . .?" Lloyd looked over at Chester in complete confusion. It was as if his battered brain refused to find any logic in what was happening.

"You don't have any idea who I am, do you, Mr. Ballou?"

"No, sorry."

"We met several weeks ago, when you came into my family's store, over by the Union of Hearts Mission." A door seemed to open, and finally some things began making sense. "You were looking for your father, and I called you a day or two later to tell you that my father and mother didn't know what happened to him. My name is Casey Charron."

"I'm sorry, but it's been a rough couple of days for me," Lloyd admitted. "Then it was you that Chester called with my phone?"

"Obviously," the woman said. "But to be honest with you, I'm beginning to have my doubts now. I'm not sure I should have come here at all."

"Now miss, don't be thinkin' that," Chester chimed in quickly. "This here a good man, but he's bunged up pretty bad. Right now you are the closest thing to an angel that he ever likely to see."

Casey Charron looked over at Chester, then back at Lloyd, trying to decide what she should do. "I'm making no promises, Mr. Ballou. If you've broken the law, I will not give you sanctuary. I'll turn you over to the police myself."

"I understand. I'll be straight with you, and then you can decide."

* * *

The walled patio garden was tiny, no more than ten feet square, simple and understated in a distinctly Asian manner. There were two stone benches along the walls, and a lovely little stone waterfall in one corner that spilled into a pond containing a variety of water plants and a small scattering of colorful fish. The plants in the long narrow beds were carefully manicured, and the one dwarf tree that rose from a plot of dirt in the center of the patio might have been tended by a bonsai master's hand. On three of the four sides, aged brick walls rose to a height of perhaps eight feet, with broken bottles embedded in cement along the top in the New Orleans fashion. On the fourth side French doors opened into a little sun room at the back of the house. This room had been temporarily converted into Lloyd's bedroom, or perhaps more appropriately, his convalescent room, for the duration.

It was the third day of his stay here at Casey Charron's little cottage on a quiet street near the north-eastern boundary of the French Quarter. This was the first day he had been allowed to get up out of bed and hobble out into the garden on his own.

He sat in a comfortably padded patio chair with his legs up on a matching footstool, drinking the strong, strange-tasting herbal tea that his hostess provided, paging through the morning edition of the Times Picayune. He knew by the position of the sun that it was late morning, but since he had been here, beginning his slow recovery in capable hands, he had lost interest in time.

Remarkably, nothing had appeared in the newspaper about the dead body in the flophouse courtyard until yesterday, three days after the fight. Lloyd speculated that might have been because the residents there seldom ever went out in that cluttered, overgrown space, and the body might have only made its presence known when it began to stink in the stifling south Louisiana humidity. Even now, the discovery rated only a few column inches on the obituary page. The body bore no identification, no one fitting that description was reported missing, and the police investigation was ongoing. Sure, as they always were.

After the fact, it occurred to Lloyd that even if the manager there had thought to link his disappearance to the dead body in the courtyard, she probably couldn't have identified him in any usable way to the police. He had given a fake name and address when he first checked in, and had always paid his rent in cash.

As for Tats, he had declared Lloyd dead from two floors up on the night of the attack, and still probably thought he had done the job Soyez sent him out to do.

Lloyd heard the latch on the French doors open and looked over to see an Asian woman in a white lab coat coming toward him. She was in the neighborhood of fifty, even tinier that Casey, with an attractive oval Asian face and almond eyes that seemed both knowing and habitually amused. Her name was Tran Ngo, and she was not only Casey's good friend, but she was also the miracle worker who had brought Lloyd back from the brink of disaster that first long, painful day.

"So, you're getting some fresh air and sun today. That's good. Better sometimes than any medicine I could give you."

Good morning, Dr. Ngo," Lloyd said. He made a move as if to rise, but settled back when she waved her hand at him.

"I'm late again today," the doctor said, as if in apology. She set her bag on a small, glass-topped table near Lloyd and rummaged around in it, finally locating a stethoscope. "My daughter had a performance at school first thing this morning, and by the time I finally got to the clinic, I already had four patients waiting."

"Early or late, I wouldn't know the difference," Lloyd said with a grin. "I don't think I've laid eyes on a clock since Casey brought me here." He opened the lapels of his robe and let her check his heart. He hadn't been fully dressed since that first day when Casey had gathered up his filthy, bloody clothes and threw them in the trash. The robe and boxers she provided had been sufficient. He thought they might have once been her husband's, but didn't ask.

"Your heart's fine, and your color's better," Dr. Ngo announced. "Pretty soon we'll start you on some kind of exercise so you can get your strength back."

"Good. I'm ready, whenever this leg will take it."

The doctor knelt and probed the large, swollen bruise on his leg, sending shock-waves up and down his leg as she poked and prodded. Although it turned out it wasn't broken or even fractured, she had cautioned him that the membrane surrounding the bone had been severely damaged. This kind of bruised bone, she explained, could sometimes take longer to heal than an actual break, and the pain might be ongoing for months. This morning as he hobbled out into the garden, using a cane for support, he got a sample of what he was in for.

Next, she cut away the bandage around his head, making little satisfied grunts as she examined her handiwork there. Two days before Lloyd had taken a quick look at that side of his head while she had the bandages off, and decided that he didn't need to be around anymore mirrors for a while. The whole right side of his head was shaved, and Dr. Ngo had repaired the torn skin with a patchwork of stitches. His ear had been half torn away by the baseball bat's insults, but she had sewn it back on and was optimistic. His ear and the skin around it were numb, and she thought that might be permanent, but he could still hear out of the ear and accepted that as a good sign.

"An inch or two over and it would have been a different story," the doctor had told him while she was working on him that first day. "You might not think so now, but you are a lucky man."

It was much the same with his fractured collar bone. She had set it by hand, giving him a wad of gauze to bite on, then put his arm in a sling, which he still wore. The rest of the weakness in his arm was due to severe bruising, and what she called "insult to the nerves." The sling gave those parts of his battered body a well-needed rest.

"Believe me, I do know how lucky I am," Lloyd said. The doctor was packing away her gear, and Lloyd was tying the robe belt back around his waist. "If it wasn't for you and Casey, I might have bled out already, or be handcuffed to a gurney in a charity ward someplace. My friend called Casey my guardian angel when she came to pick me up, but it turns out I have two."

She looked up at him. Her tolerant grin and the roll of her eyes was answer enough. He limped along after her as she started for the door, giving him instructions with every step. Take it easy with the pain killers. Get a lot of rest. Don't start getting too macho too soon. Call her if anything got worse.

"When I get better, maybe I could start coming over to the clinic and save you the driving time," Lloyd said.

Dr. Ngo stopped on the front porch and looked back at him. "It's not a good idea, Lloyd," she said. "My staff doesn't know about you, and there would be a lot of questions and paperwork if you showed up there. The government keeps a pretty close eye on us because we're a free clinic. But sometimes you have to bend the rules, in special cases. This isn't the first time I've gone off the radar, and I'm doing this as much for my friend Casey as for you. But there sure would be hell to pay if the establishment ever found out."

"Okay, but you know how grateful I am."

"Just count your blessings that you have a friend like Casey."

* * *

That evening Casey was on the phone as she walked in the door, carrying in two plastic bags with the tell-tale odors of Asian food. Lloyd was sitting on the couch in the small front room of the house, watching the local evening news on television. There was still nothing more about the dead young thug. He wondered if he might actually be lucky enough to have the whole thing behind him so easily.

Casey waved at Lloyd and mouthed the word "Hi" as she crossed the room and set the bags on the table in her small kitchen. She looked tired, and her eyebrows were knit. Although he didn't catch any of the conversation, he understood that it must not be a particularly pleasant one. She went upstairs instead of joining him, and a moment later he heard a door close.

The house where Casey now lived had been her parent's home before Katrina, and before they had moved in with their son, apparently never to return. It was a small but charming place, with a kitchen, dining room, living room and parlor on the first floor, and bedrooms upstairs. She was fortunate enough to have a narrow, gated driveway and garage on the side, saving her from the nightmare of having to search each evening for a practically non-existent parking space on the narrow French Quarter streets.

The furnishings were old but well-kept, with accessories that left no doubt about the ethnicity of its long-time residents. Every piece of furniture was protected with clear plastic coverings, and the few piece of cheap, simple art on the walls reminded Lloyd of the stylized paintings in Chinese restaurants.

Casey said she, her parents, and her brother had come to New Orleans in 1975, barely escaping the horrors of the North Vietnamese seizure of the South, and after enduring four dreary and uncertain months in a relocation camp in western Arkansas. A Catholic charity had eventually arranged to settle them New Orleans. Over the ensuing decades their lives had been difficult and frugal, living for years in the back of their small store before finally managing to purchase this little house. Casey had reached adulthood here, and now faced the difficult and heartbreaking task of having to sell both the house and the store since her parents were too old to continue their life in the city.

Lloyd struggled clumsily to his feet, using the cane and an arm of the couch to keep the weight off his bad leg. He went into the kitchen and sat down again at the small table there. Upstairs he heard Casey raise her voice angrily for a moment, but he didn't get the gist of what she was saying.

Lloyd opened the plastic bags and looked inside. One contained two small paper boxes that, from the smell, had to be Asian food of one kind or another. The other held an enormous Muffaletta sandwich and a single bottle of beer. He smiled at her thoughtfulness.

The bottle was room temperature, but was a welcome sight nonetheless. He stuck it in the freezer of the small, humming refrigerator to let it chill. It had been days since he'd tasted anything alcoholic, and he was growing tired of his daily consumption of water, green tea, and instant coffee.

Casey didn't seem to cook much, and hadn't prepared anything in her kitchen more complicated that canned soup since he had arrived here. Without any employee clever and trustworthy enough to run the store without her, she worked brutal hours, in at six in the morning and out never earlier than eight in the evening. She managed to keep Lloyd fed, and with Dr. Ngo stopping in at least once a day during what was intended to be her lunch break, he didn't want for company or caretaking. He knew the huge Muffaletta in the bag would be his supper tonight, as well as breakfast and lunch tomorrow, but he had no complaints.

It was over half an hour before Casey finally came back downstairs. Lloyd turned the television off as she dropped onto the other end of the sofa with a heavy sigh. Her eyes were puffy and red, and for a minute she seemed to be engaged in some sort of Zen contemplation of the curtains across the room. In her own good time, she looked over at Lloyd, as if suddenly discovering that she was not alone in the room.

"I'm sorry to be such poor company," she said. She looked used up, and her voice was muted. "That was my husband on the phone."

"In Canada?" Lloyd asked, not really knowing what else to say.

"Toronto." Casey paused, then added, "I was supposed to close the store for three days at the end of the month and fly up to see him."

"But it's off now?"

"He told me he will be out of town that weekend. But he didn't bother to explain why or where. Or with who." She teared up again, and turned her face away to dab at her eyes with a tissue.

Lloyd felt awkward and powerless. He thought there was something he should say or do, but he had no idea what that might be. "I'm sorry," he said finally. "I hope it doesn't have anything to do with me being here."

"No, it's nothing like that," Casey said. "He doesn't even know you're here."

"Well if that ever becomes a problem, I'm doing a lot better now. I have friends here." Those were lies, of course. There was no one else here that he could call on, and he was hardly in any shape to be on his own. But he thought he could get by if he had to.

Casey reached over and put her hand lightly on top of his. Despite her tears, she managed to give him a brief, warm smile. "This has been getting worse for a long time, Lloyd," she said. "But it doesn't have anything to do with you. I'm glad you're here, and I'm glad I was able to help you when I did. I wasn't sure at first because I didn't know if I could trust you, and I didn't know if you might bring some sort of trouble with you. But I feel better about all that now. Please stay."

"Okay then, as a favor to you Miss Casey, I'll stick around at least until I can walk across a room without falling down. But you're going to have to keep bribing me with a beer now and then."

That drew another smile and a light laugh from Casey. Soon they got up and went in the kitchen. Lloyd got the beer out of the freezer while Casey took the food out of the bags. Lloyd quartered the monster sandwich on his plate, and Casey put few dabs of fried rice and stir-fry on hers. Lloyd offered to share the beer, but she declared that it was all his.

“I think I’ll just go up and go to bed,” Casey announced after dabbling with her food for a few minutes, but hardly eating any. “I hope you don’t mind. I’m just so tired.”

“Of course I don’t,” Lloyd said. “I don’t see how you manage to work the hours you do. Go on to bed. I’ll put the food away.”

Casey nodded and rose to leave, then paused at the kitchen doorway. “It’s pleasant to have someone here for a little while,” she told Lloyd.

Chapter Eighteen

In the Army Lloyd had taken one serious beating. It happened near the end of basic training, during those heady final days when every new recruit is in perhaps the best shape of his life, and has given himself over fully to the military concept that he had been put on this earth to maim and destroy.

Throughout basic a young drill sergeant named Roger Washington, a bully by nature, had singled out one particular young trainee for special persecution. The unlucky recruit was named Darius Gold, a street kid from Dallas who barely met the height, weight, and IQ requirements to get in. His reason for being there was simple. He wanted to make something of himself, he said, unlike his good-for-nothing daddy. Lloyd could relate.

Everybody in the platoon knew about the abuse, but drill sergeants were the gods of the training grounds, or simply tyrants perhaps, and nobody dared confront them even for such blatant sins. But during that heady last week of basic, when every young recruit felt as if he had achieved Viking status, Lloyd decided the time had come to call the man out. Lloyd had a couple of inches in height and maybe fifteen pounds over Washington. He imagined righteously knocking the young three-striper around a little bit until he acknowledged that Darius Gold had ceased being a punching bag and shit-detail fall guy for the likes of him. They might even part with a handshake, he imagined, an understanding between warriors.

As agreed, Lloyd met the drill sergeant behind the barracks late at night. The fight lasted only a couple of minutes, and ended up with Lloyd flat on his back in the dust, ears ringing, brain swirling, nose bleeding, body aching from a whirlwind of kicks and punches that seemed to have descended on him like thunderbolts.

The drill sergeant stood over him for a moment, wearing an expression of amusement and disdain, seeming much, much taller with his boots planted on both sides of Lloyd's chest. He seemed about to say something, a scoff or threat perhaps, or maybe some profound life lesson that Lloyd could carry forward through his military career. But in the end Washington just shook his head and walked away.

Over the years, Lloyd had thought of that fight many times, sometimes with embarrassment, and sometimes with the righteous knowledge that at least he had tried. In the end, the only true lesson to be learned, he supposed, was that right didn't always win out.

Lloyd Ballou supposed that those few people who bothered to look at him at all mentally tagged him as one of those dark, vaguely dangerous characters who prowled the downtown streets of any major city, society's throwaways who only continued to tolerate their miserable lives out of habit.

The worn, oversized trousers and shirt that Casey had picked up for him at the thrift store didn't help his looks. She was so short and petite herself that Lloyd assumed that to her, most American men were huge. But he didn't mind. For now, the clothing matched his mood.

Walking down Bourbon Street on a quiet Thursday night, limping along with his borrowed cane, no destination ahead, he felt anonymous, almost invisible. Even the barkers outside the jazz bars and strip joints didn't bother to call out to him. Women gave him wide berth to avoid even casual contact, and cops gave him hard, unsympathetic stares, gauging his threat potential to the tourists.

He limped past the parking garage entrance to the hotel where he worked until recently. Two of his former coworkers, Beau and

Francisco, were standing on the sidewalk outside, grabbing a smoke while things were slow. These were people that he had worked alongside day after day, but neither of them recognized him, even when their eyes met briefly.

But why should they, he in his knit stocking cap, pulled down low to cover his shaved right temple, and the scraggly start of a beard meant to conceal the four-inch scar that raked down his right cheek in front of his ear?

Lloyd realized that he missed Jackson Square and the collection of old coots that he had come to think of as his friends, particularly Chester, who had most likely saved his life, or at least saved him from a prison stint. But he knew he didn't dare go back there, lest the Keystone crew of clumsy assassins realize that their work was not yet finished.

When Doctor Ngo had cleared him to get out and begin exercising, Lloyd started with daytime walks around the quiet neighborhood where Casey lived. But he soon realized that the growing restlessness and unease he felt hit hardest at night, during those insomniac hours after Casey had gone up to bed.

She didn't appear to mind his nighttime ramblings, seeming to understand that not all of the injuries he struggled to recover from were physical.

When the time seemed right, Lloyd told her everything about the attack by Tats and his minions on the third-floor walkway of the flophouse where he stayed. He hadn't even left out the part about the crushed and bloody body he left behind in the courtyard as he made his stumbling escape that night.

As for motive, Lloyd described the beating and humiliation he had delivered to the street thugs, starting with his first encounter with Tats in Jackson Square, and continuing on to the recovery of Brass Man Jake's battered old trumpet.

What he left out was the part about the strip joint he frequented, and about Soyez and the possible drug ring. It was information he felt she didn't need. He didn't want her to begin wondering if, after her remarkable kindness, she had actually taken in a stranger floundering in his own personal cesspool.

Besides, he was embarrassed and ashamed of some the things he had done. He didn't want her to know him too well, or look too deeply into his bitter and amoral soul.

When Lloyd returned to Casey's at something after eleven, he was surprised to find her still up, sitting at the kitchen table in her pajamas, drinking tea. She tried to put up a brave front, looking up at him and asking how his walk had been. But her eyes were tinged with red, and she held a crumpled tissue in one hand. She glanced down at the cell phone on the table, then pushed it away as if it was some hateful thing.

"Can I make you some tea?" Casey asked.

"Sounds good," Lloyd said, tilting his cane in a corner and sitting across from her. He still had not developed a taste for the greenish-yellow, oddly herbed tea that Casey served up, but he was working on it.

"You look tired," Casey said.

"So do you." Lloyd glanced down at her phone, knowing that it was probably the origin of her sleeplessness. Casey had only mentioned the problems with her husband that one time, but he guessed that it was ongoing and getting worse.

He didn't ask questions, and she didn't volunteer much. He imagined that the problems probably had to do with her long absence while she was here in New Orleans attempting to wrap up her parents' affairs.

Lloyd didn't know one thing about Casey's husband, but still disliked him. It seemed easy enough to believe that any man worth his salt should understand that she was only doing what was right. At the very least, he could be patient and supportive, and not leave her crying and alone in the middle of the night a thousand miles away. What a selfish jackass.

Casey set the steaming cup of pale tea in front of him, offering neither sugar not creamer. “I have to drive down to Shreveport and visit my family this weekend,” she said. “I’ll close the store at noon Saturday, and won’t be back until Monday morning.”

“I’m sure they’ll be glad to see you,” Lloyd said. “I could find some other place to crash while you’re away.” With no money, no home and no friends, he wasn’t quite sure how he would pull that off, but felt obliged to offer.

“No, no. You must stay here,” Casey said. “You’ve got a key, and Tran also has a spare. You have her phone number, and mine.” She paused a moment, then placed her soft fingers on his forearm. “I trust you, Lloyd. You should stay.”

Lloyd smiled at her and nodded, wondering if she would still trust him if she knew him better. “I’ll watch over the place.”

* * *

The first night Casey was away, Lloyd felt an unexpected loneliness. It was as if something that he didn’t even know was important to him had unexpectedly been taken away.

He called his mother, but the conversation was short and muddled. She had already taken her evening pain meds, and her speech was slurry and rambling. Tomorrow she probably wouldn’t even remember that he called.

There was no treasured beer in the fridge because Casey hadn’t brought some home from work. He tried to go to bed early, but woke within an hour, restless and wide awake. He got up finally, dressed in his dark, disheveled street clothes, and headed out.

Lloyd was growing used to the anonymity that his new persona afforded him—the shabby clothes, the stocking cap, the sprouting beard. Even the cane and limp worked in his favor, tending to make people avoid eye contact and look away quickly, lest this crippled creature ask for alms, or even simple validation that he, like them, was a person.

But in truth, he felt flush tonight. A day earlier he had found a long-forgotten twenty-dollar bill, folded small in one of the compartments in his wallet. *Keep a few bucks tucked away, boy,* his dad had tutored decades before. *Someday you'll be glad you did.*

That someday was tonight.

He bought a bag of chips and a tall-boy in a little side street market, enjoying his indulgences as he walked toward the river.

Decatur was crowded as the late evening revelers careened their way from one saloon to the next. A splash of music and loud voices blared from the open doorway of every bar, and delicious odors filled the air outside restaurants.

He eventually reached the river end of Jackson Square. At the opposite end of the square, perhaps two hundred yards away, the impressively lit cathedral loomed majestically. Distant jazz music filtered through the air like a sweet familiar siren's song, and Lloyd imagined the old men blowing on their ancient instruments as appreciative tourists stepped forward occasionally to drop their pocket change and small bills into the plastic bucket.

The music stirred a strange nostalgia in Lloyd, as if he was recalling some better, peaceful time long since gone. In a way, he thought, these actually were memories from another life. He felt an urge to go up there and find Chester to tell him he was alright, that things were okay for now. The old man might even hash some strange words together to honor the return of his own personal prodigal.

But Lloyd knew that was unwise. If it was business as usual on that end of Jackson Square, then Tats and his crew could be sliming around somewhere nearby on a busy night like tonight. He couldn't risk that, but at least he could still be a ghost, haunting the shadows, an invisible witness to the life he once led.

Lloyd limped halfway up one of the broad flagstone promenades that bordered the square on either side. The gypsy fortune tellers and bizarrely–clad mystics were thick along this side, working the passing tourists with their marvelous promises and unlikely predictions. He managed to find an open park bench there and sat down to rest his injured leg. The slow-healing wound was sending out spasms of pain from ankle to hip.

A long draft of beer helped, and he just sat there for a while, taking in the music, the atmosphere, and the pleasant feeling of alcohol coursing through his bloodstream. Gently, unawares, he drifted off to sleep.

It could have been a minute or an hour later when a sharp rap on his leg, fortunately the uninjured one, startled Lloyd awake. His nerves jolted in surprise, and he opened his eyes in time to see a black stick sweep his half-finished beer and bag of chips off the bench. He looked down to watch the beer glugging out of the toppled can onto the flagstones.

"Get moving, you worthless piece of crap!" On the other end of the nightstick stood Officer Pepper, looking as if he'd like to punctuate his order with another whack.

"Yessir, boss," Lloyd mumbled, trying to sound submissive. "Just moving along here, boss." If the cop decided to take another shot at his other leg, he doubted if he'd be able to crawl away, let alone walk.

"We don't need night-crawling gutter trash like you scaring the tourists off," Pepper said. "And clean that up before you go." He pointed the stick at the mess on the ground.

"Yessir, officer," Lloyd said, leaning forward with some discomfort to pick up the trash.

Pepper's partner this time, a solidly built young woman with razor-cut hair, maybe a Latina, stood to one side and a step back, taking in the scene with an unreadable expression. "We've gotta keep these bums out of here," Pepper told her. "Bad for the tourist trade, and they piss all over the place." The woman looked bored.

Keeping his head down, Lloyd hoisted himself to his feet with the aid of the cane and started off. Fortunately, the two cops went in the other direction. He knew what it meant when this prick of a cop changed partners so frequently, most of them new bloods, every time Lloyd saw him. None of the good cops, the seasoned, street-smart professionals, would want a man like Pepper watching their back when the pot started to boil over.

Limping back toward Decatur, Lloyd considered returning to Casey's. He thought he could sleep now, and nothing but rest was going to lessen the pain in his leg. But he wasn't ready, not just yet. As long as he was out and about, visiting old haunts, there was one still left to check up on.

A weird feeling overtook Lloyd as he turned down the block where Les Girls was located. It was something like how he used to feel as a cop when the dark unknown was ahead and he was the one who had to check it out. It was a mingling of fear and excitement, doubt and eagerness, confidence and determination.

No more than two weeks had passed since he was last here. During that time enormous changes had taken place in his life, but Les Girls seemed just the same in every detail. The neon lights still fluttered and blinked. A mostly naked dancer at the door smiled and flirted at two passing drunks, trying to lure them in. Smoke-blurred, dimly-lit apparitions moved around inside like residents of perdition. The music still blared.

Marta would be somewhere in there, still trying to make the girls keep it barely legal and doing her best to tag the undercover cops.

And perhaps Soyez was there too, the man who could deliver death second-hand with a single order. Thinking of Soyez brought to mind questions that had been churning through the back of Lloyd's thoughts ever since that night when he learned he couldn't fly.

What had Tats and his gaggle of inept halfwits reported back after the third-floor balcony battle at the boarding house? Had they declared mission accomplished, at the expense of one of their own? And had Soyez bought it, thoroughly and completely, although Tats provided no proof and Lloyd's death was never reported by name in the news?

And finally, was all of this over now?

Lloyd shuffled by Les Girls on the sidewalk across the street and disappeared back into a dim space between two buildings that was scarcely wide enough to legitimately be called an alley. The place intrigued him. It was pitch dark back in there as he explored deeper, trailing his hand along a rough brick wall and probing ahead with his cane like a blind man. The place smelled like an open sewer, and his shoes and socks were soon soggy from the thick, squishy, unknown filth on the ground.

The space ended finally at what seemed to be a brick wall taller than he could reach. On his way back out, trailing his hand this time along the wall of the building on the other side, he passed what felt like a metal door, open just slightly, rusted and jammed from years of neglect.

This place deserved further exploration, Lloyd decided. He couldn't have explained why or when just then, but he knew he'd be back.

* * *

Lloyd Ballou woke on Sunday morning feeling the best he had since before he was wounded in the balcony brawl. He was halfway to the kitchen before realizing that he hadn't reached for the cane as soon as he stood up. The leg was definitely better, despite the workout he had given it last night.

Breakfast was some warmed-over noodles he found in the back of the refrigerator, washed down with a glass of mango juice. He was getting used to Casey's food, not so much that he had developed any favorites yet, but progress was progress.

When he returned late the night before, he stripped naked in the courtyard and left his clothes and shoes outside so he wouldn't bring in the filth and stench of the alley across from Les Girls. He would have preferred to throw the whole lot away, but they were the only street clothes he had for now. Instead he stuffed everything, including his shoes and stocking cap, into the washer and dumped in an abundance of detergent.

He had scrubbed himself down in the shower last night, but took another bath this morning. Afterward he examined his battered body in the full-length mirror on the back of the bathroom door. The swelling of his leg was slowly diminishing, as was the pain. The long scar down the side of his head was also healing, but he would forever be a beard guy. The scar was there to stay, always a reminder of how whimsical death could be in its selection of who went along and who stayed.

While Lloyd waited for his clothes to finish, he made himself a cup of Casey's tea and settled down to watch the local news. The tea would never replace his beloved black coffee, but it somehow seemed to please Casey when he drank a cup with her, and he was determined to learn to like it.

It was a good news day, and the anchor on the TV was running through the usual roll-call of local crimes, events, and other newsworthy happenings.

A foxy young female was on site where yet another local festival was about to start up. The theme of this one was the local Creole Zydeco music, and the crowd was ramping up for the day-long party.

As the mug-shot of a middle-aged, stone-faced man with ruddy eastern-European complexion and eyes like bullet holes appeared on the screen, the anchor explained that he had been arrested for running a prostitution ring. Up to thirty women, most of whom spoke little or no English, had been released from semi-slavery in a late-night raid.

A new facility to serve the needs of the poor and homeless was being planned. It would be located in a renovated church building just a few blocks from where its predecessor, the Union of Hearts Mission, had operated prior to Katrina.

Until then Lloyd had been mentally planning his day, but the mention of Union of Hearts grabbed his attention. He set his tea aside and leaned forward just as J.T. Raintree's handsome, charismatic face appeared on the screen.

"All credit and praise goes to the Lord for giving my organization the means and motivation to renew this vital service in a tragically devastated neighborhood," Raintree said into the microphone being held in front of him. "The needs of this stricken community are greater than ever before, and I'm humbled by the opportunity to serve God's children with yet another outreach facility in our city."

The clip was short, but Lloyd ran it back three times, studying the man's face, tone, and declaration carefully. Lloyd had thought of Raintree many times since his tumble off that balcony, always wondering what part the evangelist and humanitarian might have in the confusing jumble of events and discoveries Lloyd had made since coming to New Orleans. Was it possible that a publicly revered figure like Raintree might actually be mixed up in such risky endeavors as drug distribution, strip clubs, and even murder?

Lloyd was realistic enough to know that he would probably never learn the truth, or even random pieces of it, but that didn't stop the questions from haunting him.

When his clothes were clean and dry, Lloyd dressed and left. He walked the French Quarter end-to-end, finally reaching Canal Street downtown. It was the farthest he had strayed from Casey's house since she brought him there, and being out so long in the daylight added to the risk. But Canal was where his bank was located, and he needed money.

He stopped at a teller machine outside the bank and was pleased to find that his card still worked. The twenty-eight hundred dollars in the account seemed like a fortune to him now, but he vowed to be frugal with it. There was no way to predict when he might have a chance to earn more. He withdrew two hundred dollars.

His next stop was a drugstore, where he bought a cheap burner phone. His battered old phone was completely dead since that morning at the concrete pier, although he did not know whether it simply needed a charge or had finally succumbed to the harsh treatment it had suffered. While he was there, he also bought a couple of pocket flashlights and extra batteries.

Next on his pilgrimage was a thrift store. The dingy old clothes he had on were good enough for lurking around the streets at night like a bum, but he knew there would be times when he would not want to appear quite so sordid. Even though Casey had come up with the old clothes for him, he was beginning to feel embarrassed when he constantly wore them around her.

Heading back to Casey's with his purchases, Lloyd pondered one final bit of risky business that he needed to take care of, and he decided that tonight was as good a time as any to get it done.

* * *

Lloyd squeezed through the rusty iron gate, hardly worrying as it moaned in protest. It was two in the morning, and the risk of anybody in a place like this hearing the noise and caring what it was seemed slim. Off in the distance he could hear faint strains of jazz from at least two different sources. The moon was up, but little light filtered through the canopy of trees into the courtyard of his previous flophouse residence. Turning on one of his small flashlights, he made his way through the weeds and uneven flagstone pavement. He was less worried about somebody seeing him, and more concerned that he might stumble over something, fall, and hurt his injured leg.

About twenty feet beyond the gate he stopped and looked down at the spot where he and Slam had landed after falling from the balcony, the two of them clinging to each other like lovers in a suicide pact. He was startled to see the puddles and splatters of blood still on the flagstones, now cured to a dark brown, cracked and curling like dry clay mud. It hadn't rained since the big fight, and nobody had bothered to even hose the dead man's blood away.

Lloyd wondered who this guy Slam, had been, where he came from and how he happened to end up in the company of alley rat like Tats. He wondered if the corpse was ever identified by the police, and if his family even knew he was dead. None of it really mattered, he supposed. There were some people who left the world a better place when they made their exit.

He hadn't concocted any detailed plan for tonight's mission. All he knew for sure was that he didn't want to hurt anyone if possible, and of course didn't want to get hurt himself. He carried no weapon except his cane, which he vowed to use only in the direst circumstances.

Going up the outside wooden stairs, he encountered only one person, a drunken old woman who hobbled up each step as if it was a gruesome challenge. She showed no sign that she even knew Lloyd was there, several steps behind her, and shuffled away down the second-floor walkway without ever glancing back.

The key to his old room on the third floor still slid smoothly into the lock and turned the latch, as Lloyd assumed it would. The management of this lice farm wouldn't be likely to change locks every time another down-and-outer moved out. He had hoped the room would be empty, but as he swung the door open, he saw an enormous mound of human flesh in the dim light, wearing only a dingy pair of boxers, lying face-down on the bed where Lloyd had spent so many miserable nights. His snores were even, rhythmic, and somehow calm, despite his bulk.

"Hey, whadda you doin' in my room?" Lloyd said. The snoring ceased for a moment, then resumed, and the man made no movement to look around or get up. Lloyd repeated the challenge a little louder, with the same results. This big fat man was down for the count, probably as drunk as the woman he'd seen on the stairs. During the weeks Lloyd had lived here, he came to understand that this place was a common waystation for hard core drunks and junkies on their downward journey to the gutter or the grave.

He closed the door and turned the latch, then carried a wooden chair to the middle of the room, just below the air vent. Climbing up on the chair with his bad leg was harder than he anticipated, and pain lanced up his thigh as he put his weight on it without the help of the cane. He still had a way to go yet.

Holding the flashlight with his teeth he fumbled at the screws above him, suddenly eager for the reassuring feel of his weapons again. Both were still there, wrapped in a worn-out tee-shirt. He stuck them one-by-one in the waistband of his jeans, then reached back in for the two boxes of ammunition he had also stashed there. Those went in his shirt for now. Next, he felt around in the small dark hole above him until he found the canvas wallet he had stuffed fat with tips from the hotel garage. He had no idea how much was in there, but knew that however much it was, it would come in handy in the days and weeks ahead. And finally, he pulled out an envelope containing the fading photos he had recovered from Billy's ravaged home. It was a strange feeling to realize that they somehow had value to him.

Chapter Nineteen

The rented house where they lived when Bennie died sat on a hillside that sloped gradually down to the meandering creek where the little boy drowned. The foundation of the house, built of local limestone, was at street level in front, but in back it was a stone wall over six feet high. There was a wood plank door in the back wall, too short for a grown man to enter without ducking his head.

When they first moved in, his mother had warned her three kids that the would-be cellar below the house was probably a favorite gathering place for rats and snakes and all sorts of evil, dangerous insects. Her intent was to scare them away from ever going inside the dirt-floored cavity, but of course Lloyd had to check the place out the first time he got a chance. There was little of interest to see in there—a few rusty yard tools, random piece of furniture beyond repair, decaying cardboard boxes of worthless belongings left behind by previous tenants. It wouldn't even serve for a clubhouse because of the damp stench inside, and the labyrinth of spider webs as thick as tropical forest foliage.

But things were different after Bennie exited their lives. Lloyd needed a place to go, away from his mother and sister, an isolated retreat where he could do battle with dark demons and raging terrors that seemed to have taken possession of his soul. He found that solace in the dark damp cellar, and there, with his knees pulled up and his eyes closed tight, he did his best not to think about anything or anybody, present or past. He never had believed in ghosts and that sort of nonsense, but sometimes it almost seemed to Lloyd that he could feel the presence of Bennie in there with him. It wasn't like his spirit was floating around in the air, draped with cobwebs and glowing faintly like the fluorescent hands on a watch. It was something more than a memory, something less than an actual part of Bennie left behind when the living, walking, talking, thinking person—the real Bennie—went away. And somehow that presence, unreal though it might be, gave Lloyd a measure of relief from the guilt he bore.

It eventually got better. Most things did, given time. A few months later when his mother moved them out of the shabby, run-down house and into a shabby, run-down duplex not far away, Lloyd made no attempt to find another dark hideaway to replace the one they had left behind.

But in the ensuing years, he sometimes wondered, irrationally, whether Bennie's spirit had stayed behind to haunt the place where he died and the strangers who replaced his family, or if he left when they left, and was with them still, as his mother desperately wanted to believe.

Both the second and third-floor windows of the old abandoned building provided a perfect vantage point from which to watch the goings on at Club Les Girls across the street. That first night he just sat there on a stack of old packing crates near a window, gaining a better understanding of the building he was watching. The ground floor was easy enough. The club was there, and on one side of the building was a narrow alley, barely wide enough for a car to pull in and park in back. All the windows on the second floor were blacked out, so he could only guess at what was there. Storage, perhaps, or even cubbies where the girls could take privileged customers for the most intimate of encounters. The third floor appeared to be apartments or bedrooms. There were curtains on the windows, and in one room where the curtains were open and a light was on, he saw part of a bed, a chest of drawers, and a small makeup table and chair. On the roof was the usual clutter of HVAC units, random wires stretched in all directions, and two satellite dishes.

Toward the back of the roof was a small structure that Lloyd though might be a stairwell.

As he watched the sidewalk out front, the usual stereotype customers came and went, all men. Most were met at the door by a woman with a predatory smile, who immediately got a fishhook grip on their arms and drew them inside.

It had been harder than he expected to access the building he was in now. The partially open side door that he had discovered on his first visit to the alley was not open wide enough to squeeze in, and refused to budge. By climbing on an abandoned stack of metal drums he was finally able to scale the wall at the back of the alley, although much pain was involved in that process. Behind the building he found a small parking area and a loading dock. Access to the area was restricted by the walls of other buildings and ten-foot chain link fences. By climbing up a fire ladder against the building, he was able to reach the roof of the dock, and from there he got inside the building through a broken second-story window.

The inside of the building was gutted and empty. Nearly all the windows were broken, and shattered glass crunched under his shoes with every step. From the look of things, Lloyd guessed that the building might have been a victim of Katrina's fury, but what purpose it served before the hurricane's devastation was anybody's guess. Exploring the place as best he could by the light of his little flashlight, he discovered that the back part of the roof was rotten and falling in. The only hope for whoever owned this place would probably be to tear it down and start over, but he guessed that sort of drastic action might well be prohibited by laws protecting historic buildings in the French Quarter. The owner was probably stuck with it the way it was.

It was nearly midnight now, and the traffic in and out of Club Les Girls was dwindling. Lloyd washed down the last of his hamburger with the last of his bottle of water, then went back to a far corner to take a leak. He was beginning to think about how he could get out of here now that he was in. He recalled seeing several wooden pallets scattered around the dock, and thought he might be able to stack enough of them up to get him back over the brick wall. He dreaded the discomfort that would accompany that little task.

When he got back to his window, he noticed a man on the sidewalk outside the door of the club, talking to a tired-looking dancer who looked like she would love to be almost anywhere but there. It was Tats, and he had his trademark backpack slung over one shoulder. He seemed to be trying to talk the woman into something, but from the look of things, she was having nothing to do with it. She kept stepping back from him, slapping his groping hands and resolutely shaking her head. She took a last pull on her cigarette, tossed it into the street and went back inside. Tats laughed out loud, as if it was all in good fun, and took a drag on his own smoke.

Lloyd raised his hand like a kid playing cops and robbers, pointed one finger at Tats, and let his thumb fall like the hammer of a revolver. "Pop!" he muttered, smiling to himself.

* * *

Lloyd raised the glass of wine, his second, took a drink, and smiled at the woman sitting across the small round table. She seemed to be watching the glass, not him, and he knew a scolding would be coming along pretty soon.

"I'll stop at four," he said. "I promise."

The woman shook her head in mock disapproval. "That's too many, but okay, just this once." Then she smiled too, letting him know she was only toying with him.

Tran Ngo looked pretty and relaxed tonight, dressed modestly in a cotton blouse and skirt instead of her usual clinic whites. She wore just a few touches of makeup that accentuated her almond Asian eyes and small, delicate lips. During her visits to Casey's house to care for his wounds Lloyd had guessed her to be in her late forties or early fifties, but tonight she looked younger.

"I'm glad you called, Tran," Lloyd told her. "Things were getting so dull around Casey's house that I was starting to talk to the fish." Although Casey had only planned to be gone for a couple of days to visit her family, she had called him at her house to let him know she had decided to stay longer. She hadn't really explained why, and he didn't ask, but it was clear that things weren't going well for her.

"That's one of the reasons Casey called me. She thought you would be getting bored and lonely, and might enjoy getting out with a friend."

A young waitress with snow white hair and thick, colorful makeup carried a tray over and began to fill up the top of the table with small dishes and bowls of odd-looking food, none of which Lloyd could easily identify.

"See, I told you it would be interesting," Tran said.

"And you were right," Lloyd said.

"Tapas is really the trend in New Orleans, and you did say to order for both of us." Tran studied his face and seemed amused by his reaction to the small, unfamiliar helpings of food. "But you don't have to like everything. You're a man, so you're forgiven if you only eat the meat dishes."

Lloyd was glad to give it a try, even though it wasn't the kind of food he would have expected in an old refurbished nineteenth century saloon like this one. He picked up some kind of meat tart in a pastry shell and took a bite. Unfamiliar, but tasty, he decided. Tran started off with a bean sprout and yoghurt concoction on top of a slice of cucumber.

"Casey also asked me to tell you why she's staying away so much longer than she expected," Tran said.

"I've been wondering," Lloyd said, "but I didn't feel like I had any right to ask about her personal affairs."

"That's partly right, Lloyd. She is a very private person, and she doesn't know you well. She's embarrassed to tell you herself, but your lives are intertwined now, for a time, and she though you should know at least the basics."

Intertwined. It was an interesting choice of words.

"Casey's husband in Canada has started the procedure for a divorce, and last week his lawyer sent her the first stack of paperwork. His grounds are abandonment, which is so terribly unfair to Casey. He knew she came here because her parents needed her, and he knew she planned to go back to him as soon as she could. But Casey understands, finally, that he doesn't want her back. This abandonment thing is merely a ploy to make him the injured party, and to take everything they have for himself."

"The guy's a real gold-plated bastard, isn't he?" Lloyd said.

"Yes, but we don't always make good choice when we fall in love, do we? I'm a classic example of that."

"And me too, I suppose," Lloyd admitted. "But now I can see why Casey was too embarrassed to tell me about this."

"She is embarrassed, and humiliated, and ashamed, and angry, and feeling a dozen other emotions, too. She still loves him, even while she hates him."

Lloyd didn't say anything. All the replies that came to mind seemed cliché.

"She'll come back, and time will pass, and she will heal," Tran said.

* * *

By midnight, Lloyd was back in his observation post in the building across from Les Girls. It was a chilly night, and a drizzling rain had started. No girls stood like bait outside the front door, and few customers came and went. The place might as well be closed, but no girls left. It was a tough game, and most of them probably needed the money for the next toot, for hungry kids at home, or for some worthless boyfriend who waited in a shabby apartment to confiscate her nightly earnings.

Lloyd began to take mental notes about the things that would make this surveillance job a little easier. A chair would be good, maybe one of those folding canvas lawn chairs that collapsed and slid into a bag. A pair of binoculars might come in handy, although he'd have to buy them cheap in the French Market. Toilet paper might be called for once in a while, and a plastic poncho would be welcome on rainy nights like this.

It had also occurred to him that he needed a second way out, just in case. All the windows on the first floor were boarded over and it was a pretty long jump from the second floor to the ground. A hundred feet of heavy rope, knotted every couple of feet, would do the trick for that.

Lloyd considered how reassuring it would feel to begin carrying around one of the hand guns he had recently retrieved, but the risk was too great. He still moved around the French Quarter in his rumpled bum clothes, and the cops were always rousting people like that for the slightest provocation, or for no reason at all. He could imagine what righteous delight Pepper would get at patting him down and finding a loaded gun on his person. If there was any cell in the city jail that resembled a Bastille dungeon, Lloyd knew that was where he would end up.

At something past one in the morning, a long dark Cadillac SUV turned into the alley between Les Girls and the building next door, disappearing behind the club. The alley was dark, and Lloyd was too far away to read the license plate. The driver never came around to enter by the front door, so Lloyd decided he must have gone in through some back entrance. That was good information to have.

It started raining harder, and for a long time no customers came or went from the front door of Club Les Girls. By two a.m. the dancers began to come out, in their street clothes now, carrying umbrellas that threatened to turn inside out with every gust of wind that blew down the canyon of buildings. A few minutes later the neon lights out front went dark.

Lloyd sat for a moment, watching the sheets of rain blow by, listening to the sound of the wind threading through the broken windows of the decaying building. It was a long way back to Casey's house, and he debated whether to wait it out or resolve to get soaked on the deserted streets. Add a sleeping bag and pillow to the wish list, he thought.

He had made up his mind to go, and to hell with the weather, when a light blinked on in the third-floor bedroom directly across the street from where he was. Marta came to the window and stared out. For a moment Lloyd had the unsettling feeling that her gaze was somehow penetrating the darkness of the abandoned building and fixing on him. But he knew she must be simply watching the rain.

Marta reached one hand behind her for a moment, doing something he couldn't see, then she raised both hands and moved the straps of her dress off her shoulders. As it slid smoothly down to the floor, she remained where she was, still staring out. Her body was about what Lloyd would have expected, somewhere between slim and emaciated. Time, drugs, and the life she led portrayed her story on the canvas of her body.

A man was moving around in the room behind her, undressing. Marta said something but didn't turn away from the window, not just yet. Eventually the man joined her at the window, naked to the waist, and Lloyd was not particularly surprised that it was Rudy Soyez. He gripped her arm, none too gently, and pulled her away from the window, away from her reverie, beyond Lloyd's view. Neither of them even bothered to turn the light off. Maybe that was part of their thing, Lloyd thought.

Lloyd glanced down the street at a streetlight and decided that the rain had let up enough for him to pack up and go.

When he got back to Casey's house, he saw the suitcase at the bottom of the stairs and knew that she was back, earlier than he expected. The light was on in the kitchen and a half-empty teacup sat on the kitchen table, but it was cold to the touch. He heard no sounds of her stirring around upstairs, and decided not to call up and let her know that he was back. Making as little noise as possible, he went to his small improvised bedroom by the garden and got ready for bed.

Chapter Twenty

Kelly had stayed awake, waiting for Lloyd to come home, which was unusual. The TV was off, and the house was quiet. A half-empty pint of whiskey sat on the table at her elbow. Beside it was a sweaty tumbler with several ice cubes melting in the amber liquor. Her eyes were red, as if she had been crying earlier, but there were no tears now as she told him to sit down and pointed to a sofa across the room, far from her.

"I've been trying to work up the nerve to tell you this, Lloyd, and I guess tonight's the night."

Oddly, the announcement came as no surprise to Lloyd. As his wife began to spill it all out, he felt only a life-weary melancholy, tinged with a measure of relief that this moment had come at last.

"I didn't know her name or anything about her. Not where she worked, or how they met, or when they were together, or why she somehow became a part of our lives. I guess I felt like if I didn't know any of those things, then maybe she didn't really exist. Like having something terribly wrong inside of you, but not wanting to go to a doctor and hear it said out loud."

Casey hardly looked at Lloyd as the story of her failed married unfolded. Mostly she gazed down into the delicate porcelain cup that she cradled in both hands, as if she might find solace in its warmth, and answers in its scattering of tea leaves. Occasionally her eyes drifted to one side, to a manila envelope that apparently contained the sheath of official papers her husband had sent her to sign.

"I guess I learned that from my mother, what a woman should do, or not do, at times like that. My father had his faithless years too, and they got through it, so I suppose I hoped that Scott and I could, too. Now, when it's too late, I see that it was actually a hateful example of *what not to do* at times like that."

Lloyd felt uncomfortable hearing all this. He had known this woman for less than a month, and yet she was opening up her heart to him with such complete intimacy. It wasn't like he had learned anything of value from his own divorce. All he could have told her was that there was lots of pain and ugliness ahead, which wasn't what she needed to hear.

But here they were, sitting at the kitchen table, their breakfast plates still in front of them, her tea and his coffee growing cold. And he was getting far too deep a look into the soul of a woman who was in many ways still a stranger to him.

"One thing that surprises me is that I'm the one who should be hating him. I should want to see him absolutely destroyed for what he's done. But it's the other way around. I always thought I was a good wife to him, and yet he hates me, and wants to take everything we had, everything we built together in fourteen years of marriage. The divorce papers say I abandoned him. What kind of cruel joke is that?" Lloyd watched her glance down to the manila envelope like a third hateful presence in the kitchen.

Again and again, Lloyd thought of things he might say, words of consolation, snippets of presumed wisdom, or simple validation that Casey's husband must be among the vilest of men. But he knew that she wasn't telling him these things because he might have valuable advice to offer. They just had to be said to somebody, and he was there.

"My brother thinks I should hire lawyers in Toronto and fight him for my share of everything, the house and all our other properties and investments. It's a lot of money. We lived well. But I just don't have the heart for a prolonged fight like that, and I'm afraid of the type of person it would turn me into."

Without asking Lloyd whether he wanted more coffee, Casey took his cup over and refilled it from the pot on the counter. It was one of those ancient percolators that people used back in the seventies, but it looked almost new. An appliance like that probably hadn't seen much use over the decades in a traditional Asian household like this. As Lloyd stirred in the appropriate dosages of cream and sugar, Casey took their breakfast plates to the sink and started running hot water. She was one of those people who couldn't remain idle for long.

"Thank you for watching over the house while I was gone," Casey said unexpectedly.

"Are you kidding?" Lloyd said. "After all you've done for me? I was honored that you trusted me enough to let me stay here alone."

"I do trust you, Lloyd, and I'm glad you're here."

They lapsed into small talk about her visit to her family, mostly just to keep the silence at bay. When the dishes were finished, she went upstairs to shower and dress. Later he went with her to help reopen her parents' store after several days' absence. The heavy iron bars over the windows and doors had kept intruders out, but some of the fresh produce, meats, and dairy products had spoiled while she was gone. While Casey was busy tending to customers and taking care of the business side of things, Lloyd did the yeoman's work of cleaning out coolers, sweeping and mopping floors, and stocking shelves.

It was hard work, the first he had done in weeks, and by eight that evening when Casey locked the door and they got in her car, Lloyd was aching and exhausted. They took home some of the leftover Asian food that Casey had been selling to her customers all day, and that was supper.

Casey asked him about how he spent his time while she was away, and Lloyd talked about his various excursions around the French Quarter and downtown, leaving out his nightly vigils in the abandoned building across from Les Girls. From the start, Lloyd had vowed to himself that he would not lie to this kindhearted woman. But that didn't mean he was ready to tell her everything, at least not yet.

But was silence a lie? He didn't know.

Vague ideas about how he should deal with the people who had nearly killed him, the same people who might well have done something similar to his father, were beginning to develop shape and substance. Right now, though, it would only alarm Casey if he started filling in the picture, and revealing to her the darker side of who he was. She deserved better than that, especially now when her own burden was so overwhelming. Lloyd wondered if a time might soon come when he too would need to leave her.

He woke in the middle of the night slumped down on the couch in the living room. He and Casey had come in here after supper to watch a movie, but after the day he'd put in at the store, he didn't last long. Casey was long gone, and it was dark and quiet upstairs. Staggering to his feet, still half asleep, Lloyd checked the locks and deadbolts on the front and back doors just as he once had done when he had a home of his own. All was well and secure. He shrugged out of his shirt and jeans in his own room by the patio, then piled down on his bed and was back asleep in a moment.

* * *

The next morning was bright and lovely. Lloyd was awakened just past dawn by the sound of the footsteps upstairs. A few minutes later Casey came down, already wearing her street clothes, and Lloyd took his turn at bathing. By the time he came back to the kitchen, she already had a light breakfast, croissants, fruit and juice, laid out on the patio table.

"I put the coffee on," Casey told him. "It should be almost ready." They might still be somewhat strangers to one another, but she had learned that much about him. "Scott never was a coffee drinker, so you'll have to tell me if I'm making it right."

"It's been fine," Lloyd said. "What's the occasion?"

"Nothing in particular," Casey said. She smiled at him, but looking at her face, he could tell that sleep had not come as readily for her. Her morning cheer seemed to be a front.

"When my parents lived here, they used to eat a lot of their meals outside, just like they did back in Viet Nam. They brought me over to the U.S. when I was very young, but I remember the little postage stamp patio and garden behind our house over there that looked like this. Maybe that's why my father designed this one the way he did, so it would seem like home." She smiled again, and Lloyd realized how seldom he had seen a smile on her face.

Lloyd went in the kitchen for coffee, and when he came back out, everything was ready. He sat across from Casey at a small wrought-iron table and buttered a croissant.

"I have to go to the store early this morning, and I'll probably be back late," Casey said. "I'm getting quite a few deliveries today, and I have to check everything and stock the shelves. Plus, my helper, Estrella, has disappeared again. I'm worried that immigration might have caught her because it's been over a week. Or she might be hiding from her husband again."

"I'd like to go help you again," Lloyd said.

"No, that's not necessary. You're still recovering."

"I want to, Casey. I admit that this busted body is not up to par yet, but I'll do what I can."

"Okay then, I could use the help. But only if you promise to stop and rest once in a while."

Her mothering made it Lloyd's turn to smile. "I promise."

It was easy enough to learn the routine up front in the store, but considerably harder to keep an eye out for the pilfering that was bound to occur in a neighborhood like this. With most of the kids and teenagers, he simply made them put things back or pay for the small items that they guiltily stashed away. But when one bedraggled old man started to leave with a can of beer bulging in his pants pocket, Lloyd ignored the petty larceny and rang up a dollar from his own pocket.

Casey was all over, signing for deliveries from the supply trucks, opening the cartons and pricing the contents, and stocking the shelves. Both she and Lloyd worked the deli counter. It was a new experience for him, and it felt good to finally be paying her back for her many kindnesses.

When they closed up that night, Lloyd was worn out again. Casey built him a hero sandwich to take home for supper, and ladled up a container of some kind of noodle concoction for herself.

Things were pretty much the same all week. Lloyd went to work with her every day, overriding her protests, and every night he went to bed feeling the righteous exhaustion of a hardworking man. By Saturday morning, he was looking forward to Sunday, when the store was closed.

Lloyd was pleased and surprised by how comfortable he and Casey were becoming with each other. It had been a long time since he had spent so much time around another person, but he didn't miss his solitude. She didn't talk a lot, although she and Tran had long phone conversations almost every evening, mostly in their own language. She hardly mentioned her husband to him, but he did catch his name from time to time when she was talking to her friend in Vietnamese.

The Saturday trade was steady all day, and Casey spent a lot of her time up front with Lloyd. One thing that interested him was the diversity of language of the people who came into the store. For his part, Lloyd relied primarily on the cash register totals and a crazy mix of hand gestures to communicate with customers whose English was poor. Casey was more effective. Besides her fluent Vietnamese and English, she seemed to have some command of Chinese, especially for food items, and her Spanish wasn't bad.

By late afternoon beer sales started increasing. Casey had finished most of her other work and was staying up front to help Lloyd at the register. It was nearly dark outside, and people were beginning to get off work, so business was brisk. Because they were busy, Lloyd hardly noticed the three young men until they were in the store and slouching back toward the beer coolers along the wall opposite the checkout counter.

"Uh-oh!" he said in a low voice. He immediately turned to face the cigarette racks behind the counter.

"What is it?" Casey asked, startled by his abrupt about-face. Out of the corner of his eye, Lloyd saw her hand drop to the shelf just under the counter where a .38 revolver laid ready.

"I recognize a couple of those guys, the ones back by the coolers," Lloyd told her. "From that night."

"The night you got thrown off the balcony?"

"Yep. One was there for sure, and probably the other ones too."

Their quiet talk was interrupted when a short, husky Mexican came up and set two twelve-packs of off-brand beer on the counter. His filthy jeans and denim shirt attested to the fact that his vocation had something to do with mud. He pulled a folded stack of cash out of his front pocket and peeled off two twenties. Casey rang the beer up and gave him his change.

"I don't think they recognized me, but I need to go in back just in case," Lloyd said when the Mexican had gone. "Don't worry if I don't come back right away. I have an idea."

Casey was startled by the intrigue, but said nothing more as Lloyd threaded between the close rows of shelves and through the door to the back storage and office area.

By the time the three young men left the store, Lloyd was outside waiting in the shadows on one side of the building. As they walked under a street lamp, he clearly recognized one of them as a member of the posse that Tats usually brought with him to haunt the dim alley near Jackson Square. Another one brought to mind a dim memory of a half-scared, half excited face, seen only for an instant, on the balcony outside his rented room. His nose didn't look quite straight, and Lloyd thought this one might have been the recipient of his desperate swing of the confiscated baseball bat before he and Slam went over the side. The third didn't look familiar, but hanging out with the other two made him suspect enough.

He let them get half a block ahead before falling in behind. He ducked his head as he passed under the first streetlight, but quickly realized that no precautions were probably necessary. Each of them had taken a beer out of the sacks they were carrying, and they seemed to be more interested in roughhousing and talking in loud, boisterous tones than they did in checking their back trail.

After two blocks they crossed the street and took a right onto another side street. Lloyd hurried up, worried that he would lose them, but when he reached the corner they were still in sight. He hurried his pace and closed the distance with his prey. Just before they reached the end of the block, they turned right again and went up a sidewalk into a run-down house. It was a long and narrow clapboard building, as were the other houses nearby, and even in the near dark it was easy to see the neglect and decay, again like its fellows. Stopping out front for a moment, Lloyd noticed that all the lights were on, and through thin shabby curtains he could see people moving around inside. Through an open window he heard a woman shrill out some profanity, and the sound of laughter followed.

Lloyd went to the end of the block, crossed the street, and walked back on the other side. It was Saturday night, party night, and judging from the noise they were already making, he could only imagine how rowdy this place would get before the night was over.

When he was with the KCPD, he and his fellow officers knew to never barge into a place like this alone. If a complaint was called in, they went in with plenty of backup, and full-scale warfare still erupted sometimes.

A dark form approached down the sidewalk, and Lloyd took a step back to give the passer-by plenty of room. He and the other man eyed each other suspiciously, and the man seemed to hesitate when he was still a few paces away. Lloyd couldn't tell whether the man was expecting trouble or ready to hand some out, but he passed on by.

It served to remind Lloyd that he was in a tough neighborhood, and he was taking an unnecessary risk just standing out here any longer. But he knew where the house was now, and this would not be his last visit.

His cell phone rang when he was halfway back to the store. He reassured Casey that he was alright and nearly there.

* * *

"They run with Tats," Lloyd explained to Casey. They were in the car on the way back home, and Casey was driving. "I don't know much about any of them except that they help him peddle his drugs on the street, and do a lot worse things than that if he tells them to. Like shoving a guy off a third-floor balcony in the middle of the night."

He couldn't read her reaction to what he was telling her. She kept her eyes on the street ahead, handling the wheel with both hands at ten and two like she was taking a driving test, her face expressionless.

"When you took me in, Casey, I didn't have much on my mind except not dying under a concrete wharf," he said. "But now that I'm getting better and stronger, I keep thinking that these punks shouldn't get away with what they tried to do. They shouldn't, and the people who sent them after me shouldn't."

"But what can you do, Lloyd?"

"I have no idea," he said. "I know I can't go to the police. All I could tell them would be a lunatic story with no evidence and no witnesses, weeks after the whole thing happened. And at the first sign of trouble, Tats and his bunch would disappear like mist. I'd be left trying to explain how I ended up in a flophouse courtyard with a dead man under me to break my fall. They shoot nasty stuff into people's veins for things like that.

"All I've got going for me right now is that they think I'm dead, and if I had any brains, I guess I'd settle for that. I'd go on back home and try to figure out how to put my life together again. Right now, you and Tran, and I guess my pal Chester, are the only people in this city that know I'm still alive. And that's something else I have to worry about. If I decided to stay here and do something reckless and crazy, I might drag you right into the middle of it just because you were kind enough patch me up and let me sleep in your parlor. What good sense I still have tells me that it's time for me to leave."

"I'm not afraid," Casey said softly. "I have my own dragons to deal with, and yours don't scare me. Maybe you should stay a little longer and see if the answers come."

Chapter Twenty-One

On a routine call to the run-down riverside district of Kansas City, Lloyd and his partner, Tony Achilles, found the foaming, writhing, moaning remains of a young man of about twenty. He died before the ambulance could get there, the needle still dangling in his arm.

"We had to buy from new guy 'cause you took our regular guy to jail," a filthy, rancid girl of maybe fifteen explained to Lloyd and Tony as they helplessly watched the life seep out of her companion. She wore her blond hair in frizzy dreadlocks that looked like they hadn't been washed for weeks, and held a a man's brown overcoat tightly around her against the cold.

"So this is our fault?" Tony challenged.

"You an' him, or whoever hauled Mario in. He was a straight-up guy. We could trust his H."

"What's this man's name?"

"Dean. Dean something. We hooked up a couple of days ago, and we were on our way to San Diego. I got some friends out there."

The ambulance came and the attendants loaded up Dean Something's body as carefully as if he had typhoid. Somewhere in the confusion the girl disappeared, but Lloyd and Tony didn't care.

Two days later another patrol found her in the same alley. San Diego was off the itinerary for good.

From his vantage point in the empty building across from Les Girls, Lloyd spotted Tats and one of his flunkies going into the bar. They brought a girl with them, a plump young blond, so wasted that Tats' companion had to keep her upright and steer her along with an arm clamped tightly around her waist. Soon she would probably be completely unconscious, and Lloyd did not want to even imagine what kind of circumstances she would find herself in when she woke up tomorrow.

Lloyd snapped a picture of her through the zoom lens of Casey's Canon, although he wasn't sure what use he could ever make of it.

This was his first night in the warehouse since Casey came home a week ago, and he had told her that he probably wouldn't be back until very late. She would have to tend to the store alone tomorrow, which she assured him that she could manage.

It was a slow Tuesday night at Les Girls. The usual kinds of customers came and went occasionally—rumpled business men drunk beyond the limits of good sense, rowdy young guys bursting with hormones, old loners submitting to the lure of girls young enough to be their children's children.

At one point during a lull, Marta, came outside and joined a couple of the dancers on the sidewalk for a smoke. She wore a sleek satin dress that shimmered like treasure in the glow of a streetlight, and her long black hair stirred in the breeze. Lloyd recalled her invitation to show him the daytime sights of the city in her true and guileless persona, Mary Lucchesi, and he wondered again what that was all about. Was she just wanting to spend some time with a man that didn't involve sleaze and sex and hard cash, or to find out more about what he was up to and how much of a threat he posed? Lloyd supposed it didn't matter.

But now the exotic mystique that she brought to the table the first night they met was gone. She was Rudy Soyez's woman, and hopelessly entangled in all the evil that fact involved—prostitution, drugs, abductions, and even murder. She belonged to the man who might be responsible for the death of Lloyd's father, and who also thought he had successfully ordered the murder of Lloyd himself. Something cold and dark rose within Lloyd when he considered this reality in such harsh terms.

When the familiar dark SUV turned into the narrow alley beside the bar, Marta tossed her smoke in the street and went back inside.

The two dancers out front tapped at their phones for a few more minutes, then went back in. For a few minutes the street was empty and quiet, except of course, for the distant cacophony of music a few blocks away on Bourbon Street. Lloyd finished the contents of one of the water bottles he brought along, then tossed it across the littered floor. He had a package of Oreos in his backpack, but decided to save them for later. Since he hadn't been back here in well over a week, he planned to stay late, at least until the bar closed, in case anything interesting and unexpected happened.

Without warning, the metal door of the bar blasted open, slamming violently against the brick wall outside and jolting Lloyd from his momentary reverie. As if propelled by some unknown force inside, the blond girl that Tats and his friend had dragged in a few minutes earlier erupted through the opening, staggering on rubbery legs, waving her arms in the air and shouting hysterically. Off balance and out of control, she fell forward on her hands and knees, scraping her flesh on the rough pavement. A couple of the other girls hurried after her, helping her up and trying to calm her.

But the blond would have none of it. Shouting, "No! I won't!" she wrestled in the grasp of the other two girls, trying to break free.

"Let her go," a calm voice said from the doorway. It was Marta. "She'd be nothing but trouble."

The two dancers looked over at Marta, then obediently released their captive. The blond took off like frantic, fleeing prey, racing clumsily toward the lights, noise, people and salvation so close ahead on Bourbon Street.

Lloyd wondered if the wrecked blond girl would remember any of this tomorrow, and possibly learn a lesson. Or would she just wake up in pain, wondering how she had managed to do so much damage to her knees and palms. And he wondered if she would ever realize that one of biggest turning points of her life might have been when she fled the hellish life that two strangers had almost led her into.

Eventually Tats and his sidekick came back out, each carrying a backpack over one shoulder. They talked briefly outside, then split up, heading in opposite directions up and down the street.

Lloyd had a pretty good idea what the backpacks contained, and the timing of the players seemed to work. *Tats and his stooge arrive carrying empty backpacks. Less than half an hour later, Soyez shows up and parks in back. Allow a little time for Soyez to collect yesterday's take from Tats, and give them a fresh supply of crap to peddle on the street. Then out comes Tats and friend, ready to go pollute the bodies, minds and souls of the usual local druggies.*

It all made sense, but Lloyd knew that if his speculations were wrong, he could be headed down a dead-end street. He had to be sure.

The next night Lloyd left the camera and anything else of value at Casey's house, and went out in full homeless bum attire. He was glad that she had already gone upstairs because he knew she would be curious, and he didn't want to have to explain his bizarre plans.

Passing down the length of the French Quarter, he limped along the back streets, knowing that at this late hour the police wouldn't tolerate his kind mingling with the tourists and staggering drunk partiers over on Bourbon. He kept his head down and exaggerated his clumsy limp, getting better and better at his non-person role each time he hit the streets in this getup.

When he turned down the street where Les Girls was located, nobody was standing outside the bar, and he managed to slip into the dark alley beside the abandoned building unnoticed. Once there, he knew he was unseen and safe. But tonight he stayed in the alley instead of making his way to his usual vantage point. For the first couple of hours it was business as usual across the street. Tats arrived at what seemed to be his usual time, between eleven-thirty and midnight, accompanied this time by a different flunky, but no new recruit for the pole inside. A half hour passed, but the black SUV with the tinted windows, presumably driven by Rudy Soyez, never arrived.

Lloyd hoped that Soyez's absence didn't mean that there would be no exchange of cash for goods tonight, and that his time spent in the filthy, stinking alley was not in vain.

The two punks finally emerged some time past midnight, both their backpacks appearing heavier than when they went in. As before, they paused outside to talk for a minute, the only difference being that this time Lloyd was close enough to overhear the conversation.

"Alright, shithead," Tats said. "This is your test run. You wouldn't be here at all if Bobby hadn't decided that he could be a mule at night and a purse snatcher in the daytime. I hope that little weasel is getting corn-holed right now over at the NOPD lockup. But, you're sure about the handoff, then?"

"Back side of the Spee-Dee Parking lot, over by the tracks. Dark blue Nissan Sentra with custom rims. Ask the driver his name, and only hand the pack over if he says Tyrone."

"Okay, and you'd be smart not to take a peek in that backpack to see what's there. You can't tell anybody what you don't know. And don't get any ideas about getting rich quick. Anyplace you tried to sell what you got, we'd find out, and you'd end up on a float trip down the Mississippi. Face down."

"Hey, Tats! I'm your guy. I wouldn't try nothin' like that."

"You don't get my trust 'til you earn it, shithead," Tats said.

They parted then, and Lloyd stayed in the alley until Tats was nearly to the corner of the block before stepping out of the alley and turning in the opposite direction.

Some of the cops Lloyd worked with in Kansas City knew the looped belt trick but few ever used it, or at least never admitted to using it, because it was too risky, a lawsuit waiting to happen. But it had its advantages. It could put a guy out quick by restricting his breathing and the blood flow to his brain. If you did it right it seldom left a mark, and you could make that particular weapon simply disappear by threading it back through the loops on your pants.

The biggest drawback was that with a little too much enthusiasm, you could put somebody out permanently without intending to.

The kid had his earphones in, music blaring, and it was easy enough for Lloyd to come up behind him undetected. By the time the loop settled over his neck and Lloyd drew it tight, it wouldn't have done the kid much good to be carrying a full arsenal of weapons. All someone tended to think about in that first instant of panic was trying to claw that thing from around his neck.

It took a remarkably short time for the kid to pass out. As soon as Lloyd felt his body begin to sag, he loosened the belt, hooked his hands under the kid's armpits, and drug him into the shadows outside a closed car repair shop. Fortunately, there was no foot traffic up or down the street. There were no bars or restaurants on the block in either direction, and little reason for anybody to be walking along here. This late at night, even in the French Quarter, it was smart to restrict your carousing to the populated, well-lit areas.

Lloyd didn't even bother to take the backpack off the kid. He pulled the zipper and folded the top flap back, then took a look inside using a small pocket flashlight. The pack was filled with zip-up plastic bags of varying sizes and contents. The larger bags were filled with marijuana, the smaller ones with two or three kinds of pills. Each bag was marked with a mix of letters and numbers, code for the ultimate recipients of this cargo, he supposed. Lloyd pulled out a few small zip-up bags that he had brought along for this purpose and took small samples of everything.

He knew he couldn't figure out what it all was, nothing except the weed, but if he needed to he'd find a way to get the stuff identified. Even Tran might be able to do it for him if the need ever arose. But the clear message here was that the kid was transporting drugs, picked up at Les Girls, and almost certainly provided by Rudy Soyez. Who they were delivered to was not his concern, but where Soyez got them, and where they came from before that, definitely interested him. After all, this wasn't a police investigation. It was personal.

By the time Lloyd finished gathering his samples and closed the pack, the kid showed signs of coming around. In preparing for tonight, Lloyd had considered taking the backpack and tossing it in a dumpster someplace, or taking whatever cash the kid had on him to make it look like a robbery, but decided against both. For now, he didn't want to make any waves or stir up any suspicion until he knew more about how this little chain worked from end to end. Then he would decide what he wanted to do about it.

He left the kid lying face down on the sidewalk, stirring around weakly in the shadows, no doubt trying to figure out what just happened. Chances were that he might not even remember the loop of the belt around his throat, and the sudden bloodless darkness that followed.

Lloyd moved away a few dozen steps down the street, acting now as guardian until the kid was back on his feet and walking again, still shaking the fog out of his mixed-up brain. He'd have a hard time trying to explain to Tats, or whoever, how he hadn't opened the pack and had no notion about why a pill or two was missing from a few of the bags.

When his prey reached the next street corner, Lloyd turned and started back to Casey's house by another route, again limping with every step and leaning heavily on the cane.

Is this why they killed you, Billy? Lloyd wondered. *Because you stumbled into the middle of this setup? Is that why they came after you in the middle of a hurricane, and let the chaos of nature take care of what they left behind? And is this why they came after me as well, just because I wouldn't leave?*

As before, Lloyd had left his clothes outside that night, still reeking with the stench of alley slime, but Casey already had them in the washer by the time he woke up.

The coffee was ready when he shuffled into the kitchen, eyes only half open and his brain still in neutral. The whir and clatter of the washing machine woke him much earlier than he had planned to get up.

"Did last night's adventures include crawling through the New Orleans sewer system?" Casey asked as she poured him a cup. She didn't seem upset or even annoyed, but he could tell that she was open for an explanation if he chose to give here one.

"I was following a couple of those guys I told you about, and at one point I had to hide down an alley. It was pretty disgusting in there." Lloyd spooned sugar and creamer into his coffee, then sat down and tried it out. "Sorry about the clothes. I was going to wash them this morning."

"You should burn them," Casey said. "I picked them up with a good set of kitchen tongs, and then realized that I would have to throw the tongs away." Instead of the casual pants and shirt outfits that she usually wore when she went to work at the store, she was far more dressed up this morning in a light gray pants suit and silk blouse.

"Is the store closed today?" Lloyd asked. "Is it a holiday or something?"

"No, I'm just going to open late. Hopefully around noon. I have an appointment this morning. With a lawyer."

"About the divorce papers?"

"That, and some other things." Casey brought her tea to the table and sat down across from Lloyd. She looked attractive and business-like this morning, and Lloyd realized how sloppy he must appear to her. After his shower last night he toppled straight into bed, and this morning his hair pointed in all directions of the compass.

"My lawyer in Toronto plays golf with Scott sometimes, which shouldn't matter, but I'm beginning to wonder if I'm getting the kind of advice I need from him. Tran recommended somebody here, and we talked on the phone for an hour last night. He's recommending a different strategy that makes a lot more sense to me." She looked down at her watch, then said, "I'll tell you about it later, but I have to go now."

On an impulse, Lloyd said, "Leave me the key to the store and I'll walk over and open up for you."

Casey looked at him with an expression that managed to convey both her pleasure and uncertainty at his suggestion. "But you were up so late, and it's a long walk."

"I need the exercise," Lloyd said.

Casey took the store key off her key chain and laid it on the table. "I guess it's time to get one made for you." She gave him a bright smile and turned for the door.

Eventually Casey showed up at the store, coming straight there and changing into her everyday clothes in the back storage area. Business was brisk, and she pitched right in.

"I feel like a mom who's sent her kid out for the first time on his bike without the training wheels," she said. "How did things go?"

"Well I was fine with the cold cuts and sandwiches," Lloyd told her. A small, elderly Vietnamese man stood on the other side of the counter, patiently waiting for his change. "I even opened some quarts of potato salad and slaw so I would have something for sides. But I didn't even make a pass at the hot foods. I'm afraid your Mexican and Asian regulars weren't too happy about that."

They worked steadily for the next hour, she dishing up the re-heated food from yesterday and slapping meat on bread, he running the register and, as always, keeping a sharp eye on their slight-of-hand clientele. When the lunch rush was over, Casey went back to the cooler for a couple of bottles of beer. Lloyd was surprised to see her tip a bottle back and take a long, satisfying chug.

"I know. I know," she said. "You've never seen me drink, have you? But today's been a whirlwind."

"How did it go with the lawyer?" Lloyd asked.

"He was a little creepy," Casey said, "and I started imagining how well he must do with some the distraught, soon-to-be divorcees who come to him for help and consolation. But he knew his business, and suggested a plan I like. And he didn't make a pass at me."

"Maybe he's just not into Asian chicks," Lloyd said with a grin. Casey gave him a faux offended shove, but didn't honor him with a response. An ancient, wrinkled black woman finagled her battered walker through the door and bought a pack of Marlboro's. At her age, why not?

"Tell me about the plan," Lloyd said.

"My biggest worry is that Scott will try to grab a share of my practice, or maybe even try to take it all, because I *abandoned* him," Casey said.

"Your practice?"

"I started it with a friend from medical school, a Vietnamese immigrant like me, and we've done well. We provided some specialized cancer testing, but I'd bore you to death trying to explain it to you. My partner is willing to buy me out, and of course he's on my side. If Scott manages to get his hands on practically everything else, this will be all I have to start my new life with. But I'm afraid to just turn it into cash. Scott and his lawyers will smell the money and go after it like a pack of wolves."

"Sweet guy," Lloyd said.

"Isn't it odd how someone you've loved and trusted and planned your future with can turn into such a bitter enemy so quickly? I think that's the part of this that is so remarkable to me. I know I have to be practical and take care of myself. I have to fight for what's mine. But there is also that other side of things that I will never understand. Is this the way it always happens, Lloyd?"

"I don't understand it any better than you do," Lloyd said. "But when there's treasure involved, it usually seems to end in a brawl."

"Well this lawyer—his name is Clay Bissel—has come up with a plan that seems like it will work. He wants to tie up my assets, particularly my half of the practice, into a daisy chain of two or three shell companies set up here in New Orleans. That way Scott's lawyers will have to deal with the legal system down here, which I've heard is strange and complicated. He's also found some tiger shark of a lawyer in Toronto who's promised to pile as much grief as possible on Scott up there. Detectives, scandal, counter-suits. The whole arsenal of sleaze."

"Wow, you went from 'Let him have it all' to 'Lock and load' pretty fast."

"I finally got mad," Casey said. "I came down here to honor my parents and take care of them in their old age. But he used all those good intentions against me, just so he could, well, you know what, with that woman."

"Good for you, Casey," Lloyd said. "And I bet he'll get a lot less 'you know what' when she figures out what kind of shooting war he dragged her into."

Lloyd slept for a few hours after supper that night, then got up after Casey had already gone to bed and headed out.

He picked up Tat's trail up the street from Les Girls, and followed him up to Bourbon Street, where the party was still going on. Because of the crowds, he closed up the distance between himself and Tats, which he knew cranked up the risk of being discovered. Tats was a lot more cautious than his flunky had been the night before. He wore his pack with his arms through both back straps, and had another strap around his chest in front.

At one point Tats paused to look into the window of a souvenir shop, lit a cigarette, and turned his head briefly to check out his back trail. It was a smart move, and Lloyd had no smooth counter to it. If he stopped, Tat's alert level would shoot up, and if it happened a second time, the young thug would know for sure that he was being followed.

Lloyd veered to the left into the street, which was blocked off nightly to accommodate the revelers. He fell in behind a couple of young women, dressed in their skimpy party outfits, drunk and ready for whatever the night brought their way. Almost. Lloyd said something lewd, and one of them looked back at him and gave him a disgusted look. He veered away again, and reached the other sidewalk before casting a look back where Tats had been. He was lost in the crowd, and tonight's surveillance was over.

But there would be other nights, and he didn't always have to be a shabby bum with a scraggly beard and a limp.

* * *

Somewhere in the late-night hours Lloyd had fallen asleep in the folding canvas chair he had added to his surveillance roost across the street from Club Les Girls. It was past three, and the club was closed. The lights were out in the upstairs bedroom, but the window was open, its curtains performing an eerie, somehow graceful dance in the breeze that blew up from the river. The street was empty, and for the first time Lloyd could remember, even the distant music had silenced for the night.

Half awake, half asleep, his thoughts drifted to Marta. He wondered again what she actually wanted that night when she drifted over to his table and sat down. His cop instincts told him that it was nothing good, and she would only use whatever he revealed against him. But as a dreamlike fantasy began to take form in his mind, he imagined them walking through some previously unexplored part of the city, an area of modest but well-kept old homes, the neighborhood where she grew up. She was Mary once more, telling him about the simple life her family led, the modest local sites that were landmarks in her life, the small, innocent moments and pleasures that would someday become her happiest memories. She needed him to understand that, more than anything, she yearned to somehow go back in time and be the naïve and innocent girl, daughter of a refinery worker, while the future still whispered promises to her.

It was ridiculous, he thought, to believe that she was actually reaching out to him that night, as if he might be able to cleanse her somehow, to kidnap her from this life, strip away all the bad things she had become, and leave her clean again.

If that was her goal, she had chosen the wrong savior. He was too near the bottom of the sewer himself, and had yet to figure a way out.

The curtains on the window across the street rose briefly on the breeze, and he thought he saw a shadowy form just inside. He had almost convinced himself that it was just his imagination, but then the door across the room opened, letting in a splash of light that outlined a slim form near the window. The door closed again, but the form remained there for a while. Soon the dark SUV rolled slowly out of the alley, turned right, and was gone.

* * *

Lloyd's sleep patterns started to suffer, broken as they were between his nighttime vigils at Les Girls, and his daytime work helping Casey out at the store. For several nights he had continued tracking Tats in fits and starts, picking him up one night from the place he had broken off his pursuit the night before.

Tats' patterns, to Lloyd's thinking, were dangerously predictable, but it did make his surveillance easier. Leave Les Girls at about the same time every night. Use the same route to his delivery at the side door of a souvenir supply wholesaler down near the French Market. Head toward an older residential area to wherever he managed to park his aging blue Camaro, and drive away. He kept the backpack with him even after his delivery, and Lloyd guessed that it must contain the payments Tats received, as well as his own stash for street sales and personal consumption.

A few daytime trips down Ramon Street on the way to work convinced him that Tats did indeed stay in the shotgun row house a few blocks from the store, where Lloyd had followed the three young men recently. More often than not, Tats' Camaro was parked out front during the daytime, which is when his kind slept, like roaches and vampires.

He decided he had learned about all he could about Tats and his crew without actually going inside to take a look around. So that came next.

Lloyd decided that his vigils in the building across from Club Les Girls had become pointless, and thought he might need to take a break. He still got glimpses of Soyez from time to time, but what could he do about it, short of buying a sniper's rifle somewhere and putting one in an eye socket from the third floor window? Without a car he could not follow Soyez when he left, and he rejected the idea of using Casey's car for that purpose. She already had enough challenges without getting tangled up in this.

He would make one more trip to the abandoned building, he decided. After that, he would change his focus to helping Casey navigate through the nest of problems that she now faced.

He arrived at the normal time at his perch across the street from Les Girls, and ate a fast-food supper in the folding chair as he watched a couple of the bar girls outside flirting with three young men. By their short hair and trim physiques, Lloyd took them for sailors, on leave and out seeking some pleasure in the other sin city. The girls finally teased and taunted the trio through the big metal door, but they were back outside in five minutes. Lloyd figured that they had either found out what a thimble full of beer cost in a sleazy joint like this, or discovered that the dancers inside weren't all the seductresses they had expected.

The night proceeded according to the usual routine, which was thoroughly familiar by now. Neither Tats nor Soyez showed up, but that was not unusual. They didn't come every night.

When the neon lights finally blinked off and the girls started straggling out the front door to go home, Lloyd stood up and stretched, then took his chair over to a litter-strewn corner where he stashed it. He was already thinking about how good it would feel to pile into bed in the small first-floor room by Casey's back patio.

He took a quick look at his watch on the way to the stairs, but stopped before starting down. The evening hadn't passed faster than expected. They were closing the club early tonight. That was a first. Even on slow nights the lights never went out before two a.m., and if business was good they stayed open until three. But it was only twelve forty-five. Lloyd puzzled over that for a moment, then decided to take the folding chair back over to the window, opened a can of Coke, and waited.

Lloyd was watching the third-floor room across the street, expecting the light to go on soon. He didn't pay much attention when the black BMW sedan turned a corner and cruised slowly down the street, but it caught his attention when it stopped at the curb outside the club. In a moment, Marta stuck her head out the door, nodded, and went back in.

A smile came to Lloyd's face. So Soyez had some competition then, he thought. He had come to believe that Marta was Soyez's woman exclusively, paid for and owned as completely as the SUV he drove. If that was true, then it would go pretty hard for her and the man she was fooling around with if the big, ruthless thug found out she had something going on the side. But why should he be surprised? Wasn't that what people like this did?

The car backed up a few yards and turned into the narrow alley beside the club. Lloyd found himself feeling eager to see what Marta's other man looked like. He must be younger, handsome and pumped, if little Mary Lucchesi was willing to take this much risk to arrange a rendezvous.

At least ten minutes passed before the light in the third-floor room blinked on. A woman and then a man came in, but he couldn't see them clearly through the sheer curtain. It wasn't Marta. When she came over to close the window, he saw that this woman was a little shorter, and her hair seemed lighter. She was young, very young, and her face looked nervous and afraid. She still wore her skimpy dancing outfit.

The girl struggled with the window, trying to close it, and finally the man came over. He was shirtless already, revealing a hefty belly salted with gray hair. He was older than the girl, decades older. He tugged on the window until it slipped reluctantly down into place, then closed a pair of heavy blinds tight.

During that last instant before the blinds were closed, Lloyd realized that he knew this man, and it changed everything. Reverend J.T. Raintree liked them young and nasty, it seemed.

Chapter Twenty-Two

There were two of them, young black kids in their late teens with nothing to lose, and a hatred for cops that probably ran as deep and hot in them as their own lifeblood. They had just robbed a convenience store north of downtown Kansas City, in the vicinity of where Lloyd and his partner, Tony Achilles, were on patrol that night.

Lloyd and Tony were only two blocks away when they got the call, and they spotted the thieves on the street almost immediately. When the police car pulled up there was no good place for the young thieves to run, so the pair stood their ground, probably deciding to lie or fight their way out of the predicament as best they could.

Lloyd was out of the passenger door first, his weapon already drawn, but one of the kids kicked the car door before Lloyd was completely clear of it. It slammed Lloyd hard and painfully in his shoulder and shin, and his gun went flying. It was a rookie move, and Lloyd wondered what kind of price he'd have to pay for it.

Tony was around the front of the hood in an instant. Both the young thugs had knives, but the one closest to Tony barely got his out before finding himself sprawled on the sidewalk, dazed and hurting. The second one dropped his blade, staring at Tony with a look of resentment and resignation. Tony decked him too, just for the principle of the thing.

"Man, that felt sweet!" Tony said to Lloyd, grinning, nursing the knuckles of his right hand.

Just looking out the dirty plate glass window at the Yamaha parked outside in the lot gave Lloyd a warm feeling of satisfaction. "Man, I really owe you for bringing my bike down from Kansas City," he said to the man sitting across the table.

"Yeah, you nearly owed me a funeral a couple of times coming down through the Ozarks," his companion said. Anthony Achilles took a good hard pull on his sweating beer bottle, then grinned at it as if it was a woman he wanted to charm. "Once she nearly laid down on a tight curve, and another time I was just inches from going airborne off the side of a mountain."

"And both times you were only going the speed limit, right?"

"It was probably the speed limit someplace, maybe out in the flatlands of Texas, but just not where I was at the moment."

"Well, you're here now, all in one piece and that's what counts."

Tony took another drink. "Abita. I love the stuff," he said. "Maybe you could start shipping me a case a week of this stuff until I say stop."

They were sitting in a little roadside beer joint called Fellas, a concrete block building that was reputed to have survived not only Katrina, but the previous half dozen hurricanes before her. The management kept score, and had a wall dedicated to photos of the parties that had gone on while nature did her damnedest to get inside and stir things up. Fellas was located several miles east of New Orleans along the river road in a little berg called Chalmette. Across St. Bernard Highway was the sprawling Chalmette Refinery, blocking the view of the Mississippi River beyond with its metal towers, impressive tangles of oversized metal pipes, and vast acres of storage tanks. In this vicinity, the background stink of processed petroleum and flaming waste was a way of life. This was a working-class suburb of New Orleans, bereft of the attractions, charm and affectations of its famous historical neighbor so close by. Few tourists roamed this far out of New Orleans unless they wanted to visit the battleground where Jackson whipped the British in 1814 after the war between their countries had already ended. A cousin that Anthony was staying with lived here in Chalmette, and owned the bar they were drinking in right now.

"I mean it, Tony. I really do owe you, brother," Lloyd said. "I haven't had anything with wheels for months, and sometimes it's damned inconvenient being a pedestrian, even in a place like New Orleans."

"Hey, you needed me, and I came. Papa taught me that that's what a man does for a real friend. Besides, I should be used to pulling your johnson out of the grinder by now." Tony had never let him forget the liquor store robbery thing, and over time it had taken on epic proportions when he told the tale.

"Okay, I owe you *big*. For the bike, and for throwing your body between me and certain death."

"And you really will owe me if I pull this other thing off," Tony said with a grin. He raised his beer bottle in the air as a signal to the waitress across the room, and she nodded. "The whole thing sounds like a lot of fun, and it's good to come down here and see some of the family again."

"Tony, I think you enjoy the good things in life more than anybody I know," Lloyd said, lifting his bottle and taking a serious drink. "And the bad stuff seems to just blow off of you like dust. Of the four of us, you're the only one who seemed to land on his feet after the shooting."

"Aw hell, I was getting tired of being a cop anyway. It was all that stuff about walking the blue line all the time. No fights just for the fun of it, no getting drunk and tossed in jail, no slapping around some bitch if she two-timed you, or kicking the other guy's ass. Guess I'm not made to live like that. Don't get me wrong, I'm sorry that one of us, or maybe more than one, capped that old man on his own back porch. But you've got to go on living, don't you?"

Tony was a lean, hard, handsome Italian with coal black hair, ruddy features, and a ready smile that could turn as cold as dry ice when his temper surged. He had grown up in the old northeast section of Kansas City, which was Italian turf and reputed to be one of the toughest parts of the city. His father ran a locksmith business, and by his own admission, Tony started young as a street punk and low-level thug. But he had never done anything bad enough to keep him from signing up with the KCPD about the same time Lloyd joined. They had gone through the academy together, and rode as partners from time to time over the years. Lloyd enjoyed working with him because he was always entertaining, and very good at what he did. If Tony had your back, you could count on him all the way.

After they got fired from the force for the killing of the old man, Tony started a security service, and eventually branched out into detective work. Lloyd had worked for him for something short of a year.

Over time, Tony had expanded into electronic surveillance, and that was why Lloyd called him. He only requested advice, and maybe the loan of a few pieces of gear. But the job caught Tony's interest, and he decided it was high time for him to pay a visit to New Orleans. As an afterthought, Lloyd asked Tony to ride the Yamaha down since he now had someplace to keep it.

"When do you want me to do this thing?" Tony asked.

"The sooner the better," Lloyd said. "Tonight, or tomorrow night would work."

"Just not tonight. My aunt and uncle are planning a big spread for the whole clan, and after, I'm going out with my cousins to look for trouble." Tony had myriad relatives here, and just about any event was reason enough for a big family feast. Although his grandfather had moved his family to Kansas City decades ago, Tony had spent many summers here as a boy, and still considered it to be like a second home.

"Okay, tomorrow then," Lloyd said. "I'll call you in the morning."

"Not too early. I'll be recuperating."

* * *

The next night Lloyd sat in his observation post in the abandoned building across from Club Les Girls, trying to keep his nerves in check. Soyez arrived a little earlier than normal, drove down the dark narrow alley, and parked in back, as was his habit. From time to time the bait girls came out in twos and threes to have a smoke, check their phones, and troll for suckers. Drunks went in, drunks came out, and blaring music spilled into the street every time the metal door opened. Tats and one of his crew showed up with their backpacks, stayed inside a half hour or so, and left again, heading off in opposite directions as soon as they hit the street. Lloyd never got a glimpse of Marta, but he knew she must be there. She was always there.

The third-floor room across from him stayed dark, with the window open and the curtains closed.

On the way here tonight, Tony told Lloyd that one of his cousins had actually known Marta when he was growing up over in the Italian part of town. The way he described her, she was everybody's punch, starting in junior high. So much for the heartwarming legend of sweet little Mary Lucchesi, Lloyd thought.

It was business as usual at Club Les Girls, with only one exception. Tonight, right now, his friend Tony Achilles was lurking around the upper floor of the building, up to some serious mischief.

Lloyd had done his best to reconnoiter the building in preparation for tonight. Once, after everyone had left, he even climbed up the fire escape in back to check out the roof, but the double locks on the metal door up there kept him from actually going inside.

Lloyd had determined that the roof was the only safe way in because the front and back doors surely had alarms. Tony only chuckled when Lloyd told him about the locks up there. "I was cleaning my teeth with lock picks in my daddy's shop when I was five years old," he said. "I'll get in."

Apparently, he did get in, but now, an hour later, Lloyd was beginning to wonder if something might have happened to keep him from getting back out again. Lloyd considered what he should do if Tony didn't eventually come out. He'd have to go over, of course, but how long was long enough to wait, and how would he get in when he did go over there? Should he take his gun, as Tony had, and would he be willing to use it if they had already captured Tony? Questions without answers swirled around him like bats.

A mild evening breeze had kept the thin curtains on the window across the street gently stirring. Unexpectedly though, one of them now swept back more abruptly, and an arm emerged. It stayed out only long enough to flip Lloyd the bird with a long, upraised middle finger, then withdrew back inside.

* * *

Tony was pumped. He was working on his third beer in fifteen minutes, and his grin was so wide it seemed ready to split his skull in half. He and Lloyd were leaning forward across the small table so they could hear one another above the music and noise of the bar, their heads so close they had to lean back a little to take a drink.

"I swear she came so close to me that I could have reached out and pinched her," Tony said, "but she never knew I was there. The bulb was burnt out in the hall, and I was behind some boxes. She went into a room for a couple of minutes, then came out and went back downstairs. Maybe there's something wrong with me, but I kind of get off on the razor's edge stuff." Tony raised his bottle and drained the last half of it, trying to catch the waitress's eye while he was still pouring it down.

"I know," Lloyd said. "That's one thing that made it so interesting riding shotgun with you." Now that the setup was in place, Lloyd vowed to himself to keep up with Tony drink for drink for as long as he could. "But this gig was a lot more dangerous than most of the jobs you probably take on. It's not like getting some shots of a wife coming out of a motel room with the wrong man, or catching some bartender slipping twenties into his pocket. I told you about this guy Soyez. He's nobody to mess with unless you're ready to take it all the way."

"Yeah, my cousin Arturo has heard of him. His family was big in the rackets up in Chicago. He popped some guy up there over a personal beef, but the guy was an inside man, which should have been the last stop on the line for our guy Soyez. Instead he was just banished because his uncle was his capo, and so he moved to New Orleans. He's not mobbed up down here, but he's got some kind of understanding with them. Out of respect for his family, they let him do his thing cause it's small compared to what they've got going on."

The waitress shoved through the crowd with their new bottles, and Lloyd paid. Six dollars a pop, plus tips, so he was already out about fifty dollars, and they had just started out. He would never have picked a place like this for a debriefing, but Tony's batteries seemed to re-charge in these rowdy environs.

"Tell me about the setup," Lloyd said. "What you put in there, and how it works. I don't know squat about that stuff."

"The camera's not as big as a cigarette lighter. It's motion activated, and switches from normal to infrared depending on the light in the room. The battery should last two to four weeks, depending, and when it goes dead, I'll have a good excuse to drag my tail back down here and switch it out. But here's what's really cool. The signal goes out through their router to the internet, and that's how we get to watch the show. If anybody swept the system, they'd find it soon enough, but I've got an idea that doesn't happen too often at The Girlie-Girlie Club, or whatever that toilet bowl is called."

"So where did you put it?"

"There's a shelf high up in one corner. It's covered with junk and dust, so nobody's been up there looking around for a while. I mounted the camera in one eye hole of a Mardi Gras mask. Pretty slick, huh?"

"Definitely."

Push came to shove between two guys nearby who were arguing about The Saints, and one of them staggered back, taking out the little round table between Lloyd and Tony on his awkward journey to the floor. Lloyd managed to snatch his beer up in time, but Tony's went flying, slinging beer on his shirt and jeans.

And so it begins, Lloyd thought.

Tony stood up and handed Lloyd the small canvas bag of tools and tricks that he had taken with him into Club Les Girls, then turned to face the man who had started all this ruckus. If this guy hadn't already figured out the intent of that cold grin on Tony's face, he was about to make an unpleasant discovery.

Chapter Twenty-Three

Lloyd's occasional dreams over the decades about his little brother Bennie reflected his own endless turmoil about this seemingly pointless tragedy. Some were echoes of the guilt that he would never completely escape, and others were filled with only love, tenderness, and nostalgia. Then there were the ones that revived the absolute terror that he felt at that moment when he realized that his little brother was truly and irrevocably dead.

Bennie sitting on the couch, smiling as he watched the routine family activities going on around him. Bennie begging for a quarter to ride the mechanical horse outside the grocery store. Bennie eating a peanut butter sandwich and getting it all over himself.

Other were filled with fog, confusion, and darkness, with powerful rushing water somewhere nearby, and a child's haunting pleas for salvation. In most of these, Lloyd stood paralyzed amidst the chaos, helpless even though he knew Bennie was perishing someplace close by.

The most painful dreams, the ones that could still bring him to tears by their sheer poignancy, were the ones that made Lloyd face the guilt that he knew he would carry to his death. He and Bennie walking down a long dirt road, holding one another's hands. Bennie seeming enraptured by everything around him, the trees and flowers, the birds and animals and bugs, even the wind and the clouds floating lazily above them. Bennie stopping to look up at Lloyd, his face as innocent as a cathedral cherub, and saying, "Now that I'm gone, you have to live my life for me."

But how?

Chester was sitting on a bench facing the cathedral, scarfing down what was left of a sub sandwich that Lloyd suspected he probably fished out of a trash can someplace. His disheveled clothes were the same ones that Lloyd had last seen him in, or others just like them. His chin and cheeks were covered with at least a week's stubble, and he smelled the way he always had, of liquor and body odor and slow physical decay. The new cane leaning against the bench beside him caught Lloyd's eye. It was a classy looking gentleman's walking stick, crafted from well-lacquered walnut, with an elaborate silver handle shaped like a lion's head. It was clearly a hand-made treasure. Lloyd wondered if he had stolen it, then felt a tinge of shame for doubting his friend's integrity. Chester was not a thief.

Across the way the old music men were just settling in for tonight's session. No crowd had gathered yet, but that would happen soon enough when the first note from Brass Man Jake's trumpet speared the early evening solitude of Jackson Square.

Lloyd was sitting on the other end of the same bench Chester was on, unrecognized and ignored. He wore the same second-hand pants and shirt that Casey had first bought for him, and his dark knit cap was pulled down low over his ears. His hair was almost shoulder length now, and his beard was thick, tinged with unwelcome gray. Just another homeless guy loafing around Jackson Square.

"Want to trade sticks?" Lloyd said, trying to disguise his voice. For tonight's foray he had brought along his own beat-up cane, and faked the limp that had been all too real weeks before.

Chester gave him a cursory glance, then looked down at Lloyd's battered cane. "You crazy man," Chester said with a chuckle, "if you think I trade for that chewed-on old toothpick you got there. This here a gentleman cane. I found it fair and square in the weeds down by the river, and nobody around lookin' for it neither."

"How about if I buy you a whole muffaletta, all your own, and a tall boy to wash it down with? Then could I have it?"

The offer was so bizarre that Chester took another, closer look at him, staring straight into his eyes this time. "Why you rascal you!" he said finally. A broad smile spread across his face and he reached over to give Lloyd a hard slap on the shoulder. "I been tellin' so many people you dead that I nearly commenced to believin' it myself. Where you been, boy?"

"Still staying with the pretty Asian angel that took me in," Lloyd said. "Mostly I've been recovering from what those sewer rats did to me."

"But you back now? You know them boys is still around, don't you? Maybe if they see you, they kill you again."

"I don't plan to give them the chance, Chester. It's my turn now."

Chester gave Lloyd a conspiratorial grin and asked, "So you up to something then? You gonna kill them first?"

"Not really," Lloyd said. "It's more like what you told Brass Man when they stole his horn. 'The white boy's gonna wish he was dead, but he won't die.' "

Chester cackled out loud, and slapped his knee at the thought of it. "I wish I see that!" he said. "I jus' wish I see it!"

"You will if things work out the way I've planned," Lloyd said. "You'll be right there with me making it happen." He stood up and motioned for Chester to join him. "Come on, my friend. Let's go get a little something better to eat than whatever that is you've got there."

Half an hour later, when the waiter at Rascal's Place set the two big platters of fried catfish and fixings in front of them, Chester's face lit up. "I hadn't seen this much food since Christmas," he said.

"Yeah, I'm starving," Lloyd agreed. Considering their appearance, the waiter made Lloyd show him some money before he took their order.

Chester's first deep-fried fillet was nearly gone before Lloyd had the paper napkin spread on his lap. "I like them crawfish, an' gumbo, an' etouffee, an' all that other Nawlins cookin' jus' fine," he said, "but give me a mess of catfish any ol' day."

Lloyd had to agree. Back when he worked at the hotel, Rascal's has been his favorite go-to place on payday when he was feeling flush and craving comfort food.

They ate without talking until they had taken the edge off their hunger. Chester had decent table manners, and always said *please* and *thank you* to the waiter. He might be living on the streets now, Lloyd thought, but it was clear that he hadn't forgotten what his mama taught him.

By the time their plates were nearly empty, Lloyd was ready to get down to business. "I found out where old Tats stays," he announced to Chester. "I watched the place from time to time, and even slipped in late one night after everybody was passed out on drugs or booze or whatever. Turns out Tats and a couple of his buddies live there, and sometimes they have girls in, but not too often. They use a lot of heroin, and other stuff too, and when they fade out for the night, they're down for the count. I could have made bad things happen to every one of them that night, but I had something else in mind."

"You ain't no assassin like them, boy," Chester agreed.

"No sir, but I've figured out that I can be one mean bastard when somebody shoves me off a balcony. So, I decided to have some fun with this little prick, and persuade him that the climate here in New Orleans isn't healthy for him anymore."

"I like what I'm hearin' " Chester said. "An' you say you want me to help out?"

"If you want to, Chester."

"If I want to? Pssshaw! I'd crawl on broken glass to come to this party."

"Alright then. We're in business," Lloyd said. He took an envelope out of his back pocket and passed it across to Chester. There's some money in there, and a list of things I want you to buy and bring with you. I also need you to get a poem ready for our boy, something that'll make him wet his pants for years to come every time he thinks about it."

"I feel the inspiration comin' on already," Chester grinned.

"And there's just one other thing. I need you to find a woman for me and bring her along with you."

Chester looked puzzled. "For after?" he asked. "Ain't that little Chinese girl takin' care of you that way?"

Lloyd had to laugh out loud at that question, picturing his prim and modest hostess ever 'taking care of him that way.' The one time he had even tried to get a kiss during a quiet, relaxed evening on the sofa, she had reminded him, with some embarrassment, that she was still a married woman. He was reluctantly realizing that he was falling for Casey, and perhaps she was headed in the same direction, but he knew there was no course for him but to wait until she was a free woman once more. And then maybe a while after that.

"No, not for that," Lloyd said. "I want an older woman, the uglier the better. A hooker or somebody on the street, or anybody else you can scare up. I don't care, as long as she's got some sense. Tell her I'll pay her fifty dollars when the job's done. And you'll get the same."

"I know just the woman for it," Chester said. "My brother's old lady. She ugly as a catfish, and fat as an oil drum. Most times she goes around bein' ugly and nasty for free, so I'm satisfied she'd take fifty dollars just to be her own self. Maybe after, she even let me sleep on her foldaway again."

"The address is in the envelope, Chester. Meet me there at two tomorrow night. We're going to have some fun."

* * *

Lloyd sat on a moldy old couch along one wall of the room, shifting occasionally to avoid a maverick cushion spring that was determined to pierce his flesh. He held his .38 casually in his right hand, in case someone tried to interfere in tonight's entertainment, but he didn't think that was likely. His eyes were fixed on the man lying immobile on the bed a few feet away, and he thought he had never known a human being's eyes could open so wide. This must be what sheer, overwhelming terror looked like.

His rubber gloves and Guy Faulk mask lay on the couch beside him. He had hoped to find a disguise more appropriate for the occasion, but this was the best he could do. His work was over now and he was out of the man's restricted line of sight, so he could just sit back and savor the experience.

Tats looked so helpless and petrified that Lloyd almost felt a twinge of pity for him, wallowing in his own stinking waste, no doubt convinced that his life would end here tonight in some terrifying way. But all Lloyd had to do was recall what it felt like to fall twenty feet through the air to bring the ice back into his bloodstream.

Chester's sister-in-law hovered over the man, her face only a few inches from his, her mouth fixed into a nearly maniacal grin. Her name was Birdie, and she wasn't nearly as ugly as Chester made her out to be. But she sure did know how to make herself up to look like an honest-to-goodness voodoo woman. She wore a long shapeless black gown draped over her substantial frame, and a long handkerchief was tied around her hair. The necklace of small bones and chicken feathers that she had on dangled above Tat's face like a promise of doom.

Tats tried to scream, but with his own hand fixed securely over his mouth, the only sounds that came out were muffled and mournful. Lloyd watched and nodded his head with satisfaction. Super glue did work as well as ropes and gags for a job like this.

Without warning, maniacal laughter filled the room. Tats raised his head as much as he could manage, bringing his pillow up with it, and his gaze shifted to the tall man standing at the foot of his bed. Tats had seen this old black man countless times before in Jackson Square, but didn't recognize him now. Chester's face was painted coal black, with white ovals around his eyes and a wide white grin painted around his mouth. He wore a battered old top hat perched askance on his head, and a long black tuxedo coat covered his disheveled street clothes.

Chester had told Lloyd earlier that he'd need twenty more dollars for the rental of the hat and coat. Lloyd saw now they were worth the investment.

Raising his fancy cane and pointing it at Tats, Chester began his soliloquy in a deep, ominous voice.

Baron Samedi tired to see you ugly face
In the light, above the ground
In dis same old hoodoo town.

Birdie produced a straight razor from someplace and drifted it lazily in front of Tats face, like a merchant displaying her wares. Tats' eyes fixed hypnotically on the shiny, flat, five-inch blade.

Dim light from the candles they had lit in their prisoner's bedroom flickered and danced, casting a host of exaggerated swaying shadows on the walls and ceiling. The air was filled with the musty odor of smoldering herbs.

He send Bokor take you wit him soon,
Into the dark, into the deep bayou
Where sun don't go,
An' no white boy life don't stay so long.

Birdie lowered the razor down, out of Tats' line of sight, and drew the backside of it slowly, almost gently, across his throat. His body jolted as if he had just been electrocuted, not sure that his throat wasn't slit, not yet at least.

He look at you, he see jus' meat a'walkin'.
He give you bitter bloody drink that steal you mind.
Make you crazy like a man on fire.
Make you sorry mama squeeze you out.
Let dem gators chew on you for a while.
But you don't die, not all de way.
Never really die, jus' wish you could.

The back side of the blade trailed in swirls and tickles down Tats' chest. Unfortunately for him, he slept naked, so everything he had was just right there. Birdie raised his privates with the flat of the blade, then glanced up at Chester, rolling her eyes and shaking her head to scorn its size. She reached down and gave it a little pinch with her rubber-gloved fingers, and Tats' body jolted again.

He trade you to his wife Queen Marie,
For snakes an' worms, an' sweet Oleander.
She open your belly and put a chicken in dere,
Not one happy chicken sure.
Still live an' peckin'.
Then she sew you up tight.
Proud of her work, show it off.
Show all her people her fine work.
Show all dem zombie dey got some screamin' meat a'comin'.

Birdie teased and toyed with him, making him believe over and over that the razor had done its worst. She poured red food dye over her glove and the razor, raising them high in the air like a gruesome offering to the dark powers. Then finally she lowered her head so her eyes were only inches from his, so close that her necklace teased and tickled his bare and hairless chest. Again, Tats writhed and moaned, his screams smothered within. When she spat into each of his eyes, even Lloyd shivered in surprise, imagining the shock and disgust of such a defilement.

Bokor he comin' for you soon,
You stinkin,' nasty, wurfless man child you.
Bes' you go on run off someplace far away,
Hide you little boy thing deep in de groun'
So Lady Marie don't find it no more.
Bes' Baron Samedi not see you face one more time
In dis ol' hoodoo Nawlins town.

When it was over, Lloyd draped a pair of skid-marked underwear over Tats' eyes so he couldn't watch them quietly gather up their props and leave. Lloyd imagined him lying there through the terrifying remnants of the night, glued to his own filthy bedding, until his clueless, catatonic buddies in the front room woke at last and found him there.

They walked to Birdie's car, parked across the street, and put their boxes of voodoo wares in the back seat. Chester was feeling good. He was going to sleep the rest of the night on the fold-away bed at Birdie's house. He was back in her good graces until he messed up again. Lloyd was going to walk back to the store, where he had left Casey's car.

"You done good, boy," Chester said as he accepted the cash Lloyd held out to him. "Jus' like somethin' the mayor mighta concocted."

Lloyd looked at him, a quick smile of amusement playing across his face. "I'm not quite sure why you never wanted to tell me straight out, Chester," he said. "But I get it. Finally."

"There's a time for everything in dis old life," Chester said. "Dough have to rise before it can be bread. Your daddy mayor, he'd be proud of you, Lloyd Ballou."

* * *

A shaft of sunlight found a gap in the banana leaves outside in Casey's courtyard, probing between the almost-closed curtains, and prickling Lloyd's closed eyes, pestering him awake at last. He stirred groggily and took a look at the clock on the bedside table. Eleven forty-five.

He sat up on the side of the bed, rubbed his eyes, and raked his hair back with his fingers. Time for a trim, he thought. He tugged on his jeans and shirt and padded barefoot out into the front room.

Casey was sitting on the couch watching a local TV channel, sipping her tea. When she heard Lloyd stirring, she got up and went into the kitchen to start his coffee.

"Good morning, you lazy, lazy man," she said lightly. Her breakfast dishes were in the sink, and Lloyd wondered why she wasn't already at the store. Then he remembered that it was Sunday, their day off.

"Morning," Lloyd said, still half asleep.

When the coffee was ready, she poured him a cup and fixed it the way he liked it. That was one of the many small things she had started doing for him, and Lloyd had to admit that she now made better coffee than he did. He followed her into the living room and they sat in their usual places on either end of the couch.

Sipping his coffee, feeling the caffeine go slowly to work, Lloyd watched the weather and accident reports with little interest. Then a story from the young female reporter on the screen grabbed his attention.

"A New Orleans man is in the psychiatric ward of Charity Hospital today after a bizarre incident at his Ramon Street home. According to the patient, the devil broke into his house last night, held him prisoner, and tortured him for hours before friends finally rescued him."

The woman stifled a smirk as she continued to read from the teleprompter.

"Police are calling the incident a 'practical joke gone terribly wrong,' and they are interrogated the man's roommates in an attempt to sort the whole thing out."

Footage of the outside of Tats house appeared briefly on the screen, but apparently the TV station didn't get a crew on the scene soon enough to get a money shot of the paramedics rolling him out.

"Twenty-two-year-old Freddy Parks was found about ten this morning tied to his bed and super-glued to his mattress."

A bad photo of Tats, clearly an old mug shot released by police, showed briefly before the camera went back to the reporter sitting primly behind her studio desk.

"As a further insult, the victim's hand was glued across his mouth, which was why he was unable to call out for help after the assault. Parks was incoherent when the police arrived. The roommates claimed that they had all gone to sleep about midnight, and had no idea who had done this to him sometime during the night.

"Drugs were found in the house, which I suppose shouldn't surprise anybody," she added as an editorial aside before ending the report. "The roommates are currently in police custody pending further investigation."

Casey looked over at Lloyd from her end of the couch. "Why the grin?"

"I don't know," Lloyd said. "I guess I like to see people like him get what's coming to them for the things they do."

Casey studied his face before speaking. "He must have done something very bad to deserve this."

"Seems like it."

"Ramon Street is near the store. It's in the same direction that you followed those three boys that night, isn't it?"

"You know the city better than I do," Lloyd said with a shrug.

Casey continued to look at him for a few seconds, as if waiting for him to say more. But Lloyd kept his eyes on the television. "This is something I shouldn't ask too many questions about, isn't it?" she asked finally.

"Probably so."

Chapter Twenty-Four

Once during his tenure with the KCPD, Lloyd Ballou had witnessed the raw randomness of fate at its whimsical worst, and the memory of it had returned to his thoughts many times in the years since.

A traffic cop working I-70 out near Royals Stadium had stopped a motorist for some minor violation, hard at work to meet his monthly ticket quota, and because the driver was giving him grief, he made a routine call for backup. Lloyd and another officer showed up in separate squad cars, but by the time they arrived the first cop already had his guy handcuffed and bent over the hood of his car. A patrolman named Caldwell pulled in behind Lloyd, and although there was not much left to see or do, they still got out of their cruisers and started forward.

A car coming too fast, a sweet little BMW driven by a pretty little brunette, late for class and impatient with the slowing traffic, clipped the side of Caldwell's cruiser. It wouldn't have been all that serious, but the cruiser's side mirror broke free and went shooting through the air.

It all happened in an instant, the screech of brakes, the scrape of metal against metal, the muffled sound of the mirror slamming into Caldwell, and the hard spray of blood that plastered Lloyd's back. Instinctively Lloyd leaped toward the shoulder as the BMW careened past with an impressive display of screaming tires skidding sideways on the pavement.

Lloyd's shocked gaze turned back to Caldwell, splayed out on the asphalt, twisted and broken by the mirror casing buried in his back.

It wasn't until later, after the body had been taken away, the damaged cars towed, the brunette hauled off to jail, and the undamaged cruisers back in service, that Lloyd started to dissect the miraculous tragedy he had witnessed.

But for Caldwell walking behind, it would have been Lloyd bundled in a body bag on the ground and loaded clumsily onto a gurney. If Caldwell had taken another sip of coffee before he started to this place, or stayed in his car a moment longer to check in, or decided to unwrap a stick of gum before getting out, or any one of countless other possibilities that ran through Lloyd's mind . . .

But he hadn't, and that made all the difference. Day by day, moment by moment, that was how life worked.

It was one of those scalding, humid New Orleans days when not a trace of a breeze stirred, and after just a few minutes outside, you felt like you had wandered into a sauna with your winter coat on. Casey and Tran were spending the day across the river in Algiers, where they planned to stock up at an Asian food supermarket, have a leisurely meal at one of their favorite Vietnamese restaurants, and spend the evening with friends. Casey told him they might stay overnight with a friend.

With the house to himself, Lloyd had decided not to stir out of the air conditioning all day, and not to lay down the remote or leave the couch unless he was hungry, thirsty, or nature called.

A week had passed since the Tats-meets-the-Baron melodrama. Since then Lloyd had held one late-night vigil in his observation post across from Les Girls, but none of Tats' minions had showed up to make their regular deliveries. He had also spent a couple of evenings with Chester and the others at Jackson Square, and the alley beside the cathedral remained empty of dealers and scammers and garden-variety punks.

With Tony's camera planted and Tats out of the picture, Lloyd was satisfied with the progress he had made. But one challenge remained, and it was certainly the thorniest. How could he bring down Soyez, and then, perhaps later, the big guy himself, J.T. Raintree? One after another, a string of scenarios traipsed through his mind, but all seemed either too risky or too ineffective to seriously consider. He finally came to the simple conclusion that he knew too little about the man to put together any workable plan.

He realized that he had to start by learning more about Soyez. He needed to find out where he lived, what his daily routine was, what other sleazy characters like Tats he had working for him, and what other locations they might have like the Union of Hearts Mission to store their wares. Before, when Lloyd was afoot, he would have little chance of finding out any of that, but now he had the Yamaha, he felt empowered. It would take time, but he had all the time he needed.

And he also had a final solution if all else failed. They had tried to kill him, hadn't they, and were probably responsible for his father's death in the middle of a raging hurricane. Perhaps nothing but death would stop them, and if that made him an assassin, he thought he could live with that.

The sun was down when Lloyd woke from his second long nap of the day. On the television, Clint Eastwood and Eli Wallach were carrying a crate of explosives down a hill so they could blow up a bridge. There was a text on his phone from Casey telling him that they were staying overnight at their friend's house in Algiers. A half-finished Bud Lite on the side table was warm, flat, and undrinkable.

His quest had continued to churn in his thoughts as he slept, and he woke with a mission for the night. It was Sunday, and Soyez usually came to Club Les Girls on Sunday night. Tonight Lloyd would slip into the deep shadows in the alley beside the strip club and get the license and VIN number for the SUV that Soyez drove. Tony should have no problem getting the numbers run, and it might give Lloyd a good starting point.

The street outside the club was clear, and none of the girls were loitering in front, so Lloyd proceeded without hesitation toward the alley. He had done this so many times that now it was almost second nature to him. He turned into the alley, and not bothering with a flashlight, moved through the familiar darkness toward the barrels and the wall in back.

The rope settled around his neck so suddenly that it seemed to simply materialize there. Instinctively his hands grabbed at the restraint, but it was too tight to get his fingers under. He couldn't yell, couldn't breathe. His head felt heavy and dull, and needlepoints of light began to dance in front of him. Arching his spine, he reached back over his shoulders and clawed at the meaty hands of his captor. But a hard slam into a brick wall put a stop to all that useless struggling.

"Cut that shit out if you ever want to breathe again." Lloyd felt the heat and smelled the stale blend of liquor and cigarettes on the man's breath close behind him. Lloyd let his arms fall and laid his head against the wall. He wasn't sure if his nose was broken, but it was bleeding. The pain would also be along soon, he knew. "Better. Now just stay like that." A little slack came in the rope, and Lloyd savored the primal joy of drawing air into his lungs again.

Lloyd had only heard Soyez mutter a few words months ago during his visit to J.T. Raintree's house, but he felt sure that's who the brute behind him must be. Who else would attack him here?

Fingers fumbled along his torso in a clumsy frisk, then probed in his hip pocket and took out his wallet. A dim light glinted behind him for a moment, then went out. "Well, what do you, know? Lloyd Ballou!" Lloyd felt his wallet and phone being snatched from his pockets. "How do you turn this damn thing off?"

"The little button on the top."

"You should have stayed dead the last time we killed you, Ballou. Then you wouldn't be in a mess like this. You'd be out of our hair."

"I could still make that happen," Lloyd said, his voice harsh because of the rope. "Let me walk out of here and I'll be four states away by morning."

Soyez made a throaty noise that could have been a chuckle or a snarl. "My choice was to slit your throat and toss you over that wall back there. It might take days for anybody to find you, but the stink would have been bad for business. And besides, somebody wants to have a talk with you first." As he spoke, he let go of the rope looped around Lloyd's neck and pulled his arms behind him. Lloyd heard the zip of an electrician's tie and felt the plastic band bite into his wrists.

"Now here's how it goes," Soyez said. "We walk across that street and into the alley. I've got two guns and two knives on me, and if you try anything, I'll still get to do it my way. The only difference is I'll have to get rid of your body someplace else. Got it?"

"It's not complicated," Lloyd said. The panic was draining away, and he was beginning to think again.

"Go ahead and be a smartass while you can, Ballou. Just like your old man. But his clock ran down, too."

The street was still clear when they went out, and Soyez walked just behind Lloyd, his hand gripped tightly on the tie that bound Lloyd's wrists.

"So how did you get onto me?" Lloyd asked.

"I never was sure Tats had really killed you. That little degenerate would lie even when the truth was easier. But you were gone, and that's all we really needed anyway. Then when I heard about that thing that happened to Tats at his house, I started wondering. Where have you been hiding out?"

"Here and there."

As they reached the sidewalk on the Les Girls side, a middle-aged couple rounded the corner down the block, coming his way. But Lloyd didn't try anything, knowing there was nothing they could do to help him.

"I went by the boarding house and talked to the broad that runs it. She said the coroner only hauled one body out of there, and she didn't recognize him, which means it wasn't you. That little shit Tats still has to answer to me for that one if he ever gets out of the looney bin. But it's like I said, you disappeared and I decided you must have left New Orleans, just like Raintree told you to."

That one mention of the TV evangelist's name answered the suspicions that Lloyd had held for a long time. Raintree was all-in on this mess, just like his hired man, Soyez. But whether Lloyd would live long enough to do anything about it was suddenly up for debate.

When they reached the back of the alley, Soyez made Lloyd lay down in the back seat of his SUV and fastened another tie around his ankles.

Just before Soyez wrapped a towel tightly around his head, Lloyd got a glimpse of a slender form backlit in an open doorway. It was Marta. She didn't move or speak, although she must know what fate awaited him.

Soyez climbed into the front seat, and started describing his detective work, of which he seemed proud.

"So last week one of the girls saw a man go back into the alley and never come out. You probably didn't see her because she had slipped down into the alley for a sniff. She told Marta about it, and Marta told me. The next day I went over and I found your little nest up on the third floor. I figured it wasn't the cops because of the beer cans all over. You were my next guess. I remembered how interested you were in the club."

"Busted," Lloyd said. "But I didn't find out anything about what went on inside. If you cut me loose and dump me out of your truck, I swear . . ."

"I don't take chances, and I settle my scores. Hell, Ballou! You're an ex-cop, and you've got a grudge to settle. I can't take a risk with someone like you."

"I was a lousy, crooked cop, Soyez, and they tossed me out after I screwed up and shot an old man. I just missed having to go to prison for it. The local law here wouldn't listen if I went to them, and I bet you and Raintree have contacts inside anyway. I'm not stupid. I know you could get me busted, and I've heard bad things about the prison system down here."

"Yeah, we set your old man up that way," Soyez said, chuckling at the recollection. "If he hadn't died first, he'd probably be bent over a sink right now, making some big, hairy monster happy."

Lloyd thought he might be able to get some idea of where they were going, or at least what direction, by remembering the turns, but he quickly realized that was pointless. And what would he do with the information anyway? The realization was slowly settling in that his moment of opportunity might never come. Soyez seemed to have some experience along these lines, and probably wouldn't make any mistakes that would give Lloyd his chance.

Their speed seemed to increase, and Lloyd figured they were on a freeway now. Soyez made a short call. "Yeh, we're on our way." Pause. "Thirty, maybe forty minutes." Pause. "No, no trouble at all." Pause. "Alright, I'll see you there." They started up a long grade that Lloyd figured was the river bridge.

Soyez drove on, listening to the radio now, for at least a half an hour, maybe longer. Lloyd thought they had left the city, and because of the sweeps and curves of the road, he guessed they must be on a secondary highway. The sound of other vehicles close by became more rare. Finally the SUV slowed, and Soyez took a right turn onto what might be the worst road in Louisiana. Foliage raked along the windows from time to time, and every few yards they dipped and bumped through deep, water-filled potholes. Lloyd drew a mental picture of the desolate bayou country that they must be passing through now.

"Almost there," Soyez announced, as if it was something Lloyd should be looking forward to. He wasn't.

The SUV stopped at last, and Soyez got out. He pulled the blindfold off and slit the tie around Lloyd's legs, dragging him out of the back seat like a side of meat.

They were parked in a small clearing in front of a metal building that looked to be about twenty feet wide in the spackled moonlight. There were no outside lights, but a window on one side of the door threw a rectangle of light out onto the ground where they were standing. Beside Soyez's Cadillac sat a long, low silver Mercedes that had J.T. Raintree written all over it.

Soyez took a long-barreled automatic out from the back of his belt and worked the slide once. "I'll be glad to cut you in half if you give me a reason," he said.

As they went in, Lloyd saw that most of the building was being used for storage, but there was a small ten-by-ten office in the front. Raintree was sitting in a folding canvas chair in the office drinking coffee from a mug that read "Help heal the helpless" and bore his picture.

"Any trouble, Rudy?" Raintree asked.

"Nope. He walked right up and surrendered."

"Sit down, Lloyd. Over there." Raintree pointed to a folding chair similar to his. He was dressed classy casual, in a knit shirt and khaki's, as if he might have come straight from the country club to make this meeting. Lloyd sat down, but it felt awkward with his arms still restrained behind him. For a moment he and Raintree sat there studying one another.

"You know you do resemble your father," the evangelist said at last. "A little taller and a little huskier. And much healthier. He had a beard too, you know."

"I didn't know, and don't really care. I hadn't seen the man in thirty years."

"How much do you know about the trouble Billy got himself into here in New Orleans?" Raintree asked. His voice was calm, almost reassuring, as if he was consulting with a follower.

"Not much. I found out he died, so I came down here to see if he had any money, or any property I could sell to help my mom. She's got cancer, and the bills are piling up."

"You told me that before. Very noble of you, Lloyd. So you didn't know that Billy was just one step away from homeless himself? That he was stealing from my community service organization to get the drugs he needed, and that he had raped a young black girl near where he lived?"

"It doesn't surprise me, not after the way he treated us."

"Wasn't Sarah Bradley able to help you at all? She worked with your father for a time, and she should have been able to tell you some of these things." Raintree drank from his mug, then set it aside on a gray metal desk. "I'd offer you something, but I suppose it wouldn't be wise to free your hands. So, about Sarah . . ."

"I called her twice, but she didn't want to have anything to do with me. She sounded old on the phone, and it seemed like she was pretty scared. She said he was there in the mission with her and some other people when the hurricane blew in, but when the building started to fall apart, he took off. She didn't know what happened to him, but was pretty sure he died during Katrina."

Raintree exchanged glances with Soyez, who was standing off to one side, holding the gun casually at his side. Soyez rolled his eyes and shook his head, as if he thought everything Lloyd said was a load of crap . . . which it was.

"If you didn't learn anything about your father, why did you stay in New Orleans, Lloyd?" Raintree asked.

"I almost left," Lloyd said. "But then I got a job and I was getting some action from a lady bartender I met, so I stuck around. There wasn't anything to go home to. No job, no wife, no place to stay." Then he added, "But I'd sure like the chance to reconsider that decision now."

"I'm sure you would," Raintree said. He got up and poured more coffee, added cream and sugar, and topped it off with a healthy shot of bourbon from a bottle sitting on the counter.

There was something creepy about the calm and deliberate way in which Raintree interrogated him. Unlike Soyez, who would have his doubts if somebody told him the sun would come up tomorrow morning, there was no reading Raintree. When Lloyd first met the evangelist months ago, he had pegged him as pompous and most likely a fraud, but tonight there was something about this man's calm that made his skin crawl.

"If you didn't find out anything about anything, Lloyd, why did you spend so much time across the street watching what went on at Club Les Girls? What did you think you would find out if you stayed there long enough?"

"I don't know anything about that," Lloyd said. "I went in there a couple of times to watch the strippers. But the drinks were too expensive, and the girls were mostly ugly or fat. It was a waste of money. Maybe the local cops had the place under watch."

"And tonight?"

"I stepped into that alley to take a piss on my way to a sports bar around the corner, and that's when your guy here grabbed me."

Raintree leaned back in his chair and took a drink of coffee, staring at Lloyd as if every word he spoke deserved serious consideration. Lloyd stared back, trying not to allow the fear to show in his face, and trying to avoid the realization that he would never leave this place alive. His hands started to tremble but he leaned back, pinning them against the chair. All that helped him stay strong was his determination not to give this bastard a moment's peace of mind.

It occurred to Lloyd that beyond everything else Raintree wanted to know, about Billy and Sarah Bradley and about what dark secrets Lloyd himself might have unearthed, Raintree might be worried most about what Lloyd knew regarding the things that went on in that sleazy little upstairs room when he paid one of his visits to Club Les Girls.

"I had hoped you would be a little more help to me tonight, Lloyd," Raintree said at last, "and that we might find some middle ground to deal with this situation. But I can see that's not going to happen. I suppose I could let Rudy here go to work on you with his pliers and car batteries and what-not, and I know he would enjoy persuading the truth out of you. But in the end, there's nothing to be gained from that."

The evangelist rose again, and as he started to the door, he glanced over at Soyez and said, almost sadly it seemed, "He's all yours, Rudy."

Raintree was almost out the office door when Lloyd called after him, "So you're a man of God, huh?"

Raintree paused in the doorway and looked back, his gaze filled with cold disdain. "I was once, until I figured out that it would never get me what I really wanted."

* * *

A dozen thoughts and memories seemed to race through Lloyd Ballou's head almost simultaneously, each with such vivid clarity that it was almost like he was there again.

That moment, staring down at Kelly's sleeping face, and realizing that he loved her.

Racing up that long hill that never seemed to end, bawling and screaming and peeing on himself, feeling as if the world had suddenly become an empty place and that there was nobody anywhere to help him with his little dead brother.

Climbing on a bus to New Orleans, squeezing into a seat beside an old man who reeked of various vices, and thinking, at least for a moment, that he was on a fool's errand.

The squalid bayou water in his shoes squished with each step he took. The electrician's tie had rubbed his wrists raw, and he could feel the blood dripping from his fingertips. Lloyd had always admired others who had faced their own end eye-to-eye, and wondered now how he would handle it. Okay so far, he decided.

Despite her swollen, seven-months-along-belly, Lloyd thought his sister Kat had never looked prettier, or happier, when he surrendered her hand to Robert on a steamy July afternoon in the Methodist minister's living room.

Once, astride the Yamaha, riding wide open, the wind needling his face and the engine growling between his legs like a living beast, he could remember thinking that he should just keep going like this forever.

The path was narrow and seldom used, leading across overgrown hummocks and stretches of soggy lowlands. From time to time the moonlight penetrated the trees and spotty clouds, revealing nothing ahead but more of the same. The light from Soyez's flashlight flickered and dimmed, making it clumsy going for Lloyd, who was in the lead. The bayou was a dark presence that engulfed them, filled with unrecognizable odors and sounds. He had fallen once, feeling like a vine had reached up and deliberately snagged his ankle. With his hands bound he had trouble getting up, rolling and wallowing in the slippery mud until Soyez stepped up and gave him a hard kick in the back to encourage him along.

His mother sat on the side of her narrow bed in her tiny cell-like nursing home room the last time he saw her. Her thoughts blurred and wandered, and nothing that came out of her mouth made much sense. She'd had chemo the day before, and was on a cocktail of drugs to battle the side-effects. She began crying as Lloyd bent to kiss her, and he had to unlock her thin desperate arms from around his neck. Kat stayed in the room to distract her while Lloyd slipped out the door.

"You're not squawking and begging like some of them," Soyez said. "That little accountant was the worst, I think. I ended up shooting him before we got there, but then had to drag his sorry ass all the rest of the way."

Soyez was enjoying this business a little too much. Lloyd thought about answering with something defiant and insulting, but decided not to waste what little time he had left.

The last time he saw Casey he was on the couch and she was at the front door, her purse over one shoulder and a larger canvas bag over the other. She gave him a smile and a quick wave that warmed his soul. As she turned and went out, his gaze swept across her trim little rear, as a man's eyes were prone to do. How could that possibly have been just this morning?

"At least you'll have some company out there. Let's see. There's one of Tats' stooges who decided to try a little sample of the product he was delivering. But he was too stupid to be much company for you. And a slut from the club that said she was going to the cops. She might be more to your liking. And a guy that tried to steal my ride. I don't know anything about who he was. And a couple of others. It's a good place to make stiffs go away forever. You'll see what I mean."

Lloyd tripped over a cypress knee and fell again, landing hard on his right shoulder without his hands to break the fall. Soyez stepped up and gave him another cautionary kick, managing to find the place on his leg where he was injured when he fell from the balcony. Lloyd winced and shuddered, but didn't give his captor the satisfaction of hearing him cry out in pain.

"Damn you, Ballou, can't you keep your feet under you?"

"I can't see anything with that crappy flashlight you brought," Lloyd said.

"Yeah, I forgot to get batteries." He hooked a hand under Lloyd's arm and pulled him to his feet. "But at least the moon's up."

"So, is this where you brought my old man?" Lloyd asked as he started up again.

"How could I?" Soyez said. "Just think about it. Katrina was still hammering away. The reverend took off in a chopper the day before, and the rest of my crew were scattered all over town, nesting up like rats. I was riding it out alone in an old warehouse we'd rented for food distribution. Billy surprised the hell out of me when he showed up afoot in knee-deep water in the middle of the storm, babbling something about how I had to drive over to Union of Hearts and help the bums there. He was broke up and half drowned, and I figured he was out of his damned mind. I hadn't seen him for over a week, not since the police got after him for that rape thing. All I could think of was getting rid of him any way I had to."

"What did you do to him?"

"That was a problem, I admit. I didn't want to just shoot him there, and then sit around waiting for the cops or the National Guard to show up and find his stinking corpse with a bullet in his head. But the river was close, just three blocks away, so I hauled him over there. I was going to shoot him and throw him in the river. But he saved me the trouble, and jumped in himself. I saw him come up once and I took a couple of pot shots at him. Then he rolled under the water and I didn't see him again. And that was that."

"I wish I knew all that a while back," Lloyd said.

"I bet you do," Soyez said with a cold chuckle. "But it's no use to you now."

They crossed another long stretch of lowland, the shallow water they trudged through as black as coal, the mud beneath sucking at their feet. Then Soyez flashed the light up ahead for a moment, and Lloyd spotted a hummock rising from the marsh. A few twisted trees managed to survive on its uneven slopes, and vines and weeds flourished around them.

That's the place, Lloyd thought. He wasn't sure where that thought came from, but the certainty of it went through him like an electric charge. His knees weakened and his sphincters knotted. A cold wave of fear enveloped him, and he fought back the impulse to turn back to Soyez and begin pleading and negotiating for his life.

Slowly Lloyd felt his courage starting to return, materializing in his veins and flesh like molten metal. Everybody died, and few had the chance to decide when or where or by what means. In the end, it was what you did when you saw it coming straight at you that showed who you were and what kind of life you had led. Everybody died, and it was his turn now.

Lloyd straightened his back and moved forward without hesitation.

"Ready to meet your new friends, Ballou?"

"Why the hell not?" Lloyd said. He started up the shallow incline onto the slight hump of higher ground.

"There's a deeper channel on the other side of this little hill, and that's where they live. I'd swear these gators know me by now. I've sure brought them enough grub."

Near the top of the incline Lloyd fell again, this time on purpose. He moaned in pain and muttered a bitter "Shit!"

"That's not going to work again, Ballou," Soyez told him. "Get up." He punctuated his command with a couple of hard kicks. Lloyd struggled to get up, but fell again.

"It's my ankle," Lloyd said. "I think I broke something."

Soyez stepped up closer and gave him another kick. "Can you get up now?"

Lloyd tried again and failed.

"Aw hell!" Soyez took a handful of the back of Lloyd's shirt and dragged him roughly across the level part of the hummock, then dropped him carelessly on his back. Lloyd looked to his left and saw that he lay just a couple of feet from a steep embankment that led, he guessed, to the channel below. The plan, it seemed, was to shoot him here, then tumble his body down to the alligators waiting below. Or maybe Soyez would not even bother to spend a bullet on the kill shot.

Soyez stepped to the edge of the embankment and started pulling something out of a plastic bag that he had brought along and tossing it in the water. Lloyd realized that it was raw chicken leg quarters, bait it seemed, to draw the alligators into the vicinity. At the same time his executioner started calling out, "Whoo! Whoo! Come on, you hungry devils." It was a signal he had apparently agreed upon with the reptiles.

In a minute or two Lloyd began to hear splashing in the stagnant water below, as well as odd, unfamiliar noises that were something between a hiss and a snore. Alligator talk.

Soyez turned back to Lloyd, towering close over him with one foot between his legs, the flashlight glaring down on his face. "You want a bullet?" he asked. "Some do, some don't. Either way, it don't take long. They'll drag you right to the bottom." When Lloyd didn't answer, he went on. "I know I'll probably go straight to hell for saying this, but I enjoy this part a lot more than anybody should."

In that eerie moment that Soyez took to savor his gruesome pleasure, Lloyd saw his chance and took it. He clamped his legs around Soyez's ankles, shoved hard against the ground with his right elbow, and rolled abruptly to the left. The gun went off. The bullet hit the ground so close to Lloyd's head that it splattered dirt into his ear.

Soyez was right about one thing. It didn't take long. An instant after he toppled sideways over the edge of the embankment there was a desperate cry, truncated abruptly. The water thrashed and churned violently for a few seconds. Then the night was quiet again.

"Are you still enjoying this part?" Lloyd mumbled.

* * *

Soyez took the failing flashlight to the bottom with him, and Lloyd wasn't inclined to go in and look for it. He twisted and writhed until he had made it to his knees, and then to his feet, encouraged to make a quick job of it by the occasional splashing sounds down in the water.

He felt a growing elation wash over him during the walk back in the moonlight. Struggling to make peace with the certainty his own impending death, and then to realize that the danger was gone and his life would continue, was a remarkable experience. That kind of thing could turn a man's life around, Lloyd thought, and maybe even make him turn to religion. Unexpectedly, he glimpsed a mental image of Sarah Bradley and his Aunt Charmaine, sitting in the shade of the old woman's back porch praying together, praying for him even though it made him uncomfortable at the time. Had they prayed for his salvation, he wondered, and was this the kind of salvation they had in mind? It was something to think about, although he knew that battlefield conversions didn't always take when the bullets stopped flying.

He kicked in the locked door of the metal building where he had met with Raintree, then located a pair of snips that easily bit through the electrician's tie that bound his hands behind him. He was free at last, although it would take a little while for his damaged wrists to heal. Before leaving the building, he started a fire in the back, where crates of toys and cheap tourist goods were stacked nearly to the roof.

Lloyd remembered seeing Soyez toss his keys in the passenger seat of the SUV, and he was pleased to find his phone and wallet also lying there. He thought about turning on the phone, then decided to wait until he was far away from this place to do that. Just in case.

The rising sun was just beginning to lighten the eastern sky by the time Lloyd neared the approaches to the river bridge. He decided to turn the phone on then, and it immediately began its usual pings and tones.

There was a new text from Casey telling him that she was running late and would go straight to the store to open up.

He also had a phone message from the 816 area code, and Lloyd recognized his friend Tony's number. "Bingo! Call me soon as you can, goombah."

Lloyd left the Caddy on a quiet side street a few blocks outside the carefully monitored boundaries of the French Quarter. He dropped the keys on the driver's seat, and left the window down. It would be a nice ride for somebody, and not likely to ever be reported stolen.

Chapter Twenty-Five

Sarah Bradley's sitting room had an aged, elegant old-world charm, with its frayed period furniture, crocheted table doilies, and dusty portraits of long-dead ancestors, all probably residents of this same pillared plantation house over decades and centuries past.

She kept no hired help, but managed to scare up a few snacks and iced tea for her guests. The crackers and shrimp dip were still in their grocery store packaging, and the tea came in cans. Clearly, she didn't spend much time obsessing over Old South etiquette.

Today was the first time Lloyd had persuaded Casey to set aside her inhibitions and risk riding behind him on the Yamaha. Sarah Bradley's home seemed the ideal destination, just 45 minutes east along the coast, and no crowded, dangerous interstate highways along the route. For the first part of the ride Casey clung to Lloyd as if he owned her fate, but finally she began to relax and enjoy herself.

"I felt like somebody had given me my life back the first time I saw that video on the news," Sarah was explaining to Lloyd and Casey. "To see his holiness J.T. Raintree in a shabby little room molesting a scared young woman . . . I wonder if the authorities will ever find out who spread those videos all over the news and the internet?"

"My guess is that they won't," Lloyd said. "It must have been some slime ball who owed the Reverend some serious payback." Casey gave him an odd sideways glance. She had her suspicions, but hadn't asked any questions yet. Lloyd had already resolved to lie to her this one time if she ever did.

"I'm still hoping they'll find Rudy Soyez, too," Sarah went on, "but I suppose it doesn't matter so much now."

"He wouldn't stick around for a mess like this. He's gone for good." Lloyd put a dollop of shrimp dip on a cracker and wolfed it down. He had promised Casey a seafood dinner somewhere along the way, and he was hungry.

"What are your plans now, Lloyd?" Sarah asked. "Now that you don't have this other business hanging around your neck like an anvil?"

"It seems like here is where life wants me to be. I've got my eye on a little grocery that's up for sale," he said. He knew she must be burning with curiosity about the relationship between him and Casey, but he honestly wouldn't have known what to say even if she asked. Casey's divorce was still churning through the legal systems in Montreal and New Orleans, and Lloyd Ballou had yet to claim that first kiss from this particular married woman.

"Then you've decided to put down roots here?"

"Yes." It felt good to finally be certain about something.

"Then that leads me to another matter that I've been thinking about," Sarah said. "I've had my lawyer looking into what it would take to get your mother brought down here. Is that something you'd be interested in?"

"Sure, but she's in a nursing home. I don't have a place of my own, and couldn't take proper care of her even if I did."

"I could help with that," Sarah said, dismissing Lloyd's hurdles. "I have a special room upstairs, much like a hospital room with all the necessary equipment. I had it put together when my own mother was in her last days. A few years later my Aunt Andrea lived there for months before she went on to be with the Lord. I wouldn't bring this up to you, Lloyd, if I didn't have this option to offer you."

Lloyd just looked at Sarah Bradley for a moment, not knowing how to respond. "Are you sure you know what you're offering?" he asked finally. "She has cancer, and she's dying slowly."

There's a hospital fifteen minutes away when we need it, and another bedroom upstairs for a full-time nurse. Your mother would get better care here than in a nursing home, and it's something I really want to do."

A host of reasons why this wouldn't work ran through Lloyd's mind.

"Come on upstairs with me before you make any decisions. You come too, Casey, since you might be a part of this."

Casey was as puzzled as Lloyd, but they both rose and followed Sarah up the broad oak staircase and down a carpeted hallway. They stopped at the last room and Sarah opened the door. The room was high-ceilinged and larger that Lloyd expected. True to Sarah's claim, it contained a variety of medical paraphernalia, and two hospital beds were positioned to provide a view of the gardens outside.

As they entered, a middle-aged woman in nurse's whites lay her knitting aside, rose from a chair to one side, and left quietly through a door nearby.

"You already have a nurse?" Lloyd asked.

"We already have a patient," Sarah told him.

"Another relative?"

Sarah crossed the room and stopped beside the bed. She raised a skeletal hand from the blanket and stroked it with her fingertips. "Yes, but he's not my relative. He's yours, Lloyd," she said.

Casey took Lloyd's hand and they moved forward to the side of the bed. She was crying now, and Lloyd could feel his own throat constricting. No words came to him as he got his first glimpse of the withered form in the bed before him. It was impossible. It couldn't be him. He was dead.

"After all the things that should have taken his life during the hurricane and after," Sarah said, "it was something completely unexpected that brought him to this. He knew he was sick for a long time, years maybe, but he didn't do anything about it. He thought of it as payback, something he deserved."

Lloyd looked at Sarah, then back down at the man in the bed. The covers were drawn up to his chin, with only his head and hands out. He looked like he could easily be a hundred years old, or even corpse, dead and mummified already. His chest rose and fell slightly at alarming intervals, as if each breath might be the last.

"He wasn't a good man for most of his life," Sarah said, staring down at Billy Ballou with a soft, affectionate smile. "But he became one. Let's bring your mother down here so they can be together again."

Lloyd stepped forward, and his eyes met Billy's for the first time in decades. He felt the tears gather, but fought them back. It was too late to cry for this old man, dead or alive.

"I never thought I'd see you again in this world," Lloyd said, "but now that it's happened, I've got some things I want to say to you."

Billy Ballou's eyes sagged closed, like those of a dying cowboy in a B movie. Then they opened again, his gaze fixed on his son. He nodded slowly, and that crooked little sneering grin played across his face.

About the Author

Greg Hunt's strong roots in the mid-west and deep south have inspired him to write a number of novels set in Missouri, Louisiana, Tennessee, and Mississippi.

Over the past four decades Greg has published many novels, including historical, frontier, Western, and other genres. A lifelong writer in many guises, he has also worked as a newspaper reporter and editor, a private investigator, a technical and free-lance writer, and a marketing analyst. Greg served in Vietnam as an intelligence agent and Vietnamese linguist with the 101st Airborne Division and the 23rd Infantry Division.

He now lives in the Memphis area with his wife, Vernice.

Now Available!

MORE ACTION/ADVENTURE WESTERNS BY GREG HUNT

For more information
visit: www.SpeakingVolumes.us

Now Available!

ACTION/ADVENTURE WESTERNS BY AWARD-WINNING AUTHOR JIM JONES

For more information
visit: www.SpeakingVolumes.us